Books by Hans G. Schantz

The Art and Science of Ultrawideband Antennas,
2nd edition, Artech House, 2015
1st edition, Artech House, 2005

The Biographies of John Charles Fremont,
Kindle Direct Publishing, 2015

The Hidden Truth:
A Science-Fiction Techno-Thriller,
Kindle Direct Publishing, 2016

A Rambling Wreck:
Book 2 of The Hidden Truth,
Kindle Direct Publishing, 2017

The Brave and the Bold:
Book 3 of The Hidden Truth,
Kindle Direct Publishing, 2018

THE BRAVE AND THE BOLD

BOOK 3 OF THE HIDDEN TRUTH

HANS G. SCHANTZ

2018

www.aetherczar.com

The Brave and the Bold
Book 3 of The Hidden Truth

by Hans G. Schantz

ISBN-13: 978-1-7287-2274-0
ISBN-10: 1-7287-2274-8

Cover Design by Steve Beaulieu at Beaulistic Book Services

10 9 8 7 6 5 4 3

To "[t]he fond and the faithful few…"

TABLE OF CONTENTS

CHAPTER 1: THE ART OF DECEPTION

The interrogator looked right through me. Then he glanced down at the dancing needles of the polygraph. "There appears to be a pattern of deception here," he observed, looking back up at me. "Let's start from the top one more time. Is your name Peter Burdell?"

"Yes, it is," I answered. I imagined the scratching of the needles on the instrument in front of me trying to burrow into my soul.

After a long pause, the interrogator continued. "You were born on October 29, 1986?"

"Yes." More silence. More scratching. I tried my best to amplify the tension and stress.

"You graduated from Lee County High School in 2005?"

"Yes." I suppressed the temptation to fill the silence with more babbling and allowed free rein to my discomfort. I imagined myself teetering at the edge of a cliff and savored the intense anxiety. I felt the hairs rising along my arms and on my back. These were the control questions against which the interrogator would compare my responses to the relevant questions. If I could amp up my discomfort high enough on the control questions, it might mask the more subtle signs of deception on the relevant questions.

"Are you sitting in a chair?"

"Yes." I imagined a swarm of bees stinging me, buzzing around my head, crawling in my ears while I did my best to remain impassive. My sphincter tightened.

Finally, the examiner asked, "Your parents are dead?"

"Yes." Another control question. I allowed myself to relive the emotions of that awful day. I felt tears welling in my eyes and a sick feeling in the pit of my stomach.

"They were killed in a drunk driving accident Thanksgiving weekend in 2004?"

"Yes," I lied, sticking to the official story. This was surely another control question, so I gave free reign to my anger. I relived the outrage at the discovery of how the Civic Circle murdered my parents. The cabal that changed the past to control the present so they could rule the future would do anything to hide the truth.

And now, I would do anything to stop them.

My opportunity was coming. The Civic Circle would soon host their Social Justice Leadership Forum on Jekyll Island off the coast of Georgia – the biennial meeting where the world's movers and shakers gather to decide which way to move and shake.

My path to the Social Justice Leadership Forum was through my summer intern position at Tolliver Applied Government Solutions – TAGS. That job required a security clearance. The security clearance required that I successfully pass...

"Is there anything in your background," the interrogator interrupted my thoughts, "that would disqualify you from getting this job?"

"No," I answered. Finally, we were back on relevant questions. I visualized myself lying on the beach. The waves were slowly moving in and out... in and out... as the sun beat down from overhead.

"Besides what you already told me, have you ever lied to get out of trouble?

"No," I answered, imagining the beautiful blue waves slowly lapping at the golden sand. I had to dampen my physiological responses on the relevant responses so the interrogator would be convinced I had nothing to hide. I could feel myself calming down.

"Besides what you told me, have you ever stolen anything else?"

"No," I replied, catching myself as I began to calculate the value of the many hundreds of books I'd helped steal from the Tolliver Library before it burned down. Relax, I willed myself. Focus. Calm. A peaceful alpine meadow, the green grass under a brilliant blue sky. I imagined the opening scene of *The Sound of Music*.

"Do you have any conflicts of interest that might impact your work for TAGS?"

I pretended to think about that a moment. "No," I lied. TAGS was a subsidiary of Tolliver Corporation, founded by my ancestor Jake Tolliver over a century ago. The family had never forgiven Mom for running off with Dad, but lately Uncle Larry had been trying to lure me back into the family. In a weird sense, I think Larry was avenging himself against my father by inculcating me in what passed for Tolliver family values – the Machiavellian quest for power and status within the Civic Circle. Dad would never have approved. Larry had arranged my job at TAGS working as an assistant to the company President, Travis Tolliver, but Larry intended me to be his spy at TAGS, and hopefully within the Civic Circle, too. I continued my focused relaxation.

The interrogator interrupted my peaceful reverie. "Do you have any reason to believe the Civic Circle was involved in your parents' death?"

Uh-oh. That was a dangerous question. "No," I lied. He knew. Now he was deliberately trying to provoke a response to detect if I knew. What was he up to? I had a momentary image of Nazis searching through my mental abbey.

"That was the weekend of the Tolliver Library fire," the interrogator observed dryly. "Do you have any knowledge of who may have started that fire?"

"No."

Of course, my interrogator knew all about that fire. He stared as if trying to peer into my skull. I relaxed, and focused on the beach again. The sun warming me, the waves moving in and out slowly in time with my breaths.

Eventually, the interrogator continued. "About the incidents of this past year at Georgia Tech... You were involved in the student protests for social justice, were you not?"

"Yes, I was." Of course, at the same time, I was also a key player in the efforts to subvert and undermine the social justice protests.

"Your linear circuits teacher, Professor Muldoon, said you were a 'menace' and 'not to be trusted.' Is his assessment correct?"

"No."

"Did you, in fact, cheat to obtain an advantage on his midterm exam?"

"No."

"You worked for Professor Wu Chen in the Gamma Ray Astrophysics Lab, correct?"

"Yes."

"Do you know his whereabouts?"

"No," I lied. I'd smuggled him out of the physics building right under the noses of the Civic Circle's Technology Containment Team, and, with the help of another "Friend of George," I took him safely to the Chinese restaurant that served as the front for the Red Flower Tong in Atlanta. The Red Flower Tong was a Chinese fraternal organization – they called themselves "the Brotherhood." I also suspected they had ties to organized crime. They had a fascinating history stretching back hundreds of years. The Civic Circle itself had roots back to a much older Chinese entity now calling itself "Xueshu Quan." Some called him a god, others called him a demon. Whatever he was, hundreds of years ago during the Chin Dynasty, Xueshu Quan taught his secrets to monks at a monastery in Fukien Province, including the basics of electromagnetic theory, centuries before those concepts were rediscovered in the West. These closely-held secrets and others gave the monks great power and capabilities. They easily defeated a much bigger force of enemies, and earned the gratitude of the Emperor. When the monks refused to join him in an attempt to overthrow the Emperor, however, Xueshu Quan turned on them. Xueshu Quan almost wiped them out. A few scattered survivors banded together as the Red Flower Tong, preserved many of Xueshu Quan's secrets, and swore to avenge their fallen comrades. The Red Flower Tong continues to fight against Xueshu Quan and the Civic Circle today.

"Did you have any reason to believe he was an agent for a foreign power?"

"No." Another completely truthful answer. The Red Flower Tong was not a foreign power. Not exactly. The Circle had concocted that espionage cover story to justify their manhunt for him when they discovered he had a connection to the Tong.

The interrogator continued his questions. "You also worked with Professor Marlena Graf?"

"Yes."

"The professor behind that rather remarkable declaration approving of sexual harassment in the workplace?"

Approving of sexual harassment? Hardly, but it wouldn't help for me to take issue with the interrogator's characterization. "Yes," I answered. Professor Graf stood up for Professor Chen when he became the subject of a social justice witch hunt for wearing a sexist shirt to a press conference. Then, when the Civic Circle began to realize that Professor Chen had friends in the Tong, Professor Graf was targeted along with him. First, they tried to recruit both professors to work at a secret government facility in Nevada where they could be more closely monitored. When that failed, the Civic Circle concocted an espionage case against Professor Chen and accused Professor Graf of being his accomplice.

"You said that the last time you saw Professor Graf was at the reception at GammaCon in Chattanooga. Do you know where she is now?"

"No," I lied. I'd helped Professor Graf vanish, with the assistance of my best friend Amit, my uncle Rob, and Sheriff Gunn. The Civic Circle attempted to poison the professor. Amit and I swapped out the poisoned beer to convince the Civic Circle their poisoning had succeeded, and then Uncle Rob laid out a false trail up in Great Smoky Mountains National Park. Professor Graf was safe and sound, hidden at Uncle Rob's place up in the mountains – Robber Dell. That was our secret refuge. If the Civic Circle knew about it...

"Your uncle's place. Up in the mountains. That's where you're hiding the professors, isn't it?"

"No," I lied, before seeking my safe refuge back on my imaginary beach. I didn't like the implications of that question. I couldn't imagine being asked that question unless the game was up, and the interrogator knew, or strongly suspected, that I'd been busily disrupting the Civic Circle's plots.

"Have you heard of Oliver Heaviside?"

"Yes," I acknowledged. This interrogation was running through a minefield. Heaviside was one of the pioneers of modern electromagnetics. His contemporaries, James Clerk Maxwell, George Fitzgerald, and Heinrich Hertz were all killed before they could bring Maxwell's remarkable theory to fruition. Perhaps the Civic Circle dismissed Heaviside as a harmless eccentric, but from his cottage in Devon, he'd taken an intriguing step forward. Heaviside discovered how electromagnetic waves exchange energy as they pass through and interfere with each other. His simple yet counterintuitive result extended Maxwellian electromagnetic theory in directions the Civic Circle found dangerous. They suppressed Heaviside's work and removed all mention of it from period texts. I became aware when I found a mention they'd overlooked in an old book. The Circle found evidence of my search, but they thought a friend of my father, Jim Burleson, was the one poking into their secrets. They killed him, and my parents, too, to make sure their secrets were safe.

"Have you ever had any dealings with the Red Flower Tong?"

"No," I lied. The interrogator knew I'd been in contact with Professor Chen's allies in the Red Flower Tong and was using his knowledge to provoke a response.

"What about the Ordo Alberti?"

"No," I replied.

I saw a smug smile develop on the interrogator's face. "Clearly you know of the Albertian Order, though, don't you?"

Blast. I should have pretended confusion instead of denying it outright.

"No." I insisted. The Albertians were a secret order of Dominicans. Their motto was "Investigare, Cognoscere, Defendere," or "To Investigate, To Understand, To Defend." They and the Red Flower Tong both fought a secret war against the Civic Circle, trying to unlock the hidden truth. The Ordo Alberti had rescued and shielded great scientists, like Ettore Majorana, who'd fallen under the scrutiny of the Civic Circle. They'd tried to rescue Professor Graf, almost derailing my own plan to save her. No interrogator would risk mentioning either the Albertians or the Red Flower Tong unless they were certain I already knew all about them.

"Have you heard of Angus MacGuffin?"

Oh, shit. "No." I suppressed my anxiety with difficulty. Angus MacGuffin had been erased from history by the Civic Circle. His memoir, *Suan Ming or the Art of Chinese Fortune Telling*, one was of the books I'd saved from the Tolliver Library fire. The contents were explosive and the Civic Circle would summarily silence any and all who came close to the secrets it contained or even the name and history of the author. Focus. Calm. Relax. It was getting harder to do.

For an interrogator to mention Angus MacGuffin, author of the suppressed memoir describing the history and methods of the Civic Circle and the Circle's closely guarded tie to Xueshu Quan..."

"Do you know of Xueshu Quan?"

"Who?"

"Xueshu Quan," the interrogator repeated, apparently relishing my discomfort.

"No." I replied, realizing the game was up. No way would an interrogator mention Xueshu Quan. No way. As I tried focusing intently on my imaginary beach, there were storm clouds on the horizon. Anyone who knew anything about the mysterious Mr. Quan had a bad habit of ending up dead. The too-bright light above me was drying out my eyes. I blinked.

The interrogator looked neutrally at me, as if my eye-blink were yet another sign of my guilt.

"Xueshu Quan," the interrogator said the name slowly, calmly, coldly. "The Red Flower Tong." He stared at me. "Ordo Alberti." He was just saying the names, not asking questions. I remained silent. "Angus MacGuffin." He looked at me with cold contempt. "I'm not seeing confusion in your responses. I'm seeing familiarity. It's plain as day. You claim you've never heard of any of these?"

"No," I lied. With an effort, I slowed my breathing and returned his stare. I could feel the calm and relaxation pervading my body. Was he lying about my reactions? Or was I truly giving myself away somehow? I suppressed the urge to fill the silence as the interrogator's eyes drilled right through me.

"Your responses indicate a pattern of massive deception," the interrogator insisted. "I submit that you are part of a terrorist conspiracy to attack the Civic Circle. Isn't that right?"

"No," I lied.

He scrutinized the wiggling needles I could hear furiously clawing away at the instrument's paper, and he shook his head sadly. "I submit that you and your band of conspirators helped Professor Chen and Professor Graf evade the authorities, and even now you are helping shield these fugitives from justice. Isn't that correct?"

"No," I lied.

The interrogator looked down at the scribbling of the needles on the graph, snorted in contempt of my evasions, and continued.

"Your friend, Amit, and your uncle, Rob Burdell are part of this conspiracy you call 'the Reactance,' aren't they?"

"No," I insisted.

"I submit that you have access to the secret memoirs of Angus MacGuffin, and that you are even now trying to unlock the technical secrets and uncover the hidden truths that the Civic Circle and its Technology Containment Team protect from public scrutiny. Isn't that correct?"

"No," I lied.

"We have evidence that you and your 'Reactance' conspirators plan to infiltrate this year's Social Justice Leadership Forum on Jekyll Island and the G-8 Summit on Sea Island. Is that correct?"

"No," I lied."

The interrogator stared at me, not even bothering to glance at the readings he insisted revealed my deception.

There was a knock at the door.

Amit let himself into the double-wide trailer.

"Sorry I'm late," he apologized.

The interrogator, my Uncle Rob, stood up and smiled, "You have good timing. I just finished my third grilling of Pete. I think he's got it down pat, if he'll remember to be 'confused' instead of denying something outright."

Amit stared intently at the polygraph. Finally, he asked, "How exactly does this lie detector test work?"

"A polygraph exam is not really a test," Rob explained. "It's an intense interrogation. The main reason for the polygraph is to frighten and intimidate a subject into making a confession or admission."

Amit looked skeptical. "I thought it detected some kind of physiological reaction associated with lying."

"There's no such thing as a lying reaction," Rob clarified. "At best, a polygraph detects nervousness. The 'reaction' that brands you as a liar only indicates deception about half the time. Anyone can pass any lie detector test simply by duplicating the physiological response to fear on demand at the appropriate time. The polygraph records your blood pressure, your heart rate, and what's called your galvanic skin response."

I held up my right hand and examined the black electrodes attached to my first and third fingers. "So, it's just measuring the electrical resistance."

"Exactly," Rob confirmed. "The more you sweat, the lower the resistance between your fingers. The polygraph can literally see you sweat. The pneumograph tubes around your chest and stomach record your breathing." He unfastened them from me. I stood up, and Amit took my place in the chair.

"Any number of innocent stimuli cause the exact same reaction that would brand you as a liar," Rob said, fastening the tubes around Amit. "The more well-developed your conscience, the more likely you are to flunk a polygraph examination – the more hardened your conscience, the better your chance of passing it."

"So, how do you beat the polygraph test?" Amit asked.

"To pass a polygraph examination, you have to know how it works. There are two types of questions: relevant and control. The relevant questions are the ones the interrogator really wants to know. You have to show no reaction whatsoever on the relevant questions. On the control questions, you want to establish a baseline of high stress and nervousness. The examiner compares your reactions. If the relevant questions show a greater reaction than the control questions, that's considered a sign of deception."

Rob showed us the traces. "See? These are the traces for the control questions, and these are the traces for the relevant questions."

I couldn't make much sense of the squiggles. "Where's the indication of massive deception you mentioned?"

"I lied," he said with a smile. "The control traces are somewhat elevated compared to the relevant traces, like it should be for an honest person who comes in nervous and calms down over the course of the examination. At worst the interrogator might call it ambiguous and bring you in for a redo, hoping the added pressure would yield some admissions."

I thought about the implications. "So it's all a game of intimidation?"

Rob nodded his head in agreement. "The interrogator uses the lie detector as a tool to intimidate the suspect into a confession. Sheriff Gunn was telling me when lie detectors first came out, they'd connect a suspect to a photocopier by some wires and when the interrogator thought the suspect was lying, they'd push the print button. Out would pop a copy of the paper they'd loaded with the message, 'He's lying.' They got a lot of suspects to confess that way."

"Where'd you get the polygraph?" Amit asked.

"The FBI let us borrow it," Rob grinned.

"Really?"

Rob nodded. "Sheriff Gunn has been making friends. The local Feds hate the new regime. The honest ones, the loyal patriots, they're being eased out everywhere to make room for the new breed, the compliant ones who won't hesitate to do their masters' bidding. They ship out the good agents to career-killing dead-end jobs at backwoods offices like Knoxville, so they can fill the important offices with more trustworthy, compromised agents. The good guys are networking, comparing notes, doing favors for each other, like letting Sheriff Gunn borrow this polygraph."

Rob settled back into his chair. "Ready, Amit?"

"Oh," Amit suddenly remembered, "Rick was waiting by the gate when I arrived, so I let him in. He's dropping off your truck, Pete." I'd left it in Chattanooga when Sheriff Gunn insisted I ride home with him. Amit handed me a data CD. "Here's the latest public news and the overnight intercepts. The Civic Circle can't decide whether Professor Graf ditched them in the Smoky Mountains to join Professor Chen in Charleston, or whether Charleston is a false trail to distract them while they both hide away in some Smoky Mountain cabin. The Civic Circle's Technology Containment Team seems convinced their Russian contractors managed to poison Professor Graf, though."

"So far, so good, then," Rob nodded. "The plan's working." I bit my tongue to keep from pointing out that Rob's plan had been to abandon the professors to the Civic Circle. They were both alive because I'd defied my uncle and insisted on executing a rescue with or without him. He'd acknowledged he was wrong though, so there was no point in my rubbing it in again. Rob handed me some keys. "To the cruiser," he explained. "Rick'll drive it back to the Lee County Courthouse."

"OK." I headed out the door, wondering what Rick would think of finding himself driving one of Sheriff Gunn's cruisers, like a real deputy sheriff.

"Is your name Amit Patel?" I heard Rob ask as I shut the door behind me. I walked over to my truck.

Rick stepped out as I approached and tossed me the keys to my truck. I looked him over. "Nice outfit, Deputy Rick." Apparently, driving the police cruiser wasn't going to be a novel experience for him after all.

He glanced down at his uniform and looked up with a grin, shifting his hand to rest on the holster at his side. "You don't want to run afoul of the law hereabouts, son," he said in a fair imitation of Sheriff Gunn.

"No, sir," I assured him, reaching out my hand.

Rick relaxed his lawman pose, and suddenly he was my old friend from high school shop class once again. He took my hand in a strong grip. "How you been, Pete? School treat you well?"

"Kept me busy, both inside and outside of class.

"Yeah," he acknowledged. "I heard something about those protests at Georgia Tech. Figures you were involved."

"What do you mean by that?"

"Stuff's happening," he explained. "Your uncle's in the middle of it. Last summer, Mr. Burdell, he'd take you and

Amit on up in the hills most every weekend. 'Just camping,' he told the rest of us."

I remembered it well. We'd meet up with the sheriff, Mr. Garraty, and some of Rob's other friends to practice escape and evasion, marksmanship, and small unit tactics all over the nearby hills and hollows.

"This past year, he's been taking me and a few of the other shop rat gang 'camping,' too," Rick explained with a knowing look on his face. "There's a fight coming, isn't there?" Rick dared me to deny it. "He's getting us all ready."

I hadn't known Rob was busy recruiting more cells into our organization, but it was no surprise. I wasn't supposed to be talking about it, though. "What makes you think there's a fight coming?"

"My eyes are open," Rick said. "I see what's happening, parts of it, at least. The Preserving our Planet's Future Act – that was just the beginning of it. It's not just the terrorists killing President Gore and President Lieberman's 'Gore Tax' driving the price of gasoline and everything else way up. That's just an excuse to take more money from our pockets. They're trying to take over. Completely."

"Who's trying to take over?"

"The elites, of course," Rick answered. "The big shots, like your uncle, Larry, and the rest of the Tollivers. The Civic Circle. You know?"

I knew exactly what he was talking about. The Tollivers had never forgiven Dad for stealing Mom away from them. Uncle Larry had tried to recruit me into the Civic Circle – a way of getting even with Dad. Dad stole his sister from him, so he aimed to steal me back. In recruiting me, Larry revealed a part of their hidden agenda.

You know how they say conservatives think liberals are stupid? Socialism has been tried time and again. We had the "National Socialism" of the Nazis and the "International Socialism" of the communists. Both sides centralized power in the hands of the state, crushed opposition, and ruthlessly killed their enemies. The Nazis exterminated around

20,000,000 "race enemies." The Nazis were amateurs, though, compared to their communist rivals, who slaughtered something on the order of 110,000,000 victims. Government power is a necessary condition for mass slaughter, and the historical correlation between absolute power and absolute corruption and devastation is undeniable. If liberals were smart (or so reason some conservatives), they would understand the danger posed by government power. Therefore, liberals must be dumb.

What if conservatives are wrong? What if liberals aren't actually stupid – at least not all of them? Many in the elite are there because of social connections and inheritance. Once there, though, how do they stay there? At any time, some eager young interloper with cleverer ideas and a better work ethic might undercut their position and usurp their power. How then can the elite increase social stasis, decrease social volatility and mobility, and enhance their chances of remaining on top without requiring an honest victory over the competition?

The answer is simple: socialism.

The devastation that inevitably follows when absolute power leads to absolute corruption? An acceptable risk if it allows them to be the ones with absolute power.

Their redistributive welfare schemes that never seem to cure poverty? They buy votes and build a bureaucracy vested in perpetuating the status quo.

Feminist policies that never manage to eliminate the "wage gap?" They get women out of the home and into the workplace, weakening the threat of families as a rival to government power, lowering the birthrate, and ensuring that what children are born get sculpted by the public school system to be proper citizens with the "right" values and attitudes. They get women looking to the government as a surrogate husband.

Educational loans to help everyone get a college education? They encourage students to incur vast amounts of debt they will never be able to repay, putting them in fiscal bondage for life, while funding the elites' cheerleaders and propagandists in academia.

Environmental policies to "save the planet"? They're specifically designed to throttle industry, slow down progress and enforce a social stasis in which the elites' positions will be secure.

For every "benevolent" policy of the enlightened liberal elite, there's a sinister hidden agenda to tighten the elite's grip on power.

"Yeah," I replied to Rick, "I know."

"They're trying to take over," he insisted. "They fly off on their fancy jets to their exotic foreign resorts to hobnob with Hollywood stars and lecture us all about how we need to learn to live with less. For the planet, they say. Then they leave us with less, and they skim off the rest to fund their next scheme to change the world and buy 'em more votes."

I nodded. Rick got it. I could see why Rob was bringing him into the Reactance.

"They're fencing us in with regulations, and harvestin' the sweat off our brows and the shirts off our backs in taxes," Rick continued. "Don't matter if you vote Democrat because you think they'll help the little guy, or Republican because you think they'll get the government off your back. The end result is always the same. We keep losing our country bit by bloody bit."

I hadn't realized Rick was so passionate and so clued in to what was going on. "What do you think we should do about it?" I asked him.

"I don't know, exactly," he acknowledged, "but if you think they're going to give us back our country without a fight, you're sadly mistaken."

I nodded.

"Mr. Burdell, he's got a plan," Rick continued. "I don't know the details. He keeps all that pretty tight. No 'need to know.' He gets us to help him though, when he needs it. Like with that missing scientist lady."

"You think he had something to do with that?" I asked.

Rick rolled his eyes at me. "The sheriff and your uncle, Mr. Burdell, round up me and most of the other reserve deputies to run off to Chattanooga just as this scientist lady you were workin' for at Georgia Tech goes missin'? And somehow I gotta drive your truck back here for you a few days later? I may not be in the loop on the whole story, but I can put two and two together and get four."

I couldn't lie to my friend. I remained silent.

"Don't worry," he assured me with a grin. "I won't say nothin'. I gotta go get ready for tonight."

"Tonight?"

He looked at me. "I thought you were involved." He looked at me more intently, uncertain whether I was really ignorant or merely refusing to say what I knew. "Never mind. Need to know and all."

I resisted the temptation to ask him what was going on, and I handed him the keys to the cruiser. "See you around, Rick."

"Later!"

I was going to have to ask Rob how Rick fit into our day's plans in particular and the Reactance in general. I mean, I knew Rob was busy working out how to take down the Civic Circle, and I knew he was using his business activities as a cover for his plans. I'd figured he was collaborating with Sheriff Gunn and some of their veteran buddies. Rob recruiting his employees, including my high school friends, into some kind of covert militia – the scale of it took me by surprise.

Seemed Amit and Rob were still busy with their interrogation in the trailer, so I headed to the barn to check on the professor. Rob didn't want Amit knowing about the refuge buried underneath the barn. Until Amit and I went off to our summer jobs, we were maintaining the fiction that Rob and I were occupying the trailer and Professor Graf lived in the apartment in the barn. That fiction was for Amit's sake. Rick may have put the pieces together to figure out what was going on, but neither he nor anyone else were supposed to know we were hiding the professor. When Rob and I had left her, she was reviewing her calculations in the kitchen. That's where I found her.

"Hi, Marlena." I was still getting used to calling Professor Graf by her first name.

"Hi, Pete," she looked up from her book. "Ready for your polygraph exam?"

"I think so," I assured her. "The concept is easy. It's the practice of consciously controlling breathing, heart rate, and nervousness in general that are the challenge." I looked at Fox News playing on the TV in the background. "Isn't that distracting?"

"Yes," she acknowledged, "but I was stuck anyway, and I just can't help myself. Every hour they recap the top news, and America gets to learn the latest developments in the manhunt for the Chinese spy, Professor Wu Chen, and his missing femme fatale, yours truly. They're saying the most vicious things about him seducing me or me seducing him – ridiculously salacious speculations woven out of no evidence whatsoever."

"There's no reason to subject yourself to that nonsense," I pointed out. "Amit compiled a digest of the online press and the Civic Circle's internal reports." I handed her the CD.

"Thanks," she took the disk. "I need to see it, though," she gestured toward the TV. "I need to keep reminding myself that I really am a wanted fugitive, that I really have broken all my ties to my past life. You get used to being able to search for the specific information you want, online, instantly," she said, a tone of frustration in her voice. "Having to sit back passively while some clueless talking-head gatekeeper feeds you a stream of information, most of which you don't care about..."

"It wouldn't be a good idea for us to show too great an interest in your case through online searches," I pointed out. "They monitor everything, and if they start to focus on who's paying attention to the news about you..."

"I know," she interrupted me, "I know. It's just that I'm used to keeping up to date in astrophysics, looking at who's citing my work and who's publishing what in my area. Every morning I'd check the latest. Now, I can't do that."

"If you get Amit a list of what you want to keep up with, he can roll that into all the other searches he distributes across all the hotels running his software. We have to hand-carry it up from town, though. With our satellite internet out here, it's just too easy for them to keep an eye on our data and activity. The hotel Amit's family runs and the network Amit built up provide much better cover for hiding potentially suspicious data streams like that."

"That's just part of it," Marlena looked off into the distance – the weight of the past few weeks evident in the weariness that showed on her face. "My old life is gone. I can't go back. It's finally sinking in. I'm a prisoner here."

I started to protest, but she cut me off.

"Oh, I know. You and your uncle have been very nice to me. I'm grateful you saved my life. I'm grateful you've provided me with a refuge here to hide, but... I can't leave. It's a prison. A very nice prison with friendly jailers, but a prison nevertheless. I'm angry at the Civic Circle. They may have failed to kill me, but they did manage to take my life away. I'm frustrated there doesn't seem to be anything I can do about it."

There wasn't much I could say to that, because it was all true. I thought she knew I loved her, but I wasn't sure. I wanted to tell her how I felt, but with her in such obvious turmoil, the timing just didn't seem right.

I finally noticed the book in her hands – the original proof of Angus MacGuffin's *Suan Ming or the Art of Chinese Fortune Telling,* quite possibly the most valuable, or at least the most dangerous, book in the world. "We do have copies, you know."

"Yes," she said holding it up guiltily, "but I just wanted to take a break from deciphering the physics and try to get a better feel for who he was and what he thought. I get a stronger connection to him holding the original proof instead of a copy."

The book was a confusing mix of mysticism and a memoir of MacGuffin's experience in China in the 1920s and 1930s. MacGuffin's Chinese contacts had provided him with some ancient documents. He'd translated them to yield some seemingly "mystical" prose that turned out to describe Maxwell's Equations. The MacGuffin manuscript included the suppressed ideas from Heaviside that got me into trouble in the first place, and used them as a springboard into even more fundamental physics. I made a good start translating them, and lately Marlena had been picking up where I left off. "Making any progress?"

"No," she acknowledged. "I've been reading MacGuffin's account of his time in Buenos Aires. His last few months he spent compiling his notes and manuscript in the library, and relaxing in cafés with friends. After all the stress and turmoil he faced in China, it must have been like a vacation for him. I'm glad he got to enjoy his last few months before..."

...before he returned to the U.S. in 1940 to be brutally slaughtered by the Civic Circle's agents. Knowing how MacGuffin's personal story ended made bittersweet the obvious pleasure he'd found in the Buenos Aires chapter of his life.

"He got to be good friends with Ettore Majorana," I pointed out. The brilliant Italian physicist had fled the Civic Circle's attempts to recruit him in Italy and vanished, re-emerging under the name "Mr. Bini" in Buenos Aires to build a new life with the assistance of the Albertians – the secret order within the Dominicans that aids and protects scientists.

"The man who called himself 'Mr. Bini.' You've convinced me he was really Majorana. It's MacGuffin's other friend I'm curious about," Marlena explained, "Jorge."

I had a vague memory of the name from when I read through MacGuffin's manuscript last year. "That writer MacGuffin ran across in the Argentine National Library whose apartment he visited for dinner?"

"You remember him after all," Marlena smiled. "You recall what he had to say about MacGuffin's book?"

"That the book was without beginning and without end because there always seemed to be more pages added to it?"

"Exactly," Marlena nodded. "MacGuffin said Jorge had a real gift for understanding the more esoteric concepts from the Chinese scrolls. The three of them – MacGuffin, Majorana, and Jorge spent hours talking in their favorite café, having dinner in Jorge's fourth floor apartment. Maybe Jorge wrote something about the experience."

"Wasn't Jorge working in the library? That doesn't sound as though he had any kind of a success as a writer. Any writer who's any good at all can make a living off his work, right? And anything Jorge wrote would probably be in Spanish. Our priority should be to find where MacGuffin hid his source material – the original scrolls and the Nexus Detector."

Marlena looked skeptical. "I still have trouble buying the concept of a device that can detect a Nexus – a time and place where reality itself begins to... to fork into different paths."

"Weren't you telling me about the 'Many-Worlds' interpretation? The quantum-mechanical concept that if I flip a coin, there's a universe in which it came up heads, and a universe that came up tails? Two universes where once there was one?"

"By its nature, that's a completely untestable hypothesis," Marlena pointed out, "and at any given moment every atom interacts with its neighbors in various quantum mechanical ways – many universes springing into being for every atom, for every sub-atomic particle in every minute instant. Holy Occam's Razor – talk about hyper-complexity! That's why my attitude toward quantum mechanics has always been to ignore the philosophy and get on with the physics – to 'shut up and calculate.'"

"We have MacGuffin's account of how this Nexus Detector worked in Chinese history," I insisted, "and we know today the Civic Circle has been using one to track down and eliminate their enemies who might divert the course of history from the Civic Circle's preferred path."

"Whatever MacGuffin may have done with his Nexus Detector and his scrolls, that was in 1940. Unless they were carefully preserved, the Georgia humidity has probably taken a toll on the scrolls. How can we possibly track down this 'thorny friend' MacGuffin entrusted everything to sixty-five years ago? At least Jorge was a writer. There's a chance he wrote something about his experience. I think Jorge is a lead worth checking out," Marlena insisted.

After the initial elation of escaping the Civic Circle's attempt on her life, she'd been stressed and depressed at the growing reality of cutting ties to her past life and living in hiding. Her passion for hunting down Jorge was the first genuine enthusiasm I've seen in her in a few days.

"Will do," I humored her. It'd be a null result, but it wouldn't take long to run that one to ground.

She flashed one of those brilliant smiles that just melted me inside. I had a crush on her from the first time I saw her in class. I kept wishing that the obvious passion she had for physics might someday be directed toward me. We found ourselves on opposite sides in the social justice protests at Georgia Tech. Amit and I infiltrated the social justice movement, and I had to maintain appearances. One magical evening, we'd forgotten about the politics and protests and simply worked together to unravel some of the physics in MacGuffin's work. I thought we'd really made a deep personal connection, but the apparent political divide was too much for her.

Then, I'd learned the Civic Circle was on their way to eliminate her and Professor Chen. Rob insisted Amit and I bug out back to Tennessee. I'd defied him, saving both professors, with some help from Rob and Sheriff Gunn at the end. Why did I do it? Because the Civic Circle killed too many people – my parents, people who'd helped me in my research and paid for it with their lives, scientists whose passion to push the boundaries made them a threat to the Civic Circle's control. Because I'd had enough. Because I couldn't live with myself if I let the Civic Circle kill yet again, even if it cost me my life. And because I was in love with her.

Marlena had cut her ties with her former life. Sure, it looked as though we might be able to retrieve her cat, and maybe we'd be able to let her mom know she was alright, but in hiding. All her friends and professional acquaintances, all her belongings, all her work and her career, she'd had to leave behind. She'd been grateful for what I'd done, and friendly enough to me in the few days since she'd arrived in Uncle Rob's hidden refuge, but there was still a wall between us. She was still reeling from the dislocations in her life. I wanted to tell her how I felt, but at the same time, I thought I needed to give her space to adjust, to come to terms with her new life. I'd been waiting for just the right moment to let her know how I felt about her. It never came. Now I was about to leave for my meeting with the Red Flower Tong in Atlanta and to start my summer job in Huntsville.

"Marlena," I began, reaching out and holding her hand. She glanced down and then back up at me, but did not pull her hand back. "I need to tell you something, to let you know where I stand."

"I know, Peter." She smiled gently and pulled her hand back. "This is all so strange for me: discovering a whole new layer to reality, finding a hidden war taking place for control over science and society with you and me right in the middle of it. I don't know yet exactly what my place... or your place will be in this new grand design."

I moved closer to her, but then there was a knock on the door.

Amit let himself in. Again.

My moment was lost. I turned toward Amit. "That was quick."

"What can I say? I'm a natural," Amit explained. "Breezed right through it." He looked at the two of us. "Interrupting something, am I?"

"No," I lied.

Rob came in just behind him. "I still don't like you going to visit the Tong solo. Professor Chen may be a friend of sorts..."

"I know," I interrupted him, "but the Red Flower Tong is dangerous, probably criminally so. All the more reason we not expose anyone else to harm. I have a relationship with them, already. I need to be the one to talk with them. If you came with me it would give them a link to you, to your place here, and to everything else we're trying to do."

Rob didn't like it. He looked like he'd swallowed a bad batch of his own moonshine. With my father dead, he'd stepped in to fill the void. Now, though, I'd defied him to rescue Marlena and Professor Chen, after he insisted I leave them and run home. He was having to adjust to dealing with me as an equal instead of as a subordinate. I needed to be conciliatory.

"I don't like having to do it, either, but the job is mine, and I'm the one who has to do it." I could see that hit home. Rob was big on accepting responsibility, sucking it up, and doing your duty. "I'll use the burner phone to let you know when I'm done, and I'll be heading on to Huntsville to start work Monday morning."

Rob paused as if he were about to say something. Then, he just nodded. "You have a long day ahead of you. Best get going."

"Take care of him for me," Marlena smiled, "will you, Amit?"

"Keeping Pete out of trouble is a full-time job, Marlena, but you know me. I'm always, always up for it," Amit insisted.

I'm certain the double entendre was entirely intentional.

I turned Amit back toward the door. "Let's go."

CHAPTER 2: INTO THE DRAGON'S DEN

"'Take care of him for me?'" Amit hopped back into the truck after closing the gate to Rob's place. "Did you make it with her, after all?"

"A gentleman never tells," I replied.

"That would be a 'no,' then," Amit seemed amused.

Amit could really get on my nerves sometimes. He'd landed a kind of Golden Ticket to the Civic Circle's Social Justice Leadership Forum – an internship within the Civic Circle itself. Of course, he'd get invited to their Social Justice Leadership Forum. Amit was now one of their up-and-coming social-justice leaders. Me? I'd been rejected for that opportunity, but I was still going to the meeting thanks to an alternate plan. Uncle Larry greased the skids to get me into TAGS as the personal assistant to his cousin, Travis Tolliver, who ran the company in Huntsville, Alabama. That was my ticket to the Social Justice Leadership Forum.

Larry had been working for years to get Tolliver Corporation into those "leadership" circles, so he, Travis and other Tolliver executives were among the invitees. In fact, TAGS was providing the IT support for the meeting.

I got the feeling Larry didn't entirely trust Travis and wanted me to spy on the Huntsville operation. That was fine by me, so long as I could infiltrate the Social Justice Leadership Forum and help disrupt their scheme to fool the country into a pointless Middle East war. Uncle Larry was my source for that information and my main conduit to the Civic Circle and their plans. I needed to stay as close to him as possible, and if Larry was willing to pay me to be his spy within TAGS and the Civic Circle, that was fine by me.

I still wasn't sure why Amit wanted me to drive him to Atlanta. I was only heading to Atlanta for my meeting with the Tong en route to my summer job in Huntsville. Amit asked me to drop him off at a hotel near the airport, to catch a flight up to Washington, D.C., first thing the next morning to start his internship with the Civic Circle. He could just as easily have caught a flight from Knoxville instead of spending half the day driving to Atlanta with me. His motives became clear only when we arrived in Atlanta just after lunchtime with several hours before my scheduled dinner with the Tong.

"Take I-285 east," Amit said with a hint of pleasure at my confusion. "Exit here," he added a few minutes later. I directed my truck south on Georgia 400.

"Take this exit to Lenox Square Mall," he directed mysteriously. "I have something to return before I go."

Amit pulled a shopping bag from his suitcase. "Three hundred fifty dollars of perfume is amazingly compact," he observed.

"You were serious about hitting on girls at perfume counters?" I hadn't really believed the stories he told me.

"Watch and learn, my friend. Watch and learn. You need to identify that perfume the Albertian babe was wearing," Amit pointed out, "the one you dubbed 'Perky Girl.' We need to be able to identify her again so we can reach out to the Ordo Alberti. They had you blindfolded the whole time, so the only way you'll be able to tell if you meet them again..."

"...is if I recognize the perfume," I completed Amit's thought. "Surely the Albertians will have someone on Jekyll Island to keep an eye on the Civic Circle. We might get lucky."

"Exactly," Amit confirmed. "Plus everything went down so fast at the end of the semester that I never did get a chance to finish this particular exploit. I need a wingman to run interference on her supervisor, anyway. Follow my lead."

Exploit? Wondering exactly what I'd gotten myself into, I followed him into the big department store and down the escalator to the perfume counter.

"Hi, Heather," Amit caught the attention of the girl behind the counter. "I have some bad news for you."

"Ah, yes, it's... Amit," she replied with a bright smile. "What's the problem?"

"I had to call it off with Alexa," Amit replied sadly. "She wanted to cancel her trip to Venice for the Victoria's Secret lingerie shoot. She was insisting on moving in with me in Washington, D.C."

"Really?" Heather asked. "That sounds like she was really into you."

"Yeah," Amit acknowledged, shaking his head, "but a lot of those model types are real prima donnas – flighty, temperamental, looking for an anchor, you know?"

I could see Heather nodding her head in agreement.

"Can you believe anyone would pick a summer in Washington over a summer in Venice? Walking along the canals, eating gelato on a hot summer day, weekend excursions to the Alps. Some of my best memories..." Amit said wistfully. "Would you really pick Washington over that?"

"I haven't been either place," Heather replied, "but it sounds wonderful."

"She was just too pushy, trying to get too serious, too soon," Amit said in sorrow. "Wanting to move in together, talking about baby names for goodness sake.... It's just too fast, too soon. We're too young to settle down. This is the time of life when we experiment, we take chances, don't you think? I mean, you're not getting married anytime soon, are you? You and your boyfriend – you're not engaged are you?"

"No," she said, seemingly amused by all Amit's banter, or maybe she was just being polite.

"I thought so," Amit smiled at her. "A fellow free spirit. Anyway," he said, placing the bag on the counter, "the romantic send-off I'd planned for her just isn't happening now, and I'm going to have to return these."

"Oh, that's too bad," Heather replied. I figured she probably worked on commission. Did they deduct returns from her paycheck? Not the kind of thing Amit would be concerned about.

"Yeah, and I just wanted to give her a little something to remember me by," Amit said sadly.

A $350 "little something?" I saw Heather checking the returns against his receipt. The other lady, an older matron who must have been in her forties, started moving toward us to help Heather.

"Now's your turn," Amit said softly to me. "Go to the other end of the counter and ask the old dragon about the Albertian girl's perfume."

I moved to intercept her. "Excuse me, ma'am." I saw her nametag, "Dee, can you help me?"

"One moment please, sir," she brushed me off as she continued to help Heather process the return. I figured helping Heather ward off Amit's advances was probably on Dee's agenda as well.

"Thank you so much for all your help, Heather," I could hear Amit at the other end of the counter. Looked like they'd finished up.

"Ma'am?" I caught Dee's attention. She disengaged and came over to me. Amit was not through with Heather, however. He faked out Dee by doubling back. I could hear Amit and Heather talking, but I had to focus on Dee and my own questions now. "I'm trying to identify the perfume a friend of mine was wearing. Can you help me?"

"That blouse really looks slimming," Amit was saying to Heather down at the other end of the counter. Was that what he called a neg? A backhanded compliment intended to puncture a girl's ego? I mean, Heather didn't look like she needed to worry about trying to look more slender. Her ratios approached geometric perfection. I could see why Amit had singled her out for this elaborate pick-up attempt.

I couldn't pay more attention to Amit and Heather just then, because the Dragon Lady was asking me questions.

"How did it smell? Musky? Floral? Citrusy?"

"I don't know if I can describe it," I admitted.

She reached under the counter for some samples.

"I just love how you don't really care what people think of how you look," Amit was telling Heather.

"This one?" Dee asked me.

"No."

"How about this one?"

"Closer, but no."

Finally, the fourth sample reminded me a bit of what Perky Girl had been wearing.

"All I can say is that sure is memorable," Amit was saying as I began my next round of samples.

"Like that one," I told Dee, "only not as... as..."

"Musky?" she asked, looking sternly down the counter at Heather and probably wishing she could save her young charge from Amit's predations.

"I suppose so."

She pulled out several more samples.

"What time do you get off?" Amit was asking Heather. "I still have the reservations I made for dinner, if you don't mind being a last-minute substitution."

"That's it!" I wafted some more toward my nose. "That's the one."

"Your young lady has exquisite taste," Dragon Lady confirmed. "That's an exclusive mix from a small Zurich perfumery. You wouldn't normally find it in the U.S. Is your young lady European?"

"I suppose so." That did seem likely. She had a vague hint of an accent.

Despite confirming I was looking at the smallest possible quantity of the perfume they could sell, I was not happy with the outrageous price tag.

"Catch you later," Amit was saying.

I hoped Heather – and getting a sample of Perky Girl's perfume – would be worth the cost and hassle.

"You found the right perfume?" Amit seemed surprised his scheme had actually worked. "Let me sample that." He took a good whiff so he'd recognize it too. "Nice stuff. She must be a classy babe."

"So how'd the pick-up with this Heather go?"

"I am so going to score," Amit said confidently. "I can sense it."

"Awful expensive way to land a date," I pointed out.

He smiled. "I'm on expense account. The Civic Circle is picking up the tab for the whole evening. Dinner and hotel room. Thought I'd take advantage by playing some 'Alpha Provider' game."

He saw the puzzled look in my eyes and answered my unasked question. "I'm the exotic foreigner, moving in elite circles, dating supermodels, but unwilling to be tied down to any particular girl," he explained. "That's like chick crack. I'm so far beyond her boring boyfriend or any other guy she's ever met, she can't help but try to make a play for me."

He seemed confident.

"I have a dinner of my own in a couple hours with the Tong. You'll be OK?"

"Just fine," Amit confirmed. "I can practice picking up numbers from girls on the other side of the mall until Heather gets off shift in three hours. I need to get my play card filled so I'm ready when we're back in school this fall. Let me get my bag from your truck, though."

* * *

I returned to the Chinese restaurant where Professor Chen had introduced me to the Red Flower Tong just over a week ago. They were expecting me. The manager himself stood behind the servers' podium. He bowed deeply. I returned a curt nod. "Please follow me, sir," he said respectfully. The black eye I'd received as a result of his screw-up on my previous visit had mostly faded. The Tong seemed a ruthless bunch, but they had a certain sense of honor. They were in my debt for having saved Professor

Chen, and the manager compounded their debt by his mistreatment of Professor Chen and me. I had a feeling he'd be facing some kind of brutal retribution if only I insisted on it, so I didn't. In retrospect, that was a smart move, because it meant his bosses in the Tong felt all the more obliged to even the scales in their dealings with me. I was confident they'd extracted whatever toll from the manager they thought appropriate in the week since my last visit.

The manager held open the door, saying something in Chinese, and bowing deeply. I noticed no one returned his bow. One of the men replied, a hint of anger in his voice.

"Our guest has arrived," the manager said in a fearful tone. Good help must be hard to find.

"You are dismissed." My eyes adjusted to the dim lighting as the manager beat a quick retreat, and I saw the speaker was Mr. Hung. Professor Chen had referred to Mr. Hung as his "uncle," but I had the impression the relationship was a figurative description of relative rank within the Tong. I saw Professor Chen was there, too, along with a couple of the bodyguards I'd met last time. There were a few new faces, including another distinguished-looking older gentleman. "Mr. Burdell," Mr. Hung continued, "Welcome back to the Red Flower Pavilion. I have the honor to introduce my own uncle, Honorable Shan Zhu."

Mr. Hung was some kind of local big shot, and this new Shan Zhu must be his boss. I returned the bows and shook hands. "An honor to meet you, Mr. Zhu," I acknowledged. He said something in Chinese.

"You may call him, 'Honorable Shan Zhu,'" Mr. Hung corrected me. "Please be seated." He showed me to a place at the table. A stunningly beautiful girl in a long form-fitting silk dress served tea. She must have been new, because I certainly would have remembered her if I'd seen her before.

I took the offered tea. "Thank you."

"My pleasure, sir," she answered demurely, but with an inviting smile before shuffling away with small steps constrained by the tight dress.

"You like her?" Mr. Hung must have noted my lingering gaze.

"She is very beautiful," I replied, neutrally.

"Her name is Ding Li. Much can be arranged for our friends."

Was he suggesting...? It was a good thing I'd left Amit behind. He'd be angling for them to throw the girl into the deal. The morality of accepting such an offer aside, I had a feeling that although the immediate experience might be quite pleasant, there would be undesired consequences.

"You are most generous," I played for time while I thought how to politely decline, "but such a lovely flower would leave me too deeply in your debt."

Professor Chen was talking softly in Chinese to Shan Zhu. Translating? Shan Zhu replied and looked at me.

"Honorable Shan Zhu is pleased to meet the 'youxia' who outwitted our enemies and saved Professor Chen," Mr. Hung explained.

"Youxia?"

"It means an adventurer... a knight who roams the countryside doing good deeds," Professor Chen clarified. "Were you able to save Marlena?"

"Professor Graf is fine," I assured him, then immediately realized that it might not have been a good idea to let the Tong know that. "She sends her regards and her thanks for your letter."

"I'm delighted," Professor Chen smiled, "to see you were as effective in your rescue of my colleague as you were in your rescue of me."

"You believe the Circle is convinced she is lost in the mountains and dead?" I was curious what their sources were saying.

He glanced at Mr. Hung who gave him a subtle nod and then turned back to me. "They believe she has died of a poison of some kind," he assured me. "While they would like to find her body for confirmation, they are convinced she must be dead.

That was good news, but it more or less confirmed what Amit had been able to pick up.

"They continue to monitor her apartment, her credit cards, her online accounts, just in case, however," Professor Chen continued. "It will be difficult for her to remain safe forever. You must caution her to remain vigilant and careful."

"We can help," Mr. Hung offered. "We have ways of keeping lost those who the Circle seeks to find. Her talents would be useful in our own work. We can offer her sanctuary."

I began to see why they were being so nice to me.

"I thank you and Honorable Shan Zhu for that generous offer," I acknowledged. "I will pass it on, when the opportunity presents itself."

"Excellent." Mr. Hung replied, while Professor Chen translated my words to Shan Zhu. "Your deeds have marked you as a worthy ally," Mr. Hung continued. "Professor Chen speculated that you might be Albertian."

"What?" I pretended to look puzzled.

"Albertian," Mr. Hung explained. "A member or agent of the Ordo Alberti."

I took that in a moment before replying. "Who are they?" I was glad I'd just been practicing how to pass a lie detector exam. I willed myself to remain calm and relax.

"They are... fellow enemies of the Civic Circle," Mr. Hung continued. "Sometimes allies, sometimes rivals of ours in the Shadow War we fight against the Civic Circle. We both usually focus our efforts against the greater enemy biding our time until the Civic Circle is defeated. The Albertians seek to unite the world in a religious dictatorship under the control of their Pope. They are few, but they have a power and an influence beyond their number, thanks to ancient teachings stolen from us by a man named Angus MacGuffin."

He paused and stared into my eyes. I took the bait. "Who is Angus MacGuffin?"

Mr. Hung continued looking at me. "We were hoping you might be familiar with him," Professor Chen interjected. "You showed me how the duality of the taijitu, the yin-yang symbol, follows from the duality of the electromagnetic field. That insight explains much about how to interpret our ancient writings."

"When the Civic Circle closed in on Mr. Burleson and your parents," Mr. Hung picked up the questioning, "They were concerned about the Heaviside research, but what they found truly alarming was a book by Angus MacGuffin, and a few other forbidden texts that had been overlooked in the Tolliver Library. Did Mr. Burleson ever speak of this MacGuffin?"

"No," I answered honestly. We'd been focused on researching the lost work of Oliver Heaviside, and we'd never have found the MacGuffin manuscript if Amit hadn't intercepted the Civic Circle's urgent instructions to their field agents to confiscate MacGuffin's work and other suppressed texts. "If there were any other sensitive books in the Tolliver Library," I offered, "the Civic Circle's agents probably took them when they burned the place down."

Of course, Uncle Rob was responsible for burning the library, once we collected all the books the Civic Circle was after. I was beginning to realize it would be a very bad idea to let Mr. Hung and his Brotherhood know how much we knew and what we had.

"The Civic Circle did not burn the Library," Mr. Hung declared.

I raised an eyebrow and tried my best to look surprised and puzzled. "But I know they burned down my house. I assumed... If they didn't burn the library," I said slowly, "then who..."

"The Albertians burned the Tolliver Library," Mr. Hung explained, "so you see they are not to be trusted. They stole our secrets, and they burned your library to the ground to make sure their stolen secrets remained out of others' hands."

"This MacGuffin, he was an Albertian?" I asked.

I saw Professor Chen look at Mr. Hung, and Mr. Hung gave him a subtle nod. "He was a missionary in China. Some of the Brotherhood trusted him with our most sacred scrolls and artifacts. He was supposed to deliver them to our friends in San Francisco. He vanished, perhaps with the aid of the Albertians, because he disclosed many of our secrets to them. He re-emerged in Atlanta in 1940, trying to disclose our secrets to the world. The Civic Circle silenced him. They took every copy of his writings, or so we thought. The last known copy was in the Tolliver Library, and the Albertians apparently took it or burned it."

Mr. Hung finished his sidebar conversation in Chinese with Shan Zhu. "That is why we find it curious that you are so knowledgeable about our ancient teachings," Mr. Hung's eyes bored into mine, a hint of accusation in his voice.

"I have you to thank for that," I turned to Professor Chen, startling him. "I saw your tattoo when I first met you. You were evasive about it, so I figured it was a secret of some kind. When I took microwave theory, I realized that your version of the taijitu looked like a Smith Chart. I was playing around with the Schelkunoff formulas for the impedance of a dipole, and thought I'd plot them on a Smith Chart. The result was the symbol you have tattooed on your arm."

"But how did you know that it came from our own ancient teachings?" Chen asked.

"My father, or perhaps it was Mr. Burleson, figured out that there was a tie-in to Xueshu Quan. I researched Chinese history, culture, and philosophy. Once I figured out the Taijitu symbol, I reviewed what the Tao had to say about it. It was clear to me that the talk of the balance of yin and yang and their mutual transformations was really describing the behavior of the electromagnetic field. Do you have some related teachings that are not publically available? Is there anything that goes beyond the conventional Maxwell theory in your ancient writings?"

This time it was Chen who translated for Shan Zhu. I was so going to have to learn Chinese to keep up with their sidebar conversations. The delay gave me a welcome moment to collect my thoughts. I couldn't let them know how much I already knew about MacGuffin. I had to keep my secrets to myself while pushing them to disclose their secrets to me.

"We have some portion of the material stolen by MacGuffin," Chen acknowledged. "The material is in Chinese, so it would be difficult for you to contribute to our work."

"I see." An excellent excuse for them to keep their own secrets to themselves. "This is all new to me. First, I learn that the Civic Circle is a conspiracy bent on taking over the world. Then I learn that the Brotherhood opposes them in secret. Now I learn that there's yet another side in the Shadow War. Are there any other players in this great game?" I might as well fish for more information.

"To the outside world, we are the 'Red Flower Tong,'" Mr. Hung confirmed. We and the Albertians are the principal opposition to Xueshu Quan and the Civic Circle," Mr. Hung confirmed. "There have been 'other players,' as you put it. Your country was profoundly influenced by Adam Weishaupt and the Bavarian Illuminati working through the Freemasons. They sought to develop your nation as a counterweight to Xueshu Quan. In the late 1820s and 1830s, however, Xueshu Quan's agents prompted a purge of key Masons in your country, eliminating their leaders and subverting their society. They swept up most of the useful remnants into their own organization which became the precursor to the Civic Circle, and they cut off ties to the remainder."

I took that in. "So the current Freemasons have forgotten their founding principles?"

"Either forgotten, or they are not acting on what knowledge they have," Mr. Hung clarified. "There are certain small cells who have preserved or recovered the ancient wisdom. They are rarely a factor.

"The Dark Ocean – the Genyōsha – of Japan. They remain powerful, but have not acted directly against Xueshu Quan and the Civic Circle in decades.

"It is the same with the royal houses of Europe. They had some knowledge of Xueshu Quan and the threat he posed. For a time, they acted in concert to cripple the power of my homeland in an effort to thwart Xueshu Quan. With the collapse of the Qing Dynasty, decades of war and lawlessness, and the rise of the Communists, they thought the threat was finished.

"Queen Elizabeth II is the last of their line to retain any significant power. Perhaps her uncle, Edward VIII, failed to pass on the secrets to her father, George VI, when Edward abdicated. We do not know. Even if she does know the hidden truth, she has failed to act upon it.

"Of course the last royal houses to make a serious move against Xueshu Quan were the Romanovs of Russia, the Hapsburgs, and the House of Hohenzollern. The result was World War I, the loss of their power, and the dismemberment of their respective empires.

"Perhaps Elizabeth is merely prudent and biding her time, but Britain lost the empire her house conquered. Now her nation is being conquered in turn by immigrants from the lands she once ruled. By her inaction, for whatever reason, she is no longer a factor."

How much of history could be explained by this Shadow War against Xueshu Quan and the Civic Circle? How many curious and counterintuitive events were their doing, side effects of their ancient struggle?

"Now, the Brotherhood is all that stands between Xueshu Quan and world domination," Mr. Hung continued. "We do not often work with outsiders, however, you have proven yourself. You saved my nephew, Professor Chen. We can help you avenge your parents killed by the Xueshu Quan and the agents of the Civic Circle. Working with us is your only option, because we are the only viable opposition to Xueshu Quan."

He paused and took a sip of tea to punctuate that point.

"You have a plan to discredit your professor. I told you we can do this. Honorable Shan Zhu is here to decide if we will do what we can do. Explain what you have in mind."

"Honorable Shan Zhu," I nodded at him and saw him tilt his head in reply. "Professor Gomulka... he is an operative of the Civic Circle, and he led the campaign against Professor Chen. He is my enemy and yours." I paused for Professor Chen to catch up in his translation. "I am in a position of trust and can read his emails. Professor Gomulka has certain... weaknesses. I believe he can be led into a compromising situation that would not only remove him but bring ridicule and contempt for the Civic Circle."

Professor Chen finished translating my words for Shan Zhu. Shan Zhu looked me in the eye as he replied.

"Honorable Shan Zhu says that a source of information is not so lightly discarded," Professor Chen translated. "If you can read your professor's emails, it would be wise to watch patiently and learn what you can from his indiscretions. 'Know the enemy and know yourself, and you will never fear the result of a hundred battles.'"

Was that from Sun Tzu's *The Art of War*? "Thanks to the professor's indiscretions, I now have other sources of information," I explained. "I also have access to his superior's email and that of others in the Civic Circle. I will continue to know the enemy, even if Gomulka is removed. I offer an opportunity to subdue the Civic Circle, to break the enemy's resistance without fighting." That sounded like something Sun Tzu might say.

I saw Shan Zhu nod as Chen translated my words and listened to Shan Zhu's reply. "Honorable Shan Zhu asks, 'What is this weakness you would exploit?'"

"Professor Gomulka has an addiction of sorts to online sex sites: he watches and downloads pornographic videos, and he participates in sex chats online. On many occasions he hits on the women with whom he's interacting. Of course, he only ends up paying more in exchange for longer chats or webcam sessions. He also has accounts on online dating and hookup sites where he frequently approaches young attractive women who invariably reject him."

"He is... thirsty," said Mr. Hung while Professor Chen translated in the background. "We can work with this – a honey trap." I must have shown my confusion on my face because he continued. "A beautiful woman can tempt a thirsty man, wrap him around her finger, and lead him where she wants. You have a word for this: a 'honey trap.'" Then he paused to listen respectfully to Shan Zhu's reply.

"Honorable Shan Zhu sees many possibilities in this," Mr. Hung explained at last. "What is your suggestion? Explain it for Honorable Shan Zhu as you explained it to me."

"Professor Gomulka will be at Jekyll Island this summer for the Civic Circle's Social Justice Leadership Forum. He will be part of the Civic Circle delegation to the G-8 Summit the following week. This summer, Professor Gomulka will meet a new online girlfriend, one he cannot resist, one he will fall in love with. She will be moving to this country to begin her new life with him, and she will need his help to receive a shipping container of her possessions. When the shipping container arrives and he claims it, the container will be full of heroin or some other illicit drugs.

"His online girlfriend will have duped him to smuggle in the drugs and equipment to keep the Civic Circle's wild parties well stocked and supplied. Or maybe he was in on the plan all along. Or maybe he was working directly for his superiors in the Civic Circle and doing their bidding. No one will be able to tell. It will be a huge scandal with Professor Gomulka and the Civic Circle right in the middle of it, pointing fingers at each other, discrediting them all. It works on many levels... We break their resistance. We disrupt their plan to lead my country into war. We win a great victory without needing to fight at all."

I could see Shan Zhu frown as Chen translated.

"Many containers ship from China," Mr. Hung acknowledged, "and we have many friends. Honorable Shan Zhu says we can prepare an appropriate... surprise for this

Gomulka. But the Civic Circle will know they have been duped. They will see our hand in this thing. There may be reprisals. The risk is great."

"We must give them what they expect," I replied. "It will confirm their own biases and expectations. At the Social Justice Leadership Forum, they aim to prepare our country for war with Iraq. Many powerful parties seek this conflict and would benefit from the destruction of Sadaam Hussein: the Israelis, for example, or the Iranians, or the Kuwaitis. The shipment will be traced to China, perhaps to a rival you can afford to put at risk. They in turn will have been hired by an anonymous third party with nebulous ties to some party with a plausible motive. Layers upon layers of cutouts. Someone is trying to influence them, to bribe them to do what they want to do anyway. They expect this. The pattern is plausible."

"Your professor," asked Mr. Hung, thoughtfully, while Chen was translating, "what will the Civic Circle make of him?"

"Perhaps they will realize he was a puppet, a victim of a con," I replied. "Then he is an unreliable fool. Perhaps the online seduction is merely his alibi and he was in league with the puppet masters all along. Either way, they will never trust him again, and his career is finished."

Shan Zhu spoke with Mr. Hung at length. Finally Mr. Hung replied.

"You saved our nephew, Professor Chen. We repay that debt by doing as you ask. Professor Gomulka attacked our nephew. We avenge him. We bring confusion and dishonor to our ancient enemy. The potential rewards are great. The risks are manageable. We will do as you ask. We will prepare a suitable 'surprise' for Professor Gomulka. The surprise will arrive at the Port of Brunswick just before the Social Justice Leadership Forum. We will trust in you to entangle Gomulka, to ensure that he shows up to claim the shipping container."

"I have your word?" I asked. I saw Mr. Hung stiffen, and I knew I'd put my foot in my mouth somehow.

"A Brother does not make promises," Professor Chen explained my mistake. "When a Brother speaks, it is a vow. Everything a Brother says is a promise. If a Brother says he will do something, then it will be done."

"Please pardon my ignorance of your customs," I bowed my head in apology. "I intended no offense."

"No offense was taken," Mr. Hung nodded in response. "We will arrange the shipment you request, the details of which we will define later." Then, he began lecturing me on communications security. "Oh, you already use Lavabit?"

"Yes." The encrypted email service was the backbone of our communications within the FOG, the "Friends of George," the covert group we'd set up among the students of Georgia Tech.

George P. Burdell is a legend among Tech students. Back in the 1920s some resourceful students got hold of an extra enrollment form and submitted it on behalf of the fictional George P. Burdell. They enrolled him in classes and took turns submitting homework and exams on his behalf. Since then, George P. has received multiple degrees from Georgia Tech. It's a running joke to page him at events where Georgia Tech students and alums congregate. When Amit and I needed an anonymous figurehead to rally the campus against the Civic Circle's attempt to take over, we used George P. Burdell's name.

"That should suffice," he nodded, "but never speak specifically about what we are doing. We are 'the waiter.' You are 'the busboy.' The cargo container is the 'fortune cookie.' This Gomulka, he is 'the guest.' Get it?"

"Got it," I confirmed. We ran through more options and permutations in our scenario code, and exchanged email addresses.

"Let us drink to the beginning of our partnership." Mr. Hung actually smiled one of his disconcerting smiles. I realized his smile bothered me because it seemed unnatural. Mr. Hung had so trained himself not to show emotion, that when he did, even a genuine smile seemed forced.

Ding Li brought a crystal decanter and poured four small glasses of the dark liquid. It smelled fruity.

"Plum wine," Professor Chen explained.

"Death to the Circle!"

I took a sip to Mr. Hung's toast. It was a bit too strong for my taste.

Shan Zhu said something in Chinese.

"Drink up," Mr. Hung translated.

I took another sip and set my glass down. "I have a long drive ahead of me," I told him. "I will need a clear head." I hoped I wasn't causing offense, but it seemed unwise to overindulge in the potent wine.

"We would gladly extend our hospitality to you," Mr. Hung offered, "should you wish to spend the evening." Ding Li smiled sweetly at me. "She is a skilled masseuse, and well-schooled in the Eight Ways of Pleasure."

Ding Li gazed at me and licked her lips, expectantly.

Oh, my. I took a deep breath and steeled my resolve.

"I must regretfully decline," I broke eye contact with her and looked at Mr. Hung at last. "I have... places to go, and promises to keep."

"How very unfortunate," Mr. Hung replied. He gestured, and Ding Li cleared the table. He gave me his contact information after assuring himself I understood online security.

I returned the bows of my hosts. "Thank you Honorable Shan Zhu, Mr. Hung, Professor Chen for your hospitality." Then, I shook their hands. Mr. Hung escorted Shan Zhu out a back way, and Professor Chen accompanied me to the door.

"Peter," the professor said softly. "The Brotherhood may be trusted to do what it says..."

Before he could finish, Ding Li somehow appeared in front of me. "I will escort our honorable guest." Professor Chen nodded and turned to follow Hung and Zhu. "This way," she held the door for me. Two guards were standing just outside. I stopped and looked at them. They seemed familiar – probably the guys who'd roughed me up the last time I was there. The last thing you want to do with guys like that is show fear. I stood impassively, making sure I could remember their faces if I saw them again. They returned my stare, doing a marvelous job of hiding how much I intimidated them. "This way," Ding Li insisted, taking my arm and leading me through another door and into the crowded restaurant.

The clanking plates and noise of conversation combined with the odors of the food and the spicy, oriental fragrance of Ding's jet black hair to assault my senses. The receptionist hastened to open the door for us as Ding Li escorted me outside.

"I work next door." She pointed to the massage parlor. "My hands very good."

I swallowed. It would be easy to accept her offer. I couldn't, though. "No, I need to be leaving. Thank you."

I started to move to my truck.

Ding Li grabbed my arm. "Will I see you again, soon?" she asked, looking up at me hopefully.

I was getting really tired of this turbo-charged come-hither business. I reached down, removed her hand from my arm, took it in mine, and drew her closer to me as if I were about to kiss her. She tilted her head back, narrowed her eyes, and closed the gap between us. I felt her silken curves against me.

I looked deeply in her expectant eyes from inches away and placed my other hand on her shoulder. "Yes," I answered. "The tea was delicious, and I will be sure to ask for you to brew some more for me when I return."

I released her, turned deliberately without waiting for her reply, and walked slowly but purposefully to my truck. I drove off, my hormones still percolating furiously. Was that business with Ding Li some kind of a test to see if I would succumb to a honey trap of the Red Flower Tong's making? Well, if so, I passed, but my head was still spinning with the thought of her as I made it to the Perimeter. While I stopped at a light, I pulled out my burner phone, and texted Rob the code to let him know I was done and safe. There wasn't much traffic, and I gunned the engine up the on-ramp to put the Tong's machinations further behind me.

On second thought, maybe that was closer to the truth. Machinations. Maybe Ding Li was a distraction, a diversion, deliberately making my head spin so I would overlook... what? I carefully reviewed my memory of the meeting.

I disclosed that Marlena was alive and well. That may have been a mistake, but Professor Chen was a good friend and colleague. He'd helped me save her. I owed him. I'm not sure I could try to deceive him on that score, even if I'd thought to try in time. Chen confirmed the Circle was still monitoring her apartment and credit cards, not that we hadn't expected that, but I should pass that on to Rob.

They volunteered more information about the Shadow War behind the scenes and the players removed by Xueshu Quan and the Civic Circle. The insight into this secret history was fascinating, but their willingness to share without some kind of quid pro quo meant it must be old news to the various Shadow War belligerents.

They seemed on board with my scheme to discredit Professor Gomulka, even offended at my suggestion that the deal should be formalized in a promise. Their code of honor was interesting. I felt as if I had only a vague grasp of the rules, yet I was playing a game of chess with a grandmaster. As I left, Professor Chen assured me yet again that the Red Flower Tong would keep its side of the bargain. I played the events over and over again in my mind so I could remember the details later.

As I reached I-75 and curved north toward Chattanooga, I still saw no hidden subtext, no reason for a deliberate distraction. And, wow, was she ever distracting.

I was in love with Marlena. I wanted her, not Ding. Amit kept insisting with picking up girls that practice made perfect, and the more you worked at it, the better you got. That did make some sense. If I got better – more experienced – with girls in general, wouldn't that help me get better at landing the one woman I really wanted? Would it have hurt to have accepted Ding's advances?

Even now I was still excited, remembering Ding's delicate hands, red lips, expectant eyes, and jet-black hair. It must have been a test, after all, to see if I could resist temptation. I passed, I guess. Now, though, I was beginning to regret it.

Would there have been any harm in accepting the Tong's freely offered gift? Ding Li certainly didn't seem to be coerced. I could have spent the evening with her, gotten up early the next morning, and completed my drive to Huntsville in time to get settled into my apartment. I might even have saved the cost of the hotel.

I still felt the tension of my stress from the meeting with the Red Flower Tong. A good massage would have felt wonderful. And what on earth were the "Eight Ways of Pleasure?" My mind ran through various speculations of what they might entail, how Ding's silk dress would feel under my hands, how it might unfasten and slide...

Suddenly, I noted headlights looming behind me, approaching fast. Another truck passed me on the right and... was that Rick waving at me from the driver's seat? I noted the Lee County Tennessee plates as the truck made the turn to continue up I-75 toward Knoxville. I went the other way on I-24 toward the turnoff to Huntsville.

It was Rick. He'd been following me. The operation he'd mentioned that he thought I was involved in? I had a pretty good idea now what it was. Uncle Rob had a surveillance team on me the whole time.

He hadn't told me.

He was doing it to me again, wasn't he?

Yup.

Sigh.

Rob had hidden his involvement in the library fire, sending me on a wild goose chase looking for the culprits. He'd hidden the fact he was training a militia to take action against the Civic Circle. He'd done his best to keep me away from any sort of direct involvement. It was a wonder he'd relented and allowed me to participate in the Social Justice Initiative at Georgia Tech, but the alternative would have been finding some other way to pay for school. I doubted he'd have allowed it if he'd known how much trouble there'd be.

I thought the last couple of weeks had marked a turning point in our relationship. Rob insisted Amit and I leave Professor Chen and Marlena to the Civic Circle. We were supposed to run home and hide as events started going south. I wasn't about to abandon anyone to the Civic Circle if I didn't have to, though. I'd saved Chen single handed, and then rescued Marlena with help from Amit and, yes, Rob and his team.

I defied him. I showed I was right and he was wrong. I demonstrated I deserved equal treatment – that I was a partner and a colleague, not a subordinate to be shielded and kept in the dark.

Heaven help me if I'd actually taken Ding Li up on the offer to spend the night with her. I cringed at the image of Rick, Rob, and his team bursting in to "save me" at the most inopportune moment.

Rob was carrying need-to-know awfully far. Having backup wasn't a bad idea. Providing me with backup and not telling me about it... I wasn't a partner. I was a tool, to be kept in the dark while he plotted how to use me.

I'd have to reassert myself with Rob. Again. I filed that away, further down my to-do list. For now, I had to stay focused on the road in front of me. Amit was already a lap ahead of me with his internship at the Civic Circle and his easy Golden Ticket to the Civic Circle's Social Justice Leadership Forum. I was playing catch up, having to sneak in the back door as a personal assistant to Travis Tolliver and working as Uncle Larry's mole inside Tolliver Applied Government Solutions and the Civic Circle

If all went well, though, I could look forward to a couple of months of research and contemplation, further piecing together the Civic Circle's schemes, understanding the ideas they'd hidden, and figuring out how to stop them.

I remember Dad saying, "Preparation is the first step to victory." Unfortunately, the path to success is never as easy as it first seems.

CHAPTER 3: AN INAUSPICIOUS START

I ate the free breakfast, and I checked out of the hotel early. The apartment office didn't open until noon, so I passed the time driving around Huntsville and the adjacent city of Madison, familiarizing myself with the area. The move-in itself was pretty quick. I had a table and a chair to use as a desk, and a cot as a bed. It was just like an extended summer camp. I carefully surveyed the apartment, looking for things I'd need, and I made a shopping list. A toilet brush and other cleaning supplies would help. Maybe a couple stools for the counter. There was a Walmart not far away, so I stocked up on groceries, too.

The challenging part was security. That wimpy deadbolt and chain wouldn't stop a serious home invader for long. I kept my rifle loaded under my bed, and Alabama recognized my Tennessee concealed carry permit – a nice change from having to go unarmed on campus. Still, I couldn't take my handgun to work, and I'd have to leave it in my truck.

Furthermore, a burglar could help themselves to my stuff while I was gone – including my rifle. Finding a clever place to hide it would cost me time if I needed my weapon in a hurry, and a gun safe was more money and hassle than I cared to tackle for a few months in an apartment. With theft the lesser of the threats, I left my rifle, loaded, under the cot.

The trickier problem was data. I wanted to be able to continue studying scans of the books we saved from the

Tolliver Library, including the MacGuffin manuscript and my and Marlena's latest analysis. I couldn't very well leave all that data around in case it was stolen, or worse, discovered by the Civic Circle's goons in a raid or search. My solution was to store everything on an encrypted flash drive.

Flash drives are small, so hiding them is pretty easy. Mine was sealed in a plastic bag to keep the moisture out and shoved up the hollow handle of a water pitcher in the refrigerator. Even if they got the flash drive, they wouldn't be able to read it without my encryption key. That's where Amit worked his cleverness. If I were ever under duress, I could give away one key which would open up a stash of soft-core pornography while randomly scrambling the rest of the encrypted data. "Good stuff," Amit insisted. "You ought to check it out. Just be sure you've backed up the rest of the data elsewhere, because you're never getting it back." A different key would unlock all our work in progress.

If you hide something and someone else searches for it, they're going to keep looking until they find it. That's why it's important to give the searcher what they expect to find. Then, they focus their time and energy on what you want them to find, and not on what you want to remain hidden.

I only had a handful of books – a dictionary and some textbooks – to prop along the edge of my table/desk. One of the books was an old hardcover novel from a thrift shop. I'd cut out a big void in the center of the book to make a hiding place for about a hundred bucks as well as a half dozen flash drives. A couple were innocuous – full of last year's school work and some family photos. A couple were full of 256MB of what Amit described as randomly scrambled data – "Let 'em try to unencrypt that!" Another couple had more of Amit's soft-core pornography stash "protected" in an encrypted compressed file format that Amit insisted provided no real security at all. The idea was that a thief in a hurry would find the stash quickly, take it or copy it, and get out. A thief with time to burn would squander it reviewing the material.

Amit and I each had standard laptops thoroughly compromised by the pervasive surveillance hooks built into all the latest gear. We compounded that by using Omnitia's Omnimail like good, compliant young citizens with nothing to hide, sacrificing any privacy for the sake of "free" email. We used them for homework and everyday communication and any casual web browsing.

Our secret work, we did on different machines. Rob was confident that the surplus military laptops we were using had none of the surveillance hooks built into standard civilian and commercial computers. "DoD isn't stupid enough to let anyone compromise their own gear, not even NSA." Amit assured me that his networking software would strip off or fake any relevant identifying information that could lead back to incriminate us.

I hoped they were both right. I wasn't so confident, though. I wanted better security and a good place to hide the notebook I used for reviewing and working on the Tolliver Library data and for communicating online.

One of Rob's carpenter friends had the answer. He built me a beautiful little bedside stand out of oak planks. If you pushed the pegs in back on either side, the thick center shelf would slide out. The end of the shelf popped out, and there was just enough space inside for my small secure laptop and a flat panel directional WiFi antenna – far more compact and efficient than the Pringles can antennas we'd been using when we first started wardriving for anonymous WiFi connections. When I wasn't using the gear, it remained safely stored and hidden.

Furthermore, I had an alarm clock with a built-in video camera. Amit got one for recording his sexual conquests in our dorm room, but I don't think he ever managed to use it for that purpose. With the built-in motion detection, though, it made a good security camera. I set it on my bedside stand, pointed at the door.

The final part of my security regime was detecting if someone had been in my apartment. There, I picked up a tip from Rob, and I carefully placed eyebrow hairs or fingernail clippings in strategic locations – on top of unused kitchen cabinet doors, between the front pages of my hollowed-out book safe. I clamped a fingernail between the closet door and the frame, so it would fall out if anyone opened the door.

By the time I finished my security preparations, got back from the store, and made some dinner, I could eat my spaghetti in the confidence that I was moved in and ready to start work. After dinner, I packed a lunch, and realized baggies weren't very good for storing leftover spaghetti noodles. I added storage containers to my shopping list, then I added note cards at the last moment. Amit taught me a trick where those notecards would come in handy. I made a second trip to the store. Satisfied I was as well settled in as I could be, I got a good night's sleep.

I showed up early for work the next morning. Turns out I could have slept in. A dozen of us were waiting to start work at 8 am. I took a page out of Amit's game plans and played Master of Ceremonies for the incoming interns. I wrote my name, phone, and email on top of each of a dozen cards. I then started passing the notecards around the room, asking everyone to add their contact information on the next line and pass the cards along. In a few minutes, everyone had each other's contact information. I'd been concerned there wouldn't be enough time to complete that exercise, since we were supposed to start at 8 am. Now I had to come up with something else to keep the momentum going.

"I'm Pete Burdell," I kicked off the introductions, trying to keep my enthusiasm up. "I'm a junior at Georgia Tech, studying physics and electrical engineering. Looking forward to a fun and exciting summer here in Huntsville."

"Hey! Great to meet you, Pete! Put 'er there!" Another student held out his hand and when I clasped it, he took my hand in both of his. "I'm Jonathan D. Rice the third, call me 'Johnny Rice,' and I'm a 'ramblin' wreck,' too! I'm a senior at Georgia Tech, studying management!" I thought I'd turned my enthusiasm up to eleven, but Johnny Rice was a turbo-charged package of relentless congeniality. "Fantastic idea of yours, Pete, with passing around these cards so we can all get each other's contact information. There's a whole wonderful city out there to explore, and I'm looking forward to taking it all in with all my new friends! Don't let me monopolize the conversation, though. Who are you?"

Taken aback by Johnny's enthusiasm, the rather attractive girl sitting next to him replied, "I'm Kirin. I'm a sophomore in management at Georgia Tech." She seemed a bit timid.

"Wow! What a small world!" Johnny enthused. He'd completely pre-empted my own game plan to be alpha intern, and was doing it way better than me. Kirin was awfully cute, and I was looking forward to getting to know her better.

By the time Johnny had worked his way around the lobby, I could only sit back in awe of his performance. He'd solicited everyone to introduce themselves, teased out a bit more information, and made everyone feel comfortable and at home. He'd helped a couple of Auburn students realize they both went to the same school, casually defused some tension with a hard-core Alabama fan, and even found something nice to say about Vanderbilt's lackluster football program. He was a natural. I was having to work at being outgoing, and the difference was obvious.

I got up and walked over to the receptionist, "Hi," I glanced down at her name, "Julie, is it? I'm Pete Burdell. We were all supposed to be here at 8 am to start work, can you check to see what's going on?"

Julie assured me that "Rachel from HR" would be with us "soon." I reported back to the group. Johnny thanked me, as if I were his assistant, and launched into a round with everyone telling their proudest accomplishment. I simply couldn't compete with Johnny, so I settled into the role of being his number two, helping him out and following his lead.

At 8:45 am we were "...still missing a few folks. Rachel will start with you when everyone shows up." Johnny was still going strong.

An hour later no other interns had arrived, and Rachel finally made an appearance, interrupting Johnny, who was in the middle of encouraging everyone to share the most embarrassing thing that had ever happened to them.

"Why have we been waiting so long?" Kirin asked Rachel.

"Oh, orientation takes me a full hour, and I didn't want to have to do it twice if someone came in late," she explained. "I guess they're no shows."

I thought about Rachel's math. A dozen of us kept waiting nearly two hours in order to save her from potentially wasting an hour of extra work. Assume 2,000 hours per year. She'd have to be making... I did the math in my head... nearly a quarter million a year for that decision to make economic sense. I got the impression that math and analytical reasoning might not be among Rachel's core talents.

I sat through orientation – an explanation of basic policies, company rules, timekeeping, security, and the like. Rachel gave us a checklist and a stack of forms to complete. She clicked busily on her computer in the back of the small conference room while we filled out paperwork. I saw the reflection of Microsoft Solitaire in her glasses when she looked up in mild annoyance to answer the occasional question. Hanging out with Johnny and the rest of the intern crew in the lobby had been way more fun. Finally satisfied with everyone's paperwork, Rachel handed out work assignments.

"Off for a fun and exciting day of productive achievement!" Johnny led the crew into the hallway and pulled out a floorplan to help folks figure out where to go.

I looked at mine. IT Assistant reporting to Dan Humphreys. I confronted Rachel with my offer letter.

"Hey, Rachel," I held my offer letter in front of her, "I'm supposed to be 'Personal Assistant to the Chief Executive Officer,' reporting directly to Travis Tolliver." Uncle Larry had greased the skids at corporate to get me into that position.

"Oh, that's not right," she said, condescendingly dismissing my offer letter. "We don't have a 'Chief' Executive Officer, anymore. We no longer use the term 'Chief' out of respect for Native Americans. You need to read the Diversity and Sensitivity section of the Code of Conduct in our Employee Handbook before you make any more stupid or offensive mistakes like that."

I was not about to let myself be out social-justiced by any lame HR poser like Rachel. "The indigenous peoples of the Americas and their communities are rather diverse," I reminded her in good social-justice fashion, "and generally prefer to be referred to by the name of their particular nation or tribe. Does the Employee Handbook really require disrespectfully lumping together those diverse communities of peoples as 'Native Americans'?"

Rachel was taken aback that I'd doubled down on her own social-justice virtue signaling. "I'm not sure if that was considered," she said tentatively.

"Does the Employee Handbook also explain the change in my job assignment?" I pushed my offer letter further under her nose while I had her on the defensive.

I saw the smug look return to her face. "You must realize there's no way to eradicate the misogyny afflicting corporate institutions like ours without recognizing the oppression intersecting the identities and rights of employees. It's, like, really that simple."

That was both non-responsive and didn't make any particular sense, so I cocked my head and waited calmly for her to continue.

"The issue of misogyny in our workplace," she finally added, "must be framed within a culturally-informed, feminist, survivor-centered, locally-focused, collaborative approach that doesn't rely on the dictates of a distant corporate office alone. The historic oppressions of the traditional patriarchal workplace require remediation to ensure that the most consequential opportunities are made available irregardless of gender."

I parsed the buzzwords and checked my interpretation with her. "You unilaterally modified the job offers made by Tolliver corporate HR up in Tennessee."

"Exactly," she beamed, "to take into account local conditions. Women continue to be underrepresented in science, technology, engineering, and math. Mr. Tolliver himself is eager to empower the contributions of promising young women like Kirin. He chose her personally to work with him, right outside his office."

Yeah, I bet he did. I'd been admiring those curves, I mean contributions, myself in the lobby most of the morning. And playing personal assistant – effectively being a glorified secretary – was going to be more "empowering" for Kirin than actual technical work?

"You know," she continued, "Mr. Tolliver will be attending the Social Justice Leadership Forum later this summer, and Kirin is going to have the chance to accompany him – meeting some of the most powerful and important people in the whole world. What a fantastic experience!"

What a fantastic monkey wrench in my plans... I didn't know what to say.

"You need to get to your boss, you know," Rachel said helpfully. "You were supposed to be there hours ago."

Yeah, because YOU kept all us interns waiting... but of course I couldn't say that. Travis Tolliver and Rachel had between them undone all Uncle Larry's careful maneuvering to get me to the Civic Circle's Social Justice Leadership Forum. Obviously, Rachel wasn't going to be any help. I took a deep breath to collect myself.

"Where do I need to go?" I interrupted her as she'd already turned to head out the other door.

"Where are you working?" She looked at my assignment. "You're working for Dan Humphreys in... it?"

"No, 'eye-tee,' not 'it.'" I corrected her.

"Oh," she said dismissively. "You'll have to ask Julie at the reception desk. I can't possibly keep track of everyone." She turned and left.

Fifteen minutes later, I found Mr. Humphreys.

"You're late," he welcomed me to his office.

"HR ran long," I explained. "They gave me a list of things to do," I showed him my checklist.

"Well then, get it done. And take this." He handed me a cell phone. "That's the help-desk line. You know computers, right? Answer the phone. Solve their problems. If you get stuck, have 'em call me," he handed me a card with his number. "It better not be that they forgot to plug their computer in or failed to try rebooting or turning it off and on again! OK?"

"Yes, sir," I replied.

I stood in line again to get my photo taken for my badge. The keys office appeared to be closed early for the lunch hour I didn't have time to take yet, so I thought I'd skip a step or two ahead and call to arrange to get my domain login and email account set up. Just then the helpline cell phone rang. I canceled my own call and pulled out the helpline cell phone. Missed call. From my own number. Great.

I found Mr. Humphreys just as he was locking his door to go for lunch. "What do you want now?" he welcomed me back.

"Any minute now," I pointed out, "this phone is going to start ringing with interns needing to get email and domain accounts set up. You want to take this back," I handed him the helpline cell phone, "or would you rather show me how to set up the accounts?"

He looked at the phone and back up at me in annoyance at my unreasonable request. "You're one of the kids with the clearance, aren't you?"

"It's provisional. I'm supposed to have a polygraph exam later this week."

He looked at me... mulling it over. He unlocked his door and settled back into his chair with a disgusted grunt.

Clickity-click, click-click, click, bang! He punished his enter key to vent his frustration at my interruption of his lunch. Password entered, the server woke up. He opened a file on his desktop and clicked. I heard a laser printer whine down the hall. Finally, he stood and trudged his way down the hall to the printer. I followed. He picked up a printout and turned around, apparently miffed that I was now blocking his way. I stepped aside and followed him back up the hall. He snagged a key from behind a picture hanging on the wall. "This is the spare server room key." He gave me the impression that if I were halfway competent, I'd have figured that out on my own. He unlocked the adjacent door and returned the key to its hiding place. I followed him in the room. A couple dozen fans hummed from three racks of servers. He lowered himself into the chair and logged on.

"Here's a list of all the new intern accounts that need to be created," he said, placing the printout beside him. "Click here to create an account." He led me through the process of creating my own domain account. Then, he showed me how to create an email account on the company's Outlook Exchange Server. "Got it?"

"I think so," I took his seat and studied the screen a minute. "So, will my login credentials allow me..." but when I turned, he was already gone. I poked my head out the door and looked down the hall. His door was shut and punctuated by an out to lunch sign. "If you need assistance, call..." It was the number for the help-line phone I was carrying.

I decided I'd best keep myself logged into his account so I could be sure I could get some work done. It was some kind of server version of the Microsoft OS, but it looked and behaved a lot like Windows XP. I poked around the display and power settings to make sure I wouldn't get logged off for inactivity.

It was a good thing I had. In poking around the keyboard I suddenly found myself looking at the desktop for a different server. It took me nearly ten minutes to figure out that the print-screen button toggled the monitor, mouse, and keyboard to connect to a different server. I eventually found the original server I'd been using. I couldn't figure out why there were two dozen servers. None of them seemed very heavily utilized, and some seemed completely idle – no CPU cycles, and no storage. I had to get back to work, though. And I had to figure out a way to exploit the access Mr. Humphreys had just given me.

I had a brainstorm. I pulled up Mr. Humphrey's account information and my own. I compared the two side-by-side. He was a member of a bunch of groups, "Administrators," "Exec Council," "Finance," "Proposals," "IT," "Contracts," "Production," and a dozen more. I added myself to the same list of groups. That ought to give me the same privileges. I'd have to test that another time, though. I got to work on the list of intern accounts.

An hour later, I had set up everyone's account and finished eating most of the lunch I packed. Hungry as I was, cold spaghetti didn't appeal to me, particularly if I had to eat it with my fingers from a baggie. I should have transferred it to one of the storage containers I got from the store on my second trip last night. Better yet, I should have brought my Boy Scout mess kit. I printed out login and password information for the rest of the interns – one page for each.

I passed through the break area on my way back to the badge office. A partial plate of sandwiches was on the table. As I examined the food hungrily, someone grabbed one.

"Can anyone help themselves to one?"

"Sure," the woman explained. Seeing the look of confusion on my face, she elaborated. "When the executives have guests, they sometimes cater lunches. They bring the leftovers here when they're done. Help yourself."

The turkey and cheese in a croissant roll were even tastier for being free. I finished it off as I arrived at the badge office. I passed out a few of the login information sheets to the other interns waiting in line to pick up their badges. The rest, I left with Julie at the front desk. I figured all the interns would know how to find her.

I found Mr. Humphreys back in his office. "The intern accounts are set up," I confirmed.

"Yeah, OK," he replied absentmindedly, continuing to focus on the screen. With his left hand he reached out for a stack of printed emails and passed them to me. "Take care of these," he said.

"Do I get some kind of desk? A computer? A place to work?"

He looked up, as if considering my request. "There's a table in the server room, and a couple shelves of PCs in the back. Get one set up for yourself."

After the first computer failed to boot and the second didn't seem to work at all, I realized I was working from his junk pile of problem computers. I took the network card from one that didn't work at all and tried it in a computer that wouldn't connect to the network. Success! Then, I started looking through the email printouts – automated notices of printers with low toner levels.

"What now?" Mr. Humphreys did not deign to look at me.

"Where do I find the toner cartridges I'll need to replace these?"

Humphreys sighed deeply in frustration at being saddled with an intern who couldn't figure things like this out on his own. "There's a storage cabinet in the server room. Look there. The empty cartridges go in the bin in the server room to be recycled."

"Thanks." I found the stash of toner cartridges. There was a plastic cart in the server room, so I loaded up the five cartridges, consulted my building map, and headed out on my rounds.

My first stop was in one of the temporary, modular buildings that had taken over the parking lot next to the main building. I doubted I had solved the traveling salesman problem and identified the optimal route between my destinations, but since I was trying to understand the layout of the place, I didn't mind.

I poked my head in the door. "Hello?"

A young woman with her hair tied back in a long ponytail popped up from behind some clutter. She reminded me of one of the meerkats at the Nashville zoo scouting for predators. "May I help you?"

"I understand your printer needs a new toner cartridge?"

"It does?" she asked.

"Automatic notice," I explained, holding up the printed email notification the printer had sent.

"Oh. Over there. She pointed behind another stack of boxes to where a printer sat in the corner.

I wheeled my cart in, wondering how anyone could accomplish anything in a lab full of clutter. The only work station was her desk, itself piled with books and papers. "So, what do you do here, if I may ask?"

"This is the Space Elevator Lab," she explained proudly.

That didn't make sense to me. "Elevators for space stations?"

"No," her eyes lit up at the prospect of explaining her work to someone new, "it's an elevator that goes all the way from the ground up to a counterweight space station in geosynchronous orbit. It's the easiest and most cost effective way to lift people and cargo into space. By the time you're in geosynchronous orbit, you're more than halfway to most anywhere in the solar system!"

"That'd take a heck of an elevator cable," I noted.

"Exactly!" She beamed at me. "I have the solution. See everyone else is working on a cable to go all the way to geosynchronous orbit. There's nothing known that can handle the strain of supporting its own weight over that distance, let alone carry any cargo."

"You invented a stronger cable?" I thought about some of the work I'd been reading about. "Carbon nanofibers, or something like that?"

She nodded. "Exotic materials are a part of the solution," she confirmed, "but the real answer is to use a shorter cable."

"How can you use a shorter cable? Geosynchronous orbit is a fixed distance, isn't it?"

"The cable only has to be long enough to accelerate the propulser to escape velocity." She smiled with delight at sharing her clever idea. "See, everyone is trying to use beamed power solutions with lasers or microwaves. It's not terribly efficient. My idea uses the cable itself to guide RF power from the ground to the propulser."

I hadn't heard of a 'propulser' before, but it was clearly some kind of a rocket.

"There's a concept called a 'G-Line' after Goubau, the guy who discovered it. You can send RF power up along a single cable with the right properties. Beam power up to the propulser, accelerate at about 10 gees, and you can hit escape velocity in a few hundred kilometers instead of needing thousands of kilometers of cable."

"So, the rocket, or 'propulser' has a big spool of this cable that it..."

"No!" she interrupted me. "The cable is all on the ground. No sense making the rocket carry the dead weight until it has to."

I could see how that did make sense.

"You beam the power up to the rocket. See, exhaust velocity is proportional to the square root of the temperature. There's only so hot you can get it with chemical fuels. There's no particular limit with the microwave thermal propulsion concept. For example, using hydrogen, you can get a specific impulse of 700–900 seconds and a thrust/weight ratio of 50-150."

That may have meant something to her, but I was no rocket scientist. I had her print a test sheet to confirm her printer was good, and I needed to be on my way to my next stop. "So, how do you work on this stuff here in this lab?" I gestured toward all the clutter.

"I'm packing up and moving out to the Nevada Test Lab!" She was clearly excited about the possibility.

Another one? The Civic Circle's Technology Containment Team had a very specific MO. If they caught researchers moving into dangerous areas, they gently dissuaded them or gave them excellent opportunities to discontinue problematic work – time to drop what you're doing and accept this fellowship to work in an exotic locale doing something completely different! Of course, scientists and engineers being who they are, often become attached to their ideas and want to see them through no matter what the costs. Then the Civic Circle arranges for an appointment to their Nevada Test Lab, so the work can be kept bottled up.

Of course, if you got too far along paths they didn't want followed before they noticed you, they terminated your project – and you, and your collaborators – with extreme prejudice. That's what happened to my parents. Maybe I could dissuade her.

"Are you sure you want to go out to Nevada?"

"It's the opportunity of a lifetime," she replied enthusiastically.

"Good luck with that!" I offered as I wheeled my cart out of the room and into the hall. Maybe I could warn her? She didn't seem the least bit troubled by the prospect – she seemed genuinely excited about the opportunity to work in the Civic Circle's technical gulag. It troubled me, but there didn't seem to be anything I could do.

At my second stop, I fumbled with the printer until I figured out how to remove the toner cartridge.

"It doesn't need to be replaced," the man sitting in the office across the hall said.

"Oh?"

"It's printing fine," he explained. "It isn't even low yet."

I double checked the email printout. "I got a report that this printer needed a new cartridge." I handed it to the man. "Am I at the right printer?"

He looked at my printout. "Yeah, you got the right place, but you can't trust those printers. A couple weeks after a new toner cartridge goes in, they start complaining about low toner, but they'll go months without a problem. Even then, you can usually shake the cartridge and put it back and get another few days out of it."

"Thanks." It hadn't occurred to me that the printer might be biased toward false positives in reporting low toner status. I continued my rounds, checking all the printers on my "low toner" to do list. Sure enough they printed a test sheet just fine. Even the one cartridge I'd already removed worked perfectly when I popped it into a printer to check. I decided not to open any more new toner cartridges to replace ones that still seemed to be fine. I needed to ask Mr. Humphreys whether he wanted me to really replace toner cartridges that were still working.

When I got to his office, Mr. Humphreys was gone – his door closed and locked. I still had another hour on the clock, so I unlocked the server room, and I settled in. That took all of five minutes. I went down the hall and helped myself to some office supplies – a pad of paper, a couple of pens, a pad of Post-It notes and my very own red Swingline stapler. Fifty minutes to go.

I remotely logged on to all the printers that reported low toner, and I made a note of their page counts. I wanted to see how many more pages they'd print before they really needed new toner. Forty-five minutes left.

I logged on to the servers and started poking around, trying to figure out what they were all doing. Not much, it turned out. Three racks of servers, about twenty-five servers in all. I amused myself by logging the available disk space and CPU usage. One was being used as a file server and had duplicate hard drives running a backup routine. It had quite a few open shares and the drives were a bit over half full. Another server had Quickbooks and finance data and about 25% usage on the drive space. The rest? They were mostly idle.

I found only one server chewing up any significant amount of CPU time. It was running a program called "VirtualDan.exe." There was a compiler on the server, and the source code was there as well. I started taking a look and found script after script concatenated together. Individually, each one was pretty simple. One script checked for activity on

Mr. Humphreys' PC. If there wasn't any by 9:00 am, it first checked his vacation and holiday schedule, then sent out an email to his boss, "Running late this morning," along with a randomly selected reason drawn from a large list of options. If his computer was active after 5:15pm, it sent a text "Finishing up something important at the office, home soon," to a particular phone number. Activity after 6pm triggered a "Taking longer than I thought," update to the same message.

One script scanned incoming email for keywords like "problem," "trouble," "fix," "broken," and a host of others, waited five to ten minutes, and then sent out a randomly selected message from a list including, "I'll take a look," "I'm on it," "I'll look into it," and a bunch more.

Another script automatically performed a database backup restore whenever another email address sent a help desk request. Then, this script sent a randomly selected reply from another list: "No problem, fixed it," "Try it now," or "Let me know if that fixed it for you."

Continuing down the list, it was clear Mr. Humphreys had completely automated his job. Anytime he did anything for anyone, he wrote a little script that would do the process automatically the next time. Forgot your password? Virtual Dan would email you a reset link with a "personal" note admonishing you to be more careful in the future. Printer not working? Virtual Dan assured you he'd take care of it tomorrow, unless it was Friday, in which case he'd work on it Monday. The script even checked holiday and vacation schedules and used appropriate versions of the messages.

By that point, I'd put in my eight hours, and there wasn't more I could accomplish today at work. I headed home to be greeted by my barren apartment. I made a quick check to confirm all the little tells I'd deposited – the fingernail clippings and so forth – were still in place.

I was exhausted. It wasn't that I felt physically tired. Instead, I felt soul sick as I surveyed the ruins of my plans. My easy vacation until I got to the Civic Circle's Social Justice Leadership Forum on Jekyll Island was no more. It didn't look as though I'd get to go at all, thanks to Travis Tolliver and Rachel deciding to "empower" Kirin by giving her my job.

I could probably get Uncle Larry to help, but I was supposed to keep that relationship secret. Our deal was that I should show up to Jekyll Island as an "independent" observer and use my involvement with TAGS – Tolliver Applied Government Solutions – to funnel insights and intelligence back to him. In exchange, Larry had offered me a nice chunk of cash that would completely cover a year at Tech – even more if I continued to hold on to my Social Justice Initiative Scholarship. I got the feeling he didn't completely trust Travis Tolliver, and he wanted me as a back channel. I'd never met Travis so he didn't know me from Adam, and there are any number of Burdells in the hills and hollows of Southern Appalachia. I didn't think he'd make the connection between me and the arcane Tolliver family lore about my folks. Still, if I asked Larry to directly intervene on my behalf, my pretense of anonymity would be gone, Travis Tolliver would know there was a connection, and I could kiss Uncle Larry's cash goodbye.

I thought about what to do.

I had to find out about the TAGS contract with the Civic Circle. I didn't have to be Travis Tolliver's personal assistant to get there, only figure out how I could get on the install team. I probably had a decent shot, since I was working in IT already, and any big job needs lots of cable pullers to do the grunt work. That thought made me feel a bit better.

I reheated the spaghetti I'd packed for lunch and ate it for dinner. I couldn't solve my problem and get a ticket to Jekyll Island tonight, but there were things I could be doing, and I needed to start doing them. I'd feel better for having accomplished something productive. I removed my secure laptop and my directional antenna and went wardriving.

I waited until I was a few miles away from my apartment to start searching. I quickly found a number of residential WiFi nodes that were completely unprotected – people not bothering with the extra hassle of securing them. My problem was, I didn't want to park on a residential street, have the neighbors get suspicious and call the police on me. Finally, I found a coffee shop that seemed to have a couple of unsecured networks available from the parking lot. I went inside, bought a cup of decaf, and got to work. I was still able to close the link using my high gain antenna pointed in the right direction.

For the first time in a couple of days, I had an anonymous Internet connection. I fired up TOR – The Onion Router – to bounce my traffic through its network of anonymous nodes. That would make it much harder for anyone to trace my traffic back to me.

Amit's family owned the local Berkshire Hotel franchise near our hometown back in Tennessee. He parlayed his experience helping his folks run the place and developed a software package to help hotel managers monitor their networks for criminal behavior. It had been adopted throughout the chain. He'd leveraged his access to keep an eye on the Civic Circle's field agents. They seemed to be a secret society within the FBI and answerable only to the Director and the Inner Circle of the Civic Circle. When Amit found one of them staying at a hotel running his software, he arranged for them to get promoted to Double Platinum status in record time. He then collected all their data packets. Lots of it was encrypted, but Amit managed to crack a good fraction of it and keep an eye on what they were up to. If nothing else, we usually had a good idea of their activities and travels.

In addition, Amit set up a Virtual Private Network or VPN at certain hotels. Amit's hack allowed us to log in to the hotel's server and then access the Internet, distributing our traffic across the profiles of the hotel's guests. I logged into one of Amit's hotels and from there reconnected to TOR for my outgoing traffic.

The resulting link was slow, but as secure as we could make it. The Civic Circle had tracked us back through TOR once before, using a clever exploit. We weren't going to fall for that particular trick a second time. In case they had some other devious ideas up their sleeves, we wanted their trail to lead somewhere safely far away from our actual location. If that failed, I was in a coffee shop a good block away from the homeowner who left their Wi-Fi unsecured. I'd have a decent warning to pack up and clear out if one of their tactical teams swooped in looking for me.

I found Amit's update from earlier that same night. He'd arrived safely and was in a hotel. To be safe, he'd found a deli and logged in to an open WiFi across the street. He'd been by the apartment building where the Civic Circle had arranged accommodations. It had an excellent line-of-sight to other nearby apartment buildings, so he didn't anticipate any trouble finding an open WiFi node and checking in regularly. Amit had already set up a dating profile using photos he'd found and biographical information from Hungarian supermodel Reka Kozma. "It's only been up an hour and I'm already getting hammered with messages from hungry guys," he complained. I looked at one of the pictures of her in a bikini, and I could see why. Using the handle "Sapiosexual Gal," Virtual Reka said she liked older, more mature men, with a deep commitment to social justice. I had to go to the dictionary to discover that "sapiosexual" meant she found intelligence attractive. Amit had loaded Sapiosexual Gal's profile with all the terms Gomulka was using to search the site. If he didn't find her himself and reach out in a week, Amit would have Reka ping him.

I wrote up a brief note to Amit and Rob. I summarized my meeting with the Red Flower Tong. The operation was a go, and I gave Amit his deadline to get Professor Gomulka to fall for "Reka." I passed on the new insights about the secret war against the Circle and how the Circle was keeping an eye on Marlena's apartment and credit cards. I also noted, for Rob's benefit, that I wasn't happy being the unwitting object of Rob and Rick's secret "op." We could discuss that later, though. Local HR had blocked my attempt to go to Jekyll

Island as Travis Tolliver's assistant, but I'd be working on going anyway as an IT grunt. Not much to report.

I unplugged my laptop, and I was about to power down and head home when I recalled my promise to Marlena to check out this anonymous writer friend of MacGuffin's, "Jorge." I searched "Jorge Buenos Aires writer library," using Duck Duck Go – a search engine that, unlike Omnitia, didn't log all searches by user and pass the results on to Homeland Security.

I stared a moment at the results on my screen. Then, I plugged my laptop back in. This was going to be a long night.

Jorge Luis Borges (1899-1986) was an Argentine writer and a giant in Spanish-language literature. Perhaps it was just a coincidence? Jorge isn't that rare a name. I dug deeper.

Borges began working at a municipal library in 1938. That aligned with MacGuffin's description. Then I saw it: "The Garden of Forking Paths," a short story from 1941.

In Borges' story, a Chinese professor, Dr. Tsun, living in England, serves as a spy for the Germans during the First World War. Having discovered the location of an artillery park, his attempt to communicate the location is thwarted. Evading capture, Dr. Tsun goes to the house of Doctor Stephen Albert, an eminent oriental scholar.

Dr. Albert is honored to meet Dr. Tsun, because he has been studying the career of Dr. Tsun's illustrious ancestor, Ts'ui Pên, who resigned a governorship to undertake two tasks. First, Ts'ui Pên claimed he would write a vast and intricate novel. Second, he said he would construct a vast and intricate labyrinth. Ts'ui Pên was murdered before completing his task, leaving behind a "contradictory jumble of irresolute drafts" and no sign of an actual labyrinth. He left behind a cryptic note: "I leave to several futures (not to all) my garden of forking paths."

Now, Dr. Albert believes he has solved the mystery. The novel is the missing labyrinth. The novel describes the "garden of forking paths," a universe in which all possible outcomes happen. The paths diverge with each choice we make and a new universe arises within which we experience the consequences and face still further choices.

Dr. Tsun sees his pursuers approaching and shoots Dr. Albert. Captured by the British authorities and hanged for espionage and murder, Dr. Tsun has nevertheless succeeded in his mission, for the newspapers tie his name to Albert – the village in northern France that hosts the artillery park. And so, despite the best efforts of the British, Dr. Tsun succeeds in communicating the location of the artillery park to the Germans.

The events of Borges' tale seemed inspired by MacGuffin's experience. The Chinese angle, the threat to Dr. Albert – a reference to the Albertians hosting and protecting Majorana? MacGuffin's own manuscript... was that also a garden of forking paths, a "contradictory jumble of irresolute drafts?" And the physics... the many-worlds hypothesis was first proposed by Hugh Everitt in the 1950s. This "multiverse" idea only reached mainstream thinking in the 1970s. Yet an Argentine writer incorporated the notion in his 1941 story. Either Borges was as gifted a physicist as he was a writer, or he was profoundly influenced by MacGuffin and Majorana.

I knew Marlena was smart, but her intuition on the importance of this lead was almost spooky. We really needed to learn more about the Ordo Alberti. MacGuffin mentioned them in his manuscript, but that was more than sixty years ago. What was the Ordo Alberti doing today? Still rescuing scientists if their attempt to save Marlena was any indication. Where did they keep their scientists? What were they researching? Were they really trying to turn the World into a religious dictatorship, like Mr. Hung had claimed? I didn't know, but Marlena's suggestion had just given us another line of research that might answer these questions. I wrote up a summary of my findings and sent it off to Amit, Rob, and Marlena.

It was late. I needed to pack up, head home, and get some sleep. I had a busy day of IT grunt work ahead of me, not to mention a plan to devise to get myself to Jekyll Island.

CHAPTER 4:   WHERE WE GO ONE...

Instead of productive work, the next morning found me sitting in yet another mandatory orientation seminar.

"There's no 'I' in teamwork," Rachel opined. "We need to hire the right kind of people, people who can work together as a team. That's why a big part of our job in HR is to screen out applicants with problematic viewpoints. We have many wonderful people at TAGS, but some of our nerds are, well, a bit quirky. They suffer from Asperger's and autism. Our top priority is to make sure our people don't find themselves exposed to toxic interpersonal interactions."

The diversity seminar was a combination of social justice virtue signaling and exhortations to comply with social justice group-think.

"If we make the wrong hire, we could find ourselves in a position where someone is triggered daily by a coworker with an oppressive perspective," Rachel spoke with genuine enthusiasm. "Social justice considerations aside, these negative interactions and micro-aggressions can cost the company lots of time and money from employees taking sick leave to recover from toxic workplace stress. Good HR not only helps build a just and equitable workplace, it makes good business sense, too! This proactive approach to employee satisfaction is rapidly becoming the industry norm, and we're glad to be leading the way!"

I'd heard it all before, of course, but it was interesting how Rachel twisted it around to make Human Resources in general, and herself in particular, the heroic champion of the oppressed and the arbiter of social justice. I spent my time reading through the company Employee Handbook and the even less fascinating Tolliver Corporation Safety Manual.

Mr. Humphreys was not happy when I handed the helpline cellphone back to him first thing that morning. "I'm supposed to be in a polygraph exam to finalize my clearance," I explained.

He still didn't like it.

"The polygraph examiner isn't going to want me answering calls in the middle of the exam," I pointed out.

He finally bowed to the inevitable.

My polygraph exam was right before lunch. Uncle Rob made a much more intimidating interrogator than the bureaucrat who questioned me. My exam began with a magic card trick and the interrogator using the lie detector to demonstrate how he could tell when I lied about the card he'd forced me to choose. I tried to look impressed and willed myself to a high state of anxiety as he went through the control questions. Then, I relaxed as he questioned me about my trustworthiness and my background. I was calm and confident I'd passed with flying colors.

"I see some indications of deception here," my interrogator explained.

"How so?" I wondered which question raised a red flag with him.

"Is there anything else you need to tell me?"

No particular question? Did he actually have a concern, or was he just fishing? I pretended to think intently and slowly began to shake my head. "No, sir. I can't think of anything else relevant."

The interrogator glared at me. "I'm going to have to schedule you for a follow-up session tomorrow afternoon." He wrote the time on a slip of paper. "Remember: your exam is confidential, so don't be discussing it with anyone."

"Yes, sir." Then I did the math. There were just six of us interns going through the clearance process. The interview was about an hour long. The interrogator was conducting a follow-up session with me tomorrow instead of fitting me in later today? I had a feeling everyone's initial interrogations were "inconclusive" and we'd all have to come back for another hour-long session tomorrow. Since we weren't supposed to talk about it, we wouldn't be comparing notes. It was all just another trick to increase the pressure and convince us to divulge any incriminating personal information – if we thought he was on to us, we may as well 'fess up. The realization that the follow-up interrogation was another trick made me feel better.

I recovered the helpline cell phone from Mr. Humphreys. I wanted to ask him what to do about the toner cartridges, but he was heading out for lunch. I finished my bag lunch and got to work on the rest of my toner list. It was clear that the printers were crying wolf. I got out a postal scale and measured the weight of some new cartridges to establish a baseline. Then I weighed the cartridges in the recycle bin. They were lighter, but varied all over the place. I took one of the lighter cartridges, loaded up the printer down the hall with paper from the recycle bin, and ran the cartridge dry. Good thing I used paper from the recycle bin – I went through a sizeable stack. That gave me an empty cartridge to weigh, and a decent estimate of pages per toner cartridge.

I took the page counts I'd pulled from the printers the previous day, and the pages per toner cartridge estimate I'd just derived, and I calculated an estimate for toner cartridges used. Maybe Mr. Humphreys could help me track down how many toner cartridges the company ordered?

Somehow he'd gotten back from lunch. His door sign indicated he was back on site, and if he was needed, to call... the helpline cell phone number.

This was really getting annoying. I suppose I could have called him, but I didn't want to annoy him if he was "busy" playing hooky somewhere.

I wrote up my toner results. I figured the company could save a couple thousand dollars per year by waiting for cartridges to actually run out, instead of replacing them whenever the printer sent out a low toner alert. By the time I was done and had emailed my results, I had an hour left, and Mr. Humphreys was still a no-show.

I had an hour left and had completely run out of anything productive to do. I used my administrative privileges to look for any documents on the file server relevant to the company's Civic Circle contract supporting the Social Justice Leadership Forum on Jekyll Island. There it was. I got the Request for Quote, TAGS' Quotation, and the Purchase Order. The most interesting information was stored in Travis Tolliver's personal folder.

The Civic Circle had ordered a state-of-the-art file server with many terabytes of capacity. TAGS itself only needed a couple terabytes for a complete backup. The "data vault" project was only part of the overall effort. The Civic Circle also wanted TAGS to update the IT infrastructure all over Jekyll Island – the Jekyll Club Hotel, a large number of historic cottages, even a couple of hotels. Everything was to be coordinated through a secure data center in the basement of the Jekyll Club Hotel. The plan called for Mr. Humphreys and a couple of TAGS' network engineers to supervise the final acceptance of the system from a contractor who'd be doing the bulk of the installation. Additional "special services" of an undefined nature were also on the invoice. It didn't look as though there was much need for a junior assistant like me on the project.

The installation plans and network design had already been completed by yet another contractor. I resisted the temptation to look up "Delta Data Design." Their logo was a distinctive triangular spiral. I made a mental note to track them down later.

By that time, I'd put in my eight hours at TAGS. Somehow, Mr. Humphreys had slipped out behind me without my noticing. The sign on his door now read "Heading

Home, But Always on Call." Of course, the number was for the helpline cell phone I was carrying.

I'd been considering another round of wardriving when a text from Amit made it required instead of optional. He texted how "really exciting" his new job was. That was the code we agreed upon for "unable to communicate through secure channels." I sure hoped he wasn't busy entertaining some new lady friends, because it meant I had to take over running Virtual Reka for him.

I turned off the helpline cell phone and left it at home. No sense letting it track me around. I figured if Mr. Humphreys had any complaints, I'd tell him I didn't know if I was authorized to work overtime. One microwaved leftover spaghetti dinner later, and I was on the road. This time, I headed west into the neighboring city of Madison. I found a McDonalds with WiFi. It was slow, but since the TOR connection I was using for anonymity was even slower, I figured it wouldn't matter.

Virtual Reka's bulging "Sapiosexual Gal" inbox was an eye-opener. There were guys wanting to fly Reka out for romantic weekends. One offered up his private jet! Hardly any of them said anything to indicate they actually read her listing. With her supermodel looks, I guess not many guys cared. And do girls actually swoon over guys who send them pictures of their... Anyway, it took me nearly an hour sorting through the messages before I realized there was a search box. I got a hit on "Rousseau2k," Gomulka's user name on the site.

Gomulka's note made me feel even more sympathy for what girls put up with. His message was cringe worthy: part begging for attention, part bragging about his intellectual achievements, his professorship at Georgia Tech, and his importance as "an architect of the coming social order."

Sigh.

And now I had to write back to him.

I put on my Virtual Reka thinking cap.

"Wow, Rousseau2k! You are real professor who teach next generation social justice? How rewarding that is to you! You are brave man to share with me your real identity, too! My real name is Reka Kozma. I move to US in a few months and live in Atlanta for exciting modeling job. I sure you have pick of college girls you teach, but if you have time, I love to meet you when I get there. It makes me feel all warm know you be there in US, and I might meet you there. Love and Kisses, Reka."

That ought to do the trick.

I figured some extra security wouldn't hurt, so I reset the connection. Once I was back online, I reconnected through TOR to one of Amit's hotels, and through TOR again to a server we'd been using as a drop point. Rob had left a note for me. He thought Amit was fine, but perhaps under scrutiny as he was starting up his new internship for the Civic Circle. He also said he'd be coming through Huntsville on his way to meet Marlena's mom. Sarah, one of the students who'd worked for Marlena, had come through for us. She'd been watching Marlena's apartment and looking after her cat. She'd also been a "Friend of George," part of the FOG – the anonymous group who'd banded together in the name of Georgia Tech's most famous (if fictional) alum to defend the school from the Civic Circle's attempted takeover. "George P. Burdell" had arranged with Sarah for her to take the cat to Marlena's mom, along with a few items Marlena most wanted. Rob would be passing through to make the pickup – handing off a note from Marlena to her mom and retrieving Marlena's cat, laptop, and other property. Rob also said we'd talk about why he didn't tell me in advance he had me under surveillance when I met the Tong. Good. I sent him details on a good rendezvous location.

Marlena sent a polite note thanking me for the information on Borges and asking for anything else I could find on him. She didn't say "I told you so," but the subtext was there.

Finally, I searched on Delta Data Designs. They were a part of Delta Designs, "Architects to the Stars," their website proclaimed. Their practice ranged from Hollywood to the Hamptons, and they had a who's who of impressive clientele from media, finance, and politics. "Discreet and Secure," they trumpeted their expertise in safe rooms, video surveillance, and the highest possible level of residential security.

The news items I found told a different story, though. "Plane Crash Kills Architect, Partners," it proclaimed. The principals in the company all died in a plane crash last fall, along with a half dozen senior members of the firm. They'd been heading back from a job at a client's residence on a private Caribbean island when their plane went down without a trace. "The Bermuda Triangle," speculated one article. I suspected more mundane culprits.

I began to see how TAGS ended up the contractor on the Jekyll Island job. In ancient times, kings blinded their architects to keep their secrets and so that no one else could have a palace of the same splendor. Apparently unexplained plane crashes were the modern method of choice. I wondered what secrets the "Architects to the Stars" took to their watery graves. Knowing too many of the wrong people's secrets drastically shortened your life expectancy.

With Larry's efforts to raise Tolliver Corporation's profile among the Civic Circle, TAGS was in a great position to move on up and replace Delta Designs. I could only hope that this one job wouldn't expose us all to so many secrets that we met the same fate as the Delta Designs team. What was the cost-benefit tradeoff? Surely they couldn't kill all the contractors after every job? Talk about making it hard to find good help! Since TAGS was just starting out, we'd probably be fine. I was glad I was only a short-term intern and not working for TAGS full time until my access to secrets caught up to me.

I wrote up my notes and left them on the server for the rest of the team. On my way back to my apartment, I swung by a book store, and I paid cash for a couple collections of Jorge Luis Borges' short stories to read.

It was clear we had the right guy.

"The Book of Sand," was the title of one of his short stories in which a Scotch Presbyterian antiquarian and Bible seller traded the titular book to Borges – a book without beginning and without end. A book with seemingly infinite pages and endless content. "Affirming a fantastic tale's truth is now a story-telling convention; mine, though, is true," Borges proclaimed. Consumed by the book, Borges forced himself to be rid of it, hiding it in the dusty stacks in the basement of the Argentine National Library on Mexico Street in Buenos Aires where he once worked.

In another essay, "The Analytical Language of John Wilkins," Borges described a taxonomy of animals allegedly taken from an "ancient Chinese encyclopedia" entitled "Celestial Emporium of Benevolent Knowledge." The list divided all animals into fourteen categories:

Those that belong to the emperor
Embalmed ones
Those that are trained
Suckling pigs
Mermaids (or Sirens)
Fabulous ones
Stray dogs
Those that are included in this classification
Those that tremble as if they were mad
Innumerable ones
Those drawn with a very fine camel hair brush
Et cetera
Those that have just broken the flower vase
Those that, at a distance, resemble flies

I had to chuckle, because Borges' parody captured exactly the spirit of MacGuffin's own often-confusing translations of his ancient Chinese sources.

Borges' "Scotch Presbyterian" who found "The Book of Sand" may have been from the Orkneys instead of from

Appalachia, but I was convinced to a certainty that Borges had met MacGuffin. His stories were peppered with elements drawn from or clearly inspired by their relationship. Was another copy of MacGuffin's manuscript actually buried in a library in Argentina?

It was late. Tomorrow I'd pass on my new discovery to Marlena and the gang.

* * *

I finally caught Mr. Humphreys at his desk. He greeted me cheerfully. "What the hell do you want?"

"When I have the helpline phone overnight and I need to answer a call, I may have to work overtime. Is that OK?"

He gave me a look like I was trying to cheat the company.

"I suppose so," he grudgingly acknowledged, "but you better make it quick to minimize the hours billed."

"If I run into trouble, or if I get a serious problem I can't handle, I need to be able to contact you," I pointed out. "It's OK if I call your cell phone number?"

Mr. Humphreys seemed even less happy about that request. He nodded his assent.

I capitalized on my momentum with him by sharing my analysis on the printers. "I think we can save at least $2,500 a year by running toner cartridges completely out instead of replacing them the first time the printer emails us a 'low toner' warning." I was already thinking how I'd spend my $250 bucks – my 10% cut for a successful suggestion, according to the Employee Handbook.

"Yeah, I saw your email. That just makes more work, though," Mr. Humphreys pointed out, "having to monitor the levels in detail. You're making more work for me, once you head back to school. It also means that printers will actually run dry, inconveniencing our users."

"It's not that much more work, I countered. "And there are any number of other printers. If one runs dry on a user, they can always use a different one."

"Time and inconvenience cost money – probably more money than you'd save." He grunted disapprovingly. "The answer is 'no.' Get back to work, and replace all those toner cartridges you should have replaced yesterday."

I'd hoped to impress Mr. Humphreys with my initiative to persuade him he should take me to Jekyll Island as part of his team. This wasn't working out the way I hoped. Time for Plan B, the direct approach.

"I understand TAGS has a contract to do network upgrades and IT for the Civic Circle's Social Justice Leadership Forum this summer on Jekyll Island, and the G-8 Summit a week later on Sea Island. Could you use me on the team?"

"No," he said, dashing my hopes. "Get back to work."

I was getting really frustrated. Having just sat through orientation and read the Employee Handbook, I was an expert on the company's policies. I had one last card to play. On to Plan C.

"You know," I pointed out, "if I submit my toner savings idea as a formal suggestion, even if you don't like it, you're obliged to pass it on to your manager, the VP of Operations. She just told us during orientation that she's always on the lookout for new ideas to save money. I bet she'd jump on this one."

He looked at me like a snake eying his prey, got up, and closed his door.

"Yeah, she would," he glared at me, "and she'd count it against me on my next performance evaluation for not having noticed it first. They always do that with suggestions – they're a down-check on the department head who was 'wasting' money, and they ignore 'intangibles' like wasted time, effort, and inconvenience, in favor of what they can quantify, in this case, a couple thousand bucks of extra toner.

"That's exactly how the previous Chief Operating Officer lost his job. A guy submitted a bunch of suggestions, showed something like a quarter million in direct process cost reductions, and the safety violations totaled up to another quarter million. They count it as a minimum $10,000 savings for every safety-of-life suggestion per person no longer at risk, and hand over a $1,000 check to the person who spotted the problem and made the suggestion. The guy figured out that the overhead crane could drop a load on any of a couple dozen folks working in the assembly building. Let me tell you, the only thing the company hates worse than having to pay to remediate a safety issue is having to fork over a $50,000 check to some smart ass technician who showed he was cleverer than his bosses. They canned the ass of the COO for letting that happen.

"You think I haven't noticed the printers crying wolf? You have weeks to get around to changing the toner cartridges after the printers start warning you. No one really cares because in the grand scheme of things, the opportunity cost of working around a printer that's gone dead when you've got something important to print, on a deadline maybe, is far more expensive than what you'd save by squeezing the last couple of pennies out of a toner cartridge."

I hadn't thought about it that way. He had a point.

"Let me tell you a story," he began, "about another bright-eyed young engineer who worked hard, and was always looking for an opportunity. After three years of extraordinary service, he applied for a promotion that would have meant a nice raise and recognition for all the hard work and the many nights he'd stayed late fixing the consequences of others' stupidity. His boss came into his office and said, 'Your work's been outstanding, and you're the best qualified network engineer in the whole company. I have to tell you, though, that the word has come down from on high. We don't have enough women in senior positions. For the time being, only women are going to get promoted into management around here.' That young engineer was heartbroken that everything he'd done didn't matter because of some stupid diversity quota."

He looked at me and let that sink in. I had a pretty good idea that young engineer was sitting right in front of me.

"So, he found another job at a smaller company that he thought would be less bureaucratic, and he redoubled his effort to make up for the lost time. He was promoted to Director of IT in short order. His work made the difference in landing a couple of big contracts, and he managed them to successful conclusions. He even went to school nights and weekends and picked up an executive MBA. Then, the position of Chief Operating Officer opened up. He had the inside track, and no one else at the company was even remotely as qualified for the job. The CEO came into his office and said, 'We don't have enough women in senior positions, and you're too important to the company in the job you have now.' The company hired an outsider whose primary qualification – as far as I can tell – is that she's a woman."

Mr. Humphreys looked me in the eye and added, "It's remarkable how liberating it is to realize that there is no correlation between one's effort and one's reward.

"Take it easy. Enjoy your summer. I'll be leaving you in charge of IT for the whole company while I'm on Jekyll Island. You'll get some great experience and responsibility, and I'll write you a solid recommendation letter. Or you can try to fuck with me by submitting this crap suggestion, and so help me, I will bury you. What's it going to be?"

I had to think about that a moment. "I don't really care for either option you're offering me. I want to work with you, not screw you over, so I won't submit the suggestion. I do want to go to Jekyll Island, though. How can we make it happen?"

"We can't. It ain't gonna happen. Now go get those toner cartridges replaced, like you should have done yesterday."

Damn. Strike three and I was out. I grabbed my list of printers and got back to work.

I was replacing the toner cartridge in the printer outside the robotics lab when a familiar man walked by. "Professor Glyer?" I'd inadvertently blurted out his name before I realized it.

"Yes?" He paused to look at me.

Professor Glyer had lured Marlena to the astrophysics conference, GammaCon, in Chattanooga with a promise of a job offer at the University of Alabama, Huntsville, apparently so the Civic Circle could try to poison her. What was he doing here?

"Well, what do you want?"

"Sorry, sir," I recovered. "I didn't realize you worked here. I thought you were at the University of Alabama at Huntsville."

"I left UAH to work at U.S. Robotics last year," he explained, "and now I'm starting up the Robotics Lab here for TAGS."

I needed to get out of this discussion before he remembered seeing me at GammaCon in Chattanooga. "Your printer will be ready in just a minute, sir."

"Thanks." He continued past me into his lab.

The coincidence troubled me. What were the odds? I mean, Glyer had a tie to Huntsville, but still? And offering Marlena a job in astrophysics at UAH? Not only was he no longer on the faculty, but his work was in robotics, not astrophysics. More pieces of an unclear puzzle.

The next printer on my list was outside a lab full of hefty spirals of copper tubing and high voltage equipment. In the back of the lab, I saw familiar looking tall things with domes on top. "Are those Tesla Coils?"

"Of a sort," the man in the lab looked up from his work to answer me. "They're actually equipment for a Zenneck surface wave launcher."

"A surface wave?"

He smiled, clearly happy at the opportunity to explain his work. "Most radio waves are 'space waves.' Their energy propagates away in all directions over the surface of a sphere around the source. The energy goes as the inverse square of the distance."

I nodded. That was basic physics.

"A surface wave propagates along the surface – along a plane. The energy is concentrated in the plane, so it propagates over the circumference of a circle. The energy goes as the inverse of the distance instead of the inverse distance square."

I thought about the implications. "The energy in a surface wave falls off more gradually than in a space wave."

"Exactly!" he confirmed. "You get much stronger signals with a surface wave than with a space wave."

That puzzled me. "Why don't people use surface waves instead of space waves, then?"

"It only really works well at lower frequencies," he explained. "By the time you get up to the frequencies used in most wireless systems today, the loss in typical ground is so big that you can't propagate far at all. That's why you've probably never heard of it."

"Radio started off at low frequencies, though," I pointed out. "Why didn't they use the technique in early radio?"

His eyes lit with a passion. "They did. Only, the powers that be suppressed it. Tesla wanted to use surface waves to send wireless power to the world. He got investors, including J.P. Morgan, to fund construction of his Wardenclyffe Tower on Long Island in 1901. But then Morgan pulled the plug on the system, so Tesla never got the chance to see if it would work. They dynamited his wonderful tower in 1917 and sold it for scrap to pay his debts."

Wasn't Morgan one of the architects of the Federal Reserve? I wondered if I'd just uncovered yet another example of Civic Circle manipulation of science and technology.

"Why didn't someone else pursue the idea later?"

"They did. The theory was worked out by a brilliant radio engineer, Jonathan Zenneck, in 1906. These surface waves are called 'Zenneck Waves,' in his honor. Another famous physicist, Arnold Sommerfeld, worked out the theory of ground waves, confirming Zenneck's work. The concept was revisited in the 1930s, but yet another radio engineer, a man named Kenneth Norton, convinced everyone that there was a sign error in Sommerfeld's theory. In the Sommerfeld-

Norton theory, the ground waves attenuate quickly and don't have the marvelous performance Zenneck predicted."

That name – Kenneth Norton – it seemed vaguely familiar. I had a different question, though. "Why wouldn't people have noticed that the real world behavior doesn't match the theory?"

"Most of the time, behavior does match the Sommerfeld-Norton theory. It's tricky to launch a pure Zenneck wave, but that's what we're working on."

Just then, the helpline phone rang. I had to excuse myself to reset a user's password. I had a feeling there was something I was missing. It wasn't just the sheer improbability of it all – yesterday's lady rocket scientist with an idea to make space elevators obsolete before they had even been invented, and now today, running into Professor Glyer and the guy working on surface waves.

* * *

By the end of my first week, I knew my way around the TAGS campus, and I'd caught up completely with what must have been a month's backlog of toner requests. It was obvious Mr. Humphreys was only working a couple hours a day at best, and had left all the rest of his duties to me. There wasn't enough IT work to keep one person fully employed, let alone two.

I'd tried to hang out with the other interns. Unfortunately, they liked to go out for lunch, spending upwards of $10 or more at the West End Grill or one of the other trendy restaurants that catered to the contractors and engineers at the Research Park. I needed to pinch my pennies and save as much as I could for school. I had no guarantee that the scholarship I had through the Social Justice Initiative would continue through my senior year, and I wanted to build up enough of a reserve to finish my studies.

The only other interns with the sense to eat in were Johnny Rice and his new girlfriend, Kirin. It figured that the most attractive girl around would get snapped up like that.

They were friendly enough when I joined them for lunch, but it was clear they were really into each other and three was a crowd.

I ate my bag lunch hidden away in the server room and took advantage of Mr. Humphreys' long lunchtime absences to poke around. I used my administrative superpowers to look into Professor Glyer's files. He had protected them with encrypted zip files. I copied them off to work on them at home.

The encryption was no problem, because Amit had shared with me a hacking tool he'd found on the dark web. It let you break the zip file encryption if you could guess a plaintext string in the file. I found online where Glyer had published a technical paper while he was at U.S. Robotics, and sure enough, it was one of his zip archives. That got me his password, which was the same one he'd used in all his other zip files.

What I found was fascinating. He'd helped himself to a vast amount of U.S. Robotics "Proprietary and Confidential" information – circuit diagrams, mechanical drawings, build documentation, bills of materials – everything you'd need to build one of their robots. What's more, I found an archive of his old emails.

Glyer had been specifically paid by TAGS as a "consultant" to attend the GammaCon conference and conduct a phony job interview with Marlena. I couldn't tell if he knew about the assassination attempt. Perhaps that aspect of the operation had been compartmentalized from him? I was ready to give the man the benefit of the doubt when I came across a host of emails on his plans to "set up a robotics lab" at TAGS.

Glyer and Travis Tolliver, the CEO, were planning to take the designs Glyer had stolen from U.S. Robotics, ship off the mechanical drawings to some Chinese vendors, and produce low-cost knockoffs of U.S. Robotics models. Between the lower production costs and the fact TAGS wasn't going to have to recoup the engineering cost of creating the designs in the first place, TAGS would make a killing. They even had a big defense contractor lined up to sell robots to the Army for bomb disposal, reconnaissance of caves and tunnels, and other applications, as soon as TAGS completed a prototype run to submit for Army testing.

As if that wasn't bad enough, I found an email Glyer sent to Travis Tolliver, proposing what he called "killbots," small robotic assassins that could penetrate a secure area, recognize a target, and either shoot them or administer a lethal injection. "Far more secure than relying on outside contractors to poison a bottle of beer! Perhaps our sponsors would be interested in funding a demonstration?"

So Glyer knew exactly what happened at GammaCon, after all. He was an accessory to attempted murder. Now, he was proposing to build and unleash a horde of Chinese killbots on whatever wrong-thinker the Civic Circle decided to target.

My summer to-do list was getting uncomfortably long. Here I was trying to save the world, and I was stuck in Huntsville, Alabama being stymied by a burned out IT guru with a chip on his shoulder. Not only did I have to persuade Mr. Humphreys to let me join the Jekyll Island team, but also I now had to figure out how to stop Glyer's Chinese killbot army. All I'd accomplished this week only put me further behind.

CHAPTER 5:   ...WE GO ALL

"Good to see you," I greeted Rob as he joined me at the picnic table. It was still early, and not many people were present in Monte Sano State Park, atop the mountain just to the east of town. "Hard to believe it's only been a week."

Rob surveyed our surroundings carefully and pulled out a small handheld radio. He pushed the transmit button twice. A moment later, I heard two clicks in reply. "We're clear," he confirmed. "I had the rest of the team show up an hour early to get into position and provide surveillance. Good practice."

I was impressed. I'd been looking for surveillance, and I hadn't seen them. Of course, if they'd gotten here first and remained motionless, they'd be next to impossible to spot.

"You've been keeping plenty busy," he grinned. "'They say you make love with professor twice – once with body, and once with mind.' Really?"

"If you think you can do better, you're welcome to take over running Virtual Reka, yourself," I replied, levelly.

"No way. I bow to the expert. You got that professor of yours hornier than a brass band on the Fourth of July. Nice work. Of course, with a body like Reka's, no red-blooded man would need much persuasion."

That was a half-hearted compliment. "Thanks, I guess." No sense beating around the bush. I had a bone to pick with him. "What's with running surveillance on me when I met the Red Flower Tong and not clueing me in?"

"Operational security." He gave his default answer for everything. "What you don't know, you can't betray."

"I seem to recall one of those small-unit tactical books you made me read say that 'surprise is best reserved for the enemy.' If things had gone south, don't you think it would have been a good idea for me to know I had some backup?"

"Old habits die hard, I suppose. I'm used to thinking of you as a kid." He grinned, sheepishly. "Treating you like one. I default to keeping secrets. Have to in this game if you want to stay alive. You're right, though. You're a grownup, too, now. I should have told you."

I was surprised it was that easy, and he'd been so reasonable. "Thanks," I nodded my acceptance of the implicit apology.

"I'm sure your father would have had some pithy saying, some words of wisdom to impart, just right for the circumstances."

"Growing up," I noted, "is when you start having things you look back on and wish you could change."

"Heh," Rob snorted. "You do a better job channeling your old man than I do." He looked off into the distance. "Roy left some mighty big shoes to fill. I'm doing my best, but in many ways, I'm not the man he was. He made it look so easy the way he'd organize a job, get all the subcontractors in line, and drive them to complete a job on time and under budget. Things would just happen. Me? I'm struggling trying to make a living and training a militia for the Reactance at the same time."

"You've done a good job keeping it all secret from me," I observed.

"We all have our part to play. Those men and boys," he gestured at the seemingly empty forest around us and continued softly, "they count on me for their living and for the training they need to stay alive when the Reactance gets down to a fight. I can't do it alone. None of us can. But we can do it together.

"Bud Garraty's running the business side of things. Some of the guys wanted to get into smuggling cigarettes or worse. I put my foot down on that. Skirting the environmental regs is bad enough. With all the expenses, though, I'm hemorrhaging cash. Had to mortgage Robber Dell to make ends meet. Heading down to Jekyll Island after July 4th. Got me a gig on the catering team for the Social Justice Leadership Forum. I'll be there with the rest of the Reactance, but it's going to cost me a couple months' income, and we're all going to have some mighty thin paychecks for a while.

"Another year of this, though, I can't be sure I can keep the wheels on. Lot of these guys been out of work for years what with the Gore Tax and the regulations killing the economy. Unless things change, it's all going to fall apart. I'll lose my place, and the whole team will be unemployed again.

Rob glanced around again and lowered his voice. "There's a lot going on you don't know, and I can't tell you, but I can give you the broad strokes. Buddies of mine, including... well just call him a senior officer I can trust. They're in... positions of responsibility. In military intelligence. In three letter agencies. Elsewhere. They have other buddies. They can all see what's going on – the corruption, the betrayal of the oaths we all swore to uphold the Constitution against all enemies: foreign, as well as domestic.

"I've reached out to a few old friends. I don't tell them who I am. They just know I trust them, and I share enough to let them know I must have served with them. I've been feeding them intelligence from Amit's intercepts, helping them figure out what's going on, who's dirty, and who they can trust. Predict an assassination or two in advance, and the information from 'the Reactance' really speaks for itself."

"You think we can trust these friends of yours?"

"I have before, with my life. We have a motto – 'Where we go one, we go all.' They've got my back just as I've got theirs. I only know a few of their names: the ones I trust and reached out to. We only communicate over secure channels.

A few of them might suspect who I am, but they don't know for sure.

"There's an enormous opportunity here. The enemy is careless and overconfident. They're hoovering in every bit of data they can, monitoring every communication they can get hold of, confident that they hold the reins of power, and it could never be used against them."

I hadn't thought through the implications of that before. "They're not only collecting what everyone else is doing, they're collecting all the evidence anyone would need to document the very crimes they're committing."

"You got it," Rob confirmed. "My friends are moving to secure the evidence. When the time is right, they'll act. That time isn't now. There are people, people in high places who are corrupt or who have been corrupted. Plenty enough to block any effort to move within the system. We already have a long list, thanks to what you and Amit have been able to uncover."

"How can your friends act upon that list, if the people who are supposed to do the policing are part of the conspiracy?"

"Quis custodiet ipsos custodes?"

I frowned as Rob rattled off the Latin phrase.

"Who shall watch the watchmen," he translated.

"Is that from the *Commentary on the Gallic War* by Julius Caesar you put on my reading list?"

"Nah," he grinned, "I read it in a comic book." The humor left his face. "My friends think they can hide in the shadows, gather the evidence, and eventually move to kick out and arrest the scoundrels. I think they're dreaming. They don't see the big picture. We've already lost, and the Civic Circle is busy consolidating their power and easing out, or eliminating, any opposition. The fish rots from the head. The only way to get them out now would be if we got a strong president uncorrupted by the Civic Circle, a president willing to use his power to drain the swamp. I don't see that happening. The only other option is a military coup, and obviously, that's guaranteeing we drop to the level of some corrupt banana republic."

"Like cutting off your head to cure a cold," I offered.

"Exactly," Rob continued. "The Circle won't allow us a real choice. They'll continue offering up a false choice between an establishment Democrat and an establishment Republican. Whoever wins, we the people lose."

"We're learning more about who they are and what their secrets are almost every day," I pointed out. "We already know enough to blow the lid off the conspiracy and show that they're the heirs of a secret society that's been working for global domination for hundreds of years."

"Who would believe you?" Rob looked discouraged. "They'd file your 'Civic Circle' conspiracy between 'Chemtrails' and 'Clinton Body Count' and let it gather dust. The Civic Circle would realize that our information came from the MacGuffin manuscript which would lead them right back to the Tolliver Library and your parents. The only solution is for the Reactance to take direct action against the Civic Circle."

Rob was going to lead us all into some kind of a military strike against the Civic Circle.

"It's too soon," I argued. "We're just beginning to get inside their decision making. The opportunities for sabotage and monkeywrenching with what we learn this summer will be huge. We can take away their power if we take away their secrets. Make it look like a disgruntled insider. There may be a copy of the MacGuffin manuscript in the National Library of Argentina." I explained my suspicions from Borges' story.

"Maybe we could work with that," Rob still seemed skeptical, "but the best option is take them on directly. If we can figure out how to decapitate the Civic Circle when they assemble for their Social Justice Leadership Forum, we might be able to make the opportunity my friends have been waiting for – an opportunity to move against the corruption."

Now it was my turn to be skeptical. "They killed my parents. I want the bastards to pay for it as much as you do. I don't want to waste the opportunity we have this summer by running in there, guns blazing, in hopes of getting lucky. Jekyll Island's a big place, and there'll be lots of security," I pointed out. "A squad of irregulars wouldn't stand a chance."

"It's more like a platoon of light infantry now," Rob corrected me with a smile. "I've been busy training them on infiltration and tunnel clearance techniques. We just need to know where and how to get in. The network plans you got suggest the Jekyll Island Club Hotel is the main node, but it could just as easily be the Sans Souci, here. There's more to it than that, though. Petrel thinks he may be on to something."

Petrel was an astute researcher Amit and I had found last year. He'd helped us unravel the story of how the Civic Circle assassinated Angus MacGuffin in 1940, and he'd been fascinated by the historical ties to Jekyll Island.

"Here's what he found." Rob handed me Petrel's report.

Greetings Anonymous Patron,

Your suggestion that the Civic Circle has roots going back to Imperial China appears correct. I believe I have uncovered certain details of when and how that happened.

James Flint was a merchant and diplomat working for the British East India Company. In 1759 he lodged a trade complaint with the Imperial Court. Flint was detained for three years. A few years later, the Chinese detained Samuel Bowen, another East India Company employee, for four years. There was ample opportunity for both men to have been recruited.

Flint teamed with Bowen. In 1764, Bowen married into the Savannah, Georgia, gentry, and purchased nearly a square mile of land for a plantation, possibly with money contributed by Flint. They introduced the cultivation of soy beans.

There were others in the area or who arrived after the Revolution, friends and associates of Bowen, with similar ties to the Far East trade, including the Payseur family. Christophe Poulain DuBignon, a French aristocrat, acquired his wealth through trade with India, and later as a privateer during the American Revolution. He started buying land on Jekyll Island in 1791, acquiring the whole island by 1800, and settling his family at "Horton House," on the island.

In 1886, the family sold the island to the Jekyll Island Club, whose principals were such men as J. P. Morgan, Joseph Pulitzer, and William K. Vanderbilt.

Attached are two maps of the island. This first map dates back to the DuBignon acquisition. Note the pit near the Horton House, and the single mound shown near the future site of the Jekyll Island Club Hotel. Compare to the second map dating to just after the DuBignon family sold the island. The pit near the Horton House is gone, and there is a more elaborate network of "Indian Mounds" and walls shown near the Jekyll Island Club Hotel site.

I believe a small outpost was initially buried in the pit by the Horton House and later, a larger outpost was constructed, now buried near the Jekyll Island Club Hotel and nearby cottages. Note how the Sans Souci Building, a condominium built by James J. Hill, William Rockefeller, and J.P. Morgan, now occupies the site of the principal mound, and other cottages were constructed on the sites of smaller mounds. For what it's worth, "Sans Souci" is French for "without a care." That may be a reference to the palace of Frederick the Great in Berlin. Or it may be a coincidence.

Wishing you well in your own investigations. Kindly let me know if you learn anything relevant.

Stay safe,

Petrel

"The radiation signature we saw in Professor Chen's data last year suggests the facility on the north end of Jekyll Island was destroyed." I studied the maps intently. "The main complex is here under the hotel and the cottages of the historic district, but there must be a half dozen back doors to the complex. Even with a platoon, I don't see how you could take the facility what with all the security they'll have."

"That's why you've got to get to Jekyll Island in advance and scout it out," Rob explained. "I'll be there with my team — got us a gig catering for the big event. Before we get there, we need you to figure out how to get in and how to block off the exits. We'll panic them into running right into an ambush."

Rob's notion of a direct assault on the Civic Circle didn't seem as crazy as it did at first glance. I could see how a small team with the right intelligence might just be able to pull it off. "The problem is, there are three ways out of or into the complex under the Sans Souci. North to the Jekyll Island Club hotel and on to any of the cottages along the river, south to the riverfront cottages there, or east and inland."

"If the Jekyll Island complex is attacked from the river," Rob pointed out, "the Civic Circle will be inclined to evacuate inland. Control this cottage," he pointed to the map, "and you're on top of their evacuation route. We'll attack in toward the Sans Souci complex, then evacuate from one of the south cottages. We need you there to scout it out for us."

This wasn't a suicide mission Rob had concocted as a desperate last chance to win the day. Executed smartly, we could be in and out quickly while the heavy security, unaware of the tunnels, never knew what hit them.

"Getting myself there is going to be challenging." I explained the difficulties I'd encountered.

"Larry wants you there," Rob pointed out. "Dump the problem in his lap."

"He also wants to hide any link between him and me," I pointed out. "Sure, he could order Travis to have Mr. Humphreys bring me along, but that would blow my cover." I left unstated that fact that Uncle Larry was offering me a fairly substantial amount to serve as his mole within the TAGS delegation to the Social Justice Leadership Forum. He wouldn't want to tip his hand, and if he did, I could kiss the money he'd promised me goodbye.

"One way or another, you need to be there," Rob insisted, "with the rest of the Reactance."

"Couldn't I just get a job on the catering team?"

"I already got that covered," Rob pointed out. "Work side-by-side with my team, and you won't discover anything new and useful. No, you need to get in on your own through your TAGS connection. We need all the boots-on-the-ground tactical intelligence we can get from you and Amit to pull this off. Where we go one, we go all. I'm counting on you."

"I'll make it happen one way or another," I promised, not knowing for sure how I would resolve the situation I found myself in.

"I have a cat to collect," Rob smiled weakly, shaking his head. "Marlena's been moping around. She says living in my beautiful underground refuge is like being 'confined in Château d'If' and how I'm her jailer."

Beautiful underground refuge? Functional maybe, but given Rob's lack of attention to housekeeping, a reasonable comparison might be made to the dungeon from *The Count of Monte Cristo*. I leapt to Marlena's defense. "She's had her whole life ripped away from her. She has a right to be upset and depressed about it."

"Sometimes life sucks," Rob acknowledged. "You have to embrace the suck, put it behind you, and get on with life, not mope and whine about it."

"I'm sure she'll be happier once you retrieve her cat for her, and a few of her things."

"I hope so," Rob said. "Sometimes that woman is just impossible."

I was secretly a bit glad and relieved that Rob was not getting on very well with Marlena. If only it had worked out that I was the one who'd get to spend most of the summer with Marlena. I had to play the hand I'd been dealt, though.

"Good luck." I shook his hand.

"Good luck, Pete." Rob surveyed the surroundings one last time. We appeared to be alone. He smiled and held out his hand with his thumb up. Then he gestured, "move out."

All around me, there was motion in the woods. Camouflage covers vanished into backpacks as a half dozen guys suddenly appeared from nowhere. An initial group of three took off back down the hiking trail. I was impressed at their stealth.

"See you around, Pete." Rob followed at a distance, and the other three fell in behind him.

* * *

It would have been tempting to take Mr. Humphreys' advice – give up, take it easy, and enjoy the summer. I could have made it my project to chase after Kirin, or one of the other cute girls interning at TAGS. There seemed to be an awful lot of them.

There wasn't much I could do to win Marlena over remotely – a long letter confessing my feelings and desires? No, that was silly. It needed to be in person, and I hadn't found the right opportunity when I had the chance. I'd be back in a few weeks for the Independence Day holiday. I'd have to make my move then.

In the meantime, I decided Amit was right. Practice picking up girls in general would help me pick up the particular one I wanted.

I forced myself to be outgoing and gregarious when I ran into attractive girls in the halls or the break room. I'd make a casual suggestion for a lunch or a dinner out. I had a couple of dates, but none of them really seemed worth the effort. I tried to keep up what Amit called an aura of "amused mastery." Maybe it would land someone interesting in my orbit – at least that's what I told myself. Between the fact I was spending most of my time in the server room, and had far bigger worries than landing a girlfriend, I had a suspicion it was going to be another lonely summer.

Where we go one, we go all? Unless I got my act together, my friends were going to go into danger without me. I had to do something about it. I just wasn't sure what.

One afternoon I managed to get myself lost in the warren of modular office buildings that had been installed in a parking lot adjacent to the TAGS facility. Somehow, IT had gotten stuck with the job of checking all the fire safety equipment. I had to verify that all the firehoses were intact, all the fire extinguishers' pressure gauges were in the green zone, and I had to initial the inspection labels.

The buildings appeared to be assembled from pieces, a bit like how two trailers come together to make a double-wide, but on a much larger scale. Every twenty-five feet I came to a new hallway, punctuated by a firehose halfway between. Each hallway was a hundred feet long with a mix of ten- and fifteen-foot-wide offices, each ten feet deep – I'd gotten bored one day waiting for a big print job to finish, so I could swap out the toner, and I'd calculated it while I was waiting.

I'd finished the fire safety inspection, but I had some inkjet cartridges to deliver, too. Somehow I'd thought my destination was on the second level of the building. Finally, I came back down the stairs. Halfway down the third hall, I came to a large room that extended to the next hallway.

"Good afternoon," I poked my head in the door. "Hello?"

"Hi, yourself." A head popped up from behind a stack of boxes. "What can I do for you?"

"Other way around. Pete Burdell from IT." I held up the inkjet cartridge. "You need a new inkjet cartridge for your printer?"

"Ah yes," the man replied. "Over there."

I got to work. "Big space you have here." I said, taking in the boxes and the clutter. A shielded screen room occupied one corner. The room looked like a storage area but there was a table pressed into service as a desk.

"There was supposed to be a team working with me," he explained, "but there's been a hiccup with the funding."

I could see some fancy test equipment sitting on lab benches. "A network analyzer?" We had an older one in the microwave lab at Georgia Tech. "You do radio work here?"

Suddenly, he looked at me as if for the first time. "How did an IT assistant get familiar with network analyzers?"

I got the new inkjet cartridge popped in. "I'm studying electrical engineering at Georgia Tech." I punctuated my statement by closing the top of the printer with a decisive click.

"What's an electrical engineer from Georgia Tech doing replacing inkjet cartridges?"

"I'm a student intern. I guess HR figured we can do that."

He shook his head ruefully and held out a hand. "Roger Thorn. I got out with my EE from Tech a dozen years ago."

That name. It was familiar for some reason. "Pete Burdell," I introduced myself again.

"No relation to George P. Burdell?" Roger asked with a smile?

"Something of a distant cousin," I acknowledged.

"Good times," Roger said. "Hard times, too. Is Muldoon still teaching Linear Circuit Analysis?"

"He is, as a matter of fact." I grinned, understanding perfectly Roger's segue from "hard times" to Muldoon. "I had Muldoon last fall."

"I got an 88 on his midterm and a 75 on his final." Roger said it matter-of-factly – not boasting, but rather glad for a chance to share his accomplishment with someone who'd appreciate it. "With the curve, I aced the class, but man, I think it was the hardest class I took there."

Finally, I remembered where I'd heard the name "Roger Thorn" before.

"I got a perfect score on Muldoon's midterm," I explained seeing the surprise and disbelief creep into Roger's eyes. "Muldoon was convinced I cheated because he didn't think I was nearly as smart as the legendary Roger Thorn, holder of the previous high score."

"Wow," he seemed taken aback. "Did you? Cheat?"

"Not in the way Muldoon was thinking." I explained how I discovered the geometric tricks Muldoon employed to make the exam easier to grade. Using Muldoon's own tricks against him made my work much faster and more accurate than even an apparently more brilliant student like Roger.

"Of course," Roger nodded in appreciation. "I should have figured that out myself."

"I finished the exam in a half hour, and I spent another fifteen minutes double checking my work. Then I got up five minutes early and turned it in to him.

"'Don't give up,' Muldoon told me. 'You have five more minutes. Keep working and you may be able to get a few more points.'

"I thanked him, told him I was done, and then I walked out of the room."

Roger chuckled in appreciation. "I wish I'd been there to see the look on old Muldoon's face. Damn, but he was one of the best teachers I ever had. He sure could be a mean old SOB, though."

"I hear you." I gestured around the lab. "So, how did you get from Georgia Tech to riding herd on this prize collection of idle test equipment and boxes?"

"That's a long story," Thorn replied, looking at his watch. "Tell you what. Let's grab some dinner at the West End Grill after work. My treat. Least I can do for a fellow rambling wreck."

"Thanks." I accepted his generous offer.

* * *

It was a bit awkward when Mr. Thorn tried ordering a beer for me, and I had to admit I wasn't 21. I chose the chicken quesadilla on his recommendation.

"Call me Roger," he insisted after the waiter took our order.

"OK, Roger." I complied. "What brought you to TAGS?"

"TAGS bought my company," he explained. "I was working on ultra-wideband mesh networks."

"Ultra-wideband?" I mean, obviously it had something to do with really big bandwidth signals, but there had to be more to it than that.

"Ewe Double-Ewe Bee," he replied.

Took me a moment to realize it was an acronym: UWB.

"Time Domain Corporation, right here in Huntsville, was one of the leaders in the industry," Roger explained. "The name tells you a lot about how it works. UWB uses short time duration impulses to convey data, determine location, or take a radar image. It's a completely different way of doing wireless. That's why they killed UWB, the big well-funded startups like Time Domain, and my own little company."

"TAGS did it?"

"Well, the FCC, for starters. The original experimental and demonstration work assumed operation around 2 gigahertz with about a gigahertz bandwidth. All the legacy companies making money off that spectrum raised a stink about it, even though the power levels were the same as the FCC allows for unintentional radiators. The FCC used that as an excuse to bump up the frequency to the 3-10 gigahertz range, making it that much harder to implement a practical system.

"My company was leveraging the technology developed by Time Domain and others. We pioneered an ad hoc wireless network. Imagine a phone that could work just like the Internet – making a link to whatever other nodes are available and passing a data packet on, from neighbor to neighbor, until the data reaches the destination. With a UWB link, it would look like noise, unless you had the right protocol to decode it. The physical layer itself would be secure, and there'd be no central switchboard where you could try to tap the messages. Secure, private, surveillance-free communications, at least between peers in a local area. We had it working, too: we built a dozen prototypes and got our first production batch of a thousand chips in to build the first units.

"Then, TAGS bought us out at a great valuation. They paid 10% down with a payment plan for the rest and a 10% royalty on gross sales. Only, within six months, they'd bankrupted the company, so the payments stopped. I only got a dime for every dollar I expected. And the sweet royalty? Ten percent of net sales on sales of zero... You don't need a Georgia Tech degree to figure out that math."

Roger told me the story of how it all played out, just in time for the waiter to bring our orders.

"You're sure what happened was deliberate?" I asked, and then took a bite of the delicious chicken quesadilla.

"You can't ever be sure about something like that," Roger acknowledged, "but it's happened before. Ever hear of Edwin Howard Armstrong?"

He must have seen the look of confusion on my face.

"He invented frequency modulation – FM radio."

"That I've heard of."

"You see," Roger was clearly eager to share the story, "he invented the regenerative radio receiver, but a charlatan named Lee de Forest won it from him in a patent battle. Then, Armstrong came up with the super-heterodyne architecture that's still used in most radios today and an improved super-regeneration concept. He made a mint off his ideas, and became the largest single shareholder in RCA – the Radio Corporation of America."

I remembered Amit had told me a bit about that. "RCA – they were formed as a compromise when the Navy tried to take over wireless after the First World War. One government-sanctioned company to control commercial wireless in the United States. Kinda like how the government merged all the Internet companies to form Omnitia."

"Exactly," Roger seemed pleased I already knew that part of the story. "AM radio has lots of problems with static: noise and interference. Frequency modulation was considered as an alternative, but a radio genius named John Carson 'proved' that FM was no better than AM. Most everyone lost interest, but not Armstrong.

"He figured out that if you used a wide bandwidth, you could make an FM signal much better, with much less noise and static than an AM signal. Awfully similar to the idea behind UWB, actually. Armstrong demonstrated it to his friend, David Sarnoff, the president of RCA. Sarnoff put

Armstrong's FM through test after test, and it kept beating the socks off AM performance.

"Soon it became obvious that Sarnoff was just trying to string Armstrong along. FM was clearly superior, but AM radio was a cash cow for RCA in the 1930s. Sarnoff was taking all the money he made off AM radio and spending it to develop television. If RCA embraced FM, they'd be destroying their own successful market.

"FM proved its worth in World War II, and not long thereafter Armstrong had a host of customers setting up FM radio stations and selling FM radio receivers. It was clear that RCA's monopoly over radio was about to come to an end, and television was still in its early days, operating at a loss."

Roger took a deep breath. "RCA got the FCC to yank the spectrum out from under Armstrong and his customers. On the basis of an analysis by FCC engineer Kenneth A. Norton on secret military propagation data, they took away the 40 megahertz band spectrum, and bumped FM up to near 100 megahertz. They gave the prime spectrum between to television, and the FCC administrator who oversaw the decision ended up a few months later with a remunerative executive position in radio. With the stroke of a pen, all the investments Armstrong's customers had made in radio gear became obsolete. To add insult to injury, the new FM rules demanded stations use low transmit powers, so the coverage areas couldn't compete with RCA's legacy AM stations."

Kenneth A. Norton? I took a moment for me to recall the conversation a few weeks ago. That had to be the same engineer who claimed there was a sign error in the Zenneck Wave Theory. Norton had shut down attempts to revive Tesla's dream of worldwide wireless power. Now it appeared he'd helped do the same for Armstrong's FM radio technology.

Roger took another deep breath. "Armstrong fought in court. RCA stole his FM technology to use as the audio channel in television, but claimed it was different, somehow, and not covered by Armstrong's patents. And those patents were set to expire in the early 1950s. His fortune gone, one evening Armstrong opened a window, and jumped to his death."

Wow... Jumped? Or was pushed? That sure sounded like the kind of "suicide" that was the Civic Circle's hallmark. What a tragic loss... I took it in silently.

"Sorry to be such a downer," Roger smiled, taking a last bite of his dinner. "So, are you keeping busy and enjoying your summer?"

"It depends." I brandished the cell phone that now held my life in bondage. "Sometimes the job keeps me hopping, other times it's a challenge to find enough to do."

"Do you have a girlfriend?" Roger asked.

"I've been dating a couple of the other interns," I acknowledged. "But I'm really in love with a girl... back in my hometown."

"Oh," he said, waving down the waiter to get our check. "If you already have a girlfriend, why are you dating some of the interns here?"

"My girlfriend hasn't made any sort of particular commitment to me," I explained. "And I figured if I dated some other girls I'd get better at it – more likely to land the one I really want."

That answer appeared to satisfy him.

"Do you have a girlfriend?"

"No." Roger smiled, as if that were funny somehow. "Let me drop you back at the office."

I thanked him for dinner. "That was a heck of a story you told me... yours and Armstrong's." I really wanted to learn more. "Can I help you move the boxes in your lab into some kind of order?"

"Sure," he replied genially. "Stop by any time. Don't be sharing my story around, though. I'm not supposed to be talking about my deal with TAGS."

"Of course."

I stopped by the next afternoon and helped Roger get his lab better arranged. He even broke out a couple of his mesh-networking prototypes and gave me a tutorial on how it all worked.

One aspect of his invention deeply impressed me. Communications security requires encryption. The state-of-the-art approach uses mathematical algorithms to encrypt a message. The algorithm generates two mathematical keys – a public key that the algorithm uses to encrypt a message, and a private key that reverses the encryption, allowing the message to be decoded and read. In theory, it is extremely difficult to decrypt the message without the private key. In practice? The algorithms are complex, and the NSA has some of the best mathematicians and computer scientists in the world. From all the indications Amit was getting, the NSA was selectively decrypting large fractions of encrypted message traffic online.

The most important messages we share, however, are with our close friends and associates – people we spend time with. Roger's prototypes included a security process he called a "handshake." When you connected two of his devices together, they would generate and share a massive table of random numbers derived from electrical noise he insisted was better than any digital random number generator. Since the two devices shared a common random number table, they could use it to encrypt and decrypt secure messages between the devices that couldn't be cracked by eavesdroppers without violating the physical security of the devices themselves. You couldn't very well stream video or vast amounts of data using the technique, but Roger's prototypes could store enough random data for many hours of voice conversations and a virtual eternity of text messaging. Then, when the random bit bucket runs dry, you mate your phone up to your friend's and refill it with a new matched collection of random numbers.

"Why isn't this 'Handshake Device' standard on all cell phones?"

Roger smiled at my naïveté. "Because it's absolutely secure, and absolute security is not in favor these days, except for military and government communications."

The helpline phone rang, and I was off to help someone who'd locked themselves out of their account. Deep in thought, I almost got myself lost again on my way out of the modular building complex.

There was definitely something going on here.

"Once is happenstance, and twice is coincidence, but three times is enemy action," Dad liked to say. Roger's UWB wireless and the Zenneck Surface Wave wireless power guy. I needed to get his name, but that was two. There was the lady rocket scientist who figured out space elevator cables only had to stretch high enough to launch an electromagnetically-propelled rocket to escape velocity, instead of all the way to geosynchronous orbit. That made three. Oh, and Professor Glyer was busy working on his killbot army.

The pattern was becoming obvious.

TAGS wasn't just a typical government contractor. It was an unofficial arm of the Civic Circle. TAGS collaborated with the Civic Circle's Technology Containment Team to hire or acquire ambitious inventors and entrepreneurs pursuing technologies they viewed as a threat. They also served as an incubator for technologies TAGS wanted to develop for their own purposes, like Glyer's killbots. I wondered if Larry and Travis appreciated what their company was doing. Were they actively involved? Neither had much of a technical background. They could easily be doing "favors" for their Civic Circle patrons without fully comprehending the reasons, implications, or consequences.

There were only so many productive things I could do to fill the downtime between helpline calls. I'd have loved to spend the time reviewing some of the material we'd saved from the Tolliver Library, but I didn't feel comfortable using work time or a work computer to do it. Too risky. I'd finished the Borges book, but there were only so many books available from the bookstore that were relevant to what I needed to learn. I'd reverse engineered Mr. Humphrey's VirtualDan.exe scripts and used them as a model for VirtualPete.exe on a different server. So far, all VirtualPete.exe did was send me text messages when Mr. Humphreys arrived or left the office.

When I got bored with coding, I reread the company's manuals. I was on my second read-through of the Tolliver Corporation Safety Manual when I spotted it: my ticket to join the Reactance on Jekyll Island, if I played my cards right. It seemed fitting that my way out of the boring bureaucratic morass I seemed to be stuck in might come from mastery of the bureaucratic rules. I double-checked the building layout. Yes, all was as I had remembered. To pull it off, though, I was going to need some assistance from Uncle Larry.

CHAPTER 6:   INDEPENDENCE DAY

July 4 fell on a Tuesday, so I decided to take off work early on Friday and make a long weekend of it back home in Tennessee. It was a good four-hour drive – five including the time zone change. The summer sun was getting low in the sky by the time I unlocked the gate and drove up the narrow incline to Robber Dell.

No one was in the trailer, so I headed on over to Uncle Rob's barn. "Hey Pete!" Amit beamed as he opened the door to the apartment wing of the barn. "Good to see you!"

"Likewise," I acknowledged, following him in. "I really missed talking with you. I was getting worried about all the cryptic 'can't talk this channel is monitored' messages."

Rob was shaking his head. "He's been telling us all about it." Rob turned to Amit. "Give Pete the summary version."

"When the Civic Circle put all us interns up in the same apartment complex, I should have known something was hinky," Amit began. "First, they assigned everyone a roommate. A few days into the internship, I get taken in to security, and they tell me my roomie, this Ivy Leaguer named Aaron, they're suspicious of him, and they think he's leaking secrets and has contacts hostile to the Civic Circle. 'Cool,' I'm thinking, 'I'll pull a George P. Burdell and recruit the guy – start a Civic Youth cell right under their noses.' Then, a couple of days later, I notice a change in Aaron. He's all standoffish and suspicious. Huge difference in behavior, not that he was all that normal in the first place. That's when I figured it out. Everyone gets told their roomie is questionable and to monitor them."

"Wow," I was imagining having to live under that kind of surveillance from a roommate. "That's creepy."

"Yeah," Amit acknowledged. "So, the next day I report to the security office that they were right about Aaron. I tell them Aaron is clearly trying to spy on me, and it's all obvious, and he must be a plant trying to infiltrate the Civic Circle... discredit the other guy first, you see. At least I made it clear Aaron can't be trusted not to give himself away."

"Standard technique," Rob explained. "Get everyone to spy on everyone else. You know, before the Berlin Wall fell, something like ten percent of East Germany was on the payroll of the Stasi – their secret police – spying on and writing reports on neighbors, even family. But Amit, you need to tell him the best part."

"Oh, yeah," Amit nodded. "So it's the first night there in the new apartment, and I'm looking out the window at the great view, and I'm imagining all the WiFi nodes I'll be able to access. Piece of cake. I decide I better set up in the bathroom since Aaron might come back at any time, and locking myself in the bedroom might be suspicious. I check out the bathroom, I figure out how I'm going to set up the directional WiFi antenna, and I'm heading out to get my gear when I note something funny about the smoke detector."

"A smoke detector... in the bathroom?" That made no sense to me.

"Exactly," Amit grinned. "So I get my camera and take a picture of myself in the bathroom to send my folks to tell them I've arrived and all is well. I make sure the smoke detector is in the background. The lights are dim and I use my flash. Sure enough when I send the photo to my folks, I see this red reflection from what looked like a black hole in the smoke detector."

"A camera?" Holy paranoia. "They had video surveillance in the bathroom?!?"

"Real close call," Amit looked genuinely shaken. "There I was about to set up a secure comm channel back to the Reactance right under the Civic Circle's video surveillance."

"Why the bathroom of all places?" I asked.

"Oh, that's not all," Amit continued. "Both bedrooms and the common areas had the same damn smoke detectors. Six of them in an 800 square foot two-bedroom apartment."

"The Civic Circle, they take their fire safety real serious," Rob said sarcastically, "only it's not the conventional kind of fire they're eager to nip in the bud."

"Wow, Amit," I was trying to imagine having to live in a place you know is under continuous surveillance. "I begin to see why we didn't hear much from you."

"Exactly," Amit acknowledged. "It really spooked me. If they had me under continuous video surveillance, I was worried they'd search the room and find my comms gear and laptop." He took a deep breath. "The next morning, I snuck my gear bag into my backpack. On the way into work I threw the laptop and comms gear away in a random dumpster. Couldn't take the chance of them finding it. Sure enough, a couple of days later, someone swept through the apartment. All the little search tells I planted were disturbed."

"That was a smart move, Amit," Rob confirmed. "You have to know when to cut your losses, even if it means a temporary setback like sacrificing your gear."

I heard some noise from the bathroom. The secret underground part of Uncle Rob's place was accessed by a hydraulic lift that lowered the bathroom floor down to the level of the underground complex. Then, I heard the toilet flush. A moment later, Marlena came out of the bathroom.

"You're blonde!" Her long auburn hair was gone. She looked like a different person. It took me a second to realize that was probably the general idea.

She smiled when she saw me.

"Peter! Like the new look?"

Actually, I preferred her old look. "It's certainly different. I like it," I lied.

"I don't," she replied, "but different is good when you're on wanted posters all over the country. Anyway, I've made the most amazing progress on the MacGuffin manuscript."

"She refused to tell me about it until you were here," Amit said flatly. Was that jealousy? Or just sarcasm. I couldn't tell, but Marlena ignored him, came over and gave me a hug.

"What, I don't get a hug?" Amit asked in obviously fake outrage.

"You've had plenty from what you've been telling us," Marlena countered.

Rob smiled indulgently at her. "Maybe you could start from the beginning and try to explain it to us all one more time?"

Marlena slipped naturally into teacher mode, patiently explaining the obvious. "Heaviside discovered that when electromagnetic waves interfere with each other, they exchange energy. The natural balance of electric to magnetic energy in radiation is upset. Some of the energy becomes electrostatic or magnetostatic. The energy stops momentarily and changes direction. The waves exchange energy with each other."

"She keeps trying to tell me about this stuff," Rob confided, "but it doesn't make any more sense when she explains it than when you tried, Peter. I get it, but I don't know why it's important."

Marlena rolled her eyes. "It's because physicists are all operating under the wrong picture of how reality works. They assume that energy and fields are tightly coupled. They aren't. Fields exchange energy all the time. Electromagnetic waves and fields guide energy. Fields go one way, other fields go another way, and the energy they convey goes in a completely different trajectory under the influence of the interacting fields."

"OK," Amit said, struggling to understand, "but I still don't get why this is such a big secret worth killing people over."

Marlena looked up intently a moment as she tried to figure out how to explain it. Finally, her eyes refocused on Amit. "Consider two slits in a plane. An electromagnetic wave is incident on the plane, and some of the fields and energy pass through the slits. The fields from each slit are 'coherent,' synchronized with each other because they originally came from the same incident wave. They interfere with each other, adding up constructively in some places and cancelling out destructively in others. The energy is guided along streamlines, nudged toward the interferences. You get an interference pattern of bright and dark lines if you project the light on a screen or a photographic plate on the other side of the two slits."

Amit was nodding his head. He got it. Rob, he still looked indulgent, like he was merely humoring her and us.

Marlena continued. "Now assume we no longer have the classical case of streams of energy moving through the two slits. Imagine that energy is discretized, quantized, in discrete little lumps we call photons, and suppose we lower the intensity until we have just one photon at a time passing through the slits.

"The fields still pass through the two slits and generate an interference pattern. The photon randomly follows one of the same energy flow trajectories from the classical case and ends up in the interference pattern.

"See, everyone gets wrapped around the axle asking themselves which slit the photon went through, assuming it had to go through both slits in order to generate the interference pattern and had to be in both places at the same time. Feynman said that all the weirdness of quantum reality is wrapped up in this simple experiment. It's not weird at all, though. It's not wave-like particles that can be in two places at once, or particle-like waves that 'collapse' to deposit energy in a single lump. Fields behave like waves. They generate interference patterns between the two slits, throughout the region, 'non-locally,' even when there's only enough energy for one photon to be moving through the slits. Energy behaves like particles, following a particular trajectory under the influence of the interacting waves. Each does its own thing. The quantum weirdness and confusion are gone."

"The part I do get," Rob offered, "is how apparently a bunch of scientists started working out a quantum theory along those lines and they got shut down. Hard."

Marlena nodded. "Louis de Broglie laid the foundation in an amazing doctoral dissertation in 1924. He argued that particles had a wave nature associated with them. He won the Nobel Prize for his contribution. He argued that the waves guide the matter in a common-sense way. Schrödinger took this idea as the basis of his wave theory of quantum mechanics. The wave approach was attacked and nitpicked and overwhelmed by critics. No one would take it seriously, because they were all committed to the Copenhagen Interpretation. They believed that nothing could be said about what was really going on, and all we could do is model statistical likelihoods mathematically. Von Neumann came up with a bogus mathematical 'proof' that theories like de Broglie's had to be wrong. For twenty years, no one paid much attention.

"A man named David Bohm revived the de Broglie–Schrödinger approach in the 1950s. He was invited to be a professor at Princeton University. He fell under suspicion for his communist views. They fired him, and he ended up in Brazil. There was a symposium at Princeton, run by Robert Oppenheimer – the man who led the Manhattan Project to develop the atomic bomb. They spent hours trying to debunk Bohm's approach. When they failed, one of the attendees reported Oppenheimer dismissed Bohm's ideas as 'juvenile deviationism' and said, 'since we can't disprove him, we'll just have to agree to ignore him.'"

Amit's jaw dropped. "Wow."

"Oppenheimer himself fell under suspicion of communist ties and they revoked his clearance not long thereafter," Marlena noted. "I think it was because he failed to censor Bohm's heretical ideas quickly enough to suit the Civic Circle.

It took another twenty years before a physicist named John Bell started untangling what quantum mechanics really meant. Before long, the secret was out, and physicists all over the place were beginning to pay attention.

"Today there's a small community in physics working to develop and apply and understand the pilot wave approach, but they're dismissed by the mainstream community that wants everyone to 'shut up and calculate,' and ignore any physical picture of how the quantum realm really works."

"You'd think physicists would be excited about understanding how it all works," Rob offered.

"Some are," Marlena pointed out, "but many of the rest want to ignore it because, in truth, you don't have to understand what's going on in order to apply the equations and get useful results."

I thought about what Marlena was saying. "If you have the right picture of how things really work," I thought out loud, "you have a basis for making new insights and progress."

"Exactly!" Marlena looked triumphant. "Faraday was confused by the action-at-a-distance thinking that was at the basis of electromagnetic theory as he struggled to understand it. The theory was mathematically correct, but defied common sense with charges and currents over here influencing charges and currents over there without the intervention of any intermediate process or mechanism. Faraday devised the concept of fields, occupying the space between the interacting entities and conveying their interactions from place to place. As early as 1832, he was already thinking in terms of field interactions giving rise to electromagnetic waves. Faraday discovered magnetic induction, and laid the foundation for Maxwell and his successors to develop electromagnetic theory.

"Now, we're all confused by quantum weirdness, and the simple picture Heaviside devised – fields guide energy – is the key to justifying the pilot wave approach and making sense of quantum mechanics. The pilot wave approach to quantum mechanics is just the extrapolation of Heaviside's thinking on classical electromagnetic energy flow to the quantum realm."

"So, Heaviside's discovery explains and supports the pilot wave thinking in quantum mechanics," Amit recapitulated, "but is there any actual new discovery that helps the Reactance in our fight against the Civic Circle?" Rob was nodding his head in approval of Amit's practical focus.

"The MacGuffin manuscript is the key," Marlena explained, turning back to me. "You recall the basic idea we worked out back at Georgia Tech?" She smiled again.

I remembered it of course, but for entirely different reasons. I'd been struggling to understand the physics in MacGuffin's manuscript when Marlena walked into the lab. She'd been under pressure for her defense of Professor Chen, and the full weight of the university bureaucracy had been aimed at forcing her out. She'd decided to take a break from it all and was dressed for a night out on the town. Instead, she and I had solved equations at the blackboard for hours, working side-by-side in the confined space, getting chalk dust all over each other. I'd always found her attractive, but it was then I really fell in love with her. I'd tried to kiss her, but she prevented me. A few weeks later, that love for Marlena was part of what made me risk my life to save her and Professor Chen. There was still an obvious chemistry between us.

Unfortunately, I got the impression Marlena was more interested in discussing physics right now instead of chemistry. I recapitulated what we'd discovered.

"MacGuffin noted that electromagnetic energy is in balance, with equal amounts of electric and magnetic energy in electromagnetic waves," I explained. "In terms of the field intensity, that balance is given by the free space impedance, the ratio of electric to magnetic intensity is 377 ohms. As waves interact, the balance shifts, the fields start to become electrostatic or magnetostatic, and the energy flow slows down."

"Right," Marlena agreed. "If you normalize the energy velocity with respect to the speed of light and normalize the Lagrangian – the difference between the electric and magnetic energy – with respect to the Hamiltonian or the total energy, you find they describe a circle – the "Great Electromagnetic Circle," according to MacGuffin's manuscript, because it defines exactly how electromagnetics works and the full transition between forward waves at the speed of light, electrostatics, reverse waves, magnetostatic, and back to forward waves."

That was the result I'd obtained with Marlena in the lab on that memorable evening. There was an earlier result I'd figured out on my own – the Rosetta Stone that made unlocking the MacGuffin manuscript possible.

"It turned out that the Chinese mysticism in MacGuffin's manuscript was actually a thinly-veiled tutorial on electromagnetics," I reminded everyone. "Yang was electric fields, yin was magnetic fields, and so on. When you interpret and plot the result for the impedance of the fields of a dipole on a Smith Chart, you get the taijitu, the Yin-Yang symbol."

Marlena was nodding her head in agreement.

Amit looked puzzled. "So, was the MacGuffin discussion an allegory or analogy to existing Chinese philosophy? Or was that philosophy based on actual ancient teachings on electromagnetics?"

"Chicken or egg," Rob muttered.

I disagreed. "We know the manuscript dates back to a Shaolin Monastery that was raided and burned back in the 1600s. That aligns with the legends of the Red Flower Tong as well as contextual clues in the manuscript. You'll find distorted fragments of the MacGuffin version in the accepted interpretations of Chinese writing on yang, yin, divine harmony, and so forth. I think the electromagnetics tutorial version was the original and the I Ching and other Chinese writings are distorted, half-remembered, and garbled versions of the original."

"Much as I enjoy the ancient history lesson..." I was sure Rob was lying, but there wasn't a hint of sarcasm in his voice. "...you guys need to know what Marlena's been up to the last few weeks."

Marlena lit up even more with excitement. "I figured out how electrons work: they're a standing wave turned in on itself constructively interfering to yield what appears to be a static charge."

I thought about that a moment. It didn't make sense. "A wave has to have a magnetic component to make the energy move," I pointed out.

"Electrons have a bit of a residual magnetic moment," Marlena replied, "a little magnetic dipole."

I thought about how the fields would interact. "You'd get a circular flow of energy around the electron."

"Exactly," Marlena confirmed, "and when you calculate the angular momentum, it's h-bar over two – the quantum 'spin.' It's close even in a first order calculation. There's an electromagnetic basis for quantum spin. What's more, that crossed field configuration is described in Hertz's *Electric Waves*.

Amit beat me to the obvious conclusion. "That's why they were so eager to kill Hertz. He'd already unlocked the fundamental secret to explain the quantum behavior of electrons. It was waiting right there in his book for anyone to put the pieces together."

"I'm surprised they didn't manage to get his book redacted or suppressed, too," I offered.

"It may have already pushed past the critical point where enough people had found out about it," Marlena noted, "but that's not all. If you look to where the electron fields have an impedance of 377 ohms, you find the circumference is exactly half the Compton wavelength."

Wow! I could tell Amit wasn't following why that was significant. "The Compton wavelength of a particle is the wavelength of a photon whose energy is the same as the mass of a particle," I explained, taking in the implications. "So, an electron really is just a standing wave, and another mysterious quantum property follows from 'classical' electromagnetics and energy flow."

"Exactly!" Marlena seemed happy I was following her line of reasoning. "Even more significant, I finally understand neutrinos and how Nexus Detectors work."

"Finally, we're getting to the good part," Rob offered with a smile, obviously bored by all the physics.

"It's apparently what Majorana and MacGuffin were discussing with Jorge Luis Borges in Buenos Aires back in 1939." She'd been so depressed when I'd last seen her over a month ago. Now? Marlena was almost giddy with excitement.

"The Garden of Forking Paths." I explained to Amit the story I found, and then turned back to Marlena. "So, you're saying the 'Many Worlds' hypothesis is really true? The universe splits into uncountably many duplicate copies with every quantum variation?" I was skeptical how that could work.

"Not exactly," Marlena clarified. "It turns out most quantum fluctuations or alternatives are completely irrelevant. There's a bit of tension, locally, as the two possible universes exist side by side, but almost always, they merge back together, with none the wiser.

"Even more significant divergences can happen. Did you have a turkey sandwich for lunch two days ago? Or was it ham? It could have been either. Since it makes no difference, the universe in which you chose ham and the universe in which you chose turkey have merged back together.

"Some events snowball and begin huge divergences, though. The slightest hesitation changes someone's departure time by a fraction of a second. They just miss a traffic light and now they're a few minutes further back along the road than they might have been. Then they get into an accident which blocks the road by the Veterans' Home and keeps a couple busloads of retired veterans from voting for George Bush, say, in Florida in 2000."

"There's a universe somewhere in which Bush won in 2000?" I could see Amit taking in the implications. "Closely balanced events – events that could have played out in a couple of different ways with significantly different outcomes tend to split reality into multiple copies?"

Marlena nodded. "And when that happens, at the time and place of the split, there's a huge flux of neutrinos given off – the subatomic signature of reality tearing into multiple copies on a macroscopic level."

"That's how Nexus Detectors must work," I concluded.

Now it was Rob's turn to nod. "What the Civic Circle was doing here, killing your folks, making us aware of their conspiracy, prompting us to discover the MacGuffin manuscript, it's been making all kinds of significant changes in reality. That's the sort of thing Nexus Detectors pick up, and now Marlena's going to build one for us." Rob put a hand casually on Marlena's shoulder.

Marlena shook her head. "Not exactly," she cautioned. "I have the theory, yes. Making a detector that sensitive, though, that's an engineering challenge. I don't think even our state-of-the-art neutrino detectors would pick up the signature. I need a Nexus Detector to see how it works, to reverse engineer it."

The Civic Circle had one. We were pretty sure the Albertians had a Nexus Detector, too, courtesy of Majorana and a well-funded development program. And Angus MacGuffin, may he rest in peace, hid one away just before he died. Knowing he was at risk, knowing all he'd worked for was in danger of being wiped out and erased by the Civic Circle, he'd tried to preserve his discoveries for posterity.

If only we could figure out where.

After Amit finally left for the evening, Rob, Marlena, and I went down to the refuge. I tried to get some time alone with Marlena, but Rob seemed to be hovering over her. The fatigue from my long day was catching up with me. I went to sleep.

I made myself breakfast when I woke up the next morning. Rob and Marlena must have been sleeping in. As a morning person myself, that seemed slothful, but it did give me a chance to review the data that Amit had collected and brought over yesterday. Gomulka still seemed head-over-heels in lust with our fictional Hungarian supermodel, Reka Kozma. He'd leapt at the chance to help her move into the U.S. and already paid the deposit on an apartment in the same building he lived in near campus. He was going to help her claim her worldly belongings when they arrived in a cargo container at the Port of Brunswick, and then spend an inaugural week together at the Civic Circle's Social Justice Leadership Forum on Jekyll Island. That part of our plans was all set.

It was getting close to lunch time, so I headed into town for my appointment with Uncle Larry.

"Mister Pete!" Cookie opened the door with a beaming smile. "Glad you could drop by! How's life been treating you?"

"Good work to do, and good friends, too," I answered as she gave me a hug. "Can't ask for more."

"That's the truth," she acknowledged, showing me to Grandma's living room where Uncle Larry waited. "Mister Pete is here, sir."

"Thank you, Cookie," my uncle dismissed her. "Pete, my boy. How was your drive?"

"Long and uneventful."

He glanced at the door, assuring himself Cookie had departed. "And how are you coming along at TAGS?"

"Now that's a bit of a story." I explained how my assignment as Travis Tolliver's personal assistant had been hijacked in the name of diversity by HR at TAGS in Huntsville and how I ended up in IT.

"HR is a necessary evil," Larry confirmed nodding his head. "Our people in Washington write a lot of nebulous rules about 'equality' and 'fairness' It helps make a place for otherwise not very productive people."

"Why do you put up with it?" I was genuinely curious.

"Diversity is the religion of our age," Larry explained. "Dare to question it, and you risk being burned at the stake as a heretic. You have to pay homage to it, or the peasants will come at you with pitchforks and torches."

"This diversity comes at a cost," I pointed out. "Better workers get shunted aside to make room for more 'diverse' candidates, time is wasted in mandatory 'sensitivity' seminars, people on eggshells worrying that some innocuous phrase will get them..."

Uncle Larry held up a hand to stop me. "Of course," he smiled at my naiveté. "We're experts at dealing with it. Promote a token woman or minority to the executive team, fund a scholarship or two for disadvantaged youth, sponsor a Women in Tech symposium to hire the most promising – and hottest – COGS.

"COGS?"

"Career-Oriented Gals," Larry explained. "Preferably the kind who think it's daring and empowering to be a bit adventuresome around the office, if you get my drift!"

I did. Creep.

"If you show how very enlightened you are," he explained, "you can get away with most anything. Meanwhile, the competitors who aren't keeping up on the LGGBDTTTIQQAAPP front get hamstrung by discrimination lawsuits."

"LGG-what?"

"Lesbian, Gay, Genderqueer, Bisexual, Demisexual, Transgender, Transsexual, Twospirit, Intersex, Queer, Questioning, Asexual, Allies, Pansexual, Polyamorous, and don't you dare leave one off or you're a hater!" Larry had a smug smile on his face. "It's just like any form of business regulation. The people in the know write the rules and have the resources to ensure compliance. If you're not clued in, well, the most trivial incident becomes cause for a pile-on. The activists get on your case, and you and your company's name get smeared all over the press. You have to do the ritual walk of shame, and then you have to buy off the activists with some big donations to their organizations to get them to let up on the pressure. Meanwhile, we're busy competing circles around the hapless fools and getting good press for our enlightened attitudes. Sure there's a cost to the diversity bullshit, but so long as it costs the other guys more, it's a competitive advantage."

Larry's strategy seemed to me like turning loose some hungry lions and hoping they'd be grateful and eat you last. I wasn't going to tell him that, though.

Just then Cookie opened the door and called us into the kitchen. "Just poor-do," Grandma insisted over her plate of sandwiches accompanied by a sweet potato casserole, breaded and fried okra, and green beans fried with a hint of ham. "Coffee, Peter?"

"Yes, ma'am."

Cookie must have anticipated that one, because a cup of steaming black coffee was in front of me in seconds.

"That's all, Cookie," Grandma insisted. "I'll take care of everything else. You can have the rest of the day off."

"Thank you, ma'am," she replied. "Good seeing you Mister Tolliver, Mister Pete."

"Good seeing you, Cookie," I replied. Larry ignored her.

I got an earful about Grandma's garden, and how it was going to be much hotter for the Fourth, "Just you wait and see if I'm right," and how she was going to have to use her soakers to keep the flowers from wilting in the heat.

As we were finishing up, Grandma made her usual complaints about how rarely she got to see me. I explained Huntsville was a long drive, and I couldn't make it home very often.

"Lawrence," Grandma said sternly, "you really ought to get Peter a job here at Tolliver so he can start to learn his way around the family business."

I started to explain that I actually was working for Tolliver, only for a branch in Huntsville when Larry held up a hand to silence me. "Experience outside the company will do the boy good, Mama," he explained. "And there's still some in the family with hard feelings about how his father took advantage of Amanda."

"Nonsense," Grandma scoffed. "Your sister, Amanda, wasn't the sort to let any man take advantage of her. My how that girl loved her man Roy with a passion. I never did see why you boys and your father took such a dislike to Roy."

I could see Grandma was making Larry uncomfortable discussing it in front of me. "Papa had his own plans for Amanda," Larry explained, "that didn't include her marrying Roy."

"That Roy had a good head on his shoulders, and a lot of gumption," Grandma insisted. "Reminded me of your Grandpa Tom. Family could have used some of that energy and initiative. We can't just sit on what ol' Tom built up from what his Grandpa Jake started. Gotta get some new blood into the family." She smiled at me.

I felt uncomfortable in the middle of the family squabble, but it was good to know her opinion of Dad after so many years.

"That's why Pete's here, Mama," Larry reassured her. "I'm trying to see if there might be a way he could work with us after all. We can't go letting Mike or any of the cousins know about it, though, until the time is right. Right or wrong, there's still hard feelings. They might throw a monkey wrench into the plans. Can you keep this a secret and not tell anyone?"

"Of course, Lawrence," Grandma beamed at him. "So much anger and mule-headed stubbornness. Makes my heart glad to see you mending fences with Roy's boy. Family's getting spread mighty thin these days. Too many of my grandchildren and the cousins don't appreciate it's not all spending Greatly-Grand Jake's legacy on fun and games. They have to be ready to take what we did and make it bigger and better. Like Grandpa Tom, or like your Papa did."

I noticed she left Larry off that list of accomplished Tollivers.

"I have plans for young Peter, here," Larry assured her. "Don't you worry, Mama."

"Well then," she stood up. "Let me get you boys some of my apple pie, and you can get to your planning."

A piece of apple pie and another cup of coffee later, I laid out the situation for Uncle Larry.

"I can't intervene directly," he insisted. "It's bad enough that your Professor Gomulka figured out your Tolliver connection. I cautioned him not to let it go any further. Your effectiveness in the Civic Circle depends on it not being obvious that you're working for me."

"That's not what I had in mind," I explained. "I need you to insist that the install team bring along all the interns with clearances to help out with the Jekyll Island job."

I could see him mulling that through. "Yes, I could do that. Give the young folks experience, provide a force multiplier on a crucial job, show how enlightened we are, and all that. Maybe even a good opportunity to get you or some of the other interns connected with Civic Youth."

"That's all it should take," I confirmed.

"I hope you can deliver information worth what I've promised you," Larry cautioned.

I smiled. I'd been expecting this. "I think I can earn my keep with what I've figured out already."

Larry's eyebrows raised. "Do tell."

"How does TAGS select the start-ups it acquires and the inventors and entrepreneurs it hires?"

Larry considered my question a moment. "It's mostly networking. Well-connected people see something interesting and bring it to my or Travis' attention. If it checks out, we look further, and maybe we do a deal. Lots of those scientists and engineers are babes in the woods when it comes to finance. It's easy to get 'em cheap."

I looked him in the eye. "You and Travis are being used by the Civic Circle, and you should be getting paid better to do their work for them."

He tilted his head skeptically. "How so?"

"There's a pattern in the technologies TAGS has been acquiring," I explained. "They're truly great technologies. Enormous potential to disrupt the status quo."

He wasn't convinced. I continued.

"Someone wants all these cool, disruptive technologies under their control, not so you or TAGS can make any money off them, but so they can be strangled in their cradles. They want you to fail. They will not allow those technologies to succeed. They are using you to make sure those technologies die before they can pose a threat, and they'll never allow you to make money off them."

Larry shook his head in denial. "Travis tells me we got one project going on now where we've greased the skids with DARPA – the Defense Advanced Research Projects Agency. They're the military's high-tech think tank, and they're about to fund a massive multi-million dollar communications security R&D project. We have the inside track to land the contract."

He must be thinking of Roger Thorn's UWB work.

"I guess we'll see," was all I could say to that. "I have a suspicion you and TAGS are being set up for failure."

"Nonsense," Larry insisted. "Is that all you have for me? Vague suspicions?"

I wondered if he was on board with Travis and Professor Glyer's killbot scheme. This might be a chance to shut it down. I'd have to tread carefully.

"Are you aware of TAGS' robotics initiative?"

"Of course," Larry acknowledged. "Very promising project. We just won an $80 million contract to deliver robots to the U.S. Army."

"Were you aware that TAGS is working from plans stolen from U.S. Robotics? And the TAGS design violates U.S. Robotics' patents?"

"You make it sound like industrial espionage," Larry said derisively. "It's merely reverse engineering of a competitive project. Perfectly legal. Everyone does it. And the U.S. Robotics patents were developed under research contracted by the U.S. Government. They have a license to use the intellectual property."

Ah. That was why they were so brazen about ripping off the other company's work.

"All I'm saying," I offered, "is if I could figure it out, I'm probably not the only one in TAGS to know what's going on."

"I hope you can do better than that, Peter," Larry said, "or the deal will be off."

He didn't want to listen. I still didn't know how much he really knew about the project's real goal. I was going to have to find another way to shut down Glyer's killbot project.

"I'll just have to keep my ears open at Jekyll Island and see what I can do."

"Very well." He stood and escorted me back to Grandma. I said my farewells, and I drove back up in the hills to Rob's place.

* * *

A sheriff's cruiser was parked up by the barn. That was what a professional might consider "a clue."

"Well, if it ain't my favorite juvenile delinquent," Sheriff Gunn welcomed me with a big grin as I entered the barn. "How's your summer vacation going?" He held out a hand.

"Fine," I replied, taking his hand. He always gave me a too firm grip. "How's yours?"

"The usual," he replied more soberly. "Found me some jaspers out yonder pokin' 'round. They figured to score some cheap meth from some back country pusher they'd heard tell of. Ran 'em out of the county, but that's how I reckoned I got me another meth lab up in the hills. By the time I gathered up enough on him to convince the judge to let me search him... well, it was too late for this girl he had with him. She OD'd. Sick bastard just drug her body out in the woods. Didn't even know her name. Doc Wallace has the body at his funeral home."

"What brings you out here today?"

"It's an ill wind blows nobody any good," he replied.

Marlena handed me a Tennessee driver's license. It had her picture but the name read, "Brandy Tucker"?

"Doc Wallace figured it out. The girl in the woods," the sheriff confirmed. "There was something of a resemblance. Gave me the idea. Doc's still pissed off the way the Feds made him sign off on your parents' death without letting him examine the bodies. I called in a favor with him. Doc ID'd the girl, name of Brandy Tucker. The official records will show we got us a dead Jane Doe – identity unknown – and ain't nobody the wiser. That meth head's probly goin' up for a good long spell. And Miss Brandy Tucker here, who's been driftin' through from some small hamlet nobody ever heard of up in West Virginia, is about to settle down in beautiful Sherman, Tennessee, and get a job as a barista at Kudzu Joe's."

"With a bit of work and a few other favors the sheriff called in," Rob added, "the paper trail will show Miss Brandy Tucker settled in here months before that big-city scientist lady down yonder vanished into the mountains."

"Big-city scientist lady?" Marlena eyed him. "And the best you men could do was find me a job as a barista?"

"Ain't got much employment opportunity in Lee County for big-city scientist ladies, ma'am" the sheriff pointed out with an obvious twinkle in his eye. "Particularly ones on the run from the law. Unless y'all want to make the commute all the way to the Oak Ridge Lab and apply under your real name."

"That's a one-way ticket to a federal penitentiary, or worse," Rob pointed out. "It had to be something as far removed from your background as possible. And all of us are going to have to be careful to refer to you as 'Brandy.' You, too. Any slip-up or mention of 'Marlena' could be fatal."

"I understand," Marlena nodded, "but 'Brandy' is going to be moving on to bigger and better opportunities than serving coffee before too long."

"Won't this 'Brandy's' family figure it out?" I asked. "I wasn't sure I liked the name. It would take a while for me to get used to it.

"I cain't find nobody knows the girl," Sheriff Gunn shrugged. "Made inquiries on the pretense she was a suspect in some petty crimes down here. No family still livin' I could find. Law enforcement in her hometown had no record of her since she dropped out of high school near to ten years ago. Sad case, but at least there's some good's come out of it for the Reactance."

The sheriff had lots of questions for me about my experience at TAGS. It was clear he'd been reading my updates and reports.

"Simply amazing: everythin' that happens behind the scenes," he shook his head in disbelief. "Cabals wrestlin' with each other for dominance, suppressin' technologies so we don't advance too quick for them to maintain their control."

"Oh that's just part of it," Amit explained. "I've been spending my time helping the Civic Circle recruit the next generation of Civic Youth. They're developing tests and screening techniques like what Gomulka got Georgia Tech to apply to all their incoming students for next fall."

I remembered that well. Gomulka was supposed to use the personality test results to select the next class of students to be awarded full-ride scholarships by the Social Justice Initiative. Only Gomulka got lazy and asked Amit and me to do the work for him. We did, only we creatively reinterpreted Gomulka's criteria to screen out the most promising young 'Social Justice Warriors,' as Gomulka had begun referring to them. We let a few through, but most of next year's class would be the people we'd picked according to our own criteria – solid, independent minded, well-grounded folk who wouldn't be as pliable.

"Were you able to get your finger on the scale and screw up the selection process?"

"No," Amit answered me ruefully. "Security at the Civic Circle is tight. I don't dare step out of bounds. All I could do was keep my eyes and ears open and take in whatever I just happened to run across. The big takeaway is they have a complete index on everyone in the country, keyed in to their social security number, correlated with law enforcement, financial, medical, and educational records."

"Ought to be illegal for civvies to have access to all that data," Sheriff Gunn observed.

"They have 'consulting contracts' and 'research grants' with all kinds of federal agencies," Amit explained. "Wouldn't surprise me if most of what they have is technically legal. The power in it is how they piece together and correlate the information.

"They have their fingers deep into journalism schools and the media, screening candidates and looking for those most willing to parrot the party line. You think the up-and-comers, the talking heads they show on television, the guys who get the big book deals are the ones who worked the hardest and got the best grades? That's not how the system works. When they identify particularly pliant people, they get great contacts, break big stories, and take the express elevator to the top. Question the Civic Circle's agenda, write something that threatens their narrative, and your career is stalled, or worse. That's the area I was working in – correlating online articles with their authors and helping evaluate their writing for 'deviationism.'"

"Makes sense," Rob nodded. "They want a cadre of their people in positions of power and influence. Toe the line, and good fortune smiles upon you. Opportunities open up, you get a prestigious assignment, an impressive promotion, a major book deal. Show some independence, and you get sandbagged. That's an insidious form of soft power and control."

"Exactly," Amit confirmed. "They're doing something similar in politics and law. Identifying the bright and industrious young strivers, helping along those willing to play on the team, thwarting those who aren't, and getting the dirt on anyone who lands in an influential position, so the Civic

Circle can have leverage and control over them. Remember my article on how the physical differences between men and women were all due to hetero-patriarchal bias?"

"Yes." I was amazed Georgia Tech's student paper, *The Technique*, had published that utter nonsense.

"It fits the narrative," Amit observed, "and I'm in favor as a rising young activist. They've had me expand it into a full-length treatment, and a New York publishing house gave me a contract and an advance. All part of the pattern of corruption."

"They can't possibly have corrupted everyone," Marlena, or I guess I was going to have to start thinking of her as Brandy, offered.

"They don't have to," Sheriff Gunn pointed out. "Think what it would take to stop them. Y'all need us in law enforcement to investigate and gather the evidence. We've already seen how the FBI Director and probably other key figures in law enforcement are on their team, gummin' up the works. Y'all need a district attorney willing to build and prosecute a case. They can delay, stonewall, or commit technical errors at any point to cause the case to be dropped. A favored minion gets caught red handed? Why, he gets an immunity deal to testify against someone else, and when there's not enough evidence of the bogus crime you made up, the whole thing is dropped. Y'all need a judge willin' to hear the case fairly, and jurors willin' to make an honest judgment. Corrupt any of 'em at any stage, and you're basically unstoppable. It don't take many. Just a few working together can exert effective control, block any attempts to take down one of their own, and put a hell of a lot of pressure on anyone honest enough to try to thwart 'em."

"They've got the federal level thoroughly penetrated," Rob concluded. "Now they're using that control to reshape society to their liking. Meritocracy is dead. It's not a system of the best and brightest, but of the most corrupt and compliant. That's how they systematically select their minions and promote them to positions of power, use them to advance the

Civic Circle's agenda, always making sure they have enough dirt on them to keep them in line."

I thought about honest folk like me, working hard, keeping their noses clean, and struggling to make a go against the soft corruption of a system that rewards compliance and corruption instead of skill and merit. What about all the people like me who bought the narrative – work hard, get good grades, do your job with energy and enthusiasm, and you can rise to the top? It's all a scam, because the people who rise to the top in a system like that are the ones who play ball, kiss butt, and are morally compromised in a way that makes them safe and attractive to their masters. The most evil and psychopathic are the ones who come out on top.

How long would it take for me to give up and become like Mr. Humphreys, going through the motions in a dead-end job under the control of the less competent but more compliant? I shuddered at the thought.

"The way they've firewalled their system is impressive," Amit continued. "I've seen the external files. They have 'citizen scores' – like a credit score to tell how compliant someone is. There are flags, too, to tell if they're 'safe.'"

"Safe?" I thought through the implications of that.

"If they have enough incriminating evidence on them," Rob suggested.

Amit nodded his head in agreement. "They have something they call the 'black files.' I overheard some discussions I wasn't supposed to. It's all stored on an internal network – completely firewalled, there's no external connection. Some of the data I was gathering went in, so I had limited access, but I couldn't actually look at anything, except for the low-level people whose data I was entering. College students and some low-level media types, mostly. They had video files, photos, associated with lots of the people. I couldn't look at it without drawing attention, so I didn't."

"Blackmail material," Rob concluded.

"Probably," Amit agreed.

I was appalled. "We have to stop them."

"So who bells the cat?" Brandy asked.

"All that data..." I felt an epiphany forming. "It's all secure in the Civic Circle's Arlington, Virginia, headquarters, isn't it?"

"Oh yeah," Amit assured me. "The building security is impressive. State-of-the-art system."

"Between the air gap to the data and the physical security, it's locked up tight." Rob had a grim look on his face. "I tried to poke around last year. Closest I got was sharing a smoke or two with the folks who work there. I wouldn't even try to get inside. Best you could hope for is to infiltrate and get low-level access, like Amit's done. It would take years to progress through a career there and end up with enough responsibility to get access, and it wouldn't be guaranteed even then."

"So what happens if the building burns down? Or there's a terror attack? Or a pipe bursts and destroys all their servers and hard drives?"

"They must have an offsite backup," Rob was following my train of thought. "Where would they keep it?"

"I'm not positive," I walked over to Petrel's map of the Indian mounds, "but I think I know where it's going." Rob had sketched the layout of the Jekyll Island Club Hotel, the Sans Souci Apartments, and the nearby cottages on the map. "The Civic Circle just ordered an impressively large data vault for installation in the 'network center' in the basement of the Jekyll Island Club Hotel."

Amit saw exactly what I was driving at. "Their data backup..."

"It's not completely air-gapped, though," I pointed out. "They have a data connection."

"Remote backups," Amit suggested. "They don't want to have a courier travel there every week with the latest backups."

"They send them over the Internet," Rob nodded. "Encrypted, I'm sure, but that's a vulnerability."

I was supposed to be helping out Mr. Humphreys with getting the servers and other hardware ready to install. We were going to put the system together in the lab. "A tap," I suggested. "Can we put a hardware tap in the system? Copy the raw data packets as they're going through, then pull the data out at our convenience?"

"That's beyond my skill level," Amit acknowledged.

"I think I know someone who can help," Rob said thoughtfully. "I'll take care of it."

* * *

Uncle Rob loved fires, and the Fourth of July was always a good excuse for one. He had a big barbeque and bonfire planned for the occasion. This year though, July 4 fell on a Tuesday. Amit would be flying back to Virginia, and I had a half-day drive back to Huntsville. We held a smaller, private bonfire the night of July 3.

"You know," Rob explained, "although we celebrate Independence Day on July 4, the declaration was originally signed on July 2. We're just splitting the difference this year."

Only two years ago, we'd celebrated the Fourth with a huge party at Robber Dell. It was one of my last happy memories of my family before we'd found ourselves in a fight for our lives against the Civic Circle. An Uncle Rob bonfire always helped bring me back to those happier days.

"Sure you can't stay?" Rob asked me. "The gang will all be here. Most of the Shop Rats, Dr. Krueger's coming up with his family, and Mr. Burke's planning to come."

"Too much to do at work," I explained, "and I don't have much time off." The truth was I didn't feel in the mood to celebrate. I had to get to Jekyll Island. Rob and Amit were counting on me. I had a plan I thought would work, but it wasn't surefire. The responsibility weighed heavily on me. There was only so much I could do to align the odds in my favor. Too much of my plan relied on the need to persuade Mr. Humphreys. I had a good idea how I could do that, but I couldn't guarantee his reaction.

Rob was still staring into the fire. "Pete," he began, "part of why I didn't take the Civic Circle seriously in the first place was because what they were trying to hide seemed so insignificant. So what if Heaviside showed that electromagnetic waves trade energy when they interact. I still don't get why hiding that's worth killing someone."

"Never underestimate the power of the right idea to change the world," Marlena, or rather, Brandy, noted. She was sitting between Rob and me, holding Tigger in her lap. I could hear the cat purring loudly even over the crackle of the fire. "Electromagnetics started off as a collection of equations describing how charges and currents over here affect charges and currents over there. 'Action-at-a-Distance' theory they called it for lack of any better explanation."

"That's a non-answer," Amit observed. "They may as well have called it the 'Stuff Happens and No One Knows Why' theory."

"Right," Brandy nodded. "Not a satisfactory explanation. Action-at-a-Distance explained mathematically what happened but offered no insight as to why. It troubled lots of deep thinkers all the way back to Isaac Newton, who got the ball rolling with his Theory of Universal Gravitation. One genius, Michael Faraday, speculated that electricity and magnetism might be caused by 'lines of force' pervading the space around magnets. That speculation led James Clerk Maxwell to develop the equations for electricity and magnetism that – refined by Oliver Heaviside – became what we know as Maxwell's Equations. Heinrich Hertz discovered radio waves, validating Maxwell's theory."

"Hertz died of a mysterious jaw malignancy just after he published his discoveries," I pointed out, "but it was too late. The theory was out there, and folks like Marconi and Oliver Lodge applied the ideas of Maxwell, Heaviside, and Hertz to make a success of radio.

"At the same time, Poynting and Heaviside developed the theory of electromagnetic energy flow. They explained emerging phenomena like the skin effect, AC resistance, and the physics of conduction. All that work developing a physical model of reality was swept away by emerging discoveries in atomic physics that were twisted to satisfy pre-existing philosophic biases."

"The Copenhagen School." Brandy nodded. "They gave us correct and valid equations cloaked in the mysticism of complementarity and observer-dependence, guaranteeing we'd never be able to move beyond the math to a deeper understanding. They poked out our eyes and let generations of physicists stumble about in the dark." She sounded bitter.

"They probably killed Kaiser Frederick III of Germany," Rob noted. "Same MO as the hit on Heinrich Hertz just a few years later. The Circle pushed his idiot, militaristic son Wilhelm in as Kaiser. Wilhelm launched Germany onto a collision course toward war with France, England, and Russia."

"Surely the Circle couldn't have arranged the Archduke's assassination in Sarajevo," Brandy countered.

"They didn't have to," Rob explained. "They built a powder keg. A spark somewhere was going to set it off sooner or later. The resulting conflagration devastated Europe. The flower of European manhood laid waste, with vermin like the Communists and the Nazis fighting over the carcasses."

"That's what the Civic Circle is trying to get us into in the Middle East," I noted. "Drag us into the conflict, bleed off the best and bravest, weaken the country, and make us easier for them to control."

"Exactly," Rob confirmed. "Now, with Europe weakened and America falling under their control, the Civic Circle is on the verge of achieving globally what they were working for in China – a centralized world state, firmly under their control."

"This summer will be another turning point," Amit confirmed. "The Civic Circle plans on building up support for war in Iraq. They've got half of Washington convinced that Saddam Hussein is the focal point of global terror and the other half convinced they need to go along with it or be hammered for their lack of patriotism. Weaken us further, massively destabilize the Middle East, and drive hordes of refugees to Europe to escape the chaos."

We all stared into the inferno in front of us and speculated about the inferno to come. There was a long and heavy silence.

"We're going to stop it," I said with confidence, although I was filled with uncertainty as to how we'd manage to pull that off. "When Gomulka's caught accepting Virtual Reka's cargo container full of drugs, maybe the scandal will be enough to distract them. 'Senior Civic Circle Official Caught Red-Handed.'"

"I wouldn't count on it getting enough coverage to matter." Rob pulled a flask out of his shirt pocket and took a sip. "They control enough of the media to shut down stories they find threatening. One of their own, a drug smuggler, incriminating them? It'll never see the light of day. Our only hope is direct action: get in, and take 'em out. The resulting chaos as the second tier struggles to assert control will distract them from pursuing the war."

I hoped he was right. I hoped we could do it. I hoped we could survive.

"Try some of this." Rob held out his flask.

"Careful," Brandy smiled. "He tried inflicting some of that stuff on me the other night."

I almost choked on my little sip. The raw alcohol burned my mouth. "New batch of moonshine?" I coughed.

"I prefer to call it 'artisanal craft bourbon,'" Rob grinned and took another sip.

Liquor wasn't my thing. I washed the pungent aftertaste out of my mouth with my Coke.

Amit took a sip. He struggled mightily to avoid showing a reaction, but a strangled snort still emerged, as he hastened to swallow some of his own Coke.

"How will this end?" I asked myself silently, as I stared into the flames. "In fire," I realized the obvious answer.

CHAPTER 7:   A RISKY GAMBIT

I was glad I'd come back on July 4th, so I'd have some time before work started again the following day. I unlocked the door and stepped into my too-warm apartment. I immediately turned the AC back down to a more comfortable level. I set my bag down in the bathroom, and noticed my tells were missing. The fingernail balanced on the top of the drawer? Gone. The hair stuck in the cabinet door? Gone. Someone had been through my apartment. They'd made a thorough search of it – most every little tell I'd planted was gone. It hadn't been a thief. Nothing was missing, although I'd taken most of my high value stuff including my AR-15, my laptops, and my data. The book safe where I'd laid my decoy flash drives in a neat diamond arrangement? The flash drives were still there, but they weren't in the pattern I'd left them in.

My clock/camera told the story. The motion capture showed two men in exterminator uniforms coming in the apartment. Initially I thought it was just the usual maintenance contractors spraying for bugs. The guys in the video though, set down their equipment and conducted a swift, professional search of my place. They looked Asian, and they were in and out in under ten minutes. Was this the Tong's doing? They'd been suspicious I might be holding back on them. Maybe they'd give me a clean bill of health based on this search.

A more troubling thought came to mind. Maybe they had me under surveillance. I watched the motion capture again. It looked like a search, but they'd spent plenty of time outside the view of the camera from the bedroom. They hadn't installed anything in the bedroom, but they could easily have installed a bug or even a camera out in the living room. I could no longer consider my apartment secure, and I'd have to find places elsewhere to do any work I wanted kept secret. That would only complicate my life further.

My apartment would take time to cool down, so I decided to go wardriving and grab a bite to eat, being careful to look for anyone following me. I didn't see anyone, but they could easily have stuck a tracking device on my truck.

I settled in for dinner and accessed the WiFi at a McDonalds across the street and down the block. A couple minutes of navigating TOR and reconnecting through a Berkshire Inn in Syracuse, NY, and I was online. I reported the incident to Rob and the sheriff. If I was being investigated, the next obvious associates for them to check out would certainly include Rob. Sheriff Gunn would have to ask his deputies to keep a special eye out for strangers poking around Sherman County. We didn't have a specific code for "Someone broke into my place; be careful," that I could send to Amit over an open channel. He'd already rid himself of anything suspicious, so he'd probably be safe.

Larry wasn't going to do anything about Professor Glyer's killbot project. He was delighted with the big contract and might not even be aware of the sinister implications. I wondered if he was in on it, or if Travis was keeping the details from him. In any event, U.S. Robotics was about to be underbid by TAGS on the new Army robot contract. Surely they'd be interested in doing something. I took a directory listing of all the files in Glyer's "USRobotics" folder, created a new throwaway email account, and sent off the listing of stolen files with a brief anonymous cover letter to U.S. Robotics.

* * *

"You're late," Mr. Humphreys welcomed me back from my vacation.

"I've been in the office nearly an hour already. Julie at the reception desk caught me as I was coming in. She opened another email virus, so I had to clean it off and get a scan going."

He had pulled out my resume and was scrutinizing it. "You did work pulling cable and installing a network for a hotel?"

"Yes, at a Berkshire Inn and Suites." Amit's dad hired me to help install the network at the hotel they ran, and I'd done any number of network cable installs while working for my father as an apprentice electrician.

"How long do you think it would take to train some other interns to pull cable?"

Outstanding! My scheme with Uncle Larry was already paying off. "I could show them the basics in an hour or two. It's mostly on-the-job training," I explained. "We could do some network installation here, if there's anything you like to have done. It wouldn't take too long to get everyone up to speed."

"Good," Humphreys confirmed. "Here's the list of interns with clearances." I saw Johnny's name and a few others I didn't know as well. "Start training them tomorrow morning. For now, I want you back on prepping the servers for the Jekyll Island job as soon as possible. Get to it!"

* * *

The help desk calls really slowed down after July 4th. Not much being accomplished with so many folks taking a long vacation, I figured. One of the highlights of early July was the big DARPA announcement. Roger Thorn was counting on funding from DARPA to get his ultra-wideband mesh networks out of mothballs and back on the road to development. He'd been involved in the group of subject-matter experts that defined the specifications of a DARPA program, and he was confident his solution would be an ideal fit. "They may not want it commercially available, but if DoD is using it, eventually it will be everywhere," he said confidently. I went to listen to the conference call of the DARPA announcement with Roger in his lab.

"For too long, we have rested on our laurels," the DARPA Director began. "For half a century, our country has fielded high-performance, high-complexity, high-cost systems. They are fragile, difficult to maintain, take a long time to develop, and take even longer to develop the tactical expertise needed to employ them successfully because their logistical overhead and cost prohibit frequent test and use in exercises. Meanwhile, our adversaries are evolving, iterating, far faster than we can match. They employ simple, improvised, effective techniques in asymmetric fashions to inflict disproportionate harm.

"Today that changes. Today we announce a new chapter in DARPA's long legacy of funding high-risk, high-reward projects: DARPA's Communications Challenge. Here to tell us more is Program Director Dr. Ken Frederick."

"This Director actually gets it," Roger smiled as the Director stepped away from the podium to a round of applause that sounded thoroughly artificial through the computer speakers. "DARPA keeps supporting Rube Goldberg contraptions," Thorn continued, "complicated, costly, 'system-of-systems' projects that don't break any new technical or scientific frontiers. Instead, they merely recombine existing technology in byzantine ways. For too long, DARPA has been welfare for politically-connected systems integrators. Finally, they're going back to their roots, supporting fundamental innovations, like mine."

I wondered if that was a part of the Circle's game plan: divert attention away from fundamental breakthroughs and instead squander the efforts of the best and brightest in merely recombining existing technologies in different ways. Perhaps DARPA's new leadership was going to break the cycle.

"DARPA's Communications Challenge will take back the communications domain – a domain our adversaries exploit against us. We will enable communications dominance with new breakthroughs and new technologies," the Program Director began. "We call our approach 'SLIP,' Security, Location, Information, Performance. A multi-disciplinary team contributed to the specifications..."

"I was on that team," Roger confided as Dr. Frederick droned on, "and ultra-wideband is ideal for all four aspects of SLIP. The physical layer is inherently secure and robust against eavesdropping or interception. The signals can be used for localization using time-of-arrival or time-difference-of-arrival techniques. You can perform real-time radar scans of your surroundings, getting information about the propagation environment. Performance? The potential data rates are incredible."

Finally, Dr. Frederick concluded his self-congratulatory remarks, lauding DARPA and the team of some of America's finest scientists and engineers: the best and brightest that made the program possible. He began to define what DARPA meant by "SLIP."

"First and most important is 'Security,'" the Program Director explained. "We must secure our communications from use by unknown parties, and require positive identification of everyone using every channel. We must not allow our adversaries or bad actors to hide behind online anonymity, and we must enable our military and police to monitor relevant communications through secure backdoors that cannot be exploited by hostile actors. Securing communications is 'DARPA hard,' but American scientists and engineers are up to the challenge DARPA poses!"

"That's not security!" Roger was shocked. "That's ubiquitous surveillance!"

"Next is 'Location,'" continued Dr. Frederick's online explanation, oblivious to Roger's outrage. "We must be able to locate all users of communication services in case of emergency, so we can summon paramedics – or other first responders – to take the appropriate actions. Terrorists, criminals, and other anti-social individuals will no longer be able to threaten us from their hiding places."

"They're trying to build a goddamn Big Brother system," Roger muttered as Dr. Frederick continued. "They'll be sending the police after not just terrorists but anyone else they deem anti-social."

"We need 'Information' about the users of our communications. Biometric confirmation of users' identity needs to be a part of all next-generation communications hardware to enable our police and military to positively identify the bad actors and trace hostile communications back to their source."

A stunned Roger was just shaking his head in disbelief.

"Finally, 'Performance.' We must achieve all these goals – securing our communications from our adversaries, locating them and others in need of help, identifying all participants in communications, all without sacrificing performance.

"To that end, DARPA encourages and incentivizes integrators to assemble teams of experts to compete in the DARPA Communications Challenge."

The Program Director described the competition – participants had to design a communication system to compete in a series of tests and exercises, resist attempts at anonymity, employ biometrics to identify users, locate users, and benchmark data rates. In addition, the system needed to be multi-modal to be robust against jamming or disruption, while compatible with a broad range of options including cellular telephone and WiFi.

Roger still looked stunned. "This is exactly the kind of high-performance, high-complexity, high-cost system the Director warned against! You'd have to integrate a host of conventional radio systems, biometric sensors, and radio-location gear to pull it off. It makes no sense."

It made no sense to Roger, but I had a pretty good idea what was going on. Roger's idea of ubiquitous, secure communications based on UWB was too much of a threat to the Civic Circle, even for military and government uses. They were going to shut him down by any means necessary. Would he believe me?

"I need to show you something in the screen room," I lured him to the door, made a show of setting my phone down outside, and gestured to him to do the same. He looked puzzled but he set his phone down and followed me in. I secured the door behind us, and turned on the radio he kept there, generating loud static to cover our conversation. I wished I could try an anonymous contact, but I didn't think there was time. I was going to have to take the risk.

"Remember your story about how Armstrong's FM radio project got shut down?"

Roger nodded, not understanding the relevance.

"I think the same kind of thing is happening today. You remember those professors at Georgia Tech who were in the news a couple months ago for espionage?"

"Yes," Roger still looked confused.

"I worked for them. They weren't spies. They merely started poking around in technical areas that are regarded as sensitive by... by the powers that be. Just like yours."

"The powers that be?"

"From everything you told me, DARPA was about to fund your work. I think the Director was on your side. You heard what he had to say. But someone got to him and the Program Director. They ignored what the advisory team you were on recommended, and they made DARPA sponsor this travesty of a research program instead. They're so concerned about secure communications technology getting in to the hands of civilians that they won't even sponsor the development of your ideas for military purposes."

"I suppose that could be," Roger nodded with a puzzled expression.

I think your life may be in danger," I explained. "The next step is, you're going to get an offer you can't refuse," I explained. "It'll be a nice bump up in salary. They'll send you off to some secure lab in Nevada or somewhere they can watch you, and be sure anything you do is contained where it can't possibly leak out to the public."

"How do you know this?"

"There's a researcher I met here earlier this summer with a novel idea for space elevators. She's gone now, off to Nevada." I looked him in the eye and hoped he'd believe me. I'd lost the space elevator lady, but maybe I could save him. "Same offer my professors got. Only my professors turned them down. The next step was the trumped-up espionage charge. I really don't believe that was true."

"Don't they think that one professor got lost hiking?" Roger was following the news, apparently.

"I suspect foul play. My point is, you're next. You need to either accept the Nevada job, or somehow manage to convince them you're out of research and on to something innocuous."

"I don't want to do directed research in captivity in Nevada." He looked disgusted at the thought. "I suppose I could always teach." He'd made the transition from confused to thoughtful faster than I'd anticipated, but then he was clearly a very smart man.

"Start sending out your resume. Ask for some vacation time off to do some interviews, like you've been thinking about this a while. I'll see if there's anything I can do on my side." I looked through the screen door. "Get your data and designs backed up and get me a copy. When you leave, they're going to be sure you don't take anything with you. Is there anything critical you can pack up for me now?"

Roger looked across his lab full of his life's work. There was no way I could take and hide it all, and he knew it. He was going to have to abandon almost everything he'd been working on for years. I saw him take a deep breath as he reached his decision.

"I have a current backup of my data. You should take the initial prototype boards for the pilot system, and the chips to build more. How can I get in touch with you?"

"Think of a couple creative but plausible IT problems," I suggested. "Call me on the helpline with one. I'll come. I'll figure out a longer-term plan and tell you tomorrow. If something happens today and they march you out the door," I thought a moment, "come to the Highlander Coffee House on Bob Wallace Avenue at 10 am Saturday. Ignore me, but note where I'm sitting. I'll leave when you go order your drink. Sit at my table and look for an envelope taped to the underside of the table. Grab it, hide it, and read it later, when you're sure you're in private – not at home. It will include further instructions." It wasn't a great dead drop, but it was the best I could devise on short notice.

I stashed his data backup DVD in my IT tool bag, and went to get my cart. I hid Roger's DVD in the server room with a bunch of other disks. I had a printer I was supposed to deliver, so I opened the box from the bottom and set the printer on the top level of the cart. I folded the flaps in on the bottom of the box and set it down on the lower level of the cart with the beautiful factory fresh tape intact on top. By visual inspection, no one would be able to tell the big printer box was a shell covering empty space within.

I arranged a box of ink cartridges on the top level of the cart along with the new printer. I hoped no one would find it curious why I was simultaneously moving a printer and a printer box, but then most of my co-workers took IT for granted. They weren't quite as bad as Rachel in HR who didn't have a clue what "IT" was or did, but by and large they took it for granted, never appreciating, let alone understanding, the effort it took to keep their computers connected. I was seen wheeling computers and printers around all the time. It was what IT did. The only person savvy enough to ask questions was Mr. Humphreys, but judging by the fact someone had just opened up a connection to the World of Warcraft server from his IP address, my little adventure would probably be over before his.

They moved fast. I saw Travis Tolliver and another man in Roger's lab, so I wheeled on by to drop off and set up the printer. On my way back, the coast was clear. "That connection we discussed looked like it might be needed?"

He smiled. "It's a good backup plan," he acknowledged, "but with the DARPA funding not in the cards, the company decided to fund my research out of internal research and development funds, anyway. Apparently Larry Tolliver himself, the CEO of Tolliver Corporation, wants to go forward with the commercialization!"

Oh my. That was interesting.

"I think I may need that printer back when you get a chance," he said with a smile.

I checked my watch. "Would Monday be soon enough?"

"No rush," he said. He looked around and added softly. "Thanks for the warning. You really had me going there. I'm glad you were wrong."

"Me, too. I'll see you Monday."

On my way back to the office I got a text on my cell phone: "The Dungeon is now closed." I'd continued to refine "VirtualPete.exe," writing my own set of scripts modeled after the ones Mr. Humphreys used. I'd added a script to keep an eye on the Ethernet traffic from Mr. Humphrey's office. It pinged me when he was in, when he left, and when he was "adventuring." If his online escapades were over, I had a great opportunity to catch him before he left.

He glowered as I poked my head in the door of his office. His computer was already off and he'd clearly been moments away from departure.

"Quick question before you go, sir. I just wanted to confirm that I'll be on the team to Jekyll Island."

"No," he said.

"I thought you were taking all the interns with clearances."

"I need someone with a clue to keep IT running smoothly here. You're staying." He got up to leave.

"No, sir," I insisted, blocking his way. "I'm going to Jekyll Island with you." He looked confused. Before he could say anything, I played my trump card. "I've identified $24 million in suggestions that I will be turning in tomorrow – suggestions that fall within your IT responsibilities. You think the big boss was mad about handing over $50,000 to a manufacturing tech? Just wait until he's told he has to write a $2.4 million check to an intern for my 10% cut, and what's more, it's all your fault."

"No fucking way," Mr. Humphreys was in my face.

I smiled. "Have a seat, and I'll explain."

He stood frowning at me.

"Well, at least stand aside so I can write on your white board and explain what I figured out."

He stepped back. I closed the door to his office, picked up a marker, and sketched the floorplan of the modular buildings.

"The main traffic hallways in those modular buildings go around the perimeter of the building. There are four blocks of offices, twenty feet wide and a hundred feet long. At each end of each block is a fifty-foot firehose.

"Yeah," he said, "each covers half way."

"No they don't. By the time you stretch ten feet to get to the corner, there's only forty feet of hose left at each end to put out a fire on a hundred foot long hall. There's a twenty-foot gap left uncovered."

I could see the moment he grasped the problem for himself, but he recovered quickly. "Don't matter," he insisted. "It passed inspection, so it's compliant with local fire code."

"Somehow, I doubt the inspector would have passed it if he'd realized the problem. Besides," I reached past him to where he had his own copy of the Tolliver Corporation Safety Manual, and I opened it to the relevant page, "right here, the manual says, 'In the event of a conflict between local regulations and this manual, the more stringent provision shall be followed.' And over here," I paged through to the fire safety section, "it says, 'There must be a fixed fire hose with adequate length to reach all areas within occupied buildings, or a fire extinguisher within fifty feet.' The length of the fire hose isn't adequate. If you had to put out a fire in one of the center offices along the hallway, the hose wouldn't reach."

"No way is that a $24M safety suggestion," he countered.

"It's the same configuration through all the modular buildings," I pointed out. "Eight firehoses times two levels times three buildings."

"That's forty-eight." I could see him do the math. "That's only a $480,000 suggestion, and they'd write you a check for $48,000." He grimaced. That would be plenty to get him in hot water, if the story he told me about the maintenance tech was right, but he was forgetting something.

"They set the precedent with the overhead crane you told me about. That was one problem, but there were a couple dozen people in the area who could have been killed if it fell. There are fifty people working on each of those floors."

He pulled out a calculator, but I already knew what it was going to tell him. "$24 million, or a $2.4 million check for the 2,400 safety-of-life suggestions I'll be making. Straight out of your budget. Then, you have to fix the problem. Mounting thirty fire extinguishers one each in the middle of the affected hallway should take care of it. Easier and cheaper than upgrading to 75-foot hoses, I'd imagine."

"Why the hell do you want to pass up a $2.4 million suggestion bonus check to go to Jekyll Island?"

"You and I both know there's no way in hell Travis Tolliver is going to write a $2.4 million check to an intern. It'll turn out that this is a special case where we don't count all the people who might be impacted, or maybe interns aren't eligible to get the check, or there'll be some other excuse. The amount is too big to expect the company will pay up. The only real value this suggestion has is as leverage. The Civic Circle's Social Justice Leadership Forum is the world's best networking opportunity. I really want to go."

He looked at the analysis on the white board. Trying to find a way out.

"Let me point something else out to you – an implication you might not have thought through yet." Time for me to lay the final joker on the table. "You could fix it yourself. Buy and mount the fire extinguishers. I doubt the risk of a fire breaking out right in the center of the hall is that high, though. You could wait. There's no good reason fire safety should be under the IT department. Push back. Get fire safety transferred back to facilities where it belongs. Wait a year, then point it out yourself. Or get someone else to point it out for you. Let the VP of Operations have to squirm."

I saw him flash a malicious grin at the thought. Then he scowled back at me. "I take you to Jekyll Island, and you forget all about this suggestion. Is that the deal?"

"Yes, sir," I confirmed.

He didn't like it. "You're on the team," he conceded. I could tell he hated the fact I'd successfully blackmailed him.

I held out my hand to seal the deal.

"I'm not shaking your hand, Burdell. Get this straight. I'm going to work you to death on this job. And if you end up plugged in to life support, you better hope I don't find I need to charge my cell phone. Now get out."

I left.

I made it a few steps down the empty hall before letting loose with a fist pump.

I was going to join the Reactance on Jekyll Island. My risky gambit paid off.

* * *

Monday, I got an email from Roger saying he didn't need help with his printer anymore, but to drop by next time I was wheeling through with my cart. Since he'd specifically mentioned the cart, I loaded it up with my tools and the empty printer box, and I headed over to his lab.

"Hi Pete," he said with a smile when I popped my head through his door. "I'm going to be leaving TAGS soon."

"Oh?"

"Mr. Tolliver just spoke with me about it. After the DARPA funding fell through, the company thought they might be able to fund my work. It seems the company just doesn't have the budget for it after all, though. There's an opportunity to work at a lab in Nevada, but I decided it just wasn't what I wanted to do." He had a completely straight poker face on.

"What are you going to do?"

"I gave Travis my two-week notice and told him I was going to pursue a career in teaching. He seemed happy about it. He was willing to let me work out my two-week notice, and even said I could use my computer for resumes and continue using the company email after I leave." I could see the twinkle in his eye.

Ha! I bet Travis Tolliver wanted Roger to keep using their corporate email. "How very thoughtful of him," I replied. I'd lay odds I was going to find a request to set up an auto-forward for all Roger's email to Travis Tolliver or one of his security goons when I got back to check my email.

Clearly, he was taking concerns about eavesdropping seriously, so I'd assume the same. "If you need any help clearing out all this junk..."

"Why, yes," he took a few steps. "I could use some help." His foot tapped on a box.

"I'll get started right on it." I picked up Roger's box and slid it under the printer box.

Technically, I was supposed to be searched every time I entered and left the research wing. In practice, I was in and out so often, I could be confident no one would open the printer box to confirm there was really a printer in it. I went right on through and deposited the box in the server room.

I had time to make at least a couple more trips before lunch. I figured with the rest of the week ahead of me, I'd be able to clear out anything important Roger wanted to save.

I figured wrong.

On my next trip in, I passed Thorn going the opposite direction escorted by two security guys. We studiously ignored each other. I cached the empty printer box in the network closet in Thorn's building in case I needed it.

Roger's lab was locked and secured. He'd been "reassigned" to a different office. I made an excuse to swing by and say hello a couple days later. "Any plans for the weekend?" I asked.

"No," Roger said, looking me in the eye. "I'm applying for some teaching positions and I need to be updating my résumé. I'll probably just take it easy and hang out at a coffee shop."

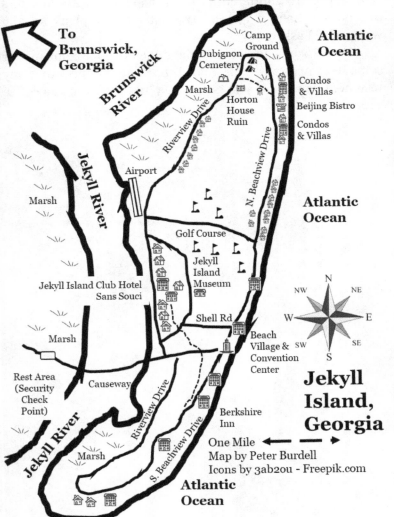

To Saint Simon & Sea Island

Saint Simon Sound

To Brunswick, Georgia

Atlantic Ocean

Brunswick River

Camp Ground

Dubignon Cemetery

Marsh

Horton House Ruin

Riverview Drive

Condos & Villas

Beijing Bistro

Condos & Villas

Jekyll River

Marsh

Airport

N. Beachview Drive

Atlantic Ocean

Golf Course

Jekyll Island Museum

Jekyll Island Club Hotel
Sans Souci

Shell Rd

Beach Village & Convention Center

Marsh

Rest Area (Security Check Point)

Causeway

Riverview Drive

S. Beachview Drive

Berkshire Inn

Jekyll River

Marsh

Atlantic Ocean

N
NW   NE
W   E
SW   SE
S

Jekyll Island, Georgia

One Mile
Map by Peter Burdell
Icons by 3ab2ou - Freepik.com

CHAPTER 8: A FAMILIAR SCENT

Security picked up dramatically at TAGS. We had an all hands meeting about some confidential material having been released to a competitor. All employees were reminded and advised not to speak with anyone, particularly about the TAGS robotics work. And there were now security screenings on entering and leaving the building. I was getting checked almost half the time when I entered or left. I was very glad I'd gotten Roger's stuff out in the nick of time.

The Saturday drop at the coffee shop went well. Roger glanced in my direction as he came in, noting my table. I gathered my things, put on a cap and my sunglasses, and left. That night, he left a comment on the blog post I'd mentioned – Roger's confirmation that he got my packet of instructions on how to set up secure email, and that he'd be in touch soon.

When Sunday dawned though, I was on my way to Jekyll Island. Naturally, Mr. Humphreys stuck me with the job of driving the TAGS van full of equipment. I'd have stopped in Atlanta to catch up with Professor Chen and the Red Flower Tong, but Mr. Hung insisted all our plans were on track. The container was already on the way, and no personal meeting was required: "The waiter will deliver the fortune cookie as planned. Be sure the guest is ready." All the other interns got to fly in the company jet. They were hanging out with Mr. Humphreys, Travis Tolliver, and a couple other senior TAGS executives by the pool at the Berkshire Inn, as I made my way up to the room I'd be sharing with Johnny Rice.

I tried not to be obvious, glancing furtively at the smoke detector as I set my bags down. The hotel room lighting was dim and the shades were drawn. I wondered. I tried Amit's trick of taking a photo of myself with the smoke detector in the background, but my phone didn't have a flash feature. In the poorly-lit room, all I got was a dark screen. Frustrated at the inconclusive test, I decided to be better safe than sorry. I'd assume the smoke detector was a camera, and they had me under observation. At least there wasn't a smoke detector in the bathroom. I sent a text to Amit: "Stopped for gas at 2:15, arrived Berkshire Inn Jekyll Island just now." I was actually staying in room 326, and the "time" was a simple one-digit-difference substitution – a bit lame, but OK for a one-time use. Amit was supposed to be arriving the next day with the rest of the Civic Youth contingent.

The good news was that Berkshire Inns all ran Amit's software, so we could easily penetrate and monitor the hotel network. The bad news was the hotel was on the south end of the island – a couple miles' hike to the Jekyll Island Club Hotel. I hoped they'd put Amit up there, at the Jekyll Island Club Hotel, closer to the action, instead of at the Berkshire Inn.

By the time I'd dropped off my bag, texted Amit, and headed back to the pool, the TAGS group was gone. Great. I whipped out my laptop, and I set up a routine to randomly web browse some of my favorite sites in background. I'd check the downloaded pages later. With that for cover, I used Amit's backdoor to log in to the Berkshire Inn's network management system, and from there, got access to the reservation data. I copied the hotel's local copy of the reservation database to my computer to take a closer look.

I pulled all the records for a month-long window around the Civic Circle's Social Justice Leadership Forum. I sorted the reservations list by block size, and skimmed. Ah-ha! Civic Youth had a big block of rooms. That meant Amit was probably staying in the same hotel. There was a block of rooms reserved for TAGS, and some other vendors. I recognized the media company doing all the sound and video work. The theatrical company putting on the opening ceremony had a small block. Then, I noted some other blocks of a few rooms, followed by a long list of individual... what the heck?

Adam Weishaupt.

Say what? I blinked my eyes, convinced that somehow they weren't working properly, but it was true. "Adam Weishaupt" had a reservation at the Berkshire Inn for room 129.

Adam Weishaupt was the founder of the Bavarian Illuminati, a secret society formed in 1776 to advance what they perceived as "Enlightenment" goals. Loosely aligned with the Freemasons, they fought against religious influence in society and may have had a hand in the founding of America, as well as the French Revolution. Mr. Hung claimed they'd been largely co-opted by the Civic Circle during a purge in the 1830s. No wait... that was the Masons. I was having trouble keeping my conspiracies straight.

Someone had a peculiar sense of humor.

I checked into the reservation record of this "Adam Weishaupt." No credit card on file. Bill to account 37911133349. The reservation was for a room on the ground floor and... an arrival date of 1 January 2001 with a departure date of 31 December 2099! Flagged for permanent "do not disturb." Housekeeping service only upon checkout or by request.

I checked the occupancy. The room wasn't very frequently occupied, but when it was, the guests sometimes checked in and out in a matter of a few hours. There were a dozen check-ins in the last month, each followed by a housekeeping request. I copied the arrival and departure times, and then I pulled up the video surveillance from the lobby.

When the most recent guest arrived, there was a five-minute gap in the video around the time the guest checked in. I looked at the other records. In each case, there was a gap in the video right at the moment Mr. Weishaupt arrived. If they had set it up to stop recording video whenever Mr. Weishaupt checked in, I was out of luck. The video gap, though, started a couple of minutes before the check-in. That probably meant the video was recorded, but then erased later. How thoroughly? I wondered. I was going to need a lot more storage space than I had on my laptop.

I went out to the TAGS van in the parking lot, where I grabbed a company laptop and a big backup hard drive. I brought them back to my room, and I made a direct Ethernet connection to the network. I used the company laptop to log in to the hotel network using Amit's backdoor. I set it to run a systematic disk copy on the hotel's security video drive. If anyone noticed and asked, I thought up a plausible rationale about an "essential" networking test.

The usual way a file deletion works is to leave the actual data on the drive and just alter the address information. Often, the actual data is left behind. The disk copy I was running made an exact copy of the drive, including whatever stray data was left unindexed on the disk. There was a chance I might be able to recover the missing video. It was going to take a while to suck all the data over the hotel network, though.

First, I went back to Amit's network security application to make sure my disk copy wouldn't show up on the network logs. While that process was running, I logged back into the security system and started scanning for Mr. Weishaupt's name. I saw no obvious scripts running. The relevant macros or commands might be stored in a database format within the surveillance app itself.

The video gaps correlated exactly to the check-in times in the reservation database. I wondered if I could approach the problem from a different direction. I checked the keycard logs for when keys to Mr. Weishaupt's rooms had been prepared. They were always close to the check-in times, of course, but didn't correlate exactly. Near as I could figure, exactly two and a half minutes after Mr. Weishaupt checked in, some process erased the five-minute window of video. I wrote a script to copy the minute of video immediately surrounding the keycard write.

I'd done all I could. Maybe Amit would have an idea or two. While I was in the system, I got codes to make a couple of universal keycards so I could open any door in the hotel, if I needed to.

Johnny was apologetic when he got back, "I'm sorry, Pete. I figured someone told you where we were heading and we'd see you at dinner."

"Mr. Humphreys has a chip on his shoulder where I'm concerned," I explained. "He didn't want to bring me along."

"What happened?" Johnny looked curiously at me.

"I can't really discuss it. Keep me in the loop as best you can though, OK?"

"Sure thing," Johnny agreed. "We're all supposed to meet in the hotel lobby for the complimentary breakfast and work assignments at 6:30 in the morning."

"Thanks."

"I can't believe we're actually getting paid to work at an ocean resort!" Johnny brushed his teeth and changed shirts.

"Heading out again?"

"Yeah," he acknowledged. "Don't wait up for me, OK?"

"If you say so."

* * *

The next morning, Johnny still wasn't back. I got up early and checked the video drive backup. Looked like the copying process was still running, but I didn't have time to work on it just then.

I took a quick early morning run along the trail leading in the direction of the Jekyll Island Club Hotel. On my way back, I saw a familiar face running toward me, but I couldn't quite place it. I felt a vague unease. It wasn't until he was almost upon me that I recognized him. I felt a burst of adrenaline. Unable to decide in that split second between flee or fight, I compromised by running past him.

It was the face that had haunted my dreams for nearly two years: Special Agent Wilson. The Civic Circle's leading troubleshooter killed my parents and would have killed Professor Chen and Brandy, if I hadn't saved them both first. I hadn't seen him or his silent partner in person since their interrogation of me, the morning after they'd killed my parents. My heart pounded as I sprinted the last quarter mile back to the hotel. I suppose I should have been expecting him to show up to the Civic Circle's Social Justice Leadership Forum, but it still came as an unpleasant surprise.

After I showered and dressed, I headed down for breakfast. I found Johnny at breakfast sitting cozily next to Kirin. Ah-ha. I think I had a good idea where he spent the evening. Since she was the only girl on our team, Kirin had a room to herself.

Mr. Humphreys directed most of the gang to head up to the Convention Center in the Beach Village to help with the installation of some new network hardware in the Convention Center Ballroom.

"Burdell," he growled. "You're with me."

It turned out the hotel had an attached warehouse – a familiar acrid smell hit my nose as soon as we came in. A dozen 55-gallon drums were set aside in a fenced off area – "Pool Chemicals Keep Out" read the sign. The 55-gallon drums were labelled "muriatic acid." Muriatic acid is just another term for hydrochloric acid. In principle, I could see it being used to keep a pool chlorinated, but more than six hundred gallons of the stuff? I'd helped Amit regulate the chlorine in the pool at his folks' hotel back in Sherman, Tennessee. We'd use some test strips and add a few pellets of chemical when it got low. Hundreds of gallons of acid seemed like complete overkill.

There was an IT room off to one side. It was well-ventilated and air conditioned. A huge bundle of cables came out near a server rack. Mr. Humphreys put me to work connecting Ethernet cables into a patch panel while he ran off somewhere. The work was simple. I kept at it diligently, but I was lost in thought. Why on earth would the hotel need such an immense quantity of acid? The stuff was dangerous. It could dissolve almost anything. Judging by the smell, it probably had dissolved or leaked from at least one of the barrels. I couldn't imagine using concentrated muriatic acid to treat a pool – maybe strip the concrete clean beside it, but not treat the pool water. A little bit would go a long way, and the quantity stored here was incredible.

Was someone planning a chlorine gas attack?

I finished patching the remaining cables and began connecting them into the switch. There didn't appear to be any servers in the rack – just a few big switches that uplinked all the connections elsewhere. All the cables were neatly labelled by room number, with additional cables for hallways and common areas. This gave me an idea.

I pulled a router out of my bag, and patched in one of the cables and my laptop. Sure enough, I hit the IP address the router had assigned to the cable with a web browser, and I was looking at a live video feed from the perspective of a smoke detector inside a hotel room. As I'd suspected, I'd just finished wiring the entire hotel for video in a separate network isolated from the main security feed.

Ethernet cables include four twisted pairs of wires, but you only really need two twisted pairs to make a valid connection. It's not difficult to make an Ethernet splitter and run two parallel Ethernet connections down the same cable. I had all the hardware I needed. Nearly a week away from the big meeting, there'd still be a good number of open rooms. I consulted my reservations list for a room near mine that would be empty tonight – 228, perfect, just one floor down and one room away.

I put on a fresh pair of rubber gloves to leave no fingerprints on the particular cables I needed to manipulate. I found the Ethernet cable for room 228 and traced it as far back into the wall as I could. I carefully removed the insulation and shielding from the cable to expose the twisted pairs. I isolated the white/orange and orange wire pair and the white/green and green wire pair. Then, I isolated the white/blue and blue wire pair and the white/brown and brown wire pair. I pushed a piece of heat shrink up the wire out of the way, and I spliced in two Ethernet cables, twisting the appropriate wires together. I plugged in my soldering iron and melted a little dab of solder on each twist. I wrapped a few turns of electrical tape around each individual connection, then I pulled the heat shrink over the top of the splice. I hit it with a blast from my heat gun to cover up my handiwork. I now had an extra Ethernet cable. I labeled it "utility," and plugged it in one of the switches. I removed the rubber gloves and let my sweaty hands cool.

I'd deliberately left the uplink unplugged, so I could be sure the surveillance system was disabled. The hotel security system used obvious cameras, and there weren't any in the basement. I decided to look around. The acrid smell assaulted my nose as soon as I opened the door of the well-ventilated utility room. I took a closer look at the "pool chemical" storage area. On closer examination, there was a door in the wall. I oriented myself. Odd room number side. First floor. End of the hall. The mysterious room 129.

I heard someone unlock the door to the warehouse. I quickly retreated to the IT room. I busied myself with one last inspection of the panel.

Mr. Humphreys opened the door. "Done yet?"

"Just finishing up," I explained.

He looked surprised that I was already done, and then he frowned at me. "Power's out on the uplink."

"I have a bad connection. I haven't been able to fix it," I explained, pointing to the dead light next to the port for room 228. "This end seems fine. It may be a problem on the other end."

He surveyed my work, grumbling at a few minor cosmetic imperfections, but all the other network activity lights lit right up. "Get up to Room 228 and check it out. We're supposed to have this online today. It's urgent."

"Yes, sir," I acknowledged, although if it were that urgent, you'd think he'd have been helping me.

Ten minutes later I was in Room 228, duplicating my splitter and connecting it to a wireless router, just like the ones already mounted throughout the hotel. My router wouldn't connect anyone to the Internet, though, only to the internal surveillance network. I hid the network name, the SSID, on the router, so my backdoor would not easily be discovered.

The rest of the day I spent working with Mr. Humphreys on a similar setup at the Westin near the Convention Center. It seemed all the hotels were being connected in a massive surveillance system in anticipation of the big meeting. We finished up, then Mr. Humphreys directed me to help out in the grunt work with the rest of the interns at the Convention Center. No money was wasted on air conditioning the place for the benefit of us IT minions. We were all tired, dirty, and sweaty from our day's work crawling around the Convention Center, laying cable, and installing wireless access points.

When we all got back to the hotel, there was a happy hour going on – the hotel was offering nacho chips and beer. The breakfast area was full of well-dressed college students. My grubby jeans and the dirty clothes of the other TAGS interns were out of place among the nicely-creased slacks. There was Amit. We made eye contact, and then we studiously ignored each other. Mr. Humphreys had abandoned us TAGS interns in his haste to head up to his room and get changed. I motioned to Johnny and headed on into the fray. He and the rest of the TAGS intern crew followed my lead.

I got a bunch of curious looks as I broke through the crowd and helped myself to some nachos and a Coke.

"So, what brings y'all here?" I broke into a group that had a number of rather attractive young women. There was a pause as they looked at each other.

"We're with the Civic Youth," explained one of the girls.

"Oh is that some kind of church summer camp or what?"

Another girl snorted awkwardly, almost choking on her Coke. I saw Amit hovering a few feet away listening to me.

"We're learning leadership skills," the first girl explained haughtily. What are you doing here?"

"Installing IT infrastructure," I explained.

"Oh," she said dismissively. "You're a techie. My father has thousands of techies like you working for him at his bank." I was no longer of interest.

"Did you get one of your dad's techies to pick out those shoes?"

"What?" She looked at her feet, and then back at me.

"They look very comfortable. Not at all what I would have expected." I'd managed to confuse her. She stared blankly at me. "See you around," I added and left. Amit and I briefly made eye contact. A hint of a grin was on his face.

Meanwhile, Johnny was talking to another group. I took a few steps over to listen.

"I graduated last year," someone was explaining to him. "I'm an activist. I protest the tyranny of the corporate state."

"So, you're unemployed?" Johnny asked. "You don't actually work anywhere?"

"Work?" he replied contemptuously. "I'm outside the oppressive bourgeoisie system of employment altogether. I'm opposed to the concept of work on many levels. I'd rather die than be 'employed.' I'm not going to waste my life lining the pockets of some capitalist fat cat millionaire while I make chump change. No way. I'm not going to become some mindless wage slave and contribute to a fundamentally corrupt and unjust system. I'm a graduate student. I live off my stipend and student loans."

For once, Johnny was speechless. He gave me a 'do you believe this guy' look. I kept a poker face and turned back to keep watching the spectacle.

"I mean, sometimes I feel like just smashing the whole corrupt system," the young activist continued, "I mean, like, walking in and just shooting everything up! Like in *The*

Matrix, you know what I mean? Doesn't everyone feel like that sometimes?"

Just then, this older girl – she must have been in her late twenties – in a polka-dot dress with unnaturally bulging eyes grabbed Shoot 'em Up's arm at the elbow. He stood in an unnatural stillness. "Get me more soda," Polka-Dot Lady insisted.

Shoot 'em Up took her empty cup and vanished without another word.

Weird.

"So you're some kind of activist, too?" Johnny asked her.

"I suppose you could say that. I'm a cognitive scientist from Harvard, Dr. Alyssa Gottlieb," she introduced herself. It was creepy the way her eyes bulged out, examining Johnny intently. Somehow, I was reminded of the guy at Dad's favorite seafood restaurant back in Knoxville, studying the live lobster tank to pick out Dad's dinner. "What brings you here?"

"Summer internship at Tolliver Applied Government Solutions in Huntsville, Alabama," Johnny replied. "I'm a senior in management at Georgia Tech."

"I've heard Georgia Tech considers itself the 'MIT of the South,'" Dr. Gottlieb smiled.

"We prefer to think of MIT as the 'Georgia Tech of the North,'" Johnny replied dryly.

"I got my Ph.D. at MIT." Dr. Gottlieb did not seem amused. "Now I'm a post-doc at Harvard."

"Why Harvard?"

"You know," she smiled at him again, "To see how the other half lives."

"So what does a cognitive scientist do?"

"I nudge people."

Johnny looked confused. She continued.

"There are an infinite number of ways to interpret complex phenomena," she lectured as if stating the obvious, "and none of them are canonical. There's no external objective reality anyone can agree on. It's only people. It's only power and dominance, but if you force people, even to do what's in their best interests, they rebel, because they're not sophisticated enough to understand what's best for them. There's a value-action gap: people's behavior doesn't necessarily align with their own best interests. If you don't believe me, look at all the dumb hicks and rednecks who voted for Bush instead of Gore."

Johnny was looking at her intently, and I suppose I was, too. Warming to a receptive audience, she expounded further.

"Nudge theory uses indirect suggestions and positive reinforcement to subconsciously persuade people to do the right thing. In my doctoral research, I nudged men to be less messy in the restroom. I painted a tiny image of a fly on the urinal at the spot they needed to aim to avoid splatter. This manipulated them to aim for the spot, minimizing splatter relative to the control urinals."

"What if the 'dumb hicks and rednecks' don't want to be nudged?" Johnny asked.

"You can't help but be nudged," Dr. Gottlieb insisted. "It works on a subconscious level. For instance, we expose the public to images of women in positions of power and authority to break down sexual stereotypes. We depict interracial couples to break down racial stereotypes. We show them same-sex couples to help them get beyond their heteronormativity."

"Heteronormativity?"

"The archaic belief that people fall into distinct and complementary genders," Dr. Gottlieb explained. "It's linked to heterosexism and homophobia."

"You might persuade or shift some people's opinions," Johnny admitted, "but not everyone is going to think the way you want. They'll tune you out and ignore you."

"Perhaps," she smiled smugly, "but with enough people on our side we can overcome the resistance. We just have to show the holdouts we can do whatever we like to them and there's nothing they can do about it. If businesses won't promote women to positions of leadership, we force them with mandates and quotas. Racists or homophobes? Make them bake a cake for the people they despise. Force them to violate their religious scruples by making the dictates of their superstitious faith subordinate to the considerations of social justice. Break down their heteronormativity by forcing them to accept the transgendered in their bathrooms. Let them know we can violate their most sacred and sensitive and private moments if we feel like it, and they can't do a damn thing about it. Break their will. Rub their noses in it. It's just like housebreaking a puppy. Once it's obvious that those so-called 'conservatives' can't actually conserve anything, everyone will fall in line.

"Democracy is far too important to be left in the hands of people who can't be trusted to vote the right way."

Dr. Gottlieb looked delighted at how obviously appalled Johnny appeared to be.

Just then, Shoot 'em Up returned and handed her a drink. "I'm a graduate research assistant in psychology," he bragged. "My professors tell me I'm the most hypnotizable subject they've ever come across."

"How very nice for you," Johnny offered, taking a step back. "I think I'll refill my own Coke, now, too."

I followed him back to the drink bar. "Who are these crazy people?" Johnny muttered, shaking his head.

"The 'best-and-brightest,' I'm sure," I replied. "Coke?"

"Nah," he grimaced, looking at the line surrounding the drinks. "I just wanted to get away from those creeps. I've had enough. I'm a live-and-let-live kind of guy. I just want to stay as far away from them as possible."

Johnny may not have been interested in 'social justice,' but I think he was beginning to realize that didn't matter. Social justice was interested in him, whether he liked it or not. I excused myself from Johnny, and crossed the lobby to the restroom, hoping Amit would take the opportunity to contact me.

I heard someone come into the restroom behind me and glanced over my shoulder to see Amit approaching. I scanned and confirmed the stalls were empty. Amit stood next to me at the other urinal.

"We're alone," I whispered softly.

"Nice neg back there on 'Comfortable Shoe Girl,'" he whispered back. "What's up?"

"Thanks. What's with that creepy research assistant guy?"

"That's my roommate, Aaron."

Ouch. I felt sorry for Amit. I flushed the urinal, so the sound would cover what I had to whisper to Amit. "Smoke detectors are wired for video."

"Figured as much," he acknowledged softly. "Seen Rob?"

"Not yet. You might be interested to know there's an Adam Weishaupt with a permanent reservation on room 129. Room gets used a couple dozen times a month. Real suspicious."

"No way," Amit snorted. "The Illuminati guy?"

"Same name. Video cuts out every time anyone arrives and uses the reservation to check in. I'm trying to recover some video. Maybe you could hit on the girl at the desk and share hotel stories?"

"I'll see what I can do," Amit confirmed. My urinal was quiet again, so Amit flushed his and added, "I hear they're bringing in the Social Justice Warrior crowd from Tech. They've asked Madison and me to speak. Cindy Ames is supposed to be there as well. Professor Gomulka will deliver a keynote speech about how those racist reactionaries at Tech derailed 'our' social justice convergence of the Schools of Engineering. They're making a big push to try again next year."

"Oh, great." I wasn't looking forward to fighting them yet again, but after the lessons we'd learned last year, I had confidence we'd be ready. "Gomulka may have other plans, though, for the evening of the opening reception. I hear he's got a lady friend arriving."

"Glad that's on track. Anything else?"

"Nope." I zipped my pants. "See you around."

I washed my hands and then walked over to the rest of the TAGS crowd occupying the far corner of the breakfast area, just in time for the hotel manager to shoo us all out into the lobby. What was supposed to be an evening reception and snack bar open for all guests had just become a private event.

We made plans to meet and go out for dinner in thirty minutes, once we all had a chance to change. By the time we reassembled in the lobby, the Civic Youth crowd was gone. The interns piled dangerously into the back of the TAGS van, and I drove us to dinner at a place in the Beach Village near the Convention Center.

After dinner we toured Jekyll Island. I stopped at the Horton House near the north end of the island. The eighteenth-century ruin was in remarkably good condition. The walls were a concrete-like material called "tabby" made from seashells. Come to think of it, many Roman ruins with similar construction lasted thousands of years.

Concrete works well under compression, but cracks easily if you put it under tension. Modern designers embed steel reinforcement bars or "rebar" to give concrete the ability to handle tension, sometimes even embedding rods to squeeze the concrete structure so that placing the concrete under "tension" merely reduces the pre-stressed compression.

What destroys most contemporary concrete structures is rusting of the steel rebar put into the concrete to reinforce it. The rust expands and cracks the concrete from within. The modern technique expands the range of application and the performance of concrete structures at the cost of requiring more and better maintenance.

The Horton House stood ready for use – put a roof on it and finish the interior, and it would be all set for occupancy. The three-century-old walls were in great shape. I wished I could spend more time looking for the pit or well that Petrel's map indicated was on the property, but the other interns were getting restless. We drove south along the eastern shore of Jekyll Island, through the historic district and back to the

Beach Village. I dropped them off and drove a mile south down Beachview Drive back to the hotel.

I had work to do.

First, I retrieved the company laptop I'd been using to disk copy the hotel security video hard drive. I set up in the room in view of the video surveillance, and I fired up a routine to click through some of my favorite web pages. I could cover my tracks for an hour or more by just randomly clicking through the links on Drudge or Instapundit. The disk copy process had been running all day, but somehow it had crashed partway through. I worked a bit on the portion I had, but near as I could tell, the security video kept overwriting the disk so there weren't any abandoned video clips waiting to be recovered.

I set up a secure channel and checked my email. Everything appeared to be on track. Rob had the network tap he promised. The setup looked to be just like the switches I'd specified for him with an extra screen to note which traffic should be copied. The Red Flower Tong promised that "the fortune cookie was on the way." I passed on the arrival information to Professor Gomulka, "love and kisses, Reka."

Then I logged into the wireless tap I'd installed in room 228 and finished configuring it. The network appeared idle. I started pinging addresses in the local block and isolated which ones were video feeds. My problem was, I had no way to tell which video feed corresponded to which room. Room 129 was a suite, which should have made it distinctive, but 229 and 329 were similar suites on their respective floors. I noted the "suite" feeds, and set up Wireshark to capture traffic from those IP addresses. I couldn't find a feed in the basement with the network room and the chemical storage area. I wondered what could be sensitive about the area.

I logged into the hotel server again. I double-checked the script I wrote to capture video when a keycard was issued for 129. It looked good. I realized there was a first floor hallway camera. I checked the login time for the last of Mr. Weishaupt's check-ins to 129. While the front desk and lobby feeds had been wiped, the first floor hallway feed was intact. I watched two people walking down the hall to 129. The video wasn't very clear, but one appeared to be a large man, the other more slight. I couldn't tell if it was a man or a woman.

I fast forwarded through the video until the checkout time a few hours later. The large man exited and walked down the hall. The front desk and lobby feeds of the checkout? They'd been deleted. I still couldn't get a good image of the man who was in the room.

I continued fast forwarding through the hallway feed. Twenty minutes later, the smaller figure exited. This time, the front desk and lobby feeds were intact. A girl, probably younger than me, walked quickly through the lobby – in a hurry to distance herself? I looked at her face. There was no purpose or passion, only a vacant look of resignation.

There were seven other uses of Mr. Weishaupt's room in the last couple of weeks: five short-term stays and two overnight stays. I think it was the same man in most of them. The girl featured in two other visits – once by herself, once with an older woman who must have been at least thirty. The woman and the girl arrived first and checked in. A half hour later, the man arrived. I couldn't be sure which of the men the video caught passing through the lobby was the one who ended up walking along the first floor hall. It was too crowded and busy. In one of the visits it was clearly not the same man. The man in this visit was taller and skinnier. Mr. Weishaupt was apparently letting friends use his room.

Another visit was with a girl I'd swear couldn't have been more than sixteen. After Mr. Weishaupt checked out, she waited in the lobby until a man came in, grabbed her roughly by the arm, and left with her. And there was a boy with a dark complexion, maybe Hispanic? I couldn't tell, because I only had the vague hallway footage of him arriving with the man. He went into the room. He did not come out. I spent another hour scanning through the video. Housekeeping came and left the room with no sign of the boy. Maybe I missed him. Sometimes the hall would get crowded and picking out individuals would get tricky. Surely the boy had to have left the room eventually. There was only one door...

I had a sick realization.

There was another way out of the room: the door to the "pool chemical" storage area in the adjacent warehouse. All those barrels of acid percolating there? In quantities far beyond what were needed to treat a pool? So strong they'd dissolve most anything? Or anyone?

I thought I'd grown hardened to the corruption of the Civic Circle and their ilk. This took it to a whole new level. I went back to the hallway video and watched the indistinct figure of a boy walk into a room for the last time in his too-short life. "You are not alone," I wished I could tell him. "You have friends. Now we know. We may not have been able to save you, but so help me, my friends and I will avenge you."

* * *

I dodged Special Agent Wilson again the following morning when I got up early to take my run. The man was awfully consistent in his habits, and apparently had a room at the same hotel. He must be using a new alias and keeping a low profile. I'd looked on the hotel's registration database and hadn't found him. Also, it was surprising he was here by himself. He usually travelled with a partner we'd never been able to identify. I was confident I'd recognize that grim face if I saw it again, but so far, Wilson's partner was a no-show. In any event, I decided riding the bike in the hotel's air-conditioned exercise room instead of running was the better part of valor. No sense giving Wilson any extra opportunities to recognize and remember me.

The rest of the week was a blur of activity. Mr. Humphreys put me to work on the most sensitive jobs – the ones he was probably supposed to be doing himself, but trusted me to complete the actual work while he lounged around or goofed off. I put the finishing touches on the surveillance network all over Jekyll Island. We were in and out of the smaller cottages in under an hour, usually. The larger hotels could take as long as half a day.

The Sans Souci building was particularly complicated. Each of the six apartments in the three-story building were beautifully appointed. The building was the first condominium in history, jointly owned by J.P. Morgan, William Rockefeller, and other ultra-rich magnates seeking privacy from the merely well-off crowds at the nearby Jekyll Island Club Hotel. From the look of the place, not much had changed in the past century.

Each apartment had its own firewall and connection to the island's secure network. It looked very secure, but there were extra Ethernet cables that bypassed the switch and continued down under the building. Whoever set it up intended that it to look private, but had probably peppered the apartment suites with video surveillance. I couldn't tell if the network connections that bypassed my switch were active, so I couldn't risk much poking around.

If Petrel's map was right though, this was the building on top of the Civic Circle's secret Inner Sanctum – The Jekyll Island Club Hotel was merely a convenient decoy for the truly powerful who would assemble here.

I also managed to get into the cottage we were confident lay at the heart of the tunnel complex. I made an excuse to check on the wiring in the crawlspace. The cottage had no basement, but there was a suspicious wall of ancient tabby in the crawlspace, just big enough to contain a ladder down to the tunnel complex below. The network closet appeared to be right over the tabby footing in the crawlspace. While I was in the closet, I drilled a hole in the floor. Rob had equipped me with an endoscope. I snaked the cable through the hole. Sure enough, a ladder descended into the darkness. I turned the endoscope back up. The trap door appeared to have a simple mechanical latch with no sign of an alarm or other sensors. It didn't appear to be locked, but it looked like it only opened from the tunnel side. I pushed the endoscope down the shaft. It terminated about ten feet down in a large room, about the size of the footprint of the cottage. A tunnel stretched in the direction of the Jekyll Island Club Hotel. Another tunnel stretched further inland. Petrel's intelligence was correct, and now we'd found a perfect ambush point right on top of the Civic Circle's secret exit tunnel.

We finished the week with a couple of days in the basement of the Jekyll Island Club Hotel putting the finishing touches on the network control center. The part of the basement we were in had the same ancient tabby walls as the Horton House, and could easily date to the same period. We were under constant supervision by security, so I couldn't do much. I did steal an opportunity to add the MAC address of the wireless router I'd installed back at the Berkshire Inn to the list of authorized network devices.

Security was so tight, they wouldn't even let us leave for lunch. That turned out to be a vulnerability I was able to exploit.

"Which would you prefer, gentlemen," Rob asked me and Mr. Humphreys, "turkey, ham, beef, or a vegetarian sandwich?" He looked sharp in his caterer's uniform as the guards escorted him in to take everyone's orders. With his hair dyed and the new mustache he was sporting, I doubted even Uncle Larry would be able to recognize him.

When he brought back our orders, he slid a box out from under the cart once he'd distracted the guards with their food. It was a switch that appeared to be just like the ones we were using, but with a key difference. It was a network tap, capable of logging and recording network traffic, and it had a vast amount of empty storage space on several hard drives hidden inside. I slid the switch we were going to use under his cart, and he wheeled it safely away.

I had a difficult decision to make. If I tried to capture everything, I'd risk filling up the drives in the network tap prematurely. It might be a couple of weeks before we had the leisure time to hack in and retrieve the data. I'd watched as even more guards escorted a server rack through a vault door to the even more secure area beyond. The massive array of disks under such high security had to be intended for the Civic Circle's new data vault. While I was supposed to be configuring the switch, I set the tap to record anything coming in or out of the data vault and the Sans Souci with priority override, including overwriting other data. Secondarily, it would capture traffic from within the Jekyll Island Club Hotel itself and adjacent cottages. There was no way I was going to try to capture all the traffic from the big hotel next to the Convention Center or the other hotels on the beach side of the island.

Just down the hall from the Network Operations Center, there was an old steel door placed in the tabby exterior wall of the Jekyll Island Club Hotel basement. Access to the tunnel and the basement of the Sans Souci? With all the security, I couldn't check it out, but I was confident the cabling from the Network Ops Center headed that way.

I hardly saw Amit at all after that first afternoon nacho bar. The Civic Youth got up early, stayed up late, and I couldn't understand what they were up to. One day, I saw them marching in unison outside under the hot sun. The matching orange jumpsuits they wore made them look like prisoners.

* * *

The day the Social Justice Leadership Forum kicked off, Kirin was summoned to attend to Travis Tolliver, and the rest of the TAGS intern crew were shanghaied into helping guests and attendees move into the cottages in the Historic District. The elite had rooms in the Jekyll Island Club Hotel, but the most elite of the elite occupied the Sans Souci or one of the historic cottages. I noted that the Chase Bank delegation had been assigned the cottage with the entrance to the tunnel complex. Attendees from Warner Brothers, Viacom/CBS, the Holy See Bank, Omnitia, and a U.S. Senate delegation occupied the adjacent cottages. I was stuck with Mr. Humphreys at the Convention Center registration desk providing Internet connectivity assistance to attendees.

As the time for the opening ceremony approached, the crowd around the registration counter increased. I didn't see as many celebrities as I'd thought. The most important had some assistant or flunky pick up their packets. I helped a few people with Internet access, but I had plenty of time to scan the crowd. A familiar woman approached the registration desk. It was Ding.

"Ding Li" she said smoothly without a trace of the thick accent she'd had when I met her months ago. "Vice President, Asia Commercial Bank of Hong Kong." She picked up a packet, and started walking my way.

"Miss Ding Li," I caught her attention as she was moving past.

She recognized me. I saw a hint of wariness in her face as she approached.

"Let me know if I may assist you with your Internet access," I offered. "The guest is expecting the fortune cookie tonight," I added softly.

"If I need you," she relaxed a bit and continued with a knowing smile, "I'll bring you some tea." She moved closer and whispered, "The waiter is delivering it this evening." Then, Ding Li turned and seemed to float into the main ballroom.

Mr. Humphreys looked suspiciously at me. I ignored him and continued greeting customers and offering to help them with their Internet access while my thoughts raced.

There was more to Ding Li than I'd thought. Her awkward halting accent was replaced by smooth, fluent English. She was... intriguing. I thought back on our last meeting. There had been something Professor Chen wanted to tell me, but Ding Li had interrupted him to lead me out. I should have noticed it before. Professor Chen had deferred to her. She was actually ahead of him in their hierarchy. No wonder I hadn't noticed her that first night when I delivered Professor Chen to them. She wasn't there. Not then. She must have arrived with the big boss, this 'Honorable Shan Zhu.' That might even put her above Mr. Hung, who appeared to be in charge of the Atlanta operation. I couldn't be sure of the exact hierarchy, but it was clear Ding Li should not be underestimated.

A beguiling yet familiar scent interrupted my thoughts. A red-headed woman walked by, stopping to talk with one of Amit's colleagues. "I'm here to pick up the credentials for the Holy See Bank Corporation, London Office." That perfume, that voice... It was definitely "Perky Girl," the Albertian operative I'd last seen in Chattanooga.

"Ma'am," Mr. Humphreys got to her first. "Y'all let me know if we can help you with your Internet access, you hear?"

"That won't be necessary," she dismissed him curtly, and walked off, without noticing me.

"I have to go to the restroom," I lied to Mr. Humphreys.

He seemed disgusted. "Well, make it quick and get back here."

I took off after Perky Girl.

CHAPTER 9: ACTIONS HAVE CONSEQUENCES

I caught up with Perky Girl just outside the main ballroom. I leaned close and whispered into her ear, "Investigare..." I began the recognition mantra of the Ordo Alberti.

She jerked around and looked at me, the surprise evident in her eyes. "Who..." she began. Then she recognized me and the shock in her face recoiled into contempt. "You." She looked around and checked that no one was in ear shot. "We warned you," she hissed at me, softly. "You let them poison her, and you let her wander off to die alone in the Great Smoky Mountains, in agony!"

"You took your time talking to me," I pointed out, quietly, not daring to raise my voice even in the crowd. "I arrived after the reception had already started because you and your friends had to play your secret agent games and kidnap me back to your lair to tell me what was going on."

She started to interrupt, but I kept talking.

"I did tell Professor Graf her beer was poisoned," I shared my carefully prepared half-truth. "She thought it was funny, so she took a big sip of the poisoned beer just to prove how ridiculous I was being. It was too late. I called you for help. The best you could offer was to let her die in peace. That wasn't going to happen with the Civic Circle's agents watching her. I faked her disappearance in the Great Smoky

Mountains to get her away from them. I made sure she was comfortable in the days that followed, no thanks to you."

I could see the cold fury burning behind her eyes, frozen in place behind an icy mask that would not let her personal feelings slip out in public.

"You could have stopped Professor Graf from drinking the beer," she said softly but with infinite contempt. "I saw you. You froze. When the moment to act was at hand, you froze, you coward."

"You put me in a no-win situation," I countered. "Wrestle the bottle out of her hand, maybe spilling the beer and contaminating everyone around? Alert the Civic Circle that someone was on to them? I'm the amateur. You're the experts. If you were expecting me to work your miracles for you, with time running out and the Civic Circle watching, you should have come up with a better plan. I did the best I could with the crappy hand you dealt me. There's plenty of blame to go around, and you're trying to shift all the responsibility to me to clear your own guilty conscience."

She raised an eyebrow. "So you're some kind of a therapist, now, too?"

I was getting nowhere with her. "I think I liked you better when you were busy playing good cop to your partner's bad cop."

She stared back impassively at me. "I think I liked you better when you were tied up, blindfolded, and unable to get in trouble. You still let her die. You sat there, watched her drink that poison, and you let her die."

I looked at her. This wasn't going to work. Two men were approaching us – a big guy I didn't think I'd want to meet in a dark alley, and an older gentleman in an expensive tailored suit. Could it be Perky Girl's partner, Bulldog, and Brother Francis?

"You tried to help," I told her. "I appreciate that. You failed, and so did I. Now, I have important information of use to you and your friends. See me when you're ready to talk about it."

Her colleagues were close enough to overhear that last message. Now that I knew who they were – or at least that they were associated with the London Office of the Holy See Bank Corporation – I could find them later... at their cottage? An idea began to form. I visited the restroom, and returned to the Internet Help Desk.

"Stop hitting on the women and get back to work," Mr. Humphreys demanded on my return.

That was certainly safer than the truth. "Yes, sir," I acknowledged. I continued to take the lead in working with the customers. Mr. Humphreys only helped when I was already occupied with someone else.

A few minutes later, I saw Uncle Larry heading into the opening ceremony and caught his attention, "Excuse me, sir!"

He motioned to his entourage to enter without him, and he came on over.

"I understand you needed some assistance with the WiFi access and wanted to check out the alternate T-shirt selection?"

He was quick on the uptake. "Why, yes, that's right."

"I'm sure I can help you, Mr. Tolliver," Mr. Humphreys interposed himself between Uncle Larry and me, recognizing the importance of my IT support client.

"You are..." Larry began.

"Dan Humphreys, sir. Director of Information Technology for Tolliver Applied Government Solutions out of Huntsville."

"That's quite alright, Dan," Larry offered genially. "I'm sure your young assistant here can help me."

"But..."

"No," Larry insisted. "I wouldn't dream of pulling you away from your important work here." He turned to me. "Now about those T-shirts?"

"If you'll come back here, sir," I offered, "I think I can help you."

Larry followed me to the room where we were storing the extra bags and T-shirts. "What's this about?"

"Pull out your phone in case someone walks in on us," I advised, "so I can be helping you with the WiFi connectivity." As he reached into his coat pocket and pulled out his phone, I placed it in a foil potato chip bag to make sure I could access it quickly, yet it couldn't eavesdrop on us. "Professor Gomulka is up to something," I explained. "I'm not sure what it is. You and the Social Justice Initiative may need to distance yourselves from him, or you risk getting caught up in the consequences of his schemes."

"That's awfully vague," Larry replied. "You're sure?"

"I warned you there was a problem with Glyer's robotics initiative, right? I told you the fix was in on the DARPA project, didn't I?"

He nodded with a grin. "We told DARPA we had such confidence in the UWB wireless project we'd commercialize it ourselves. Over the weekend, I got a call from one of my senior Civic Circle friends. His company bought out our interest. We made a tidy profit. I can't believe how quickly that deal moved. Of course, they shut down the project. You called it. You think this Gomulka tip is really solid?"

I nodded. "Here's all I know. Gomulka has taken off this afternoon when he was supposed to be at the opening ceremonies. He's attending to some 'business' at the Port of Brunswick. He's receiving a big shipment of some kind, like an entire cargo container's worth. He hasn't told anyone in the coordinating committee about it — he just slipped out to get it. It's got to be something important for him to miss the opening. Maybe it's a secret operation for the Civic Circle, somehow, but he hasn't made any provisions for something that big to come here to the Convention Center. I made a contact with the Teamsters, and he's keeping an eye out for me." Let Larry think he was getting a network of informants for the price of just me.

"More likely, it's something he doesn't want the rest of the Civic Circle to find out about," I continued. "Something he's smuggling, maybe."

"I get the picture," Larry said thoughtfully. "Gomulka's doing something major behind their backs. Something the rest of the Civic Circle might not like. If you could find out what it is, there'd be a serious reward for letting the Inner Circle know. I'd double what I promised you, if you can find out and tell me."

"I think it's too late. Whatever's happening is going down tonight. Besides, I still haven't received any of the base payment you promised me for getting myself here in a position to help. The Teamsters and the contacts I'm making for you don't help me for free."

Larry looked thoughtful. He pulled out his wallet. "With that DARPA information and the tip about Gomulka, you've earned your keep already." He started counting hundred dollar bills. "There's a thousand in cash."

He had me pegged as a greedy, money-grubbing minion. I had no problem with that whatsoever, particularly since his pocket change would go a long way toward funding my schooling. I couldn't let him think I was cheap, though. I started to point out a thousand in cash wasn't near what he'd promised me, but he cut me off.

"I know, but it's not like I carry that much in my wallet. This is all I can spare right now. Consider it a good-faith down payment toward the rest I owe you. Another hot tip like the DARPA project, or if the Gomulka tip pays off, and there'll be a further bonus on top of that."

"Yes, sir," I smiled as I pocketed the cash. "If I find out anything else, I'll send you a text asking how your WiFi is working. You complain it's still slow, and we'll coordinate another technical-assistance rendezvous like this one. Or, if you think we need to talk, you complain to me about it."

Larry nodded his agreement. He took his phone and went on in into the main hall for the opening ceremony. The registration desk had been set up in a concessions vending area. The "back room" was nominally a kitchen, and there was another vending area on the other side opening into the main hall. The counter was closed and shuttered, but I could peek through and see what was going on. The stands on either side of the ballroom were nearly full, and only a few people were milling about.

I headed back out front to the registration desk. The rush of check-ins had slowed down to a trickle. Now that the opening ceremony was about to start, Mr. Humphreys instructed me to mind the desk while he went in to the ceremony.

Now if I were in charge, I'd have shut the doors and not allowed latecomers to mosey on in, disrupting the ceremony and presentation for everyone polite and prompt enough to arrive on time. That's not how the Civic Circle worked, however. It was an organization full of people too important for such petty things as rules and schedules to apply to them. Anyone senior enough to have the discretion and judgement to make a decision about who had enough status to admit and who to turn away was busy being seen by their peers in the stands. Thus, all the stragglers were being escorted to a holding area just inside the door.

Time to put my idea into motion while everyone was distracted with the opening ceremony. I went to the back room and peeked through the crack. The opening ceremony had begun. It was some kind of weird performance. A few dozen people all shuffled in like zombies walking in step to the beat of a drum. They wore orange construction uniforms. Most were young, college-age. I spied Amit in the group. They must have recruited the Civic Youth as extras in the ceremony, and I'd seen some kind of dress rehearsal the other day. There were a few older people among them as well. They did this clumsy number in which they pantomimed some kind of rote work. Cotton-picking? Mining? Was that how they perceived the masses? I wasn't sure. I couldn't call it a dance, because it seemed so awkward. Loosely-synchronized, poorly-executed collective motion? Now there was a great parallel for the Civic Circle's "New World Order." A blurry, black and white video played on the screen in the background.

I didn't have time to try to figure out any deeper meaning, though. I connected to the local WiFi. This was risky, but I also had access to the log files, so I could clean up the records if my connection got flagged in any way. It was a chance I couldn't pass up. By the time I got connected, there was a change in the beat of the drums. I looked back through the crack in time to see a performer wearing a huge baby-face head glide down on wires from the rafters, beating enormous wings. I couldn't tell if the bare-breasted performer was male or female — I suppose that was the idea. Under other circumstances, I might have found the scene erotic, but this ambiguous androgyny? It was all vaguely disturbing.

The collective ran back toward the entrance, stripping off their loose orange coveralls. They passed underneath three ghostly figures floating, suspended on wires in front of the screen which now projected a giant image of an eye.

Now that I was connected, I had to tear my attention away from the ceremony and get back to work. I used Gomulka's credentials to send a note to the Civic Circle logistics crew:

> *Facilities issues require a last minute change of plan! Transfer the luggage and belongings of the Chase Bank delegation to the cottage occupied by the Holy See Bank delegation, and vice versa! Immediately! And contact each delegation regarding the change! Do it now!*
>
> *Gomulka*

The beat changed again as I finished sending "Gomulka's" message. I peeked through the crack in time to see a goat-man with long horns leading the group. The collective — now clad only in white underwear — cavorted in sexually suggestive ways to the deep beat of a drum. I'm sure there was some deep symbolism to it all and some profound significance for the Civic Circle. I still didn't have time just now to try to figure it out, though. I logged out, disconnected, and packed my laptop back into my bag.

Once I was all packed up, I checked on the progress of the opening ceremony. Three seemingly dead workers dangled in front of the screen, which now showed a demonic face scowling and screaming silently at them. The dangling workers transformed to scarabs. Meanwhile, scantily-clad girls now draped in translucent white veils followed the goat-man around the floor. His brides? Maybe Amit would have a better idea about what the ceremony meant.

I returned to the registration desk in the lobby. Turned out, I didn't need to rush. The registration team had closed up and gone on in to the ballroom. The ceremony went on for nearly an hour. By the time it was done, I was officially off the work clock, and supposed to attend the reception. I locked my bag in the network closet, showed my badge to the security team at the door, and went in to the reception ballroom.

The Civic Youth and other interns mingled with the elite crowd. The contrast was fascinating. Bedraggled young college students barefoot and in sweat-soaked white underwear, most only partially covered in their orange jumpsuits, mingled with men in business suits, women in elegant pantsuits and dresses, and catering staff in formal outfits. The scene was almost erotic – some of the vulnerable-looking, only partly-glad girls could have been really hot. In their bedraggled state, however, they merely looked weak and helpless. Maybe that was the idea. Maybe that was what the Civic Circle found attractive – a crowd of young people who looked as though they could be taken advantage of: easy prey for the predators.

I looked unsuccessfully for Rob among the catering staff, but I did find Amit.

"You look exhausted," I noted.

"You don't know the half of it," he snorted, softly, and looked at me through the fatigue in his eyes. "Sleep deprivation, not enough food," he shook his head. "Wake us up in the middle of the night to attend workshops and seminars on too little sleep. They call it 'Hell Week.' It's supposed to be some kind of initiation."

"Sounds like some kind of brainwashing technique."

"That's probably part of it," Amit agreed. "And testing our tolerance for disgust. We haven't showered since that first night here."

He smelled quite rank, but I wasn't going to say anything. I got him up to speed on my progress and discoveries.

"Wish I could be more helpful," he acknowledged. "I'd love to poke around inside the network you tapped. I haven't even been able to talk to the desk clerks, though – Dr. Gottlieb and the rest of the Civic Youth mentors have us always busy and under constant supervision."

"Well, carry on, and good luck," I offered.

The rest of the TAGS interns arrived about an hour after the ceremony started. I worked my way through the crowd to talk with Johnny Rice. "How's it going?"

"There was this last minute change in plans. We had to swap cottage assignments – transfer all the luggage out of one cottage and into another and vice versa. I had security people screaming at me. Then, they couldn't reach this Gomulka fellow who apparently insisted it had to be done right away. Big mess up."

That didn't sound good. "You got the job done, though?" I hoped!

"Yeah," he confirmed my scheme had worked. "These people here," Johnny gestured at the crowd. "They're all crazy, you know."

"More like idealistic," I corrected him, putting on my social justice persona. "They're all passionate about making a better world."

"Ha," he snorted. "You, too? I thought you were too smart to fall for all that bullshit. Look how they're all reveling in their exploitation of those Civic Youth idiots."

"I'm seeing the world's elite celebrating the passion and commitment of the next generation of world leaders," I said haughtily.

"World leaders?" Johnny snorted. "Ha. They're exactly the insecure, conformist types least likely to resist authority, or they wouldn't be wearing those ridiculous outfits. They're being elevated because they pose no threat to the folks who're really in charge."

Johnny had a point, but I couldn't let him know I agreed with him. "The Civic Youth will be in charge someday, leading us into the future."

"Where are the people pulling those sorry losers' strings trying to lead us?" Johnny shook his head. "No place good, I can tell that much. A world where the limousine elite drink cocktails surrounded by their powerless peasants? No, sir. Not for me. I'm going to fight it."

"What happened to steering clear, staying away, live and let live?"

"Yeah, I did think that." Johnny nodded. He paused, deep in thought. "I was wrong, though. You can't live and let live with these people. Try it, and before long they'll have you barefoot, in your underwear, and in an orange jumpsuit. That's not for me. I won't put up with it."

I was amused at how quickly an exposure to the Civic Circle had changed Johnny's live-and-let-live attitude. George P. Burdell was going to have to reach out to Johnny when we got back to Georgia Tech.

"There's nothing you can do about it," I suggested. Let me push him, I thought, and see how he reacts. "They're in control. They have all the power. There's nothing you can do but try to get along in the New World Order that's coming."

"Bullshit," Johnny snorted. "I'm my own man. I make my own decisions. You might be content to be one of their barefoot peasants, or worse, aspire to lord it over the hoard of barefoot peasants the Civic Circle wants to create, but me? I'm going to stop it."

"How?" I asked.

That finally stumped him. "I don't know," he acknowledged, a frown on his face, "but I will."

I left Johnny there, contemplating the overthrow of the Civic Circle, and I continued my search for Rob. Again, I didn't find him, but I did see Comfortable Shoe Girl. She looked far less stylish in her sweat-soaked white jogging bra and matching panties. She had one of the orange jumpsuit tops but it was too small for her – not covering much of her cleavage and showing an ample amount of midriff, including a rather dainty belly button. She was clearly uncomfortable with the amount of skin she was showing, and she had her arms across her chest.

I made a show of looking down at her bare feet and back up at her eyes. "You didn't have to double down on the foot comfort on my account," I offered. "I was fine with your other shoes."

She smiled nervously. "What, you don't like the outfit?"

"All I can say is I hope you kept the receipt," I smiled and drew a giggle from her. "Pete Burdell from Georgia Tech in Atlanta." I extended a hand.

She paused as she decided whether to reciprocate. Finally, she gave me her hand. "Jessica Marks from Mount Holyoke."

I took the initiative to grab her right forearm with my left hand and take a partial step forward as I shook her right hand. "Always be escalating," Amit liked to say.

"Where's Mount Holyoke?" I asked, now that I was standing very close.

She rolled her eyes in frustration at my provincial ignorance, then craned her neck to look up at me. "In Massachusetts. It's one of the Seven Sisters." I noticed she wasn't stepping back to open the distance between us. So far, so good.

"Seven sisters? Mighty big family. Any of them really cute? Maybe you could set me up?"

"No, silly," she grinned, "they're colleges. You study some kind of techy stuff in Atlanta?"

"Electrical engineering," I acknowledged. "Someone has to keep the world running so you and your friends can cavort in your underwear."

"This wasn't my idea," she gestured at the ludicrous, if revealing, outfit.

"I'm guessing you weren't expecting the Civic Youth's dress code. It looks better on some than it does others."

"Yeah," she agreed. "I'm tired, but I'm supposed to stay for another hour." She smiled at me.

"Tell you what," I offered. "I have a room to myself, you can crash with me, so you won't have worry about the Civic Youth people finding you and putting you through the ringer some more."

"We're not having sex," she insisted.

"Of course not," I confirmed, noting she'd broached the subject first. "You're probably too tired, anyway."

I thought Jessica was about to dispute me, but then she thought better of it.

"I need to stay until 9 pm," she said softly. "Find me, and I'll come back with you."

I tilted her head back and kissed her on her lips, then broke off. "I'll be back."

She smiled as I turned away.

Wow. I couldn't believe that had actually worked. I'd been so focused on trying to pick her up that I hadn't considered whether it was a good idea or not. I really had more important – and dangerous – things to worry about than trying to pick up a girl for some kind of hookup. Was this experience really going to help me get Marlena? I mean Brandy? I began having second thoughts about what I was getting myself into.

By the time I'd completed my lap of the ballroom, Johnny was deep in conversation with a couple of Civic Youth.

"Organic vegetables are simply better for you," a girl was trying to tell him.

"Not everyone can afford the higher cost of organic vegetables," Johnny pointed out. "Maybe you should be the one checking your privilege?"

"Organic vegetables aren't just healthier," another guy was insisting, "they help keep you from getting fat."

Johnny looked appalled. "Are you 'fat-shaming?' Are you saying there's something wrong with being differently girthed?"

The guy recoiled at the realization of his social justice sins.

"If you ask your doctor," the girl insisted, "he'll tell you it's healthier..."

"He?" Johnny looked outraged. "He? Why would you assume that a doctor is a he? Don't you think a woman could be a doctor?"

"No," the girl was almost crying. "No, of course not. Why are you so negative? I can sense your hostility, and right now, I'm not feeling very safe. I have to be honest with you."

"Well, honesty would be a nice change," Johnny said shaking his head in disgust. "You two tell me you're some kind of social-justice superstars, and I find you flaunting your organic food privilege, fat shaming the differently girthed, and misogynisticly assuming women can't be doctors."

Between the stress of Hell Week and Johnny's attack, she really was crying now.

"Let's go back to the hotel, back to my room," the guy tried to comfort the crying girl. He glared at Johnny before turning back to the girl and continuing. "We can talk it out... together... alone."

"No. I just want to sit a while and talk. You'll come with me?" She distanced herself from Johnny and the guy started to move her away toward the table.

"Nice try," Johnny told the guy, "but she's telling you while she's happy to use you as an emotional tampon, there's no way she's going back to your room with you, because there's no reason your genetic material should propagate itself into the future – certainly not co-mingled with hers."

The SJWs were too triggered and shocked to even respond. The guy moved like he was going to confront Johnny.

"It's OK," Johnny reassured him, sympathetically. "I can't imagine how frustrating it must be for you. Why, if this happened to me, I'd be so frustrated I couldn't think straight."

The guy just froze like his mental circuits were overloading.

"She's getting away from you," Johnny pointed out.

The guy turned and noticed the girl was already wandering off. He rushed away and caught up with her, his hand hovering a couple inches above her shoulder as if he were afraid to make physical contact. They limped off toward the tables at the perimeter of the ballroom, the girl crying and the guy's face red with humiliation and rage at Johnny's insults.

Johnny turned and saw me watching him. "Yeah?" He dared me to say something.

"That was cruel," I pointed out.

"Two NPCs down, a ballroom full to go," he said defiantly.

"NPCs?"

"Non-Player Characters," Johnny clarified. "The stock computer-controlled characters in a video game that you have to get through in order to find and attack the real enemy."

That was an interesting perspective. "Who is the real enemy?"

"I don't know yet," he acknowledged, "so for now, I'll just deal with the NPCs. As for you, well, I'll be praying for you." He moved on to approach the next group.

I continued my search and saw Kirin. She looked stunning, clearly enjoying the attention from Travis Tolliver and a coterie of male admirers who had her circled. No wonder Johnny was pissed off.

I finally found Rob, busing a tray. I let him know I'd confirmed the entrance in the cottage and that I'd arrange for the Albertians to be assigned the cottage we needed access to. The network tap was in place and active. I told him about the acid barrels in the Berkshire Inn's warehouse of horror. "Bastards," he muttered. "Can you get me a key?"

I was ready for that one. I slid an extra keycard into a cocktail napkin and put it on the tray he was busing.

"The bar is over there, sir," Rob offered loudly, "but you'll have to show an ID." He had a twinkle in his eye, obviously recalling how I got in trouble at the GammaCon event just a few months earlier.

"Thanks." I left Rob to his duties, and continued circulating.

I found Amit talking with a girl in a cocktail dress. It was Madison, one of our classmates from the Social Justice Initiative at Georgia Tech. She'd obviously not been through Hell Week. "Madison!" I interrupted her conversation with Amit. "What brings you here?"

"I've been invited to speak about the misogyny and racism at Georgia Tech," she said proudly. "There's a big panel discussion tomorrow just after lunch."

"What about Marcus and Ryan and the rest of the Social Justice Ambassadors from Tech?" I asked her.

"They're not invited," Madison exclaimed. "This event is only for the most important activists."

I wasn't going to dispute her, but arguably, Marcus and Ryan were the most effective activists at Tech. They'd made a huge impact collaborating to expose the universal surveillance of telecommunications. Only that wasn't exactly the kind of activism Professor Gomulka really wanted. He was suspicious of them, and rightly so, because both were key figures in the FOG. Marcus saved my butt a few months ago when I was trying to escape a Civic Circle strike team.

"I have the night off," Amit brushed some strands of greasy hair from his forehead. "Why don't we head back to my room?"

"I can't believe you!" she exclaimed. "You can't be asking me back to your room when not thirty minutes ago I saw you making out with that girl from UCLA!"

"What can I say?" Amit said, staring down at her cleavage oozing up from her rather low-cut cocktail dress. "I'm in demand, and you're looking fine tonight."

"Eyes up here!" she pointed to her face.

Amit laughed. "Be honest. You did not wear that dress here so I'd be looking at your eyes all night." He reached over and took her arm. "Two independent spirits far from home rekindling the fire?"

"You need to take a shower," Madison insisted, wrinkling her nose.

"That could be arranged," Amit agreed, amiably.

I could see her wavering.

"They say, 'What happens on Jekyll Island, stays on Jekyll Island,' you know?"

They did? Or was Amit just making that up?

"Maybe later," Madison insisted.

I was realizing that if I'd really wanted to hook up with Jessica, I should have escalated further and insisted on slipping out with her when I had the chance. At least I could help Amit.

"In another hour, Amit will have hooked up with someone else," I offered confidently, trying to be a good wingman for him. "You should grab him now, while you..."

"Peter Burdell," the loudspeaker announced, cutting me off. "Amit Patel. Please come to the information desk, Peter Burdell and Amit Patel."

Damn. That didn't seem good. Amit and I shared a look of apprehension, excused ourselves from Madison, and made our way to the information desk. "Someone wants to speak with you," one of the plainclothes security men said. "Come with us."

We were escorted to a limo which took us to the Jekyll Island Club Hotel. Two more security officers escorted us to a deluxe suite.

"Send them in," a voice commanded.

We stepped in. The minions shut the door behind us.

"My name is Bernard. Please," he said, gesturing toward the couch, "be seated." I recognized him. He was the Civic Circle representative who'd interviewed us both this past spring for the Civic Circle internship opportunity. He was also Gomulka's immediate superior in the Civic Circle hierarchy.

Amit and I sank deeply into the soft cushions. Bernard sat down in a large chair. Bernard's throne-like perch was at least six inches higher than our level. He peered down at us from his position of authority.

"You both were in Professor Gomulka's social justice class at Georgia Tech." He continued without waiting for us to acknowledge him. "The events there this spring were... disappointing." He paused to encourage us to fill the silence with nervous babbling and self-justification.

Amit and I remained impassive.

I saw a hint of a smile on Bernard's face. "I need to understand what happened there. The campus was ripe for convergence. Professor Gomulka is a skilled activist. We have our ways of... monitoring what is going on. There seems to have been a profound... change at Georgia Tech."

He had to be referring to the Civic Circle's Nexus Detector. Amit and I both put on our best "confused" faces. Finally, Amit spoke, "But there really was very little change," he pointed out. "Other than those physics professors leaving, I mean. The institution as a whole is pretty much unchanged."

"Exactly," Bernard replied. "There was supposed to be a new dean of the School of Engineering. We had allies in all the right places and a top activist in place to organize student support for the convergence. It should have happened. All the signs were there, all the trends were moving in the right direction. And yet, it didn't happen. Something acted, something interfered, to prevent it."

His insight was spooky. Did Bernard know he was looking at the two people most responsible for thwarting his schemes for Georgia Tech? Before I could divert his attention, Amit spoke up.

"There was a great deal of resistance," Amit pointed out. "Reactionary professors rallied students in counter-protests."

"There has been resistance before," Bernard observed, "but not like this."

Bernard needed a target for his suspicions. The moment was perfect. "I'm not convinced Professor Gomulka was up to the job," I said, trying to get the right tone of reluctance in my voice. "He was fixated on Alinsky's 1960s-era community organizing tactics – on working within the system to effect peaceful change. He treated the campus like a pre-converged target that just needed a nudge in the right direction to fall into place, and he didn't adapt quickly enough when it became clear the place was actually anti-converged. He faced formidable opposition, and he lacked the decisiveness and ruthlessness to force the events to a successful conclusion."

"Really?" Bernard looked skeptically toward me. "You're willing to throw your professor under the bus?"

"It's the simple truth," I insisted as calmly as possible. "The events demonstrated that Professor Gomulka simply wasn't up to the job."

"Your friend, Amit, thinks I should allow you to join Civic Youth. I have to ask myself though, how can I trust you as my subordinate," Bernard asked dryly, "when you exhibit so little loyalty to your superiors?"

"Professor Gomulka just told me what to do," I explained. "He never asked me what I thought or how we could do better. You just did, so I answered you. If you want a swarm of Ivy-League ass-kissers telling you how smart you are and how everything you do is wonderful," I countered, "then I'm not your man. If you want someone who knows the score and isn't afraid to tell you so when you ask me directly, well, here I am."

Bernard chuckled in amusement. "I thought your friend Amit was the ruthless one. It seems I may have underestimated you. You came across so polite, so idealistic, so delightfully scrupulous in our interview."

"You don't play your cards face up if you don't have to." I smiled thinly back at him. "Now you've backed me into a corner. Professor Gomulka is a fine teacher, and an effective activist, but he's not the man to crush the hard-core reactionaries at Georgia Tech."

"You think you're qualified to pass judgement on a seasoned activist like Professor Gomulka?" Bernard narrowed his eyes. "You. A teenage college student wanna-be activist knows more than his professor with decades of experience at community organizing?"

"I may not have much experience, but I do know one thing." I looked Bernard right in the eye. "Gomulka failed. The definition of insanity is doing the same thing over again and expecting a different result. If you send Gomulka back to Georgia Tech, he'll flounder about next year, just like he did last year. I'm not saying I could do better than him, but I sure as hell can see how he screwed up, and I know better than to repeat his mistakes."

"What mistakes were those?" Bernard asked.

"He was too genteel," I observed. "He wanted a dialog, a debate with the reactionary leader, Professor Muldoon. He was so busy reading his Alinsky that he forgot his Marcuse – there can be no free speech for hate speech. He treated Muldoon as a colleague, as an equal, as a fellow professor who merely had a different opinion, not as an enemy to be destroyed."

"I understand he tried to get Muldoon fired for some impropriety," Bernard corrected him.

"He never should have agreed to that discussion with Muldoon," I pointed out. "Even if his scheme to take out Muldoon had worked, it was granting equal validity to reactionary ideas. When his scheme to get rid of Muldoon backfired, the discussion blew up in his face. Muldoon rallied enough of the influential alums and regents to his side that he blocked Doctor Ames from taking over the College of Engineering."

"Dr. Ames withdrew her application when it became obvious how hopelessly reactionary Georgia Tech was," Bernard insisted.

"A nice face-saving gesture," I countered, "but let's be honest about it. After Gomulka screwed up and let Muldoon rally the opposition, Ames was through. Even if she took the job, her position would have been so weak she wouldn't have been effective."

Bernard stared at me. I stared right back, daring him to be the first to fill the silence. "So," he conceded, "what would you do if you were in my place?"

"Transfer Gomulka to a nice, safely-converged campus, and let him carry on indoctrinating more social justice warriors in a supportive setting," I suggested. "It doesn't have to be a negative – he did a brilliant job exposing the bigoted and reactionary attitudes that pervade Georgia Tech, you can tell everyone. He's being rewarded with an appointment to a more elite, but safely-converged campus. Get in someone new for Georgia Tech. A real fighter. Someone not afraid to get his hands dirty."

"Who?" Bernard looked at me with a thin smile. "You?"

"No," I acknowledged. "I can see where Gomulka went wrong, but I'm not the one to solve the problem. I can help, but I don't have the experience to lead."

"I'm glad you at least recognize your limitations," Bernard said thoughtfully. He looked at Amit. "You've been awfully quiet while your friend here has been maligning Gomulka. Do you agree with him?"

Amit paused as if Bernard had to pull the answer out of him. "Yes," he replied, reluctantly. "It's true. I've had my doubts about Professor Gomulka as well. It's as if... as if he's just going through the motions. It's like he has other plans, other agendas, and his work at Georgia Tech is just... putting on some kind of a show. I don't trust him, either."

"You, too," Bernard shook his head sadly. "Your lack of loyalty is... disturbing. I see what you're both doing. Betraying your leader. Hoping you get a new leader who will have to rely on you, to be your tool, instead of you being the tools of the leader I appoint over you. Trying to build your own power base at the expense of the man I put in charge over you. We had great hopes for you, Amit. You could have been in the elite, maybe even a full member of the Civic Circle, eventually. With great privilege comes great responsibility, though. If you can't be obedient, if you can't show loyalty to your leaders... we have no use for backstabbing wanna-be activists who don't know their place."

Bernard faced Amit. "You're fired. You," he turned to me, "You may not work for me, but you're as good as fired too. I'm good friends with Larry Tolliver, CEO of Tolliver Corporation. I'm going to have a word with Travis Tolliver. Both of you get out, and don't come back."

CHAPTER 10: THE INNER CIRCLE

Bernard moved more quickly than I'd expected. Amit's room reservation was already cancelled, and his packed bags were waiting for him in the lobby of the Berkshire Inn. As an IT peon, my reservations were in the name of the company, not me personally, so apparently my room hadn't been cancelled, yet.

We put our phones in the microwave and went into the bathroom to talk quietly, masked by the sound of the running water.

"Might be safer to work your magic with the registration system," I suggested, "and get us into a different room."

"If Bernard wanted to kill us, he could have already. Besides, the hotel is booked solid," Amit countered. "Too much chance of them spotting my handiwork."

"Someone will have cancelled a reservation or no-showed," I pointed out. "There's always an empty room or two. The Gomulka sting is going down tonight. No telling what an uproar it might cause."

"Look, Pete. Times like this, any half-way decent hotel manager is watching the reservation system and already has a dozen people on a waiting list staying off Jekyll Island who want a room here. I can't mess with the database without it being obvious and raising questions."

Amit paused, the fatigue on his face was clear. "What with the sleep deprivation and indoctrination games they've been playing with all the Civic Youth, I haven't showered or had more than a few hours of sleep the last few days. Now isn't the time for me to try some fancy database hack when the victims are at maximum alert, we're under surveillance, and I'm falling apart. I'm going to clean up and get some sleep. Get out if you don't want to watch me shower."

I had yet to see Johnny. I was pretty sure he was staying with Kirin. I let Amit crash with me in my anonymous room.

Our anonymity didn't last long, however. Somehow they tracked me down. Or maybe they pounded their way through all the doors TAGS had reserved for the interns. We were awakened just after five in the morning. "Security. Open up."

I looked through the peephole at the two plainclothes security officers and cracked the chained door open. "We're looking for Peter Burdell and Amit Patel." He took a good look at me and compared it to a photo he had.

"Yes, that's us." No point in denying it.

"Get dressed. Someone needs to speak with you downstairs."

I was a bit surprised they let us dress unsupervised, but when we opened the door there were four of them waiting for us. They'd gotten reinforcements. They were polite enough in asking us to come with them, but the unstated "or else" was clear in their manner.

They took us down the elevator, through the lobby and to a limo idling in front of the hotel. They assumed a loose formation around us – two in front and two behind – so we couldn't bolt if we'd wanted to. The limo driver opened the door.

"Sorry to get you up so early," Bernard said. "Get in. We need to talk." Sorry? As Amit and I climbed in he asked, "Do you have cell phones?" He had us surrender our phones and he put them in a foil bag in a cooler. Interesting. Whatever Bernard wanted to talk about, he didn't want it to be overheard.

"Your misgivings about Professor Gomulka appear to have been justified," Bernard explained.

"How do you mean?" Amit looked confused, although he knew as well as I what that meant. Our scheme to get Gomulka must have worked.

I was a bit slow putting on my own perplexed face, but Bernard was focused on Amit, so he probably didn't detect it.

"Professor Gomulka was arrested at the Port of Brunswick last night. He was attempting to take delivery of a cargo container with nearly a dozen young Chinese refugees.

Amit and I exchanged glances. I was just as shocked as he looked, though not for the reasons Bernard was thinking. I thought the Tong was going to be smuggling drugs, not...

"Human trafficking," Bernard was shaking his head. "And he got caught. There's no keeping it out of the papers now. We're hoping no one figures out his connection to the Civic Circle." He was clearly more upset that Gomulka got caught and about the potential for bad publicity than about the human trafficking, or its victims.

"He's claiming it was a set-up," Bernard continued. "That his girlfriend arranged it all, and he had nothing to do with it at all."

"I didn't know he had a girlfriend. Interesting," Amit said with a gleam in his eye. "I thought Gomulka would have been more discreet in indulging his indiscretions." I had to admire Amit's Machiavellian artistry. "Whatever my differences of opinions regarding his choice of tactics, Gomulka's no idiot."

Suddenly I knew exactly why Bernard was giving us the limo treatment this morning after having fired us last night. He had to make a decision. Throw us under the bus with Gomulka, or enlist our aid in saving his own skin.

"Idiot or not, Gomulka could bring us all down," I pointed out. "This is an inexcusable mess, and heads will roll. Hopefully only figuratively." I wasn't sure about that "only" part. Of course, decapitation hadn't been a preferred technique since... was the Civic Circle involved in the French Revolution, too? No time for speculation. I had to stay focused.

I had an idea.

"Yesterday," I explained, "Mr. Larry Tolliver asked me about the Social Justice Initiative at Georgia Tech. I shared my misgivings about Gomulka with him."

In other words, Bernard couldn't bury the fact that we'd been concerned about Gomulka even before these events. What's more, I had a channel of communications right around him to his leading patron.

"If we could persuade you to change your unconditional support for Gomulka, we could present a united front..."

"I may have been overly hasty last night." Bernard made his decision – better to ally with us and Uncle Larry rather than risk trying to denounce us along with Gomulka. "Loyalty to leadership is critical for any organization, but yesterday's events demonstrate your worries about Gomulka were justified. I'll be happy to reinstate you, Amit, and I think there's room in Civic Youth for you, too, Pete."

"I'll have missed last night's program," Amit sounded disappointed, but I could read him well enough to know he was thrilled to have gotten a decent night's sleep and a shower, instead. "And Pete – he hasn't been through any of the Hell Week activities..."

"Hell Week is really just intended to help build loyalty and teamwork, Amit," Bernard countered, "qualities you've both already demonstrated in abundance. A certain... flexibility is called for."

"We need to think quickly, then," Amit picked up the beat. "Gomulka either plotted this himself, or he got duped by this girlfriend of his. Either way, none of us had any idea about it, beyond a... an anxiety that perhaps not all was right with him. That maybe Gomulka's attention may have been elsewhere. Maybe that lack of commitment might explain why the Social Justice Initiative struggled so at Georgia Tech last year."

"Yes, exactly!" Bernard almost cried out in relief. "Gomulka was either neglecting his duties because he was being duped by his girlfriend, or he was busy setting up this unauthorized... activity."

"I still don't see what's going on," I claimed. "Whoever's responsible, Gomulka, or whoever may have duped him, what were they after?"

"I understand," Bernard looked a bit guilty at airing the Civic Circle's dirty linen, "some of the Thirteen and their... associates and friends have more... extreme tastes in entertainment. One of the Council of 33 owns a private island in the Caribbean where Civic Circle members can go for any manner of... indulgences. Pleasure Island, they call it. They invite Team 500 members and others. A reward for good service."

The indulgences – those were the carrot. The stick would be the threat to reveal the no-doubt well-documented "indulgences" to the public. Not that I was going to point out the obvious to Bernard. The Thirteen? Council of 33? Team 500? This was a great opportunity to learn more about the inner workings and structure of the Civic Circle.

"So, Gomulka could be making a play of some kind," Amit speculated. "A bribe?"

"Could be whoever's pulling his strings," I pointed out.

Just then we pulled up in front of the Jekyll Island Club Hotel.

"The Thirteen called an emergency meeting," Bernard explained. "As many of the Thirteen as they could find this early in the morning will be there, along with some of the senior members of the Council of 33. They wanted me there to discuss the Gomulka situation, and I thought I should bring you also. Let me do the talking. If they ask you anything, remember, we were all suspicious about Gomulka, but had no idea anything like this might happen. Got it?"

"Yes, sir," Amit and I both replied.

The chauffeur held the door for us, and more of the Civic Circle's ubiquitous security officers surrounded us and escorted into and through the lobby. Two more officers checked our IDs at the door. "They're not on the list."

"Their presence was specifically requested," Bernard insisted.

The guard vanished and a few moments later an older gentleman stepped out. "Who are these young men?"

"Civic Youth candidates with knowledge of Professor Gomulka's activities," a visibly nervous Bernard replied, "at Georgia Tech."

"Screen them," the older gentlemen told the security officers.

First they took Bernard. About five minutes later, they took me. They required me to change clothes and shower under the watchful eye of a guard. My clothes were whisked away for careful examination while I showered. Then, they returned my clothes, and I dressed. Finally, I was escorted into a conference room.

Bernard sat in a chair, his wet hair showing that he was no more trusted than me. "This is the room where the plan for the Federal Reserve was devised in 1910," Bernard distracted himself from his nervousness to play tour guide. He was still explaining the secret history of how the Civic Circle took over the nation's monetary system when the guards brought Amit in.

"Senator Nelson Aldrich, a close confidant of J.P. Morgan himself, sat..." Bernard trailed off awkwardly. "Um, ah, well... Mr. Tolliver, sir. Good to see you, sir."

Amit and I joined Bernard in rising as Uncle Larry approached. Heh, I noticed his hair was wet, too!

"Bernard," Uncle Larry said gruffly, dismissing Amit and me as insignificant. "What's all this about? I don't fund the Social Justice Initiative to be awakened at this god-awful hour of the morning to..."

"It's the Thirteen, sir," Bernard explained. "They want to meet immediately to discuss the Gomulka situation."

"What Gomulka situation?"

Bernard had made a good start at explaining the events of last night to Uncle Larry when the guards came and blindfolded us all. We were led down to the basement. I could hear the whine of the servers' fans as we passed the Network Operations room.

The steel door in the tabby wall of the basement of the Jekyll Island Club Hotel – I was confident the guards were taking us through it. We walked through a long corridor, sounds of our footsteps reflecting and echoing off the walls. Then we were led up some stairs, around a couple of corners, and we stopped. The hoods and blindfolds were ripped off us. The light nearly blinded me.

Seven... no eight robed figures sat at a table. I recognized the room from my previous visit when I set up the switch in the network closet at the Sans Souci.

"Worshipful Master," a standing robed man turned and faced the table, "the Circle is closed, yet we have four uninitiated strangers among us who have not yet sworn themselves to the Inner Circle."

"The Circle must be closed," intoned the robed figures.

"Junior Warden, swear in the strangers," the Worshipful Master ordered.

The Junior Warden approached, holding an ancient leather-bound book in his left hand and with his right hand up and facing us. "Place your left hand on the Book, raise your right hand, and repeat after me: I do most solemnly swear..."

The oath and charge were enough to freeze my blood. I took it under false pretenses, fully intending to betray my word and pay back the Circle's duplicity with my own. I could only hope the God on whose behalf I'd just falsely sworn my fealty would understand and forgive my treachery.

"Be seated," the Junior Warden finished.

"You have sworn an oath of secrecy and loyalty to the Circle," the Worshipful Master advised us. "This is a solemn oath, for you have promised to absolve any within the Circle from killing you should you disclose our secrets or fail in the faithful performance of your duties and responsibilities to us. Do you understand the oath you have sworn?"

"Yes," we all answered.

"Your Oaths shall be recorded in the Book," the Junior Deacon advised us.

"Stand up, Bernard," the Worshipful Master barked. "As Director of Academic Affairs, Gomulka is one of yours. We all want to know what the hell you and he are up to."

"Worshipful Master," the stress in Bernard's voice came through, "we've had... concerns about Gomulka for a while."

"Concerns? Why," he asked, "have your concerns not been brought to our attention before now?" Bernard seemed paralyzed. Larry stood and maintained a respectful silence. "Mister...?"

"Tolliver, Worshipful Master," Larry replied calmly. "Lawrence Tolliver, candidate member of Team 500. I'm CEO of Tolliver Corporation and I'm the principal backer of the Civic Circle's Social Justice Initiative or SJI. Like, I'm sure, many of us in the room, I was disappointed by the lack of progress Professor Gomulka made at Georgia Tech last year.

"The premise was simple: a testbed to demonstrate that complete social justice convergence was possible, even at a university in a traditionally conservative state with a strong science, technology, engineering, and math curriculum – areas that have tended to resist convergence. Despite ample funding and thorough preparation, the Social Justice Initiative failed to place our preferred candidate, Dr. Cindy Ames, as Dean of Engineering.

"We did score a partial victory, of sorts, in the campaign that led to the removal of the Chinese spy, Professor Wu Chen, and his accomplice and probably partner in crime, Professor Marlena Graf. The circumstances, though, appear ambiguous, and some are portraying the professors we removed as martyrs.

"I believe the failures of last year raised serious questions about the suitability of Professor Gomulka to lead the effort. I expressed those reservations yesterday to some on the Oversight Council in private, in anticipation of a full discussion with the SJI Board of Directors tomorrow. Last night's events... well, now my concerns about Gomulka's performance have become outright alarm and bewilderment at his actions."

"So you have no idea what he may have been up to?"

"No, Worshipful Master." Bernard, Amit, and I echoed Larry's denial.

"Gomulka was Bernard's subordinate," one of the other men at the table pointed out.

"With respect, I don't believe Bernard can be blamed, let alone me," Larry replied confidently. "As I recall, Gomulka came highly recommended by several prominent figures among Team 500, even a backer or two from among the Thirteen, or so I'm told. Bernard chose him, and I endorsed Bernard's choice on your recommendations. Now is not the time for recriminations, however. We need to understand what Gomulka did, why he did it, and converge on a consensus story to share with the public. Our formal program kicks off in a couple of hours, so we don't have time to waste."

I admired the way Uncle Larry deftly diverted attention away from himself, and by implication, the rest of us.

"Well said," the Worshipful Master cut off an angry retort from the man who'd been accusing Bernard. He glanced down at his notes. "Was Gomulka duped, or were his actions deliberate and intentional? Does anyone have anything relevant to offer?"

"Either case reflects poorly on Gomulka, Worshipful Master," pointed out another man sitting at the table.

"True," the Worshipful Master noted, "but not what I asked. Anything relevant?" There was a long silence.

"Worshipful Master, I would like to hear from Gomulka's associates and assistants their opinions."

"Indeed," the Worshipful Master agreed. "Stand up," he commanded. You on the end, who are you and what do you know about this?"

"I'm Amit Patel, Worshipful Master. I'm a candidate member of Civic Youth, a member of Professor Gomulka's Social Justice class, and I was to be his teaching assistant in the fall. I can only say that I have no idea what the Professor may have been doing. Bernard did speak with Pete and me here last night about our experience at Georgia Tech. We told

him we were concerned that Professor Gomulka was...
distracted: not giving the Social Justice Initiative the full
benefit of his time and energy."

"You," the Worshipful Master pointed at me. "Peter?"

"Yes, Worshipful Master."

"Do you have anything to add?"

"We thought Professor Gomulka was a well-meaning ally
of social justice who merely might not be the best candidate
to lead a bare-knuckles fight against the reactionary
establishment at Georgia Tech. We had no idea that he might
be pursuing some kind of... alternate agenda, or working with
some other parties at... cross purposes."

"Did he have other affiliations or associations?"

"He was very close to one of the deans at Georgia Tech." I
named him and gave details. That dean was a real weasel and
one of Gomulka's allies against Professor Muldoon. I wasn't
going to pass the up the opportunity to throw him under the
bus. I could see one of the Thirteen writing a note and
handing it to the Warden. The Warden stepped out of the
room.

"Professor Gomulka was a master of the indirect
approach," I continued. "He liked to work behind the scenes
using the Dean to influence campus administration and his
Social Justice students to create the impression of grassroots
support for his initiatives. He was a master of intrigue. My
concern was he favored the indirect approach instead of more
direct action. I could see him faking this girlfriend so he'd
have some kind of an alibi if his plan went south."

"Gomulka wasn't all that skilled at information
technology, Worshipful Master," Amit picked up on my lead.
"It should be possible to trace the supposed girlfriend's
emails back to him if he was faking it."

"Omnitia turned over all the logs they had on Gomulka,
Worshipful Master," one of the Thirteen noted. "The FBI...
our FBI," he added smugly, "haven't been able to trace it. The
IP addresses are from all over the place." Good. We'd covered
our... "Fortunately, one of the emails was sent through a

compromised node. We've traced it to a Berkshire Inn. Rapid City, South Dakota." I did my best to appear impassive, but damn. They must have cracked some of the TOR nodes and traced it back to Amit's hotel network. "That took a fair amount of computer skill. Skill Gomulka simply didn't have, Worshipful Master. He was clearly duped by a third party."

"Or Gomulka was collaborating with someone with those skills..." I got a sharp look from him at my temerity in disputing one of the Thirteen. "Worshipful Master," I added as respectfully as I could. I'd have to be careful not to be too obvious in spreading doubt and suspicion.

"Bernard?"

"Worshipful Master," he gulped. "Patel and Burdell here spoke with me last night – shared their reservations about Gomulka's conduct at Georgia Tech. In retrospect his lack of performance at Georgia Tech may have reflected his distraction by and involvement in whatever led up to this incident. On my oath, I had no idea Gomulka was procuring this... unauthorized entertainment or why he did it."

"So," the Worshipful Master snorted in disgust, "no one has any clear idea what Gomulka was up to, whether he was duped, or who else might be involved. Splendid. Do any of you have anything to add?"

We stood in silence.

"Bernard, do remind our guests about the consequences of their oaths before they leave," the Worshipful Master ordered. "You are dismissed."

The guards entered, blindfolded us, and led us back to the Jekyll Island Club Hotel, returning us to the Federal Reserve Room, and removing our blindfolds.

"I know the score," Larry preempted Bernard, "but we should remind these youngsters of the consequences of disobedience."

Bernard nodded. "Our friends are listening to everything you say or do," he noted. "Most of it goes by unnoticed, but if they turn their attention to you, they will be able to follow your every communication, your every movement, almost your every thought."

"We understand," Amit piped up, "but what if someone else leaks? What if people find out what's going on here? Couldn't we get in trouble?"

Bernard chuckled. "Who would believe it? The Circle has assets in place in many critical positions in law enforcement and the judicial system. They'll make sure that any effort to reveal the truth, let alone seriously investigate or prosecute it never happens. If it is investigated, charges won't be filed. If charges are filed, the prosecution will be sabotaged. If the prosecution goes forward, a Circle-controlled judge will throw the case out. If the case is ever heard, enough of the jurors will be Circle assets or leaned upon to deliver the right verdict. We have friends everywhere. The system is thoroughly firewalled, at least at the federal level, to protect us."

"And all along the way, the media would never cover any of it," Larry assured us. "At all. Other than a few stubborn renegades, they're all under the Circle's control in one way or another."

"You two are privileged," Bernard told us, "to have access to the highest level of power there is. You can be part of leading us all into the New World Order. You have to crack a few eggs to make an omelet, right?"

So long as you don't end up one of the eggs, like my parents did. "Yes," I confirmed, looking to Amit. "We understand. We understand, perfectly. We'll do our part."

"Excellent!" Bernard seemed pleased that suspicion in the Gomulka affair had been diverted away from him. He looked around him. "It's a great honor and a great responsibility even to be an assistant to those who are calling the shots. The history that has been made in this room... It's amazing. And now you're part of that, too. You need to live up to the trust that has been placed in you. Fail to do so, and..." Bernard paused and took a deep breath. "Well, let's just say I wouldn't want to be in Gomulka's shoes right about now."

"You're one of the TAGS interns, right? I'll tell Travis you've been assigned as a Civic Youth candidate, at their request," Larry assured me. He was doing a great job of pretending he didn't know me. "The keynote address is in a couple of hours. Be there."

"My driver will take you back to your hotel," Bernard offered. "After the keynote at the Convention Center, report back to the Jekyll Island Club Hotel."

We were silent all the way back, taking in the significance of what we'd seen. I'd been so focused on trying to absorb and understand what I'd been seeing that the enormity of it all was only now sinking in. Amit and I had hoped to nibble our way around the periphery of the Civic Circle from the outermost rings, absorbing insights and clues. Our frame-up of Gomulka, though, had propelled us right to the very center of the Cabal, thanks to Bernard's desire to use us – and Uncle Larry – as human shields against fallout from the Gomulka incident.

Bernard's driver dropped us off and returned our phones. Amit and I exchanged glances. I could tell he was thinking the same thing I was. If ever we were being monitored, it would be now.

"I'm going to hop in the shower," I told Amit.

He looked thoughtful. "I'll join you."

We went into the bathroom together. I shut the door and started the water running.

"They're probably watching, you know," I pointed out.

"So we're shower buddies," Amit pointed out, "so what. That makes them all the more likely to trust us if they think we have something to hide." He looked at the laptop I opened on the counter. "What are you doing?'

"Finding out what they're doing," I replied. "I think I can find the video feed for the meeting we were just in."

I logged in through the wireless tap. So confident was the Civic Circle in their secure, isolated network that they didn't consider how someone inside the network already could use it against them. It wasn't hard to find the feed. The meeting was over, but they'd recorded it, apparently.

I advanced the video to just before the hooded figures stood up.

"All rise," said one of the men in the video.

Amit and I watched seven figures in black robes and wearing masks enter and stand behind various chairs at the table. One of them might have been a woman – it was hard to tell. It must have been some kind of assigned seating, because half the chairs were unattended.

An eighth robed figure entered. He moved with a curious hint of awkwardness and stood at the head of the table. "What," he asked the assemblage, "is our chief care?"

"To see that the Circle is closed," the group chanted in unison.

"Pray do your duty, Junior Deacon."

"Yes, Worshipful Master," one of the men, the "Junior Deacon," apparently, replied to him, going to the door. The Junior Deacon knocked three times. A moment later three knocks came in answer from outside the door. "The Circle is closed."

"I see we are eight of the Thirteen," the Worshipful Master declared. "There being a quorum, I declare the meeting in session, and the business at hand sealed under the oaths we all have sworn. Any and all Brethren with business to present to the Thirteen come hither, and you will be heard. Be seated."

He continued after a pause. "Senior Warden, what business is before us this morning?"

The Junior Warden stood. "In the absence of the Senior Warden, the Junior Warden serves, Worshipful Master."

I saw the Worshipful Master nod.

"Our brother, Gomulka, has failed in the performance of his duties and exposed the Civic Circle to disrepute," the Junior (acting Senior?) Warden declared. He gave an account of how Gomulka had been arrested last night attempting to take delivery of a cargo container that held a dozen young

Chinese – girls mostly, but a couple of boys, also – in squalor. He lowered the lights and showed photos.

"In addition to food, water, bedding, and a rather overtaxed chemical toilet," the Warden continued, "the container held several crates of..." He paused, obviously discomforted by the news he had to share. "...of paraphernalia of a sexual nature including over two thousand condoms."

"Heck of a gang bang," someone muttered only to be silenced by a sharp bang of the Worshipful Master's gavel.

"What the hell was Gomulka thinking," one of the seated members asked, "trying to get that container through customs? They've tightened their scrutiny. You can't expect to get away with that kind of thing anymore."

"He also scrambled the cottage assignments, swapping the Chase Bank and Holy See Bank Corporation assignments at the last minute," the Warden added. "I've had to placate both delegations. I left them where they are since it would only be more hassle to switch them back.

"Gomulka insisted he was set up by this woman, Hungarian supermodel Reka Kozma." There was an appreciative whistle from someone, prompting another stern bang of the gavel. "Ms. Kozma denies any contact with Gomulka. The Hungarian National Police believe her. The FBI is trying to trace the email address now."

"Our FBI friends?" the Worshipful Master asked.

"Yes, Worshipful Master. The Director placed... trusted special agents in charge of the investigation, and Gomulka is in their custody. The interrogation is... continuing. We will be updated if Gomulka reveals anything else. The proximity in time and space to our Forum may lead some in the reactionary press to speculate that these events are tied to us. The press has been told a suspect is in custody, but we have not released his identity."

"Bring in Larry Tolliver and Gomulka's associates," the Worshipful Master commanded.

Amit and I watched the images of ourselves being led into the room with Bernard and Uncle Larry. I skipped ahead until I saw the guards escorting us out.

"What do we do about it?" the Worshipful Master opened the discussion.

"This incident merely illustrates how America remains the land of opportunity," one of the Thirteen spoke up. "We honor and applaud these wretched masses trying to breathe freely who suffered heroic hardships to reach our shores — not unlike the pilgrims of old. Their search for a better life is one of the most basic desires of human beings. These are people willing to do jobs Americans won't do. We ought to say 'thank you' and welcome them."

"Yes, of course," another replied, "but what are we going to do about these particular illegal immigrants?"

"A person cannot be illegal," countered the one I thought might be a female. Hearing the sexually ambiguous voice distorted through my laptop's speakers didn't help.

"Of course, of course," he replied.

"Perhaps," opined a deep voice, "these 'undocumented migrants' could be repatriated overseas? I'm sure gainful employment for them might be found on Pleasure Island. We appease the public voices complaining about our Open Borders Initiative with this token gesture while making sure these unfortunates have an opportunity to serve... higher purposes."

I saw nods around the table.

"Excellent," the Worshipful Master confirmed, "but what of our Brother Gomulka?"

"We're troubled by the incident, deeply troubled," Deep Voice offered. "There is no connection to the Civic Circle. If Gomulka's identity is divulged, we're unsure what his role was in this affair. He was certainly not acting on our behalf. In any event it does not reflect on the Civic Circle."

"The conservative media will be all over this," cautioned another. "Sex slaves? Human trafficking?"

"Any insinuations of a sexual nature are crazy right-wing conspiracy theories," Deep Voice explained. "Those rumors were obviously started by profoundly disturbed and repressed individuals. Such speculations are outside the realm of civilized discourse and merely reflect negatively on the character of those who share them."

"Nothing frightens conservatives more than the possibility someone somewhere might think they're not nice," someone else offered. That drew a chuckle or two.

"Exactly," another voice confirmed, "and anyone highlighting this incident is clearly a knuckle-dragging racist with deep-seated prejudice against these heroic Asian immigrants and their desperate measures in pursuit of the American dream." It was hard to keep track of who was speaking from beneath the hoods.

"If we don't provide a counter-narrative, though," Deep Voice noted, "we allow some other narrative to fill the void. Our villain of the hour is Saddam Hussein. Blame him. Saddam was offering a sordid bribe. Trying to influence us to save himself from the consequences of his action. Trying to avoid the mandates of International Justice and World Opinion. Trying to distract the world from the important work we're undertaking here. If they find out about Gomulka's involvement, why then our Brother Gomulka was clearly operating on Saddam's behalf."

There were nods from around the table.

"Very well," the Worshipful Master agreed. "We lead with the 'heroic immigrants' spin, and we let the media know that the 'real' story appears to be subversion by Saddam Hussein but they should keep it to themselves for now. We keep investigating Gomulka to see what his real motives were. Are we agreed?"

There were nods of consent.

"Now," the Worshipful Master changed the topic, "while we are assembled together, what about the Breitbart situation?"

One of the hooded figures appeared to squirm. "He declined our offer, Worshipful Master."

"Heh," Deep Voice snorted. "I told you he was no cruise-ship conservative to be bought off by a position with the controlled opposition. We're going to have to proceed..."

The Worshipful Master held up a hand, silencing Deep Voice, and then turned to face Squirmy. "You know what to do."

"Yes, Worshipful Master," Squirmy acknowledged. "He has plans to go out drinking this evening. Our... troubleshooters, the same ones who took care of the Dando problem for us, are on the job."

"Excellent," the Worshipful Master acknowledged Squirmy. "The sooner the better. This Breitbart has been a thorn in our sides for too long. I don't want to see what he can do with our Brother Gomulka's indiscretion. So, what's the status with Wellstone?"

My thoughts were racing. Who was this Breitbart character? Were they really plotting... an assassination? And who was Wellstone? That question, at least, was answered by the next speaker.

"The Senator from Minnesota remains opposed to the Iraq War," one of the hooded figures stated. "Pity... He's been a valuable asset on many other issues."

"There's no room on our team for those who won't play ball," said Deep Voice. "If anything should... happen to Wellstone, what happens to his Senate seat?"

"Wellstone only narrowly defeated Coleman in 2002," someone explained. "Governor Pawlenty will likely appoint Norm Coleman to the seat. Coleman's firm on war with Iraq."

"We may have to live with that," Deep Voice argued. "There are still too many new Senators who don't appreciate how the game is played. Wellstone has too much seniority, garners too much respect. The Senate is closely divided. He may well inspire others by his example – tilt the balance against war."

"He's flying back to Minnesota tomorrow for a political rally," one of the figures explained, "in a private jet."

There was a long pause. Were they really plotting what I thought they were plotting?

"That makes it easy," a voice muttered.

"His family is with him," someone said. "And the pilots..."

"Some sacrifices must be made," Deep Voice counselled. "Better a dead martyr than a live opponent."

"Indeed," the Worshipful Master cut off the discussion without even making a show of securing everyone's consent. "We will postpone further discussion until tomorrow night's regular meeting."

"Here?" Deep Voice asked. "Or..."

"In the Inner Sanctum," the Worshipful Master clarified. "8 pm. There being no other business?"

The room was silent with the magnitude of the decisions that had just been made.

"This emergency meeting stands adjourned."

The Warden stood and commanded "All rise!"

The images of the hooded figures filed off the screen.

"Wow," even Amit seemed stunned at what we'd just seen. "We have to get word to Rob. The Inner Circle. They were here. Right in the Jekyll Club Hotel. They're meeting tomorrow night at 8 pm."

"The Inner Sanctum," I concurred. "That had to be the complex Petrel had identified."

"What about the people the Civic Circle is targeting: Breitbart and Wellstone?"

"I'm through with standing by helplessly and watching the Civic Circle kill their opponents."

Amit nodded grimly. "We need Rob's help to save them, though."

I was very grateful the Civic Circle was too cheap to put their smoke detector cameras in the bathrooms in every room of the hotel. Amit had taken a shower last night, so he got his hair damp and changed while I scribbled out a note to Rob summarizing what we'd learned and the opportunity to decapitate the Civic Circle in one blow. We'd have to get the Albertians on board to pull it off. And maybe Rob would have some ideas about how the Reactance could save Breitbart and Wellstone. I carefully embedded the note in a cocktail napkin to hand off to Uncle Rob when I saw him. Mission accomplished, I took a hot shower and tried to wash away the disgust I felt.

Amit and I got down to breakfast early and ate our scrambled eggs in silence, neither of us willing to speak. In the background the morning news was playing.

"Customs and Homeland Security officials foiled an attempt at human trafficking last night." Amit and I both stopped eating and watched the video showing Gomulka and a group of people being taken into custody. "The victims were taken into custody by immigration officials, along with an unidentified individual who attempted to take delivery of the cargo container in which the people were hiding."

The segment closed with a cut to a beautiful announcer. "These wretched masses trying to breathe freely who suffered heroic hardships to reach our shores – not unlike the pilgrims of old – prove that America is still the land of opportunity." Her brilliant white teeth shone through a winning smile as she mouthed the same words we'd heard from the Inner Circle.

Amit and I looked at each other. "They sure move fast," he muttered.

CHAPTER 11: AN INCONVENIENT TRUTH

"Hello, I'm George Dubya Bush, and I used to be the next President of the United States," the former candidate introduced himself, earning some chuckles from the audience, recalling his narrow defeat at the hands of the late Al Gore.

Amit and I were part of the Civic Youth crowd up on stage providing a backdrop for the Governor's speech. Governor Bush's keynote featured a presentation of "An Inconvenient Truth," his documentary on the dangers of Saddam Hussein and the need for military intervention in Iraq. I got a sore neck trying to watch the video on the big screen looming over us. The Governor concluded with a mention of current events.

"Last night, we learned once again how vulnerable we are to the threat of international terror. Our diligent Homeland Security personnel intercepted an attempt to smuggle over a dozen young Chinese immigrants into the country for nefarious purposes."

The Governor cleared his throat and continued. "On one level, this incident merely illustrates how America remains the land of opportunity. We honor and applaud these wretched masses trying to breathe free who suffered heroic hardships to reach our shores – not unlike the pilgrims of old. Their search for a better life is one of the most basic desires of human beings. These are people willing to do jobs

Americans won't do. We ought to say 'thank you' and welcome them."

Amit and I exchanged glances at the familiar phrases.

"Out of common sense and fairness, our laws should allow willing workers to enter our country and fill jobs that Americans are not filling. We must not listen to the voices that would build walls and barriers between us and the world.

"Preliminary investigations suggest that this human trafficking was deliberately inspired by Saddam Hussein to disrupt our Forum. Our laws need to protect us from Saddam Hussein and other foreign actors who may try to subvert our decision-making process.

"America is a nation of immigrants, and we're also a nation of laws. God bless you all, and God bless the United States of America."

By the time I forced my way back out through the crowds to the lobby, the scrollbar was already rolling the news on the big screen television: "GOV. BUSH TIES SADDAM TO HUMAN TRAFFICKING." The screen showed images of the sordid conditions inside the cargo container and additional footage of children in immigration detention centers. I wondered what that had to do with... then I figured it out. They were pushing hard the narrative that these illegal immigrants were children who needed help. All part of the emotional conditioning to get the public to let in more voters to support the Civic Circle's agenda.

I saw Ding Li in the crowd. "I'll catch up with you," I let Amit go on ahead. I maneuvered to intercept her. "The guest choked on the fortune cookie, but the fortune certainly surprised the bus boy. What is the waiter up to? We need to talk," I insisted softly as I walked beside her.

She glanced around. "Not here. You know the Beijing Bistro?"

"Yes." I'd seen it on the map of Jekyll Island – one of the few restaurants on the north end of the island's beachfront.

"Lunch at noon," she proposed.

"See you there," I confirmed.

I caught up with Amit.

Only that morning did I realize that the Civic Circle's Social Justice Leadership Forum was really two meetings in one. There were the public sessions being held at the Convention Center in the Beach Village, but the events that really mattered were the private meetings held at the Jekyll Island Club Hotel for the elite and their special guests – who now included Amit, me, and a couple other trusted Civic Youth candidates. I wasn't sure if we'd been invited because we were trusted, or because they wanted to keep an eye on us, but I was eager to take advantage of the access either way.

We had a half hour before the sessions were supposed to start up again at the Jekyll Island Club Hotel. We decided to walk the mile across the island rather than join the line of people waiting at the shuttle bus stop, so we could have a private discussion. We secured our phones, and the words we'd been holding back all morning for fear of being overheard came pouring out.

"I still can't believe how pervasive they are," I acknowledged. "The Civic Circle controls most everything that matters."

"For now, perhaps," Amit offered a smug grin. "I assume you wrote a note to pass to Rob?"

"Of course."

"Good. Here's mine," he handed me a slip of paper. "We're going to attack them tomorrow night, right?"

It was my turn to smile. "Of course. At least, that's what I suggested to Rob. We'll need to speak with the Albertians tonight and get their approval. Only way I see it working is if we get in the complex through their cottage, and they can give us the access. It's safer than trying to distract them away, and hoping the place is empty when we strike."

"You think you can get them to go along?"

"I can ask. It'll be much harder if we have to force our way past them. I'll leave that call to Rob."

We left the road to follow a narrow walking trail. The Spanish moss hung lazily over the wooded passage as we continued sharing the details of our mutual experiences. The window of freedom was far too short. Soon we were walking past the line of vehicles waiting to get through the check point on Old Plantation Road. The guards checked our ID badges and waved us through. It was interesting how the security perimeter included the Jekyll Island Club Hotel and the Sans Souci, but all the obvious security was around the Jekyll Island Club Hotel. The hotel was merely a decoy, though. The real target, the location of the Inner Circle, was the Sans Souci.

The security at the Jekyll Island Club Hotel was more intense. The guards wanded us and searched our backpacks. Once inside, we made our way to our separate assigned sessions. I covered a session on "Population Control," while Amit was responsible for keeping the water pitchers full in a parallel session on "Information Control." Uncle Larry was a panelist in yet another session on "Economic Control," talking about the Tolliver Corporation's carrying on the legacy of the late Al Gore: carbon taxes, carbon credits, sequestration, and so on.

The Population Control session was eye-opening. Apparently the Rockefeller Foundation had funded the development of a male anti-fertility vaccine. The Civic Circle had deployed it for use in "select populations," but the presentation failed to define what populations they regarded as "select." Instead, they relied mostly on endocrine disrupters, plasticizers, and other chemicals that suppress testosterone and reduce fertility. One chart showed the precipitous decline in average sperm count over the past fifty years of their program. "In combination with the ready availability of abortion on demand," the speaker claimed, "and our efforts to raise the average age at which women chose to start families, we've similarly drastically reduced effective female fertility as well. These techniques allow us to suppress the growth of undesirable portions of our own population, while we create a more diverse and pliant society through large-scale immigration of new citizens less resistant to our enlightened control."

The ready availability of assisted fertility techniques, he assured the audience, meant that the elite, worthy, successful members of the middle class who could afford the treatments would still be able to perpetuate their successful gene lines at the expense of the rabble. That was my paraphrase, of course. I had to grit my teeth to refrain from commenting on or questioning the well-received talk.

Following the parallel sessions, there was a joint session featuring David Rockefeller, the ninety-something-year-old patriarch of the family. The plenary was held a short distance away in the Morgan Center – formerly an indoor tennis court built for J.P. Morgan in the 1920s, now a huge meeting room.

Ted Turner, the founder of CNN, rose to introduce Mr. Rockefeller. After welcoming the distinguished guests in the audience, Turner lauded Rockefeller.

"We now live in a world where we are related by economics, politics, the environment, technology, and human nature. We can no longer think of the people and problems in other parts of the world as 'foreign' to us. David certainly understood this early in the game and has been a tireless and inspirational advocate in this regard. He wears the badge of 'proud internationalist' openly, as do I. Without further ado, it is my honor to introduce our keynote speaker, David Rockefeller."

The audience rose in a standing ovation.

"We are grateful to CNN, the *Washington Post*, the *New York Times*, *Time* magazine, and other great publications and media outlets whose directors have attended our meetings and respected their promises of discretion for almost forty years," Mr. Rockefeller began. "It would have been impossible for us to develop our plan for the world if we had been subject to the bright lights of publicity during those years. But the world is now much more sophisticated and prepared to march towards a world government. The supranational sovereignty of an intellectual elite and world bankers is surely preferable to the national auto-determination practiced in past centuries.

"For more than a century," Rockefeller continued, "ideological extremists at either end of the political spectrum have seized upon well-publicized incidents to attack the Rockefeller family for the inordinate influence they claim we wield over American political and economic institutions. Some even believe we are part of a secret cabal working against the best interests of the United States, characterizing my family and me as 'internationalists' and of conspiring with others around the world to build a more integrated global political and economic structure — one world, if you will. If that is the charge, I stand guilty, and I am proud of it." He croaked, reaching for a glass of water.

"The anti-Rockefeller focus of these otherwise incompatible political positions owes much to Populism. 'Populists' believe in conspiracies, and one of the most enduring is that a secret group of international bankers and capitalists, and their minions, control the world's economy. Because of my name and prominence as head of the Chase for many years, I have earned the distinction of 'conspirator in chief' from some of these people.

"Populists and isolationists ignore the tangible benefits that have resulted from our active international role during the past half-century. Not only was the very real threat posed by Soviet Communism overcome, but there have been fundamental improvements in societies around the world, particularly in the United States, as a result of global trade, improved communications, and the heightened interaction of people from different cultures. Populists rarely mention these positive consequences, nor can they cogently explain how they would have sustained American economic growth and expansion of our political power without them."

Rockefeller's talk continued, followed by a question period during which audience members competed to see who could offer the most effusive praise to the distinguished speaker.

I was glad when it was all over and I could rejoin Amit. I'd parked the TAGS van nearby. As we were leaving, we passed through a throng of reporters just outside the secure perimeter around the hotel. I heard shouts.

"Did the Civic Circle have anything to do with this human trafficking incident?" From our distance, the answer was lost in the noise of the crowd.

"It happened just next door," another reporter shouted, "just as your meeting starts, and you say there's no connection?"

"Is this the same Gomulka," I heard another reporter shout, "who was supposed to be a keynote speaker tomorrow?"

"I see not everyone in the press got their marching orders," Amit smirked.

"A bunch of those folks are local news," I pointed out. "They probably aren't as tightly controlled."

When we got to the van, I removed the batteries from our cell phones and sealed them in a couple of potato chip bags. We were finally free to talk.

"So what the hell happened?" Amit shook his head incredulously. "I thought the Red Flower Tong was going to smuggle in drugs to incriminate Gomulka, not bring in kids to be sex slaves."

"I don't know," I acknowledged. I thought back over my conversation with the Tong, months ago. "They were supposed to incriminate Gomulka. The details were left up to them. I'd just assumed they'd be smuggling drugs."

We rode in silence north along Riverside Drive.

"So," Amit broke the silence, "how was the Population Control session?"

I briefed Amit on the content. "What about the Information Control session?" I asked him.

"Just about as appalling," Amit summarized. "I got to meet one of the Civic Circle's 'Narrative Architects.'" I listened in amazement as Amit described how the Narrative Architect began by stressing the importance of secrecy, using the example of the *Report from Iron Mountain* to illustrate the negative impact of revealing internal discussions to the outside world. Apparently in the 1960s, the Civic Circle had commissioned a study the conclusion of which was that a continual state of low-level war was essential for the government to maintain power. It leaked to the press, and helped influence public opinion against the war in Vietnam."

Today, however, the Civic Circle has much better control. Amit explained the Narrative Architect had an email list called "Journolist," to send real-time talking points out to several hundred key thought leaders, editors, academics, influencers, speech writers, and reporters. "The press," Amit said with disgust, "they don't speak truth to power. They're the power's palace guards."

"Ah." Now it was clear. "That's how that morning news anchor was using the exact talking points only a couple hours after the Thirteen decided on the narrative."

"And they were repeated in Governor Bush's Keynote. Doesn't seem to be completely effective, though," Amit pointed out. "I saw Drudge featured some local reporter who fingered Gomulka as being tied to the Civic Circle. He was all over the salacious elements of the story, and the press are having to play catch-up with him. "

"Hard for anyone to miss that the prime suspect has the exact same unusual name as one of the keynote speakers," I observed. "I'll bet that local reporter saw an arrest log, put two and two together, and it was out before they could suppress the connection."

"Nice to know the Civic Circle's control has limits," Amit noted. The Tong sure managed to get Gomulka in hot water. That firewall they tried to build broke through pretty quickly. It was all over the televisions playing in the lobby between the sessions."

By then, we'd passed the Horton House and continued around the Northern tip of Jekyll Island to arrive at the Beijing Bistro on Beachview Drive.

"You need me to pick you up?" Amit asked.

"No. I figure I can get a ride with Ding Li. Park the van in the lot by the museum and get the keys back to me after lunch, at the plenary on activism at Georgia Tech."

Amit dropped me off, and I went inside.

The maître d' saw me surveying the restaurant and asked, "Are you looking for someone?"

"Yes," I replied. "I'm looking for Miss Ding Li."

"She's waiting for you in the Red Flower Pavilion Room, sir. May I take your phone?" I handed him the folded up potato chip bag. "I will return it after your lunch," he assured me, leading me to the back room. Interesting – that was the same name the Atlanta restaurant gave their private dining room.

"Hello, Peter," she greeted me.

"Hello, Ding Li."

"It would appear we were successful. You set up this Gomulka, and we finished him off. Now, the Civic Circle is being held up to ridicule and contempt."

I was having to get used to her lack of an accent. I was still kicking myself for how badly I'd underestimated her because of her successful act back in Atlanta. A young Chinese man with elf-like features, almost a boy, approached to take our drink orders.

"Green tea," I requested. "Hot." This seemed a traditional Chinese establishment, but in the South it's always wise to specify "hot" tea if you want to avoid receiving sweet iced tea by mistake.

"My pleasure, sir," our waiter replied with enthusiasm. His intensity creeped me out a bit.

"Bring a pot for the table," Ding Li ordered.

"Yes ma'am." He gave me another deeply penetrating look and departed.

Ding Li studied me intently. "You like him?"

I had a feeling I was missing something important. "He seems competent enough."

"You have been most helpful to us." She studied me intently. "You will find us grateful. He is... available."

I suddenly realized what was going on.

"I'm not gay," I blurted out without thinking.

"Oh?" Ding Li looked surprised, but recovered. "He will be disappointed to learn that. I think he likes you." She looked deeply at me and smiled. "But you only like me for my tea?"

I returned her gaze. "I'm not sure when is the right time to embroil someone in a honey trap, but while you're in the middle of collaborating to entrap someone else in one... that's definitely the wrong time."

"That is what you think?" She looked disappointed. "You are a valued ally of the Brotherhood. We are your best friend," she explained smiling, "or we can be your worst enemy." Her expression became cold. The sudden control she had of her features was unnerving.

Just then, our waiter came with the tea. He set the pot down and carefully arranged four cups on the table.

"We'll take the hot pot," Ding Li ordered for us both before I could say anything. "That will be all," she dismissed him. "Leave us." He gave me another creepy stare before departing. With smooth and well-practiced motions, Ding Li deftly poured tea in two of the cups, leaving two empty.

"Note which two of the cups I have filled," she directed me. "You will remember it in the future?"

"Yes," I confirmed. This was like the tea ceremony I'd witnessed between Professor Chen and the restaurant manager before things went south in my first visit.

"That is your confirmation that Mr. Hung is my uncle, and I am authorized to speak on his behalf in matters pertaining to the Brotherhood. Now you take this cup," she gestured. "Pour the contents into that cup, and offer it to me."

I did as she requested.

"That is my confirmation that you are a friend of the Brotherhood, entitled to an audience and such assistance as may be fit to grant. The ritual of the tea ceremony goes back hundreds of years."

I ran through it one more time with her to make sure I had it down.

"Before you will be offered the tea ceremony," Ding Li handed me a beautifully carved jade medallion with an image of a red flower, "you must show this to the gatekeeper: the receptionist, the host, the person at the door of one of our establishments. The medallion signifies that you are a friend, worthy of an audience with Mr. Hung."

She pulled out another jade disk even more beautiful than the first. Gems sparkled from the eyes of a dragon whose tail encircled the globe. "This medallion shows that you are friend of Honorable Shan Zhu. Show this to Mr. Hung if he requires further persuasion to help you. This signifies that a favor done for you is a favor done for Honorable Shan Zhu."

This was not quite what I expected. "Thank you. You honor me with your friendship and the trust of the Brotherhood of the Red Flower Tong."

"So you do understand reciprocity after all?" Ding Li asked with a smile. "Friends do things for their friends."

"I do," I acknowledged. "We have exchanged favors to our mutual benefit. Gomulka attacked Chen and would have had him killed. We have now worked together to avenge our mutual friend by incriminating Gomulka."

"There is more we can do together, though," she pointed out. "Much more. You were brought before the Thirteen this morning. What did they say?"

I tried not to show I was unsettled by the accuracy of her information. "They questioned me regarding Gomulka. I presume they decided upon the narrative you heard from Governor Bush – it's a heroic case of illegal immigration that demonstrates why we should open our borders, and an attempt by pro-Iraqi elements to dissuade us from the righteous cause of deposing Saddam Hussein."

"Yes," Ding Li nodded. "That could have been foreseen. I know you sought to avoid this war, and you thought that incriminating Gomulka would help toward that end. I regret we are at cross-purposes here. The Brotherhood favors the dominion of the Celestial Kingdom. The Civic Circle aims to weaken your nation to impose their own global dominion using the Celestial Kingdom as their instrument. Either way, China is destined to once again dominate the world."

"If the Civic Circle secures control of China and eliminates the West as a rival to their power, the Civic Circle will be much more difficult to overcome," I pointed out.

"True," Ding Li confirmed, "we remain opposed to the Civic Circle. We, not they, are the rightful heirs to the Celestial Kingdom. While we oppose the Civic Circle and seek their overthrow, we will not stand in the way if the Civic Circle serves our ends and acts to the benefit of China.

"If your nation seeks to dissipate its strength in foreign adventures and open the walls of your country to as many foreign invaders as will come, you only hasten your own downfall. On that point, we share the goal of the ancient enemy. The Civic Circle aims to weaken your nation to impose their own global dominion using the Celestial Kingdom as their instrument. We would see the Celestial Kingdom first among the powers of the Earth. In either case, your nation stands in the way."

Just then, our waiter returned with some assistants. He placed the hot pots on the table. Ding Li dismissed him in Chinese. He gave me a look of disappointment and left us.

"What did you tell him?"

"I explained his services would not be needed. He is young. He was looking forward to a chance to serve." Ding Li selectively swept the raw materials from the platters into the three pots.

"I wish to be very clear with you," I explained, the aromas of bubbling broths and cooking meat teasing at my nose. "I will not see my country weakened, if I can help it."

"Understandable," Ding Li acknowledged, "but entirely beyond your control. Xueshu Quan has aligned his forces and made his plans. At the G-8 Summit in two weeks, the leaders of the world will join to endorse his plan as their own, and your nation will move into Iraq and dissipate itself trying to play policeman to the Middle East. The resulting chaos will unleash a hoard of migrants and refugees into Europe, destabilizing and weakening them as well – all to the benefit of the future Celestial Kingdom. It cannot be stopped."

"I intend to stop it, nevertheless."

Ding Li smiled at my naïveté. "You do not have that power, and you should not waste your strength in the attempt. Not many have access to the Thirteen. That is an asset not to be squandered. We will not stand in your way. We do not have to. You cannot stop the war. Save your strength to fight a battle you can win on ground of your choosing."

"You have agreed to not to stand in my way," I replied. "That is all I ask. I understand we may sometimes work at cross-purposes, but I would not have you and your Brotherhood as my enemies nor would it be to your advantage to make an enemy of me."

Ding Li smiled indulgently. "Yes, I did agree, and when a Brother speaks, it is a vow. As I represent the Brotherhood of the Red Flower Tong to you, I bind them as well in this matter. I tell you though, as friend and ally, you must avoid what is strong and strike at what is weak. The ancient enemy is strong. You cannot defeat him in direct combat. You defeat him where he is weak: by thwarting his plans and disrupting his alliances. That is what we have done this day. We removed his piece, Gomulka, from the board without loss to our own side. Take your victory and depart from the field. Do not risk further action."

It was my turn to smile indulgently at Ding. "We must each fight the ancient enemy as we think best."

Ding Li gave up trying to dissuade me. "Try this." She picked up a morsel with her chopsticks and fed it to me. She smiled seductively at the pleasure I found in the delicious morsel. "Help yourself," she gestured at the simmering pots of broth.

I sampled from each pot.

"Speaking of the ancient enemy," she changed the subject, "what was your impression of Xueshu Quan?"

"What?"

"You met him," Ding Li insisted. "He is the Worshipful Master of the Civic Circle, Chairman of the Thirteen, Scourge of the Ming."

"That was him?"

Ding Li smiled again. "Yes. I have never met him, myself. Those who have tell me they can feel he is... wrong. They say they can sense his unnatural evil. I think that is superstition. I think he is a man, a man chosen from among the Thirteen, not some ancient god or demon. You met him. What do you think?"

I replayed the meeting in my mind. "There was something definitely wrong about him. Something... off." I thought how I could explain it. "There is a concept in robotics called the 'uncanny valley.' You've heard of it?"

Ding Li shook her head, no. "I know of robots, but not of this 'uncanny valley.'"

"As robots look more and more human, people become more comfortable with them... to a point. When robots strongly resemble humans, but have noticeable flaws or imperfections, people feel a sense of revulsion, a distaste for them. Then, as they perfectly match humans, people like them again. That distaste, that sense of wrongness at what is a close, but not perfect representation of the human face or form, that is what is called the uncanny valley."

"Of course," Ding Li acknowledged. "We are programmed by our genes to be very sensitive to the imperfections of others. We have to be, to select a healthy mate." She was looking suggestively at me again.

What was I saying? Right. Uncanny valley. "There is a sense of wrongness about the Worshipful Master. He doesn't quite move as he should. Maybe it's a neurological disorder? I can see why people think he is not quite human."

"I had not thought of it that way. That is a potential weakness." She nodded and smiled. "See, there is much we can do together. We can reward you handsomely for your information and insights. Have you not wondered about the Eight Ways of Pleasure?"

I suppressed a guilty smile. "Yes, I have speculated on what they might entail."

"There are things a woman can do to a man," she reached out and with a single finger she stroked my forearm. "There are things a man can do to a woman." She repeated the process on my other arm with two fingers. "And, there are things a man and a woman can do together." With three fingers she touched my nose and ran her fingers across my lips and chin. She looked expectantly at me. "They are not individual techniques, but rather describe an entire family within the arts of pleasure."

"That's three," I noted.

"You are engineer. You understand math," she smiled. "Do you know permutations?"

I wasn't following her.

"They are not mutually exclusive," she explained. "The three can be done in any combination, and the eighth way of pleasure is when you mix techniques from all three together..." She licked her lips again. "...simultaneously."

I felt myself getting way too interested in what she had to say. I took a deep breath and distracted myself by thinking through the permutations. It was easiest to think in terms of binary numbers with one bit assigned to each way: 001, 010, 011, 100, 101, 110, 111. "That makes only seven," I pointed out.

She smiled. "Before you progress to combinations of the three, there is the initial stage of attraction, the building of interest, the flirtation."

Ah. I was forgetting 000. "You seem to really enjoy your work." I distracted myself with another serving.

"What is not to like?" She smiled again. "I serve in the company of heroes playing a part in the Brotherhood's noble cause. I reward other heroes who have served our cause. I inspire them to greatness."

"That is how you will spend your whole life?" I asked.

"No," she replied. "Soon I will find a hero. He will take me as his. I will bear him a son, and I will be wife and mother to heroes."

What? I froze. Did she think that I was going to...?

"Not you," Ding Li giggled happily at my look of consternation. "You are too young to be my husband. I am the favored of Honorable Shan Zhu, but he is too old. Soon though, he will find a hero for me, or I will find a hero of my own, and he will approve the match."

I wasn't sure whether to be upset or relieved that she didn't regard me as husband material. I compromised by savoring the last bite of lunch as I thought how to broach the final subject I needed to discuss with her. "The people you smuggled in the cargo container. Why?"

"You have an expression, do you not?" Ding Li looked at me "Waste not, want not? The container was coming anyway. They paid handsomely for the privilege of coming to your country. Everyone who came has a story of oppression and persecution that will rend the hearts of your investigators and ensure asylum. Then, our friends will agree to sponsor them, and we will find a place for them within our organization."

I took a deep breath and decided not to tell her that the Thirteen had similar plans. If both sides were battling it out, maybe that would buy more time for the immigrants.

"I have to be getting back," I explained. "There's a session on activism at Georgia Tech, and I need to learn what insanity they're planning to unleash on my school for next year."

"Your baizuo," Ding Li shook her head, "they advocate equality only to satisfy their feeling of moral superiority to everyone else. They call discrimination, 'affirmative action.' They call obesity, 'positive body image.' They censor those they disagree with in the name of 'tolerance.' In the name of 'equality,' they make the groups that support them superior to others. They make war and call it 'peace.' They point deer, say horse."

"Point deer, say horse?"

"You don't know story? Bad schools you have," she shook her head woefully at the state of American education before continuing.

"Zhao Gao, chancellor to the emperor, brought a deer before the court, telling them it was a horse. The Emperor laughed and said, 'That is a deer, not a horse.' Then the Emperor questioned the officials. Some said it was a deer. Some remained silent. Others, hoping to ingratiate themselves with Zhao Gao, agreed that the deer was a horse."

Ding Li paused, looking into my eyes with an almost creepy intensity. "Zhao Gao arranged the execution of all who said the deer was a deer. Thus, did he sow terror and cement his power in the court. Only an obvious and ridiculous lie serves to show where one's loyalties lie."

I understood. "Force people to lie to show their loyalty, and make them complicit in their own bondage."

"Indeed." Ding Li rose. "The specific lies they force you to say are irrelevant. It is your submission they want – the fact that they have forced you to deny the truth. That is how they demonstrate their power over you."

She led me to the door.

"It is a shame you have other plans for the afternoon," she smiled seductively at me. "Let's see what your next year at school will bring!"

* * *

The ballroom at the Convention Center was almost as packed as it had been for Governor Bush. Apparently, they hadn't had time to make signs for the new keynote speaker, Dr. Cindy Ames. Gomulka's name was crossed out, and hers was written above.

I was a bit surprised to see Amit was the lead speaker. He was clearly being groomed for bigger and better things, as an official "spokes teen" for the Civic Youth.

"I grew up colored in Appalachia," Amit began with his well-honed tale of victimization, "I came of age alone, amid a sea of white faces, a symbol to the simple Appalachian hill folk of 'the other' they saw threatening their way of life after 9/11. I became a lightning rod for their fears and frustrations, a focal point for their resentment of the oppressive economic system that for many had passed them by."

Amit's presentation was backed by well-chosen visuals projected on the screen behind him – images of the Appalachians, pictures of poorly dressed folks in front of run-down trailer homes, a school photo of a young Amit and his classmates, the shocking footage of the plane flying into the Capitol building.

"I had hoped to escape the stifling monoculture of my backwoods hometown by embarking on a course of study in the metropolitan community of Atlanta at the diverse Georgia Institute of Technology."

The screen showed idyllic images of the Tech Tower and 'diverse' collections of smiling students hanging out on campus, straight from the recruiting website.

"Alas, Georgia Tech remains barely a generation removed from the era of Jim Crow, and still harbors deep reservoirs of resentment at those who have overcome prejudice and discrimination. Bigotry exists to pull down the successful in the out group, and to justify the mediocrity of the in group. Bigotry hurts not only its victims, but also its perpetrators. Rather than strive to improve themselves, bigots seek to tear down those who are different and dare to succeed."

Amit's words were backed by images of the student protests, the "Engineering for Engineers" protestors facing off against the "Engineering for Everyone" Social Justice Warriors. He had the audience in the palm of his hand with his stirring rhetoric. He'd won admission to the Social Justice Initiative at Georgia Tech on the strength of his narrative, and it had only become more polished in the intervening time.

"I was there this past spring when the fascists said that a woman could never head the College of Engineering. I was there, marching with the students who insisted that 'Engineering is for Everyone.' I was there when a physics professor flaunted his toxic masculinity and reduced half of humanity to sexual objects. I was there when his oppressed colleague became complicit in her own oppression by supporting him. And I was there when Madison Grant exposed this toxic masculinity to the world, and the campus rose up to cast out the fascists!"

Amit had a rather creative reinterpretation of what happened, but it sure got the audience fired up. The screen behind him faded to white, making Amit an amorphous silhouette.

"I have seen the enemy," Amit proclaimed, a fist in the air. "The enemy is not the other. The enemy is he who seeks to divide us!

"As a man, I would not presume to speak to the struggles faced by women. We have among us many heroic women with strong voices, women who have overcome prejudice and discrimination to shine as examples for us all. It's my honor to introduce one of them, my fellow student and courageous crusader for social justice, Madison Grant."

Amit waved at the crowd giving him a standing ovation and then gestured toward Madison and began joining in as if the crowd were applauding her arrival. The screen faded to black as Madison came to the podium. The transition was artfully done.

Madison stood awkwardly at the podium waiting for the cheering to die down before beginning.

"Like Amit, I had no idea what I was getting myself into when I started at Georgia Tech. I was overwhelmed by the hatred and negativity. At Georgia Tech, men can do anything and women can only watch them! When they hounded Professor Cindy Ames out and refused to give her a fair hearing as head of the College of Engineering, it was a stinging slap in the face to women at Georgia Tech and around the world – a cruel reminder that no matter how far we've come, there's still a glass ceiling."

She looked down at her notes.

"That's not all! The patriarchal hegemony in science and engineering at Georgia Tech provides a breeding ground for misogynistic chauvinism and harassment! Physics Professor Wu Chen tried to normalize the sexual objectification of women!" The screen showed Professor Chen in his garish shirt with sexy women riding motorcycles and wielding firearms. Madison detailed his many sins and spoke tearfully about how the pervasive atmosphere of "toxic masculinity" deterred her from pursuing studies in science at Tech.

Next, she took off after Professor Graf. They'd artfully modified some of the images from the second press conference – made the colors more garish, removed the background of the auditorium, and added smoke effects. It made Marlena look like a model walking down a catwalk – no. Less dignified. They made Marlena look like... a stripper or pole dancer. Madison argued that women like Professor Graf were complicit in their own bondage.

"We must have diversity and tolerance at all costs! If they refuse to break their chains, if they encourage the subjugation of themselves and others to the patriarchy, they cannot be tolerated! We must not rest until they are gone! There can be no safe space for hate! No safe space for hate!"

She got the crowd fired up and chanting. I joined in enthusiastically, of course. I happened to see Johnny Rice standing off to the side, slack-jawed, shaking his head, not believing the insanity he was witnessing.

"When they told us a woman couldn't lead the College of Engineering, we said 'No!' When the Chinese spy, Professor Wu Chen, and his accomplice Professor Marlena Graf tried to tell us that sexual oppression in physics was OK, we said, 'No!' When Graf told us women should just lie back and try to enjoy sexual harassment, we said 'No!'"

The screen showed images of Marlena holding up the shirt she'd made for Professor Chen featuring sexy women scientists. The photo caught Marlena mid-word with her mouth open in a crazy looking expression. Then the screen shifted to a sober and somber looking professional headshot of Cindy Ames.

They tried to silence her," Madison closed strongly, "but you can't keep a good woman down! Now she's back! Ready to fight... and win! I give you, Doctor Cindy Ames!"

Ames rose to the podium amid yet another standing ovation. She held up both hands to silence the crowd, like a conductor preparing to direct an orchestra.

"The toxic masculinity of Science, Technology, Engineering, and Math – in other words 'STEM' studies – indoctrinates students in context-free, ethics-free, absolutist thought," she dove right in. "Traditional STEM studies brainwash students in archaic binary modes of thought, to believe that there are right answers and wrong answers instead of a spectrum of alternate truths. Traditional STEM studies train students to think abstractly, in a detached fashion that encourages them to disregard the contextuality of oppressed groups that may have different but equally valid truths to share."

The screen showed photos of vibrant and diverse students in various states of discouragement at the microaggressions suffered at the hands of their oppressive teachers and classmates.

"Traditional STEM studies hold up as a virtue such patriarchal norms as 'asking good questions,' 'capacity for abstract thought and rational thought processes,' 'motivation,' so-called 'independent' thinking, and a relatively low fear of failure. This toxic masculinity deters women and other oppressed peoples who have different values and different virtues to offer from participating in STEM."

Dr. Ames chronicled the many wrongs perpetrated by STEM studies and practitioners, from the "use of Greek letters that perpetuate the myth of the supposed deep European roots of mathematics," to the "obvious hetero-patriarchal bias in awarding research grants to overwhelmingly white, male, STEM practitioners instead of language, philosophy, and women's and cultural studies researchers."

The screen juxtaposed white male researchers in shiny clean labs full of glittering equipment with more "diverse" academics in run-down, cluttered, dirty offices and workspaces.

"My scholarship merges cutting edge techniques from the frontiers of Women's and Cultural Studies to create open, democratic classrooms, in which all students are free to flourish. Each student is unique, an individual snowflake, requiring the correct culturally inclusive pedagogy that shields them from harmful microaggressions and makes even historically underrepresented students feel welcomed."

Dr. Ames continued to extoll the virtues of her modern approach to STEM education while the screen behind her showed happy, diverse, smiling students working together, holding vials of colored liquids, standing in front of blackboards with... high school algebra? I coughed to suppress a laugh as one of the images showed a young woman pretending to solder the wrong side of a circuit board while holding the iron on what would have been the heated tip.

"The only way to get sexism out of STEM is to get more women into STEM. But that's not enough! It's time to move beyond superficial numerical measures of equality. It's not enough to have 50% women in STEM so long as STEM itself continues to poison the world with its toxic masculinity. We must change STEM itself!

"No longer can mathematics remain value neutral, educating our youth in ethics-free, absolutist thought. Math indoctrinates students that there are right and wrong answers. Math trains students in detached and calculative reasoning that disregards the contextuality of those with differing yet equally valid opinions. Math is a tool for the distribution of money, the very instrument by which we manipulate and cause vast disparities in wealth.

"The math we teach is littered with the symbols of oppression, punctuated with 'greater than' or 'less than' signs.

"In the future, there must be only equality!"

The crowd roared their approval.

"There are many champions of social justice at Georgia Tech. You've met a couple of them here today. Allies like Amit Patel, who bravely stood up for women and social justice. His provocative theory that systemic discrimination and cultural pressure are responsible for the disparities between male and female athletic performance is under contract to a major publishing house and will appear just in time for the holidays!"

The screen showed the cover of Amit's book, *Think Yourself Thin: The New Theory of How Expectations Shape our Bodies' Reality*. I noted the cover already declared it to be a *New York Times* Bestseller some four months before the scheduled release.

"And there's Madison Grant, the intrepid young journalist whose Pulitzer-nominated reporting exposed both sexism and a Chinese spy ring at Georgia Tech!"

The screen showed Madison's article in the Georgia Tech student newspaper, *The Technique*, still shots of Madison's tearful interviews on CNN, and photos of her leading protests on campus.

"I'm pleased to announce," Dr. Ames continued, "that forward thinkers in the Physics Department have merged the positions of the disgraced Professors Chen and Graf to create an Endowed Chair in Social Justice Studies in Physics. I will be at Georgia Tech starting this fall, directing the Social Justice Initiative and helping to lead Georgia Tech to a new era of tolerance, inclusivity, and equality! The era of bigotry, sexism, and racism is over! We will deplatform all the heads of the Medusa!"

The crowd went wild at Dr. Ames' impending triumph over the reactionary forces of the hetero-patriarchal hegemony that thwarted her last year. Or something like that.

On autopilot, I rose to join the herd in the standing ovation. Only then, did I realize the implications. Ames was replacing Gomulka. The Civic Circle was going all out to win the battle they'd lost last year. They were making a major, high-profile attempt to converge the campus.

The floor was finally opened to questioners who competed in gushing about Dr. Ames' bravery and her courage at leading the charge to defeat sexism and racism at Georgia Tech. Finally, I saw Johnny Rice step up to the microphone. "How can you claim to be a champion of tolerance when you propose to deny a platform and silence anyone who disagrees with you?"

"If you tolerate intolerance, then intolerance becomes tolerated and tolerance dies," Dr. Ames explained. "The one thing you can never tolerate is intolerance. You should educate yourself on the paradox of tolerance. It all follows from quantum mechanics."

Dr. Ames stared smugly at Johnny. "Reality manifests itself in contradiction. That's the lesson of quantum mechanics. The deepest truths appear to be contradictory to our limited minds. Niels Bohr called it 'complementarity.' When we reduce political axioms to deep contradictions, that's how we know we've arrived at fundamental truths."

CHAPTER 12: THE PRISONERS' DILEMMA

I caught up with Amit at a Civic Youth Workshop on Social Justice Convergence.

"The initial step of convergence is to demand inclusion in the enemy's private spaces," the speaker, a dreadlocked young woman from Berkeley, began, giving examples like women seeking access to men's clubs.

Amit sat in the back of the room with me. "What's with your friend from TAGS?" Amit whispered. "Johnny Rice?"

"The second step," the speaker continued, "is to demand the enemy change their space to accommodate us."

"I think Johnny got woke last night, in a good way." I explained what happened.

"These demands inevitably cause resentment and frustration. The third step in social justice convergence," the dreadlocked woman tossed her ratty looking hair, "is to demand the enemy stop harassing us because they don't like our demands!"

"Johnny's been chatting with the Civic Youth," Amit said softly. "He explains how he wants to understand their diverse perspectives and then he ties them up in logical knots and exposes their contradictions. He's driving them crazy."

"Step four in social justice convergence is to demand new rules or laws to remove the enemy from 'our' space because they won't fall in line with our vision for what the space should be!" Now our instructor was glaring at us for whispering in her talk. It was hard to pay attention, though, since we'd heard it all before from Gomulka. I pretended to be interested.

"In step five, you tell the enemy to get out. 'Why don't you go off and create your own space if you don't like ours?'"

"We need George P. Burdell to reach out to him." Amit whispered. I tried to figure out how we could accomplish this. I didn't want to reach out to him at TAGS — it might be too obvious to link it back to me. We'd need to track Johnny down on campus once classes started in the fall.

"The sixth and final step in convergence is to demand the enemy not create their own space after we've kicked them out of what is now 'our' space." I looked through the program. I'd noticed all the elite boarding limos and buses and heading back to the Jekyll Island Club Hotel after Dr. Ames' keynote. There was nothing on the program about sessions or activities there, though. Another secret meeting? One to which even trusted Civic Youth weren't invited?

"You!" an angry girl grabbed my shoulder. I turned around. "How dare you stand me up?" It was Comfortable Shoe Girl. What was her name? I had completely forgotten about her after Amit and I were called away by Bernard.

"I'm sorry. I got called away by Bernard. Business before pleasure." I smiled at her.

"You could have at least called or something," she pointed out.

"I don't have your number." I opened a new contact form and handed her my phone.

She stood a moment, uncertain. Then she took my phone and entered her name and number.

Ah, Jessica. From Mount Holyoke. Now I remembered. "We're heading for dinner, Jessica" I told her. "You can join us."

She looked disappointed. "I'm supposed to be at a reception for Women in Media."

"Some other time then."

Amit and I grabbed a bite to eat.

"Not bad," Amit rated my performance, "You got the number close, but never apologize to a girl. It makes you look weak and needy."

"I really have too much going on to be trying to pick up girls."

For once, Amit didn't dispute me. "I have the evening free. Maybe I'll head on to that Women in Media event." He smiled. "Good luck tonight."

I hopped the shuttle to the Jekyll Island Club Hotel.

* * *

"So, Mister High-and-Mighty's finally gonna make an appearance," Mr. Humphreys welcomed me back to the Network Ops room in the basement of the Jekyll Island Club Hotel. "What the hell happened to you? Last night, I got this call that you were fired, then this morning, you were 'reassigned' to be in the Civic Youth as an ambassador from TAGS."

"There did seem to be some confusion on that point," I acknowledged. "I figured I'd come by and see if I could help out."

"You take the support line." He shoved it my direction.

"Yes, sir."

He wasn't even trying to pretend he wasn't in the middle of another of his online games. "I put in my full shift. I may be on call, but now that you're here, I'm off duty," he explained, noticing me noticing what he was up to.

"No problem. I got it covered."

What I had in mind was going to be a bit tricky. Fortunately, it was a slow night. Everyone seemed to be attending alcohol-soaked parties, not agonizing over their Internet connectivity. I pulled up the network management software. I looked up the IP address for the router and wireless access point in the cottage reserved for the Bank of the Holy See.

I scheduled a firmware update for the router, pointing the updater to a random text file. That should thoroughly scramble the router. Then, I wrote a separate script to copy the log file and overwrite it just after the firmware update. Finally my script would erase itself. That ought to cover my tracks. I checked the timing. I had fifteen minutes.

"I need to get a cup of coffee," I told Mr. Humphreys. "Want anything? I'm buying."

"Get me a tall mocha. With whipped cream." Heh. I knew he wouldn't be able to resist my offer.

I ran upstairs, squeezed my way through the crowd to the bar, and placed my order. I saw Rob looking immaculate in his servers' uniform circulating through the crowd collecting trays of dirty glasses and dessert plates. I don't think he saw me. I looked at my watch. I had a few minutes to spare. I took my time bringing the drinks back down to the network control center.

T-minus thirty seconds.

I walked in. "Here's your tall mocha with whipped cream." I handed him his drink.

Mr. Humphreys thanked me with an inarticulate grunt.

I glanced at my watch. Ten seconds... Nothing.

Did it work? I saw the connectivity light go yellow. I pretended not to notice, and got up to throw away the drink carrier. A minute later the connectivity light turned red, and an alarm started chirping."

Mr. Humphreys glanced up at me, a frown on his face.

"I got it," I acknowledged, silencing the alarm.

His attention returned to his online adventure.

Gee. Loss of connectivity to the Holy See Bank's cottage. I tried a remote reset, which didn't work because I'd thoroughly scrambled the firmware.

"I got a bum router," I announced.

"Reflash the firmware," Mr. Humphreys muttered, his attention focused on his game.

Oops. If I overwrote my garbage firmware with the correct firmware, that would solve the problem I'd just created. I should have thought through that contingency. I quickly made a backup copy of the correct firmware so I could undo what I was about to do. Then, I overwrote the correct firmware with my garbage firmware.

"What's taking so long?" Mr. Humphreys asked.

"Checking the firmware update," I lied. "Trying it now."

I reflashed the firmware, and nothing happened because I'd just overwritten the original garbage file with the exact same garbage file.

"Still broken," I announced. "I'll run over there and replace the access point."

Mr. Humphreys finally looked up from his game, a frown on his face. "Download the latest firmware update from the support site and try that."

Yeah, that would also solve the problem I'd created. He wasn't making it easy for me to complete my sabotage. I went through the motions of downloading the latest firmware and immediately overwrote it with my garbage file. Now, I was going to need to get the correct files updated to hide the evidence of what I'd done, but time was running out. I had to get over to the cottage. Naturally, the update still failed.

"Didn't work," I announced.

"Go fix it, then," Mr. Humphreys grunted.

Finally.

I grabbed a spare router and the tool box in one hand, my coffee in the other as I headed out. The security guys at the door searched my tool box, and even looked inside my coffee cup. They were disturbingly professional.

The cottage was just a couple hundred yards away on Riverview Drive. I knocked on the door.

I waited.

I knocked on the door again.

Bulldog opened the door. "You," he said. "What do you want?"

"Your Internet is down," I explained, "and I need to fix it."

He eyed me suspiciously.

"I really need to take care of this." I held a finger to my lips. "Quietly."

He glared at me a moment. Then, Bulldog let me in.

I pulled a big foil bag out of my tool box.

He got the idea, deposited his cell phone in the bag, and took the bag. "Follow me." Bulldog led me to the living room. An old man looked up at us, raising an eyebrow. Bulldog held the foil bag out to him. The old man turned his phone off, removed the battery and placed it in the bag. He picked up a remote, turned on the TV, and cranked up the volume until it was uncomfortably loud.

"That's not necessary," I assured him. "I disabled the data connection to your cottage and all the surveillance gear runs through it."

"Better safe than sorry," he said softly, leaning toward me. I recognized the voice. It was Brother Francis, as I'd suspected. He turned to Bulldog with a gentle grin. "Please ask... Caitlin to join us. Immediately."

"Be seated," Brother Francis turned his attention back to me as Bulldog withdrew. "Now, is there anything you'd like to tell me before they return?"

I laid my cards on the table. "I need to speak with you about an opportunity to decapitate the Civic Circle."

"Why ever would you want to do such a thing?" I could see the twinkle in his eye. "I understand you are a confidant of the Thirteen, and you've even met the Worshipful Master, himself."

"You know perfectly well they killed my parents," I pointed out. "You told me as much yourself not two months ago up in Chattanooga."

Brother Francis nodded. "You have made a most remarkable use of your two months," he said shrewdly. "In only two months you have worked your way into a position in which you can rub shoulders with the Thirteen. I know many who have spent a lifetime trying, and failing, to accomplish the same. Only two months," he repeated, his eyes looking right through me. "Amazing. Unless, of course, you've been working at it a bit longer. And have some help."

Just then Bulldog and Perky Girl – Caitlin? – came down the stairs. Her hair was wet, and she was wearing a too-short green silk kimono. Our eyes met. She halted – her pale skin reddened as she adjusted the kimono to better cover her cleavage and crossed her arms in modesty. I noticed there wasn't a ring on that finger as my eyes swept down to her exposed but well-toned thighs. I looked back up in time to see her eyes flash at me in anger at the impertinence of my gaze. Bulldog gently took her arm and pulled her into the living room.

Brother Francis smiled indulgently at Bulldog, "You could have let her get dressed, first."

Caitlin glared silently at Bulldog then back at me.

"You said, 'immediately,' Boss." Bulldog did actually seem a bit chastened.

"My apologies to you both. What's done is done," Brother Francis turned back to me. "Young Mr. Burdell here was just explaining how in a mere two months from discovering that the Civic Circle murdered his parents, he managed to work his way into the confidence of the Thirteen."

"Yeah, we'd all like to hear about that," Bulldog said, looming menacingly over me.

"I'm not at liberty to discuss my secrets," I explained. "I'm here to explain to you how we can decapitate the Civic Circle tomorrow night. They will be meeting in their Inner Sanctum under the Sans Souci, next door to the Jekyll Island Club Hotel."

"Just as you're not at liberty to discuss your intimate luncheon with your charming associate Miss Ding Li in the Red Flower Pavilion of the Beijing Bistro earlier today?" Brother Francis asked.

They had a disturbingly accurate account of my day's activities. "I am no more aligned with the Red Flower Tong than I am with the Ordo Alberti," I assured him. "I am an independent actor."

"Then we're back to my original question," Brother Francis offered mildly. "An independent actor who rubs shoulders with the Red Flower Tong, and the Thirteen, and who now shows up on our doorstep with an incredible offer to 'do in' the leadership of the Civic Circle. Note, I mean that in the literal sense... incredible as in 'lacking in credibility.'"

"They got that place locked up good," Bulldog gestured back toward the Jekyll Island Club Hotel. "Guards at all the entrances, and two quick response teams – one active and the other on reserve at all times. You'd need at least a company of MOUT-trained troops to take the place. Best case, they'd take significant casualties, slaughter dozens of civilians, and by the time they finally broke through to the Sanctum, the Thirteen would be long gone through some rat hole to a safe house."

"Mowt?"

Bulldog looked at me and snorted in disgust at my ignorance. "Military Operations, Urban Terrain: MOUT. Jesus." He shook his head.

"Do not take the Lord's name in vain," Brother Francis admonished Bulldog, and then looked back at me. "You understand our skepticism?"

I was going to have to build trust by offering them a bit of the truth. "I already knew the Civic Circle was behind my parents' murders," I acknowledged. "I've been working for this moment for over a year."

"Still," Brother Francis pointed out, "you've made some truly remarkable progress. I was particularly impressed at how you managed to make the late Professor Graf vanish without a trace after so casually allowing her to be poisoned."

Perky Girl – it was going to take time for me to think of her as "Caitlin" – got daggers in her eyes again.

I started to explain, to offer the same story I'd already told Caitlin, but Brother Francis held up a hand to silence me.

"I'm honored by the trust you placed in us," he continued. "We told you the poison was lethal and you made the good Professor vanish so she could live out her remaining days in peace. That's what you told Caitlin here, after all."

"Yes," I confirmed my lie.

"Instead of taking the good Professor to the hospital? Instead of checking to see if perhaps we might possibly be mistaken and the marvels of modern medical science might cure your Professor or at least ease her pain? Your confidence in us is truly inspiring."

He was looking through me again. I remained silent. He smiled at me.

"Professor Graf isn't really dead, now, is she?" Brother Francis asked.

"What?" Caitlin asked in an almost shriek of surprise.

Bulldog looked shocked, too. He glared at me in the realization that I had fooled them.

"Your silence is all the confirmation I need," Brother Francis explained.

"Did you..." Caitlin seemed almost incoherent. "You turned her over to the Tong, didn't you?" Her anger was back.

He was wicked clever, figuring it all out. I'd give him that. I took a deep breath. "She is alive and well in a place of her own choosing, not with the Red Flower Tong. I'm sure she wouldn't mind my extending her thanks to you for your efforts on her behalf and for your offer to provide her with sanctuary. Even though you imperiled my own plan to save Professor Graf by delaying my arrival until the last possible minute."

"Too many cooks plotting in the kitchen," Brother Francis chuckled. "Sometimes an occupational hazard in our line of work. Now what is your relation to Red Flower Tong?"

"I met them when I saved Professor Chen," I explained. "Chen made the introduction."

"And they felt in your debt for your having saved their 'nephew,' Professor Chen," Brother Francis concluded. "I take it Miss Ding Li has been repaying that debt to you?"

"No." Now it was my turn to be embarrassed. "Not exactly. The Tong helped me implicate Professor Gomulka."

"That was your doing?" Now Brother Francis actually seemed surprised. "I thought Gomulka was merely dirty. It's happened before. I should have known the Red Flower Tong had their fingers in that mess."

"You arranged for that human trafficking?" I'd exhausted Caitlin's outrage. She was cold and hard. "You monster."

"No," I insisted. "I thought they were going to incriminate him with a load of drugs..."

"...and they substituted those people instead," Brother Francis nodded. "A container full of illicit narcotics would have cost them a considerable amount of money. They probably made enough money off charging those youngsters passage to America to turn a profit on the operation as well. Typical. What's more, they're probably planning on diverting their 'cargo' into their network of massage parlors and brothels." Brother Francis was a couple steps ahead of me.

"That's part of why I need assistance," I explained. "The Civic Circle plans on making them all vanish on Pleasure Island, some Caribbean island resort where..."

"We know of the place." Brother Francis looked at Caitlin who nodded. "It would be kinder to turn them over to the mercies of the Tong."

"Can you help them out?"

Brother Francis paused. I could see he was troubled.

"I can help," I offered.

"We will see what we can do." He agreed finally. "I'm sorry. Sometimes I feel overwhelmed by the deviousness of the Great Deceiver's plan."

"Oh?" I asked.

"Sexual immorality. Licentiousness. Promiscuity."

I wasn't sure what he was driving at. I said so.

"You must never forget that behind the Princes of the Earth is the Prince of this Earth: the Great Deceiver and the Great Tempter himself, Satan."

I must still have looked confused.

"I'll put it bluntly for you," Bulldog offered. "A huge proportion of young women today are f..." he glanced over at Brother Francis, "...are 'hooking up' with men who are way out of their league – men who are looking for an easy lay with a woman they'd never consider for any kind of long-term relationship. Men like variety. Women like the illusion that an important, powerful, handsome man takes them seriously."

Relationship advice from Bulldog? Beneath his thuggish exterior there was a thoughtful mind – and another example why I should never underestimate anyone based on their appearance.

"When you remove the bounds of morality," Brother Francis continued, "when you eliminate the stigma of promiscuity, you have a small number of top-tier men monopolizing the attentions of a much larger group of women. Have you heard of the 'Prisoner's Dilemma?'"

"I think so," I replied, wondering how my attempt to engage the Albertians in a plan to decapitate the Civic Circle had meandered off into a discussion of the game theory of promiscuity. "If two prisoners refuse to rat out each other they face a minimal punishment. There's some advantage to betraying the other, and the other is punished severely. So it might be to the personal advantage of each prisoner to betray the other, even though the outcome overall is worse for both. How does that apply here?"

"When men and women cooperate with each other," Brother Francis explained, "they both benefit. Each gets a lifetime monogamous mate to love and cherish. The man gives up sexual variety, the woman holds herself chaste instead of giving herself to any attractive man who will have her. All too often, that's not what happens."

"The woman who chooses to betray that social contract for the sake of sexual attention from men above her league gets what she wants," Caitlin offered, "but only in the short term. Women aren't willing to accept a downgrade. Do you think an attractive '7/10' woman is going to be happy settling down with a 7 guy when she's been sleeping with the 9s and 10s? That's not how it works. She gets bitter and angry that the 9 or 10 man is 'too immature,' 'too much of an asshole,' 'too much of a man-child' to commit to her."

"And why should they?" Bulldog pointed out. "Those 9 and 10 guys are in pussy paradise. Why should they give it up to go exclusive with any particular woman? And if they do, it won't be with the 7 who barely rises to the level of a one-night stand."

"If a woman is exceptionally self-aware," Caitlin continued, "she might realize that the 7/10 guy is all she can get and keep long-term, but he's never going to be able to fully satisfy her. More likely, she'll pass to the wrong side of 30 with nothing to show for it but a string of failed relationships, a mediocre job, and a couple of cats to fill the emotional void left by her failure to bear any children."

"Think of it," Brother Francis added sadly. "She will forsake a crown of beauty for ashes, and cast off a garment of praise for the spirit of despair. She will become the first genetic dead end in a line stretching all the way back to Eve.

"And what should men do?" Brother Francis asked rhetorically. "Suffer a passionless marriage to a woman who can never truly love him? Or worse, choose 'betray' also in the Prisoners' Dilemma of life – a life of involuntary celibacy? Or join together with their brothers to master the tactics of 'pick-up-artists' to try to enhance their apparent status, to try to become one of the elite men at the top of the hierarchy and capture their fair share of the poisoned banquet of promiscuity?"

That last sounded disturbingly familiar. Before I could interrupt and try to get the discussion back on track, Brother Francis continued.

"Both genders are increasingly choosing 'betray,'" he concluded, "trying to have it all, and in exchange receiving nothing. Lifelong monogamy is not a natural state for a man and a woman. It requires mutual sacrifice for mutual benefit. It requires social pressure to be enforced. If it's not... the consequences are disastrous. Multiply this by millions. Plummeting birth rates, plagues of sexually transmitted diseases, epidemics of mental illness and depression, male rage that manifests in violent attacks. And it's only going to get worse, much worse. Technology may improve every year, but society... and human happiness... are in decline. In large part, that's because we have abandoned the notion of monogamy."

I thought about what they'd been telling me. Something clicked. "Of course!" I shared my epiphany. "The Civic Circle doesn't seek to rule our society."

They looked at me, puzzled.

"The Civic Circle seeks to remake our society into one that is easily ruled. There is a difference. They aren't attacking the 9s and 10s as you put it. The elite will still have their choices, their sexual access, and their ability to perpetuate themselves. They will be the 9s and 10s in the new order they're building. Their goal is to wipe out the tier right below them: the middle class, that great band of aspiring 6s, 7s, and 8s who threaten their dominance. They want to secure their elite status and build a moat between them and anyone who could threaten their position. They want a society of the elite and the peasants, with no fractious strivers in between to curtail or limit their power."

"A modern-day feudal society complete with a kind of droit du seigneur," Brother Francis nodded.

"Fascinating as this is," I cut him off, "our time is limited. If you're serious about tackling the Civic Circle head-on, I can show you how to decapitate them."

"Very well," Brother Francis agreed indulgently. "Let's hear about this grand plan of yours to 'decapitate' the Civic Circle."

He still wasn't taking me seriously, but at least it gave me the opening I needed. "First, we need champagne." I handed a slip of paper to Bulldog. "Call and order this Krug vintage."

Bulldog looked skeptical.

"Do it," Brother Francis still seemed amused. "Let's see what happens."

Bulldog handed the slip to Caitlin. "I'll stay here with our guest. Please bring me some ice water. And perhaps you could change into something less revealing."

"I'll take one too, please!" I added.

Caitlin didn't look particularly happy at either Bulldog or me. As she departed, I reached for the map I had in my sock. I saw Bulldog's hand go under his jacket. "Take it easy," I assured him, pulling up my pants cuff to show him my sock with the scroll inside.

Bulldog relaxed a bit, but it was clear he was still wary about me.

I pulled out the map and unrolled it on the coffee table.

I let Bulldog and Brother Francis study it.

Caitlin returned in a few minutes, carrying a tray with the ice water, but still wearing the kimono. "The champagne is coming." She offered us the ice water.

"Thanks," I took a sip from my glass, observing her noticeably erect nipples pressing against the silk.

"Thank you," Bulldog glared at me and cleared his throat. Then, he took a sip from his glass and turned back to Caitlin. "I thought you were going to get changed."

"If this outfit is modest enough for me to wear when you introduce me to our guest," she replied, "I see no reason why I shouldn't continue wearing it."

Bulldog paused a moment in surprise at Cailin's comment. Then he looked at Brother Francis as if expecting him to intervene.

Brother Francis only smiled slightly and maintained a diplomatic silence. Bulldog looked back at Caitlin making no attempt to hide his visual survey of her revealing attire. The two locked eyes with each other and said nothing.

"Now that you're back, Caitlin," Brother Francis finally broke the deadlock, "this is a map of the area around the Jekyll Island Club from before it was built."

"Indian mounds?" Caitlin studied the map. "This layout looks like..."

"Exactly," I confirmed her hunch. "This 'wall' is now under Pier Road. Here's 'Indian Mound' Cottage – that's the one the Rockefellers built. The Goodyear Cottage is here. Dubignon Cottage is there, just on the far side of Old

Plantation Road. This cottage we're in? It's right here, built on that mound. Finally, look at this big mound, here."

"Right next door to the Jekyll Island Club Hotel – where the Sans Souci stands today," Caitlin completed the orientation.

"Only these aren't Indian mounds," I explained. "This is the layout of the Civic Circle's underground refuge. They first built a base on the northern end of the island, under the Horton House. Later, they moved the main center here," I pointed to the location of the Jekyll Island Club," and they built the hotel next to it to provide an excuse for important people to come and go. Then, J.P. Morgan built the Sans Souci right on top of the refuge. These "walls" are buried tunnels. The grade has been raised over the years to give them better cover."

"What's the plan?" Bulldog asked. "Spook 'em into sneaking out into this tunnel and frag 'em?"

"It's a bit more complicated than that," I noted. Just then the bell rang. "Please invite the caterer in with the bottle of champagne."

Caitlin came back with Uncle Rob.

"Who are you?" Bulldog asked Rob.

"You aren't getting my name," Rob replied with a confident smile, "but you can call me 'Gunny.'"

"Gunny, huh," Bulldog replied. "You a Marine?"

"Maybe," Rob sidestepped the question. "What's your name?"

"You aren't getting my name, either," Bulldog insisted.

"What should I call you, then?"

"Make up something."

"I've been thinking of him as 'Bulldog,'" I told Rob.

"Heh," Bulldog snorted. "Bulldog. I can work with that."

Entertaining as it was to watch the two of them try to out-alpha each other, we had work to do.

Caitlin looked intently at the map. "There are three ways out of the central complex: to one of the cottages north along the river, along this tunnel to one of the cottage south, or inland, right under our cottage here, terminating in the old stables – The Jekyll Island Museum."

"That's where they're hiding the quick reaction force," Bulldog noted thoughtfully. "They have a third Hummer and two Canadian LAV III vehicles hidden away in there painted black with 'SWAT' on the outside. Each is manned by three security guys."

I'd seen the two Hummers they had out in plain view on the grounds for security, but I hadn't realized they had another force hidden in reserve. "What's a LAV III?"

"Canadian armored vehicle," Rob explained. "Probably one of the ones the Army was evaluating. By now, they'll have been declared surplus and made available to civilian law enforcement and Feds. Same vehicle as a Stryker APC."

That didn't mean a lot to me, but I could see Bulldog raise an eyebrow in respect of Rob's expertise.

"So, the quick reaction force is sitting right on top of the exit, ready to defend and evacuate the VIPs, but they've left us here right on top of the evacuation route through the exit tunnel." I could see Bulldog working through the tactical implications of our position.

"Why don't you present the plan, Gunny?" I suggested to Rob.

"You're familiar with the Nakatomi Plaza incident in Los Angeles? Back in the mid-1980s?"

What? I'd studied tactics and small-unit operations under Rob's tutelage for a couple of years now, and I didn't remember hearing of any such incident. Bulldog was apparently better informed.

"A bit before my time," Bulldog grinned, "but I've heard of it. You want to get inside, cut off their comms, shoot the boss, simulate some kind of a hostage standoff to slow down the response teams, finish off the Thirteen, and exfiltrate back here while they think you're bottled up in there. You think maybe they got some bearer bonds, too?"

"Something like that," Rob said. "I have the equivalent of a platoon of light infantry under my command. I'll place two sniper teams here," he pointed to the bank opposite the Jekyll Island Club, "across the Jekyll River, and the rest of a squad to cover them. They'll shoot out some windows, create a reaction, and provide covering fire if needed."

"Not much cover over there," Bulldog pointed out. "And the range is pretty extreme. That's got to be a mile or so."

"My snipers can make headshots at that range, but they don't have to," Rob pointed out. "Just enough commotion to convince the targets to stay inside and evacuate inland through the tunnel – right into our ambush.

"One squad stays here as a reserve and to protect our entry. When the shooting starts, the other squad infiltrates the tunnel to the Inner Sanctum. We cut them off here, and either catch them as they try to evacuate, or break into the Inner Sanctum and take them out there. We eliminate the Thirteen, and exfiltrate back here with the Civic Circle's data files. We run a data line from the Sans Souci, set up a wireless link, and 'negotiate' with the rapid response teams while we get away."

"The reaction force will either cover the end of the tunnel, or move in to reinforce the perimeter around the Sans Souci," Bulldog said thoughtfully.

"Either way, we sneak out from the cottage, board a boat here," Rob pointed to a location on the river side of the island, "and we're lost in the marsh here within ten minutes."

"They have a helicopter," Bulldog pointed out.

"Which will suffer a fortuitous mechanical failure," Rob assured him. "I've got it all covered."

"The data files.... You're sure they're here?" Bulldog's eyes lit up.

"Tolliver Applied Government Solutions just finished installing a massive amount of data storage for the Civic Circle," Rob explained. "Armed guards brought in a delivery from a high security data vault in the past week. It's either the Civic Circle's complete files or a backup of them. We'll share whatever we recover with you and your Order."

Bulldog turned to Brother Francis. "This is feasible. A chance to fulfill the goals the Brethren have worked toward for centuries. We should agree... provided I get to come with Gunny, here."

"You've done tunnel clearance before?" Rob asked.

Bulldog nodded.

"I can accept that," Rob offered.

"I cannot commit the Order to this action," Brother Francis shook his head. "My vows do not allow me to shed blood, nor may I command or allow another to do so on behalf of the Order." He cut off Bulldog's objection before he could make it. "However, I will communicate your proposal to... the head of our Order. I will recommend he accept it. I'll let you know tomorrow morning what is our decision."

Bulldog and Rob continued hashing out the details. Finally, I interrupted them. "I get to go with the strike team to the Inner Sanctum, right?"

"No." At least Rob had the good graces to appear guilty. "You will need to stay out of it." He cut me off as I started to object. "Tunnel clearance is a very specialized operation. I've been working with the strike team the past month on demolitions and operations in a compromised atmosphere. You don't have the right training. You'll stay back here with the support squad covering our egress."

He promised me. He promised when the time came to take out the Inner Circle I'd get a piece of the action. Instead I was relegated to the support squad. Before I could argue, Caitlin piped up.

"What about me?"

"You'll stay here, too" Bulldog declared. "Gunny's right. It takes special training."

"You know what I owe those bastards," Caitlin snarled. "I want a piece of the action, too."

I wasn't the only one unhappy. What Rob and Bulldog were saying made sense. That didn't mean I liked it.

Before long, Rob and Bulldog were satisfied they'd completed their planning. Rob popped the champagne bottle and poured it into the glasses he'd brought. "Confusion to the enemy and death to the Thirteen."

"Death to the Thirteen!"

"I'll second that!"

"Hear, hear!"

I finished off my small cup of champagne. It tasted like a sour fruity Coke.

"I'll get word to your young associate here," Brother Francis assured Rob, "no later than 9 am tomorrow morning. Meet me on the ground floor of the Jekyll Island Club Hotel. Given the magnitude of the opportunity, I don't know why the answer won't be yes."

Rob shook their hands. "Pleasure working with you Albertians. Tomorrow by this time we'll have rid the world of the Civic Circle's leadership and be ready to exploit their secrets. I need to get back to my catering."

Rob wasn't about to share with the Albertians that he was actually off with his team to try to disrupt the assassination attempt on Andrew Breitbart.

"Yippie-ki-yay... Gunny," Bulldog bade him farewell with a grin.

"Yippie-ki-yay... Bulldog," Rob smirked back.

What was that all about?

Rob completed his round of farewells and departed.

"That reminds me," I added, "I've been here nearly an hour. I need to replace your access point, restore your Internet connection, and get back on duty myself."

Caitlin followed me back. "I'm sorry I was rude to you," she apologized as I opened the closet.

I switched out the routers as I replied. "Understandable, given what you thought of me."

"You've given me hope that the victims of the Civic Circle may be avenged at long last."

I finished connecting the new access point. The connection light lit right up.

"Thank you," she surprised me with a kiss on the cheek. "I'll show you out."

My head was still spinning a bit from the memory of her kiss and her perfume as I passed through security, back into the Jekyll Island Club, through the secure door, and down to the Network Operations Center.

"Problem's solved," I told Mr. Humphreys. "Looks like the cottage is back online."

"Just 'cause I'm lazy don't mean I'm stupid, Burdell," he replied with the grin of a predator about to devour his prey. "You crashed the access point by re-flashing the firmware. You're busted, Burdell, and now... now you're gonna pay."

CHAPTER 13: FACING FEARFUL ODDS

Oh, shit.

"What do you mean?" I tried to stall for time.

"Cut the crap, Burdell," Mr. Humphreys replied. "You faked an outage to kill the feed on that cottage. I have you dead to rights. I saw you hitting on that Holy See Bank babe earlier. Thought she'd shot you down something good, but now you're sneaking off and spending more than an hour with her? In her private cottage? On company time?"

That was not what I was expecting. Caitlin and me?

It took a moment for me to wrap my head around what he was implying. Better to take the blame for what he thought I was doing instead of what I was really up to. "Yeah, well sometimes persistence pays off," I replied smugly, playing along.

"You made it with her?" he demanded to know.

"That's none of your business," I snapped back.

"Oh yes, it is," he leered back at me. "You're going to tell me exactly what happened."

I tried my best to buy more time by looking shocked while I tried to imagine a plausible scenario of seduction. I was just going to have to make it up as I went along. I 'reluctantly' decided to fess up to my 'misbehavior.'

"I knocked on the door," best start at the beginning, I figured. "She was wearing this silky green kimono." So far, so good. "Her hair was still damp. She'd just gotten out of the shower.

"'You,' she said. 'What do you want?'"

"'Your Internet's down,' I explained to her. I had her take me back to the service closet, and I opened it up. I asked her to get me a glass of ice water."

"Yeah," Mr. Humphreys confirmed. "Get 'em used to doing what you tell 'em, and they'll go all the way with you."

"So, she got back with the ice water," I continued. "I told her to step into the closet and I'd show her how it all worked. I could tell she knew what I really meant. I told her to shut the door. That's when I knew I had her."

"You get them alone, you get them used to doing what you tell them, you get 'em in the groove, and they start to lose their inhibitions," Mr. Humphreys explained, knowingly. He must be reading the same pick-up artist sites that Amit followed.

"She had the most amazing scent." At least I'd have no trouble describing her perfume!

"Oh yeah," Mr. Humphreys replied knowingly. "Those European girls... They don't shave their pits, do they?"

Not exactly where I was heading, but in improvisation, you sometimes have to go with your audience. "Yeah," I confirmed his expectations. "Let's just say she's a natural red-head."

His mouth opened. "Even... down below?" He wasn't quite drooling, but it was clear I had his attention now.

"You're getting ahead of my story," I countered. "So I pushed her back against the wall, and she just sort of melted in to me. We kissed. She pulled off my shirt. I undid the tie on her kimono and ran my hand up her side. That's when I realized," I paused to build some dramatic tension, "she had nothing on underneath."

Humphreys was transfixed – a lewd smirk on his face.

"I turned out the light." I gave him the details of my imaginary make out session in the utility closet including some rather creative and unconventional uses for ice cubes

I'd heard Amit describe. "We did what we could, but it was tiny – too small, too awkward to do much. I could tell she wanted more. So, I asked her if there was someplace else we could go. We got our clothes back on. She called room service for a bottle of champagne, and then she took me up to her room."

Mr. Humphreys looked smug. "I knew it! I saw the catering guy deliver it."

Good thing I added in that detail.

I made up an imaginary tryst in Caitlin's room, drawing on the highlights of exploits Amit had shared with me over the past couple of years. Mr. Humphreys listened slack-jawed to my storytelling. I was certainly giving him his money's worth in entertainment value, but I was concerned he'd just rat me out to get even with me for forcing him to bring me along. I closed my story

"They're having a reception tomorrow night," I explained. "Lots of hot European women looking for a good time. I bet I could get you in."

"Oh, yeah?"

"Yeah," I assured him. There were parties and receptions all over Jekyll Island. Surely I could leverage my contacts to get him in to one somewhere. "I'll be seeing her again tomorrow. How about I see what I can do to get you an invitation?"

I could see he was tempted. He slowly nodded his head. "OK, Burdell." Then he gestured back at my workstation. "But first, you gotta clean up all the log files before you get us both in trouble. We gotta sign over this whole place to the Civic Circle people tomorrow morning."

They wanted us out before the Thirteen assembled for their meeting tomorrow night. At least that meant fewer innocent people would be around when Uncle Rob and his team came calling.

It took another hour to get everything cleaned up. Mr. Humphreys found a bunch of other network and internal logs I hadn't been aware of with traces of what I'd done. The man was scary competent when he put his mind to it. Finally, he declared our work complete. I caught the shuttle bus back to the Beach Village and then south to the Berkshire Inn and Suites.

I woke up to find Amit had let himself in. There was a note on the counter to wake him up when I got up.

"I swear she had to be on cocaine or something," he said bleary eyed. "I couldn't keep up with her."

I started a cup of coffee for him. "I'm hopping in the shower. You can tell me about her at breakfast, OK?"

Amit was doing much better once he'd had his coffee and a shower. He regaled me with his exploits over breakfast. "It's simply amazing," he said in awe. "Just being here prequalifies you to all these girls. Their inhibitions are down, they're looking for a good time, and all you have to do is isolate one and close with her before some other stud beats you to it. The cock-blocking is amazing. I could really use a wingman to help me run interference on some of these smug pricks."

"Some of us have actual work to do," I reminded him. Cell phones off and secured, we walked up Beachview Drive so we could talk in privacy.

"I wonder if they keep track of all these suspicious cell phone outages," I thought out loud.

"Maybe," Amit replied. "Everyone does it, though. It's common knowledge among the Civic Youth that if you want privacy, you need to turn your phone off. Remember we saw Bernard do it, too."

I brought him up to speed on my lunch with Ding.

"Great," he muttered. "Our Chinese 'friends' actually want the United States to dissipate its strength in stupid international conflict."

"Can't really blame them. They're allies of convenience at best," I acknowledged. "I hope the Albertians will do a better job helping us out." I explained the plan.

"We're finally going to take down the Inner Circle?" Amit seemed surprised at the thought that in a little over twelve hours it could all be over for us. One way or another.

"Not us, exactly." I explained how Rob refused to let us on the Strike Team.

"He does have a point," Amit conceded. "We haven't done any serious tactical training since last summer. I bet Rob's been drilling the guys non-stop since he got the plans in June."

I still thought it really sucked being left off the Strike Team, but if Amit and Rob both agreed, it was probably time for me to embrace the suck and let Rob run the show.

"What about that reporter dude? Breitbart?"

"He's not exactly a reporter," I began, "he's a conservative writer, publisher, and activist. He's also a collaborator with Matt Drudge." The Beach Village was getting close, and I didn't really have time to elaborate. "Rob sent me the 'all went well' code text, but of course there were no details. We may be able to get more from Rob. We're supposed to get the confirmation this morning from Brother Francis that they'll cooperate in the attack on the Inner Sanctum tonight."

As we got to the shuttle stop and lost our privacy, Amit segued seamlessly into more details of his exploits with the rest of the Civic Youth. "At the Women in Media reception, I had this drop-dead gorgeous babe eating out of my hand, eager to show how enlightened she was by hanging out with a 'person-of-color.'" He put it in ironic finger quotes. "Turns out her daddy is some kind of billionaire. Now I'm thinking I've got this heiress on the line. I mean, I could be set for life if I play my cards right. So I'm in the groove and playing like I never played before – a subtle neg, a push, a pull, escalate, withdraw. I can tell I've got her hooked, and it's time to escalate and isolate her somewhere. And then, her father shows up."

"Wow! What did he do? Did he intervene? Break it up?"

"Not exactly," Amit said, the disgust clear in his face. "He walks up to us all smooth and suave. The man was alpha, pure alpha, I mean, James-Bond-level alpha. But I figure what can he do? Anything negative he says just makes me more the bad boy rival his little girl will swoon for. So the bastard says to his daughter, 'What a nice young man you've found. You're the best piece of tail he's ever going to get, so I'm sure he'll treat you right.' Then he just leaves her with me."

I was confused. "He actually complimented you? And called his own daughter a 'piece of tail?'"

Amit rolled his eyes at my ignorance. "You don't get it. The last thing that girl wanted was to sleep with a 'nice' boy she'd just met that Daddy likes. She wanted to virtue-signal – show how enlightened she was by sleeping with the bad-boy of color who'd piss off dear old Dad. And that 'piece of tail' comment was a vulgar reminder that she was lowering herself, that her sexual market value was way above mine, that I wasn't good enough for her, and she shouldn't be selling herself cheaply. Sure enough, the spark was gone, and despite some of my best game ever, she makes a lame excuse to go to the ladies' room two minutes later."

I could see how that played out once I thought about it. "Maybe you should have rejected her then and there as too much of a 'Daddy's Girl' and tried to hook up later on the rebound?"

"Yeah," he nodded. "That might have worked fairly...." Amit looked at me with surprise, the realization dawning that for once, I was the one giving him pick-up advice.

"I do listen to your game tips, you know," I answered his unasked question with a smile.

Amit looked around and decided it was private enough to risk an admission. "I am so tired of hanging out," he confided softly, "with the 'best and brightest.' They all think they're intrinsically superior to everyone else because of their social-justice enlightenment. They verbally joust to see who feels worst about being so innately superior. Then they feel even more superior for having the refined moral sense to feel bad about their amazing superiority."

I really despaired for the future of our country if the people Amit was describing were going to be our future rulers. "One way or another," I whispered, my lips barely moving, "it'll be over tonight."

We got through security at the Jekyll Island Club Hotel and found Brother Francis holding court in the Aspinwall Room. I almost didn't recognize him. Gone was the sober, modest clergyman. In his place was a dissolute, flamboyant impresario.

"You can't just manipulate the prices of precious metals," someone was telling him. "The market's too big."

"I used to think that, too," Brother Francis began, "but not two years ago, Lord Winslow, himself, came to our bank's London Office. No small talk, no preliminaries. He is a Lord after all, and the rest of us mere peasants. 'The Chancellor of the Exchequer requires that you make the price of silver fall at least ten percent.' We were all slack-jawed in amazement. 'Gold, too, naturally,' his Lordship adds.

"Our head trader," Brother Francis looked around the room, "you boys know McNew, right?" I could see a few nods of recognition. "As stubborn a Scot as ever pinched a penny. So McNew says right to Lord Winslow, 'We can't just push a price out of thin air and make it stick! Every tosser is buying right now. We could sell our whole position, leverage all we could to short the market and it wouldna be more than a blip in the graph. It canna be done.'"

"Lord Winslow was having none of McNew's insolence. 'What are you waiting for? The Chancellor needs gold and silver to go down. This big rise is making Her Majesty's Government look bad.'"

"'How the bloody hell do you expect us to do that?' McNew asked him.

"'You do know how to trade, don't you?'

"'Aye, that we do,' McNew snapped back.

"Lord Winslow ignored the sarcasm. 'Excellent,' says he. 'You have a month to make your plans. I want silver to start falling by May the first.'

"One of the traders pointed out, 'That's a Saturday.'"

"Lord Winslow glared at him. 'Very well. You have two extra days. But silver must be falling by Monday, May the third. Oh and gold, too. But you may have until August to make gold fall.'

Brother Francis had the crowd's complete attention at this opportunity to glimpse behind the curtain and see how world economic markets were run. I looked around for Rob. A few of the catering staff were in and around, tending to their duties, but Rob was nowhere to be seen.

"So I says to Lord Winslow," Brother Francis continued, "'If I may be so bold, my Lord, why must silver fall first?'

"He looks down his nose at me and says, 'I should not have to be telling you, but I shall, nevertheless. Her Majesty's Treasury wants it to look realistic. Silver leads gold, and it went up more. The end of the bull market, and the start of a bear market must also begin with silver. You have your orders.' He turned his back and left without another word.

"Now, everyone's looking at me to tell them what to do. Of course, with my decades of experience, keen intellect, and insider connections, I know exactly how to make silver fall.

"I look at my head trader. 'McNew,' says I, 'you heard Lord Winslow. Make silver fall. I'm going to the pub for a pint, and when I get back, I want to hear your plan.'

"McNew's eyes shot daggers at me as I walked on past him, but when I came back a hour later, the ol' blackguard had a scheme outlined. 'We canna move the market on our own,' McNew stated the obvious, 'it's a raging bull out there. Canna stop that head-on. So, we gotta redirect it, wave a red cape at, use its strenth agin' it, like judo.'"

The change in Brother Francis' personality was simply amazing. In his conversations with me, he was sober, deliberate, based, well-grounded – a man comfortable with who he was and the God whose purpose he served. The man I was watching now was a decadent aristocrat, securing his place in the social hierarchy by reveling in his corruption on a global scale.

"McNew's scheme was masterful," Brother Francis said, sliding expertly from his own refined English accent back to McNew's thick Scottish brogue. "'First, we tell everyone that the dollar and pound are in terminal collapse and the bull market's never gonna end,' McNew explained. 'We make the narrative so extreme that the silver bulls all latch on to it, but so over-the-top that the professional traders see right through the hype.'

"'Second, we publish reports all about how small investors love silver. Everyone's buying silver in anticipation of the obvious gains right around the corner. That's what we tell the public. Can't hardly keep up with demand. The institutional investors and banks get a different message – the rally is being driven by retail. They'll get the right message."

"I began to see McNew's plan. 'The message that the rally is driven by the dumb money,' I told him.

"'Aye,' McNew confirmed. 'Third, we revive and push up all the balderdash about manipulation of prices. We need a wee undercurrent of fear along with the euphoria. We need the smart money on edge, so they think if the price drops, that's us banks re-asserting control. That'll crater the market for sure if we get the timing just right.'

"You see the brilliance of McNew's plan?" Brother Francis asked his growing audience. "Push a hyper-bullish story to excite the small investors, that's so obviously bollocks that the institutional investors see right through it. Convince everyone we're in the dumb-money phase of a market peak. Then FUD it all up, inject Fear, Uncertainty, and Doubt to trigger a collapse.

"You!" Brother Francis interrupted his story. I looked behind me. Rob approached at the summons. "Bring me a gin and soda."

"I'm sorry sir," Rob replied, "but the bar is not open yet this morning."

"Tonic water on the rocks then, and make it snappy!" Brother Francis bellowed, furious at the inept lout's defiance.

"Yes, sir," Rob departed, submissively.

"Where was I? Ah, yes," Brother Francis continued, "the rest of the details were technical. Crafting the reports and releases, seeding them at the right places at the right times. Dodging management and the auditors who were wondering why our trading was running at such a loss as we kept trying to drive the price down and trigger the collapse. We thought we'd forced a sell-off a week early, but the bloody dumb money bought in on the dip! Finally, May 3, right on schedule, silver dropped four dollars. By the end of May it was down ten.

"Gold was trickier. We had the advantage that silver had already collapsed, but the downside was gold has so much more liquidity. And our story wouldn't work on gold since everyone knows every Chinaman and Hindu buys gold. We had to change it.

Just then Rob arrived. "Your tonic water, sir."

"About time!" Then Brother Francis looked at me and with Rob in ear shot, he put an arm patronizingly on my shoulder. "Ah, lad! That dinner we were having tonight? Have to call it off! Swing by my cottage around noon." He turned to Rob, "You, boy! Lunch for this fine young punk and me here at my cottage at noon; think you can handle that?"

Rob was furious with him. Brother Francis was calling off the attack? What the hell were he and the Albertians doing?

"Yes, sir," Rob replied coldly, and stalked off.

"Can't find good help in the colonies," Brother Francis muttered.

I marveled at how beautifully he'd played Rob, giving him a perfect cover for the cold repressed anger Rob was no doubt feeling at being jerked around by these Albertian...

"Now where was I?" Brother Francis interrupted my thoughts.

"So, how did you crash the gold market?" one of his adoring fans asked eagerly.

"Ah, yes!" Brother Francis continued. "We spiked the financial press with stories about the explosive growth in gold

Electronically Traded Funds. How any tosser with a pound and a dial-up modem was buying shares. I mean, assets under management grew from next to nothing a few years ago to something like 50 billion dollars! This was retail with a capital R, dumb money with a capital D. This was the herd rushing in to the slaughterhouse, with a capital H! Imagine all those people buying into the ETFs! What were they going to do with their shares when the euphoria broke? Obviously, sell.

"Still, gold was harder to crash. When we crashed silver, we got a $100 dip in gold, but it recovered immediately and went even higher! The price finally broke in late August, and by mid-September the bears were finally in control."

I was entranced by Brother Francis' storytelling, while dumbfounded at the change in events. He'd been all for the attack last night, or as much as his religious vows would allow. My next step was clear. Get through the morning and meet him for lunch to get the details on what the hell had made him change his mind. And he'd neatly arranged for Rob to have an excuse to join us.

"So, Lord Winslow, he drops by again at the end of September," Brother Francis continued his story. 'You men,' the Lord began...

I heard a woman mutter about sexist, patriarchal, swine.

"You misses should save it for the masses," Francis snapped back. "We were all men on the gold desk, there. Unkink your knickers, and let me finish!

"So his Lordship said to us, he said, 'You men have served your Queen, and God, and Britain well and Her Majesty is most pleased. You are heroes. Some of you may be criminally charged, and thrown in prison, if you committed any crimes in carrying out your orders. Her Majesty's government, of course, will deny any involvement in such sordid and sorry stunts. And we will not defend you. However, other than that, you have our profound gratitude. Your excellent work has averted a greater disaster than you may know.'

"So McNew looks at Lord Winslow and back at me, and McNew says, 'Don't we get a bonus at least for our great work?'

"Lord Winslow snorted, 'A bonus? What, did you not make enough betting on the crash in your personal accounts!? You had the resources of one of the biggest financial institutions in the world at your disposal to engineer a crash. I would assume, being smart traders, that you would have profited handsomely from the crash that you knew was coming!' Lord Winslow stalked out of the room. I'd made a killing, of course – nearly doubled my personal net worth by shorting silver in May and redoubled it and then some shorting gold in September.

"Only then I noticed, all the traders were just staring at the floor. They didn't know if our scheme would work. I'd ordered them to put the bank at risk. I'd have landed somewhere else just fine, rank has its privileges, after all, but if they'd failed, they'd have been thrown out on their ears, maybe even prosecuted. I mean, Her Majesty's government could just unlimber the printing press in the basement if they needed a few billion quid to bail themselves out. Them? Ha! Risk their own hard-earned money? No thank you, my Lord! Not one of the traders on the desk had risked his own money and profited from the crash we engineered!"

The crowd was laughing at the expense of Brother Francis' traders. He looked at his watch. "Time to hear from those Americans on the latest plan to keep the rabble in line!"

The morning plenary was back again in the Morgan Center. Amit carefully checked my badge against the list of authorized attendees, and the security guards let me pass. My job was to make sure the speakers were taken care of. That was silly, because the catering staff were efficient, the water glasses full, and a pad of "Jekyll Island Club Resort" logo paper and a pen already lay neatly arranged by each speaker's chair. Must be a panel discussion. I pretended the pens needed a better alignment, and I adjusted them. Have to keep the rabble in line, after all. As the speakers arrived, I told them to let me know if they needed anything. Then, I settled into my chair to listen to the presentation.

"Hi, I'm Dr. Ken Frederick," the Chairman announced. The name was familiar. I recognized it in the next moment. He was... "I'm the DARPA Program Director for SLIP, DARPA's innovative program to assure communications dominance and protect our nation and the global order by bringing Security, Location, Information, and Performance – 'SLIP" – to next generation consumer communications products. I'm here today, though, to talk about DARPA's previous success, and how it's being rolled out even now to fundamentally change the way the public interacts with the Internet and to make it easier to gather actionable intelligence about bad actors who threaten order and security.

"As Director for the Total Information Awareness program, we faced a real challenge. A big problem with universal surveillance, is people don't like being spied upon. Oh, we can read their emails and texts and listen to their phone calls, and they'll never know their data is being scanned for keyword triggers and archived for future analysis. When that surveillance becomes intrusive, some people with archaic notions of personal privacy become uncomfortable. That was the original problem with Total Information Awareness.

"We shifted strategy by funding the LifeLog project – the attempt to create a comprehensive cyber-memory recording a user's every action, activity, who they meet, what they say, everything. We thought we could get people to accept the idea of a digital personal assistant keeping track of their own life experience. Unfortunately, that idea didn't get much traction, either. We cancelled LifeLog a couple of years ago in favor of a new and stunningly effective technique that merges traditional media, social interaction, and ubiquitous surveillance. We left out the surveillance part to simply call it 'Social Media.'"

One by one, the speakers on the panel explained their role in developing and implementing Social Media. Dr. Alyssa Gottlieb, the polka-dot dress lady with the bulging eyes was there, only now she wore a more formal-looking dark blue dress. "As a cognitive scientist," she began, "I've been responsible for the experimental designs involved in the implementation." She explained something called A/B testing – give a population of users multiple versions of the same web page. Which version drives longer visits and more interaction? Upgrade the online portal, and experiment with the next generation of potential features to optimize further. "We're engaging in the most comprehensive human subjects testing campaign in history," she boasted, "and it's all going on without the oversight of any Institutional Review Board, because 'all' we're doing is just improving web pages. We're tweaking the way a website interacts with its users to optimize a stimulus-response feedback loop that addicts users to the dopamine hit they get by participating online."

"Just like a lottery is effectively a tax on people too stupid to understand basic probability," the Homeland Security official on the panel explained, "Social Media is surveillance on people too stupid to realize we're monitoring them. It overcomes the public's objections to surveillance. When the head doctors get it tweaked just right, Social Media actually makes people want to participate in their own surveillance!"

"It's a bit like how a vaccine works," the professor from the MIT Artificial Intelligence Lab offered. "You don't have to have 100% of a population vaccinated in order to get the benefit. If 70% to 80% are vaccinated, there's a kind of herd immunity that will protect the entire population. That's how Social Media works. If 70%-80% of people are busy documenting and sharing their interactions online, we catch enough of what the remaining 20%-30% are doing to maintain ubiquitous surveillance on everyone. It doesn't matter if you opt out of social media. If you're at a party, a meeting, or any activity with more than a handful of people, you're guaranteed someone there is engaged on social media capturing what you do in their own shared photos and timeline. When you add in the phone, text, and email coverage we have even of those who opt out – it's 98% of what we'd aimed for back in the Total Information Awareness program. Better yet, the people who scrupulously opt-out of social media can be flagged for extra attention through conventional surveillance methods."

During the break, I realized the Civic Circle had not thought through the implications of their scheme. They were so eager to push us all into the "open society" of their brave new world of Social Media that they hadn't thought ahead to how the tools they were building might be used against them.

It was just like how Rob had described the mechanism of universal surveillance – they were absolutely confident they would always be in control, so the fact that their data was being collected, too, didn't concern them. The architects of this Social Media concept didn't realize that putting everyone's data on public display was a two-edged sword. The masses' data would be on display for the elite, true, but the elite's data would be on display for the masses. Could the elite hide their perversions, their contempt, and their arrogance as they used Social Media and wrestled for approval within their own social circles without revealing themselves to society at large? That was too far away in the future for me to be concerned about. For now.

After the coffee break, we were back for another session.

"We've been talking about Social Media for surveillance and security," Dr. Gottlieb began again, "but the power of Social Media for social control cannot be underestimated. Social Media cripples attention span and the ability to focus. By constantly bombarding people with external stimuli, they never develop an internal narrative. In extreme cases, their emotional development can be arrested at the level of a three-year-old. They lose the ability to interact and empathize independently of that external stimulus. By controlling that external stimulus, by curating which messages are emphasized and which are suppressed, we create a classic stimulus-response feedback loop that nudges or even controls their behavior."

"The marketing opportunity is incredible," bragged the fresh-faced young CEO of "Omnibook," the new division of Omnitia that had rolled up Facebook, MySpace, and FriendFace just months ago. As one of the CEOs of the companies involved in the merger, he was a natural pick to run Omnibook. "We monitor every click, every interaction. We can put cookies on your computer that let us track your online activity, even off the Omnibook website."

The CEO explained the technical details of how it all worked. He was another one who seemed on the wrong side of the uncanny valley. It didn't help that he had a distinct resemblance to Star Trek's Mr. Data.

"We make surveillance pay for itself," he explained. "Psychographic microtargeting lets us identify the specific users most receptive to a customer's message and place the message right under their noses on our own site or in affiliate advertising on any site on the web.

"We place your ad for veterinary services only under the noses of pet owners, sell diapers only to those with babies, and promote diet foods specifically to those trying to lose weight. In a week of use, we know who you are better than your mom. We know our users' wants, their needs, their desires. We know where you shop, what credit cards you carry, where you like to eat, and whether you're a value or high-end consumer. And we can use that power for good – blocking the flow of bad ideas and bad information, and reinforcing messages of peace, harmony, and inclusion. What we're building is a revolutionary new way to collect comprehensive information on most of the public. Then, we can use that information to nudge the public in socially desirable directions."

Professor Gomulka – or maybe it was the Dean – had told me about the nude photos taken of all freshman attending Ivy League schools in the 1940s into the 1970s. Under the guise of a scientific study of posture, the Civic Circle's academic agents had gathered blackmail material on a generation of American leaders – the generation filling this very conference room. What they were planning with Omnibook was far, far more invasive and wide reaching: a complete log of everyone's activities, even their most private thoughts, opinions, and beliefs. And it was using all that information to automatically "nudge" us toward the Civic Circle's agenda.

In the question period, it was obvious the audience understood the implications. "What you're doing in Silicon Valley is just amazing," gushed one questioner, "but, I don't understand. These young people…" She looked puzzled. "They're just giving you incriminating photos, sharing their most intimate messages, providing you with all the information anyone would ever need to manipulate them, even blackmail them or control them later in life. I don't get it. Why?"

The Omnibooks CEO looked at her. "I don't know why," he said with a smirk on his face. "They 'trust me.' Dumb fucks."

The audience got a good laugh at the naïveté of the public. I managed a smile that masked my revulsion at the scheme.

As the uproar died down, I saw the next panelist had a grim expression on his face. "Silicon Valley is not monolithic," he interrupted. "We've always had a very different view of privacy than some of our colleagues in the valley. Privacy means people know what they're signing up for, in plain English and repeatedly. I believe people are smart and some people want to share more data than other people do. Ask them. Ask them every time. Make them tell you to stop asking them if they get tired of your asking them. Let them know precisely what you're going to do with their data."

Another panelist rolled his eyes. Mister… Doctor? Frederick stood up. "I see we're running a bit long, and we certainly don't want to stand between our audience and their lunch." He turned to the speaker. "I'm sorry we have to cut you off, but I'm sure we'll all be able to hear further from you some other time. Let's all thank Mr. Steve Jobs and the rest of our panelists."

From the angry looks the Apple CEO received, I was concerned for his life expectancy. I didn't have time to worry about it just then, though. I made a beeline for Brother Francis' cottage as the applause was dying down.

Caitlin let me in.

Rob was already there, going at it with Bulldog, "This is chicken shit, and you know it."

Bulldog was apologetic, but adamant. "I don't like it either, Gunny, but I'm not at liberty to discuss it with you. Brother Francis will be here in a moment. He wanted to explain the situation to you personally."

"Nothing Francis has to say can change this chicken shit into chicken salad," Rob insisted. "We gave you the plans and proposed a joint operation. We take the spearhead, and share and share-alike in the recovered data. Now you're calling it off?!?"

The two glowered at each other: Rob demanding an explanation, and Bulldog holding his ground and insisting Brother Francis would explain everything. Fortunately Brother Francis arrived in time to avert their coming to blows.

"What's the meaning of this?" Rob demanded angrily.

Brother Francis held up a hand. "We don't have much time before you are missed, and I have much to tell you." He turned to Caitlin. "We're secure?"

Caitlin looked offended. "Of course. We have an epic lunch time story of yours playing for the benefit of the Civic Circle. You're currently enlightening us all on how you played wingman for Prince Charles at a polo match, covering for him, so he could have a discreet liaison. We have," she glanced at her watch, "42 minutes."

"Ah, that one. Very well," Brother Francis said. "I insisted that I be the one to speak with you, Gunny," he assured Rob. "I conveyed your proposal to the head of my order last night.

I recommended that he approve it. I became concerned that he did not endorse my recommendation immediately. This morning, I learned why.

"The Superior General believes that this opportunity is 'too important to be left to an unknown band of American irregulars.' Last night, he dispatched a platoon of 'Fidei Defensor' to lead the attack. They are arriving this afternoon, and will execute the attack this evening on your original timetable."

Before Rob could explode at him, I asked, "These are what, Swiss Guards?"

"No ceremonial palace guards could hope to pull this off, particularly without having trained for the operation," Rob pointed out.

"They're an elite unit of the Pope's own Swiss Guard," Brother Francis explained. "They help defend the faithful in trouble spots around the world, and they have much experience in irregular warfare. Think of them as... 'the Vatican's ninjas.'"

"Vatican ninjas? What is this, some kind of Declan Finn Pius Thriller?" Dad had been a big fan and had all of Declan Finn's books.

"I assure you, they're entirely real," Brother Francis insisted, "although I can also assure you they do not rappel down cathedrals, burst through stained glass windows, whip automatic weapons out from under their cassocks and mow down villains like in that ridiculous movie adaptation."

"I don't care how good they are," Rob said flatly. "Tunnel clearance is a specialized operation, and if they haven't trained for it, they're squandering the opportunity and throwing their lives away. They can't just waltz in there, shoot the place up, and hope to walk out again."

"One does not simply walk into Mordor," Bulldog muttered.

"There is evil there that does not sleep." Brother Francis nodded. "The Great Eye is ever watchful."

I should have figured the Albertians for Lord of the Rings fans.

"We all know as much, Gunny," Brother Francis assured Rob. "My companion... you call him Bulldog? He tells me you are the sort of man who knows what it means to have to take orders you do not like from leaders whose judgement you find... questionable. That is the position we find ourselves in, and we control the access needed to make the plan work."

Rob glowered impassively at Brother Francis.

"Isn't it better that someone take this opportunity to strike a blow at the Civic Circle even if it's not you and your group?" Caitlin offered.

"I could ask the same of you, you know," Rob offered. "One anonymous call alerting the Civic Circle and the game would be up. I can veto your attack plan as easily as you've vetoed mine."

"We have done wrong by you, I know," Brother Francis acknowledged. "I will do all in my power to make it up to you. That is because I believe you are an honorable man: a man who will not betray a friend over a slight, or lose a war to spite even a feckless ally. I think you are a man with whom we can do business, Mister Robert Burdell."

He knew who we were. Of course – they certainly knew who I was, and fingering Rob from a list of my known associates would be trivial. There was a threat underneath Brother Francis' honeyed words. If we crossed the Albertians, they could surely do the same to us. There was also an olive branch as well – a promise to work together.

"Very well," Rob acquiesced to the inevitable. "Are we to sit this one out? Or do you have a suggestion for me to consider how we might assist you?"

Bulldog stepped forward. "The earlier refuge. The one on the north end of Jekyll Island, under the Horton House. While the main raid is underway here, we can penetrate the facility there. Perhaps there is more of value there? A backup of the primary facility here under the Historic District?"

"I rather doubt it," I offered. "Our information is that the facility had a fission reactor that suffered some kind of catastrophic failure about a hundred years ago."

"Someday," Brother Francis stared intently at me, "you are going to have to explain your sources of information."

"Someday, perhaps," I acknowledged, "it won't be today, though. I doubt there's much but ruins there. I would be curious to see it. The safest time to go spelunking would be when the primary target here is already under attack. Don't we have a dosimeter?"

Rob nodded slowly. We outlined a plan. We'd go to the north end of the island. Brother Francis had arranged a party at a condo complex there as an alibi. We'd make an appearance, sneak out, and return when we were done. Jekyll Island was less than a mile wide at that point. We'd cross on foot along a trail and meet up with Rob and his team at the Horton House to kick off the operation. They'd arrive through the marsh by boat bringing all the gear and taking away any loot we might find.

We worked out the details.

"I need to be getting back," Rob looked at his watch. "A gesture of trust – one you have not earned, but nevertheless, I offer. You should know that the Civic Circle attempted to assassinate a journalist last night – Andrew Breitbart. The attempt failed, and nothing has been seen of the assassins since." He paused. "They will not be seen again. The Circle's security may be on alert."

Brother Francis nodded. "That is good to know, but how can you be sure the Circle's killers will not be found?"

"The Civic Circle has means to dispose of unwanted bodies," Rob explained. "We used them." The drums of acid in the warehouse attached to the Berkshire Inn? I thought that through. If the bodies were found, the prime suspect would be whoever within the Civic Circle had access to the warehouse and knew of the drums. I approved.

"Thanks for sharing that with us, Gunny. Sorry the guys upstairs are being such dicks," Bulldog apologized. "We'll try to make it up to you." He held out a hand.

Rob took Bulldog's hand and gave it a hearty shake. "See you at the Horton House, tonight."

Caitlin closed the door behind him. "Lunch?"

We dug into the tray of sandwiches Rob had left for us. Caitlin handed me one, and I noticed a diamond ring on her hand. "You weren't wearing that last night. Who's the lucky..."

The expression on Bulldog's face gave him away.

"That's because I got it last night," she smiled in sheer delight. "'Bulldog' finally proposed, and I accepted."

The happy couple looked at each other as I congratulated them, Caitlyn with her arms around Bulldog, holding him close. "With all the hatred in the world," I told them, "I'm glad to see there can be love as well."

"Hatred, I can deal with," Bulldog explained. "I like hatred... if it's from the right people and for the right reasons. Your goal in life shouldn't be for no one to hate you. Way I see it, your goal should be to make every sordid degenerate monster out there foam at the mouth at the mention of your name. I know that may not be very Christian of me."

"'All men will hate you because of me,'" Brother Francis quoted scripture, "'but he who stands firm to the end will be saved.' I think our Father in heaven will see fit to forgive you."

"I still have trouble believing the world stands so close to the brink," I made a confession of my own. "I never thought there could be such evil or that it could work so openly."

"They believe themselves beyond good and evil," Brother Francis explained. "For them, there is only power. No beauty, no virtue, and truth is any narrative that supports the power structure and furthers their control.

"Do you know the Story of the Tower of Babel?" he asked.

"Men tried to build a tower to Heaven," I answered. "God objected and foiled the scheme by making everyone speak different languages."

"The Story of Babel is the story of utopianism," Brother Francis explained "Men sought to build so high as to reach heaven, to ascend above the heights of the clouds, above the very stars of God. It is the same unbounded pride that led to the totalitarian disasters of the 20th century. The same limitless arrogance that threatens to overwhelm us today. What Friedrich Hayek called the 'Pretense of Knowledge' – the notion that anyone could arrogate to themselves the omniscience of the divine and know enough to successfully engineer and control society.

"Even our enemies understand the symbolism. A few years ago they built a parliament building for the European Union explicitly modelled after the Tower of Babel. They openly defy God. They talk of building systems and institutions 'too big to fail,' never realizing in truth they are so big they have to fail."

"I'm not sure waiting for that failure is a viable option, Brother Francis," I noted. "The Civic Circle is creating a huge web of surveillance and control over society. What they have created will not be easy to overcome."

"No, Peter," Brother Francis shook his head sadly at my ignorance. "Satan cannot create. He can only unmake the Creator's creation. He whispered in Eve's ear, enticing her to eat of the fruit of knowledge and become like God. She and Adam did, committing the original sin – the attempt to defy the limitations of their own human nature and become as God.

"Similarly, human ingenuity and creation is a reflection of that divine spark, and Satan's minions cannot create, either, only take or destroy. They are fundamentally parasites, living off the good works of human creators, and at their sufferance. Although Ayn Rand grasped that truth in *Atlas Shrugged*, she failed to comprehend the theological roots of the conflict she so dramatically presented."

We were running out of time for lunch, and there was something I needed to let them know. "My boss, Mr. Humphreys, he figured out how I crashed your Internet connection. He... he thinks I did it so I could have... some time alone with Caitlin."

"Does he, now?" Bulldog was not amused. "And what exactly does he think happened between you two?"

I gulped, but I had to tell them so they wouldn't be blindsided if the story got back to them. "I had to explain what I was doing here with Caitlin all the while. The bottle of champagne. I made up a story of a... a romantic encounter."

"You told him you slept with me?" Caitlin was pissed.

I gave her the details of my imagined encounter. Bulldog kept looking between Caitlin and Brother Francis as if hoping for permission to smack me.

"Oh my," said Brother Francis with a wry smile. "That will cross their signals. You do realize what it means for a man of my station to summon a handsome young lad for a private lunch?"

No, I didn't.

He explained it.

"The Civic Circle likes pedophiles in positions of power because they can be so easily controlled," Brother Francis explained. "Tempt them with access to young flesh, not just young adults like yourself, but even younger children. Then, they threaten their tools with ruin and exposure. Carrot and stick. It is an ancient formula that has worked well for them."

Caitlin giggled at the expression on my face. "I think we're even now."

Brother Francis smiled. "Invite your Mr. Humphreys to tonight's party. We'll make him feel welcomed." He looked at his watch. "We need to be getting back to the afternoon sessions."

* * *

A throng of protestors surrounded the Jekyll Island Club Hotel. As I approached I heard singing. Yankee Doodle? That was the tune, but the words were different:

Civic Circle pederasts
Went down to Jekyll Island
Used up all the local boys
Then bought some more from Thailand!

Civic Circle parties hard
Civic Circle dandies
Look out for their unmarked vans and
Never eat their candies!

Over and over the protestors sang to the frustration of the media trying to cover the prestigious gathering of the world's elite. I could tell their bawdy tune got under the skin of the CNN announcer complaining about "hate speech" when he was reduced to sputtering almost incoherently that the alleged human trafficking victims were actually from China, not Thailand. "Fact check – failed," he said smugly.

I didn't get the rest of the story until I passed through security and found Amit inside. "They tied Gomulka and the Civic Circle to the human trafficking," Amit said with a deadpan expression on his face. "Drudge broke the story this morning." I wondered if that might be the fruits of Rob's rescue of Breitbart. What information had he passed on to the journalist? The Civic Circle and their media minions were clearly playing catch up. The hotel was too crowded for a private discussion.

I had just enough time to run down to the Network Operations Center in the basement and invite Mr. Humphreys to the party before heading on to the Pulitzer Room for the afternoon's Civic Youth program.

The topic was something called "Crisis Acting: How to Shape the Narrative by Quick Reaction to Current Events." The session was all about how to capitalize on current events, using them as a springboard to push the progressive agenda. After a shooting? We need gun control. After a human trafficking incident makes the news? We need immigration reform. Extreme weather event? We need more emissions regulations to prevent "climate change."

"Civic Youth may find themselves in the middle of the news at any time," the workshop instructor explained. "You all have to be ready to exploit what opportunities come your way and advance the appropriate narrative." After a break, the workshop continued with the instructor making us all roleplay what we would say to the media in the wake of a mass shooting on campus. He coached us on delivering effective soundbites that would play well in the media. Then, we had a simulated media event, complete with reporters and TV news cameras pretending to interview us. After another break, the instructor and the reporters critiqued individual performances and provided tips for improving our effectiveness. Madison and Amit did an outstanding job, particularly Madison, who was hysterical "The guns! The guns! They're killing people!" She exclaimed to high praise.

Security had pushed the protestors back from the hotel by the time Amit and I emerged and made our way back to the Holy See Bank cottage.

A limo was waiting.

Amit and I got in back.

"It's safe to talk," Brother Francis assured us as the limo turned and headed north on Riverview Drive. "You got the radio?"

"Yes, sir," Bulldog acknowledged. "Operation Gomorrah kicks off at 8:15 pm with sniper fire on the Jekyll Island Club Hotel and Sans Souci building. At 8:20 pm, sooner if there's any activity in the tunnel, Falcon will begin clearing the tunnel and heading for the Inner Sanctum."

"Falcon?" Amit asked.

"The call sign for the Fidei Defensor strike team," Bulldog beat me to the explanation. "Our call sign is 'Sparrow.' We shouldn't need to coordinate, however."

"A couple last minute updates to the plan," Caitlin added. "We have an operative standing by in the campground a couple hundred yards north. Campsite C-20. Should be the first one you get to. Your team will be leaving by boat, while we have to cross the island to get back to the party. We've cached our weapons near Beachview Drive. Your 'Gunny' provided us with your gear and we've included it in our cache. After the operation, we'll cache our weapons there and return to the party for our alibi. We'll get your gear back to you later."

"Thanks," I acknowledged. That made sense. I was glad we'd have our weapons with us in case we got into a fight when we withdrew.

We drove slowly past Horton House. I recognized Mr. Garraty and a couple of Rob's team throwing Frisbees on the grounds, providing surveillance in advance of the operation.

As Riverside Drive became Beachview Drive and we turned south along the ocean side of Jekyll Island, Bulldog pointed out the campground

"I've been meaning to ask," Amit reached out as if to touch Caitlin's red hair, "is that your natural color?"

"No," Caitlin replied sweetly, grabbing his hand. I saw she had one of his fingers at an unnatural angle. Amit grimaced.

"I dye it in the blood of my enemies," Caitlin explained. "See that you don't become one."

Who says Amit can't take a hint? He was silent for the rest of the short trip.

The limo driver let us off at the condo complex near the Beijing Bistro where I'd had lunch with Ding. "Right there," he said, giving us the condo number. "There's a big party starting up. Mingle a bit, then leave by the back door. Rendezvous here in fifteen minutes."

I had just enough time to say hello to Mr. Humphreys and circulate through the guests at the party. More seemed to be arriving every minute.

"Let's go," Bulldog said softly to Amit and me, heading toward the back room of the condo.

Amit waited a moment before breaking away after Bulldog. I followed him a half minute later.

Brother Francis opened the door for me. "Through the curtains to the balcony," he ordered. Bulldog helped me over the rail. I dropped a few feet to the ground to join Amit and Caitlin. Bulldog joined us a moment later.

"This way," he ordered. "Maintain silence."

Amit and I fell in behind him with Caitlin bringing up the rear. His hand signals were a bit different from what Rob used, but they were easy enough to figure out from context. Bulldog waited until the coast was clear and then we casually walked across Beachview Drive and into the brush. Bulldog had apparently cleared a way through the dense vegetation earlier. We stopped in a small clearing. Bulldog uncovered a duffle bag that had been invisible under a pile of leaves and debris.

"Gunny dropped this off for you," he said softly, handing us the bag. Amit and I opened the bag and pulled out our tactical vests and weapons. Meanwhile, Bulldog and Caitlin were gearing up as well. I gave my AR-15 a quick once over. We were good to go. Bulldog took point and led us down the trail, past a water tower, and toward the Horton House.

"Down and cover," Bulldog signaled, breaking right. I broke left and took cover just off the trail. I froze, wondering what he saw, and who was coming. The sun wasn't technically down yet, but the trail appeared dark and deserted.

"Move out," he signaled. It was a test? I guess we passed, because he continued down the trail without comment.

I'd counted out a mile of steps and we'd just passed the second cross trail when Bulldog signaled "down and cover," again. I broke left and froze. A long moment later, two flashes of dim red light appeared ahead of us. I saw a hint of movement and caught the periphery of two similar red flashes as Bulldog signaled back.

A dark form headed toward us.

"Right on time," Rick grinned. "Follow me."

He led us past the ruin of the Horton house and across Riverview Drive to where Rob was waiting.

"We've been all over this place the last couple of hours," Rob assured us. It's deserted. No sign of surveillance or security. Just the occasional car heading up Riverview Drive and a few tourists to see the ruins. We're ready to breach the opening as soon as Falcon gives the word."

"Good," Bulldog nodded.

I checked my watch. We had a couple of minutes to go.

I moved close to Rob for a private conversation. "Wellstone?" I whispered.

"Got word to his aide," Rob confirmed softly. "Not sure he believed me. Best I could do with everything else going on."

I nodded in understanding, hoping that was enough for the Senator to forego his sabotaged flight home.

Two clicks crackled through the radio. I checked my watch and saw it was time. Rob signaled a freeze. We waited. A few seconds later the sound of sniper fire echoed from the south.

"Squad Two move," Rob signaled.

Two men ran to the pit containing the entrance to the abandoned refuge. They ripped off the grating. Then the breacher and his assistant dropped into the shallow pit and attached charges to the wall. The other six formed up behind a blanket man, standing off at a distance and holding up a ballistic blanket to protect the rest of the team from any shrapnel. The breacher fell back, stringing det cord behind him as his assistant covered him. They took their place in the formation behind the blanket man.

"Breaching has control."

"Roger, I have control," the breacher replied. I saw him work on the detonator. "Stand by," he added. A moment later he began his count. "Five, four, three, two..."

There was a deep thud and a crack as a cloud of smoke arose from the hole and gravel and sand from the explosion began to rain down.

"Breach open!"

"Go!"

The breach team flowed smoothly around the blanket man who dropped the blanket and took his place at the rear of the formation, surging into the breach.

A minute later I saw the signal from the pit. "All clear."

"Squad One move," Rob signaled.

Another team joined us, advancing to establish a perimeter around the breach. "Secure your weapons," Rob ordered me, Amit, and Caitlin. "You photograph," he handed me a camera. "You two grab and bag," he handed Caitlin and Amit garbage bags. We followed him into the breach with Bulldog taking up the rear.

The place was a burned-out wreck, even before the breaching charges had stirred up decades or more worth of dust. The tabby walls were covered in soot.

"Radiation levels nominal," one of the guys told Rob. "Maybe a bit elevated, but not by much."

"OK. Go," Rob pointed at me. I shot photos, and Caitlin and Amit moved in behind me, cleaning up interesting pieces of the wreckage – a coil, some wires with decaying insulation, glass insulators. The place was a junk yard of electromechanical debris. Rusted iron doors stood ajar. One door, however, was shut. It looked newer than the others.

"We can't get this door open," another of the guys told Rob.

Rob studied it a moment. "Breach it."

"Yes, sir," he replied with a smile.

The breaching team leapt into action again.

"Squad Two," Rob ordered, "form up outside the first breach."

We joined Squad One outside as Squad Two's breaching team smoothly executed their well-practiced operation. Another thud and more dust and smoke puffed out of the breach.

"Breach open!"

"Go!"

The breach team surged in again.

"Let's go," Rob said.

Caitlin, Amit, Bulldog, and I followed Rob and the breaching team.

We peered in through the dust and smoke. A huge cylindrical tank a yard or so in diameter and over ten feet long filled the room the breaching team had just opened up.

"How did they get that in there?" Caitlin asked.

I took a closer look as the dust settled and the visibility improved.

"The radiation levels shot up when we opened that door," I heard someone telling Rob saying.

The cylindrical tank had fins at the other end. I shot some photos and took a closer look.

There was a squawk on the handheld transceiver.

"Sparrow," the call was interrupted by static. "...blue flames." The voice sounded panicked.

Rob and Bulldog exchanged concerned looks even as Bulldog reached for the handheld transceiver.

"Falcon, Sparrow, say again," Bulldog transmitted.

Silence.

"Rick, you're with me. Squad Two, out. Take over the inside perimeter," Rob ordered. The team surged out past us and through the first breach.

I moved faster, trying to complete my photographic survey in case we had to evacuate. "Go, go, go," I urged Caitlin and Amit to pick up the pace and gather the debris. No way were we going to remove the huge tank.

"Falcon, Sparrow, say again," I heard Bulldog try once more.

"We still have two and a half minutes," Bulldog noted to Rob.

"Something's wrong. Rick, take the package. Have Squad Two escort you to the boats," Rob insisted. "Now."

I'd been expecting him to give that order any moment since the first hint of trouble. I was already handing my camera to Rick. He neatly collected the bags of debris Caitlin and Amit had been collecting and followed the rest of squad 1 out through the breach.

"You're needed out there. It's your crew," I heard Bulldog telling Rob as I went out the breach.

I could see Rick and the rest of Squad Two, already heading past Dubignon Cemetery to the boat with our loot.

I helped Rob out.

Between us, getting Bulldog up was easy.

A blue light tickled my peripheral vision. I glanced back toward the golf course just in time to see a tiny blue flame descending behind the tree line.

"What was that?"

Rob looked. Seeing nothing, he frowned.

"There!" I pointed through Spanish moss-cloaked trees to where a blue light leapt up and then back down in a parabolic arc.

"What the..." Rob looked, momentarily dumbfounded at something entirely outside his experience. "It's getting closer," he noted at the next jump.

"If it took out Falcon, we don't stand much chance," Bulldog noted.

"Better chance defending from the cover over there," Rob gestured toward the tabby walls of the Horton House, "than anywhere else."

"I'm going to lure it down into the complex," Bulldog declared. "I'll kill it and catch up with Caitlin and the boys. Get going."

"You sure about..."

"Go," Bulldog cut off Rob. "Get your team out of here. Cover Caitlin and the boys."

The blue flame flickered through the trees in another arc. Whatever it was couldn't be more than a quarter mile away, now.

Caitlin grabbed Bulldog and gave him an intense kiss.

"Go," he smiled confidently, pushing her away. "I'll catch up."

Caitlin moved without waiting for Rob, east along the trail, crossing the island to our rendezvous with Brother Francis. I looked at Rob.

"Squad One, form up on me," Rob signaled. All around us there was motion from the perimeter as Squad One broke cover and converged to form a loose formation around Rob.

"Go," he confirmed to me. Then he looked at Bulldog. "Godspeed."

"Deus vult," Bulldog replied. He turned, took up a position in the pit by the breach, and prepared to cover our retreat, while Rob and Squad One made for the boats.

CHAPTER 14: THE ASHES OF THEIR FATHERS

Amit and I ran along the path east after Caitlin, finally catching up with her a hundred yards down the path. A hundred yards further, and I heard a three-shot burst. I looked back to see a dark figure bounding behind the dark ruins of the Horton House toward Bulldog, trailing an eerie blue flame. It seemed to throw a ball of lightning toward Bulldog. The ball narrowly missed Bulldog, exploding on impact with the damp ground, knocking him over, and setting the adjacent grass on fire. Steam rose from a basket ball-sized divot. My God, did it actually vaporize that much soil? No, that would have made an even bigger explosion. The plasma must have vaporized the water in that area. The exploding steam carved out the crater.

Bulldog was back on his feet before the thing could launch a lightning ball again. He fired another three-shot burst. I could see the figure recoil from the impact, but it kept advancing. Damn. No wonder it ran right over the Fidei Defensor strike team. Those lightning balls would be deadly in a confined tunnel, and the Fidei Defensor team wouldn't be able to carry anything heavier than assault rifles.

I gestured for Amit and Caitlin to take cover on the south side of the trail. I shielded myself behind a tree on the north side, flicked the safety off, and raised my weapon toward the target. The thing was shrugging off small arms fire, but perhaps I could get a lucky shot.

"Deus vult!" Bulldog jumped in the pit and vanished into the complex through the breach as his war cry still echoed.

"Russell…" Caitlin cried softly in despair.

Through the scope, I could see the figure – whatever it was. It paused a moment seeming to scan the horizon with glowing, fiery red eyes. Had it seen my motion? I froze, keeping my finger on the trigger guard so as not to fire prematurely, hoping it didn't see me. Then, it dropped down the pit after Bulldog. There simply wasn't anything we could do without a hell of a lot more firepower than we had with us. Time to retreat – or advance quickly in a different direction, as Rob would have put it.

Move out, I gestured to the others. Amit took point, followed by Caitlin. I took one last look at the Horton House, muffled gunfire echoing through the woods.

As I turned, I heard a motorboat engine start in the distance. Rob and his team were making their getaway through the marsh. More muffled echoes of gunfire sounded from the depths underneath Horton House. I safed my weapon, turned my back, and continued down the trail.

We made good time. The water tower loomed above us, showing we were near the other side of Jekyll Island. I heard more gunfire in the distance and then a familiar BOOM echoed and crackled through the woods. BOOM. Amit recognized the sound, too. "That's got to be the 50 cal," he confirmed my suspicion. A third and a fourth shot boomed through the woods in quick succession. "The Raufoss rounds. Somehow it followed the boats, and Rob's snipers are engaging it."

"Raufoss rounds?" Caitlin asked.

"It's a high performance armor-piercing round tipped with incendiaries and high explosive," I explained as we continued along the path, nearing the ocean side of the island. There were no more shots. "That thing may be able to shrug off regular rounds, but the Raufoss rounds will go through a half inch of steel armor easy. The snipers either got it, or drove it off, or there'd be more shots."

"Let's stop. Here's where Bulldog wanted us to cache our weapons," Amit pointed out when we reached the edge of the woods across Beachview Drive from the condo complex. There was a police cruiser, lights flashing, parked blocking the entrance from the road. I saw a couple of state troopers corralling the partiers back toward the central courtyard.

I wrapped my gun and bagged it. Then I took off my tactical vest and sealed both in a duffel bag. Caitlin looked grim as I sealed her weapon in a garbage bag and shoved it into her canvas rucksack. "We're cut off," she stated the obvious. "We can't get to the condo."

"We're going to need an alibi," Amit pointed out. "They're going to have the island on lockdown. Roadblocks, security checks. We can't just hide here in the woods until they find us, particularly with our weapons right nearby."

"I know," I replied. Beijing Bistro was just a hundred yards down the road. The police hadn't gotten there yet. "I'm going to call in a favor from the Tong."

"You're awfully close to the Red Flower Tong," Caitlin eyed me suspiciously.

"An alliance of necessity," I explained. "Same reason you're working with me, come to think of it. You weren't terribly interested in helping at first, so I looked elsewhere."

"You can't trust them," she insisted. "That Ding Li who's been flirting with you? She's one of their operatives." Caitlin drove her point home. "The Red Flower Tong was involved in your parents' deaths, too. They stole the secrets from the Tolliver Library and burned it down hoping to recover certain secrets uncovered by an Albertian named Angus MacGuffin."

Heh. Each group thought the other was responsible for the Tolliver Library fire. It was a good thing the Red Flower Tong and the Albertians were more mutual enemies than allies in their struggle against the Civic Circle. If they ever sat down together, compared notes, and realized neither was responsible, it wouldn't take long for suspicion to turn to me. I could honestly reply that I didn't burn down the library. Amit and I helped Rob steal the critical books, including

MacGuffin's manuscript, but the fire itself was set in secret by Rob. I pretended to be surprised.

"Who is Angus MacGuffin?" I might as well see what else she'd share.

"Some other time," she brought us back to the moment. "What's this favor you're going to ask of the Tong?"

I explained.

Caitlin gave me a look like she was surprised I actually had a good idea, but she didn't object. We casually crossed the road when no one was coming or appeared to be looking, and we circled through the adjacent condominium complex to the back of the restaurant. I rang the delivery bell by the back door.

"You go to front," came a woman's voice a moment later.

"I am a friend of Mr. Hung's," I explained, holding up the jade token. "I need to speak with him."

A few moments later the door opened. "Come in," Mr. Hung invited us, flanked by a couple of awfully big busboys. "What may I do for our friend?"

I explained what I wanted, and handed him one of Uncle Larry's hundred dollar bills.

He made the money vanish. "Wait here with my nephews." He departed to see to my request. The room was small, and the expressionless watchdogs loomed uncomfortably close, watching us impassively. I stared casually into one of their eyes and he returned my stare with an expressionless face that held just a hint of smugness. That wasn't a contest I was going to win. I admired their professional competence. They were standing closer than they should, but that was a necessary consequence of the cramped quarters. I could easily have landed a first blow on them by surprise. With a knife, it might even be disabling, although the other would be on me in a flash. With my empty hands though, they were confident in their ability to absorb anything I could attempt, and then they'd pound me black and blue. I pretended I wasn't the least bit intimidated by any of that while they continued to watch us.

"Follow me," Mr. Hung finally returned, guiding us to the kitchen door. "They're just leaving." He pointed to a table in a dark corner where a couple occupied themselves filling a to-go box. As the couple left, Mr. Hung gave the command: "Now."

First one "bus boy" went out with Caitlin. A moment later, the other covered for Amit. Unless someone was actually paying close attention all they'd see was the bus boys.

A moment later, I joined them at the cluttered table, as if returning from the bathroom.

"We sure ate a lot." I had to raise my voice to make myself heard over the clamor in the restaurant as I surveyed the dishes.

"Any dessert?" the waitress asked, handing over menus. Amit and I ordered coffee and Caitlin selected sweet tea while we decided on dessert.

"What happens," Caitlin asked, "if the couple that was here gets caught up in the dragnet? If anyone follows up on their alibi, the police will have two sets of diners and only one set of dinners ordered."

She must not have followed my discussion with Mr. Hung. "He made a new tab for us. It'll show we arrived more than an hour ago. Since then, we've been eating here. It's dark in here, and I doubt any of the other diners were paying any particular attention. They aren't going to construct a timeline of who was at which table for how long, let alone inventory the restaurant's ingredients to discover someone bought and paid for a meal that was never prepared."

"So now what?" Amit asked.

"Begin by assuming this is not a private conversation," Caitlin observed.

"Excellent assumption," I confirmed. We sat in silence. Knowing the Red Flower Tong would almost certainly have bugged the table put a damper on our conversation.

"We can at least get our stories straight," Amit finally broke the silence. "What about us did you find so attractive that you were inspired to invite us both out here for dinner."

Caitlin looked consumed with worry for Bulldog. I understood why. Had that thing finished off Bulldog and then taken after Rob and his team? Or had it realized Rob and his team were getting away, left Bulldog and taken off after them? I'd have expected more gunfire if it had continued across the water somehow. Unless the Civic Circle's security had managed to get the helicopter Rob's team had disabled airborne, Rob and his team probably got away.

"Obviously, I'm attempting to pump you two impressionable and naïve young Civic Youth for inside information," Caitlin interrupted my speculations.

"Using your feminine wiles?" Amit asked.

"In your case, I need hardly try," she observed dryly, unamused by his banter.

"Oh, there are many things I might do, but betraying a secret is not one of them," Amit assured her. "You'd be surprised at the secrets women have confided in me."

Caitlin gave Amit an icy look that made clear she was hardly in a flirtatious mood. Just then, our waitress returned to bring our drinks and take our dessert orders.

That milestone accomplished, I took a sip from the coffee, holding Caitlin in my gaze. "We do need to get our stories straight," I pointed out to her, "so what reason would you have to be chatting up a couple of Civic Youths?"

She looked up a moment in thought, and back at me. Then she took a deep breath, recovering her resolution to carry on despite her fears and concerns. She said something I couldn't hear. I leaned in gesturing to my ear. "I suppose I'd be asking if you knew anything about TARP," she repeated herself.

I'd used tarps all the time in camping, as ground cover under a tent, or as an improvised shelter. A couple dozen feet of paracord to support the middle and it makes a decent shelter. I had a feeling that wasn't the kind of tarp she meant. Some kind of acronym? Amit wasn't about to admit he was clueless – part of his alpha-male pick-up-artist act – so it was up to me.

"Ok. What's TARP?"

"Toxic Asset Remuneration Program," she started down the road to explanation. "It's a plan the bankers in the Civic Circle cooked up at the Social Justice Leadership Forum two years ago. You see, for the last few years, federal policy has been to offer easy loans to help otherwise unqualified buyers own a home. The Feds guarantee the loan, so the banks can't lose. They drag warm bodies in off the streets, throw money at them without regard to their ability to pay it back, and pocket a healthy origination fee for the loan. It's the Federal Reserve outsourcing printing money to every financial institution in the country. The mortgages are bundled together and the resulting securities are resold to financial institutions."

"Housing prices always go up," Amit argued. "That's a fundamental maxim of economics. Sure there are exceptions here and there, but on the whole, ten or even five years from now, the houses are worth more, and the banks can foreclose if the borrower stops paying, right? What's the problem?"

"No," Caitlin shook her head. "'Their maxims are proverbs of ashes. Their defenses are defenses of clay.' It's a bubble," she explained. "Ever hear about tulip bulbs?"

I remembered a book my father made me read – *Extraordinary Popular Delusions and the Madness of Crowds*. "Prices keep rising in a bubble, fueled by mass hysteria and delusion. Until one day they don't."

"Exactly," she acknowledged, grimly. "Same with housing prices. More and more cheap mortgage dollars chasing more and more houses. Eventually it becomes obvious the cycle can't continue. It gets harder to find the next sucker willing to buy your expensive tulip bulb. And then the house of cards comes tumbling down, and tulips are back to being pretty flowers instead of sure-fire investments."

"You know when it's going to happen? Soon?" Not only was I curious, but also, it was a much safer subject for discussion than how we'd spent the earlier part of the evening.

"Hard to get the timing exact on something like that," she acknowledged, "but the plan is for it to collapse in a couple of years, just before the 2008 election. With either McCain or maybe Bush as the Republicans' candidate and Hillary Clinton as the Democrat, they'll come to a bipartisan deal to force Lieberman as the lame duck to go along. Of course, I don't think the Republicans realize that it's all a set up. They'll play the patsy. The Republican will be "responsible" and will call for the campaign to be suspended in favor of a bipartisan committee to address the emergency. The press will portray him as panicky and unpresidential, and the committee will roll out the TARP Plan as if they just devised it. Of course, they'll come up with a name more palatable than 'Toxic Asset Remuneration Program.' Hillary will cruise to the White House, and the bankers will get the government to buy all their worthless loans and other toxic assets.

"The election is choreographed that far in advance?" Amit looked incredulous.

"It's not guaranteed, of course," Caitlin acknowledged. "Bush or McCain will be the Republican candidate. There's a faction maneuvering to replace Hillary with someone more radical – a disciple of some of the more violent 1960's radicals. They've been grooming him for a while. Gave a big speech at the 2004 Democratic Convention. An ally of the Professor of yours who got in trouble – Gomulka. Doesn't seem likely he'll get in now that Gomulka's out of favor, though."

"How does the Toxic Asset..."

"...Remuneration Program," she completed it for me. "When the bubble bursts, they'll let one of the big financial institutions fail and threaten that they'll all collapse unless the government bails them out. They'll set up a huge fund of taxpayer money to buy out all the worthless securities they've generated – maybe as much as a trillion dollars."

"That's got to be the single largest theft in history." Amit whistled softly. "So we're sitting here and you're pumping us for information about it? When exactly it's going to happen?"

"Arguably, the Federal Reserve was a much bigger theft," Caitlin pointed out. "In less than a century, the Federal Reserve has debased the currency to the point where today's dollar is worth about four cents in the gold dollars from before their 'intervention.' And the Fed's explicit policy is to continue debasing the currency at a rate of two percent a year."

Amit frowned, his curiosity getting the better of him. "How is it people don't notice the devaluation?"

"Because costs are going down at almost the same rate," Caitlin explained. "Today's highly-skilled professional makes about the same wage today – in gold – as an unskilled laborer did forty years ago. The net effect is that the purchasing power of the average worker has been on the decline for a generation. The decline itself appears modest, but only because wages and costs have both been falling at about the same rate. The difference? It goes straight into the pockets of the bankers and funds the Civic Circle's Deep State bureaucratic allies."

"I know the whole thing was planned out here on Jekyll Island," Amit observed, "but how did they push it through? Were they all in on it? Surely it was obvious to other bankers what was going on."

"Oh, it was," Caitlin confirmed. "John Jacob Astor, Isador Strauss, and Benjamin Guggenheim all suspected that Morgan and his allies were up to something. They agreed to take a cruise together back to the U.S. from Europe to discuss it and resolve their differences. Morgan became sick at the last moment and cancelled. Astor, Strauss, and Guggenheim all went down on the Titanic. The Federal Reserve was established without opposition a few months later."

Just then, the waitress brought our desserts. I asked for more coffee. It was going to be another long night.

Caitlin picked weakly at her cake, then put her fork down. I saw her take another deep breath, then force herself to continue despite her fears and worries.

"Anyway, what everyone wants to know is who gets thrown to the wolves by the Thirteen. Some big institution has to collapse to demonstrate the seriousness of the situation. The Thirteen haven't decided yet, or if they have, they're not saying who. Every one of the potential victims has their own man in the Thirteen, or in the Council of 33. One of them gets screwed, it's only a matter of who, and whether they'll get the carrot of an inducement to make them play along, or the stick of some kind of extortion or even murder to remove them as an obstacle." She seemed awfully confident about what was going on behind the scenes.

I swallowed a delicious bite of cake. It stuck in my throat. I felt a deep sense of dread in my stomach, not knowing if Bulldog, Rob, and the rest were OK. I put my fork down, too, and gave up on trying to eat. All we could do was sit tight, establish our alibis, and hope for the best. "You have an idea who it is, don't you? Who's going to get thrown to the wolves?"

"If I did, I wouldn't be discussing it with you two at a restaurant that's surely under surveillance by the Red Flower Tong. Everyone in the circles of power knows the basics. It's the details that count. If anyone asks, I'm pumping you for information — you two actually met the Thirteen. Who seemed on the outs? What was their body language? What hints can you offer? Which way are they going?"

She already had good sources if she knew that much, but it could have been someone seeing us summoned into the meeting.

"Of course, we can neither confirm nor deny that we have any information whatsoever," Amit pointed out, "assuming we took an oath of some kind, which we can't confirm or deny, either."

"I asked you, you declined to answer, I pressed, you refused, and I told you I'd make it worth your while if you came to me with any information. All part of my job as a Vice President for Client Relations at the Holy See Bank Corporation."

"So we don't have to wait to be asked about it," I clarified, "we can go ahead and report this conversation, and you won't get in trouble."

"Business as usual with the Civic Circle," she noted with a bitter smile, "equal parts power politics and behind-the-scenes treachery." I saw her smile fade as she looked out toward the door.

"Mr. Hung has someone watching for him," I tried to reassure her. "He could come in that door at any minute, and they'll bring him right here to our table."

"Don't kid yourself." I could hear the tension in her voice as she held back the emotion. "That... thing. If it took out..." She thought better of saying any details. "I don't believe we'll be seeing him again."

"I'm amazed the police haven't been here yet," Amit said. "I expected them to have the whole island locked down by now."

Caitlin gave a grim smile. "The tension these days is between the American and European wings of the Civic Circle," she explained. "The Americans are all occupying the Jekyll Island Club Hotel and the surrounding cottages. The Europeans are in the Westin by the Convention Center. The rapid response team would respond to an attack by securing the Jekyll Island Club Hotel, the cottages of the Historic District and the causeway to the mainland. Then they'd secure the Beach Village – the Convention Center and the Westin, and then work south from there. All the other hotels are on the south end of the island. It's just residences, condos and the golf course to the north. That's why..." she was about to say his name. "That's why we agreed to undertake this operation up here. Figured we'd have plenty of time. We didn't know about that... that thing."

She shivered at the memory of the ominous dark figure leaping relentlessly toward us, breathing blue flame. "A demon," she concluded. "A devil? Straight from hell. Or maybe Satan himself."

After what I'd seen, I was willing to keep an open mind. I was pretty sure, though, I knew where to look to find out more about our unexpected visitor.

We recovered many books from the Tolliver Library, using the Civic Circle Technology Containment Team's own list of proscribed books as our collection guide. One of the books we recovered was *The Devil of Devonshire*. In the 1850s, mysterious footprints appeared overnight along a hundred-mile-long trail in the southwest of England in Devon. "The Devil's Footprints" they called them. The author of the book argued that the maker of the footprints was an entity called "Spring-Heeled Jack:" a bipedal figure capable of incredible leaps who also reportedly breathed blue flame. Was there a similar stronghold or refuge in Devon? Were there many of these things, or was this the only one?

I really needed to pay better attention. Every book on the Civic Circle's list was there for a reason. I'd at least skimmed through them all, but I had no idea why most of the books were included on the list. Most of them appeared completely innocuous. Until, of course, a seemingly-mythological creature from one of them shows up to kill you.

What was it really? A robot? An ancient Chinese god? An alien? Maybe Caitlin was right and it was a demon. I needed to go back through that list of books and re-read... Why was it suddenly getting quiet? I saw Caitlin's gaze shift to the...

"Your attention please!" I turned to see a couple of Georgia State Patrol Troopers standing by the door of the restaurant. They'd finally arrived. Two more were heading back to the kitchen. I needed to work on my situational awareness. I'd completely missed their arrival. The hum of conversation and the clinking of silverware completely died out.

"There's been an incident on the island," the trooper continued. "Nobody can leave until we get the all clear. In the meantime, we need to talk to everyone here, particularly anyone who just recently arrived."

I could see his partner already talking to the receptionist. She pointed to a couple who'd just arrived. He went over to speak with them. I could hear the questions: identification, when did you arrive, where'd you come from, did you see anything out of the ordinary?

They made their rounds. When they got to our table we bumped back our arrival time by an hour, placing it comfortably before the operation began. They checked our IDs, made a couple of notes, and moved on to the next table.

We got our check from the waitress, and Caitlin picked up the tab. The troopers were talking to the wait staff, confirming everyone's stories and arrival times. They told us to wait in the front of the restaurant for further instructions. The troopers corralled the late arrivals and took them to the back for further questions.

In the close proximity of other people, we couldn't carry on our conversation. Amit struck up a conversation with a girl sitting next to us, much to the obvious annoyance of her companion. Caitlin sat lost in her thoughts and quietly mourned for Bulldog. I saw her fondle her ring and spin it round and around her finger. Meanwhile, I sat and contemplated the ruin of my plans.

The reality of it all struck home for me, standing there, helpless, in the restaurant. Maybe the debris and clutter we collected from underneath the Horton House would be worth something. I thought about that. Old Spring-Heeled Jack wouldn't have shown himself if he weren't defending something of value. Was there something in the stronghold he had to keep hidden? From the devastated look of the place, whoever had visited before us had done a pretty thorough job wrecking whatever was there. Was it merely the existence of the stronghold itself?

That raid may have been our last chance to take out the Thirteen and block the Civic Circle's plans to embroil the U.S. in a deadly war of attrition in the Middle East.

I couldn't be sure, but I thought Rob got away. All I could do was trust the plan. Rob knew what he was doing. Bulldog?

It didn't look good. The whole point of the operation was to stop the war. It appeared the Reactance had failed.

The Civic Circle was determined to bleed us of our best and most heroic young men, squandering their precious lives in the desert sands to leave our nation weakened and ripe for their takeover.

Countless more soldiers, young men just like me, would be sent over there. They would fight bravely, with courage and determination, trying to impose some semblance of order on the chaos. Some of them would never come home again.

We hadn't been able to stop it.

The puppets had rebelled against their puppet masters, but there they still were pulling our strings.

* * *

We got in late to the hotel, and didn't get enough sleep. When we went down to breakfast, the USA Today headline screamed: *MASSACRE – Jekyll Island Attack Kills 54.* The attackers broke into the Jekyll Island Club Hotel – apparently they weren't going to disclose the existence of the tunnels and underground complex – and killed over a dozen "business, media, and intellectual leaders." This was no random slaughter of hicks in the hinterlands. The elite had lost at least a dozen of their own. The story listed the prominent individuals killed. Were some of the victims among the mysterious hooded figures who made up the Thirteen? I wondered if we'd ever find out the details. The Fidei Defensor may have been slaughtered, but they took an impressive honor guard down with them. I offered a silent toast to their memory with a glass of orange juice.

The Jekyll Island attack pushed other tragic news below the front page fold: *Senator, Family, Killed in Plane Crash.* Senator Wellstone's aide hadn't taken Rob's warning seriously. I was still reeling from the enormity of all the news when I saw Amit freeze, his eyes bugging out.

I looked at him curiously.

Finally, he handed me an inside page. "It's Gomulka," he said. "Gomulka 'committed suicide' last night in his prison cell." We looked at each other, each of us understanding the subtext. Our little game was deadly serious. The Civic Circle was tying up their loose ends. Would their housecleaning extend to us?

They cancelled the final day of the Social Justice Leadership Forum. They called off Secretary of State Hillary Clinton's closing keynote speech "for security reasons." Overnight she'd been whisked off Jekyll Island by Secret Service Agents. Amid high security, Bernard called together the Civic Youth for a final meeting.

"After last night's tragic events, we need our next generation of leaders more than ever," Bernard told the assembled Civic Youth. "We're going to Pleasure Island to reflect on our losses and re-energize ourselves for the struggles to come. Then we'll be back to help the leaders of the world achieve universal peace by uniting against Saddam Hussein and the Axis of Evil at the G-8 Summit." I don't think he realized the ambiguity of just who was the real "Axis of Evil."

Bernard directed us to pack our bags and report to the airstrip on Jekyll Island to board the jet departing for Pleasure Island, the Civic Circle's Caribbean island paradise. As I joined the crowd swarming for the elevators, two security guards stopped me. "Peter Burdell?"

"Yes?" I acknowledged.

"Come with me."

I followed him down the first-floor corridor. Suddenly the guard behind me grabbed me and forced a cloth over my mouth and nose. I think I got a good blow into the bastard with my elbow before I passed out.

I came to, tied in a chair, my head covered by a hood. From what Amit had been telling me, some girls and even guys like getting tied up. They find it exciting in a perverse sort of way to be helpless. This was the second time now it had happened to me, and as far as I was concerned it was two times too many. Unlike the Albertians who'd kidnapped me in Chattanooga, these captors had my arms tied to the arms of my chair, not behind my back. I flexed slowly against my bindings, testing them.

The hood came flying off. I blinked and cringed involuntarily at the bright light shining in my face.

"Good, you're awake," my interrogator said, stating the obvious. "We have some questions for you, Peter." There was something familiar about his voice.

I glanced down and realized they had me hooked up for a polygraph exam. I kept a poker face. I didn't know the stakes just yet, or the cards in my hand, but this was a game I was going to win.

"What's this about?" I tried my best to appear confused and disoriented. We were probably in the control phase where the interrogator was collecting baseline data, so I amped up my anxiety, bit my cheek, tasted my blood, and transitioned to fast, shallow anxious breathing.

Then, I took a closer look at the man interrogating me.

It was Agent Wilson: the Civic Circle's lead troubleshooter and investigator. The man who killed my parents and so many others. Behind him stood his mysterious partner. Suddenly, I had no trouble pretending to be afraid. A couple of years ago, I had barely escaped their interrogation with my life. That was with Sheriff Gunn and a hot-shot lawyer, Mr. Burke, in my corner. Now I had to face him alone, and he had the help of the polygraph to assess my truthfulness.

Now I was having to work not to panic.

My heart pounded.

The polygraph needles danced.

"We have a spy in the Civic Circle," Wilson explained. "We have taken someone into the circle of trust who is unworthy of the honor bestowed upon them. Cooperate, and this will all be over quickly. Resist... and it will not go well for you. Do you understand me?"

I paused to take it all in and continue revving up my body's stress reaction without succumbing to my fear. "I do." I imagined ants crawling on my feet, and involuntarily twitched in discomfort. I looked around and recognized the room from the videos I'd seen. I was in room 129. Somewhere behind me was the door that led to the barrels of acid.

"What is your name?" The interrogator ran through his control questions while I imagined the ants crawling between my toes, up my legs, up my body, nibbling their way into my orifices. The ants were just about to go to work on my face when we switched to the real questions.

"Where were you last night?"

I imagined warm water washing off the ants. I was on my imaginary beach, soaking in the rays, relaxing, and calmly sharing my carefully prepared alibi. Amit and I went out to dinner with Caitlin. We arrived a full hour before any of the excitement began, had a long leisurely dinner, then the State Troopers showed up, questioned us, and Caitlin dropped us back at our hotel. I casually told them the story.

"Do you recognize me?"

"You look familiar," I paused as if trying to place him. "I've seen many new faces this last week. I don't know." He stared impassively at me, then back at his graph. Even I could tell I'd calmed down considerably. He'd been trying to provoke me into revealing I recognized him from his interrogation of me after he'd murdered my folks. I dodged that one.

"Do you know Wladislaw Gomulka?" Wilson asked.

"Yes."

He didn't bother trying to analyze my responses and launched right into his line of questions.

"How do you know him?"

"I took his Intro to Social Justice Studies class at Georgia Tech," I acknowledged, "and I worked for him as part of the Social Justice Initiative at Tech."

"But you didn't think much of his performance?" Wilson led me through the reservations I'd expressed to Bernard and the Thirteen about Gomulka's failure to execute the Civic Circle's planned convergence of the campus.

"Did you frame your teacher?"

Did he suspect I had something to do with Gomulka's downfall?

I clamped down on the anxiety before it had a chance to rise. "Frame him? What do you mean?"

Wilson paused, looked at the graph. Were the needles a twitch more active? I was certainly still much calmer now than the baseline reading he took.

"Gomulka was framed," Wilson explained. "He wasn't the type to import a container load of sex slaves. He loved people in the abstract, only, and didn't care much for individuals. He was hopelessly repressed. He could barely maintain his composure with women. The closest he's come to a sexual encounter in decades is getting off to watching porn. You see, it's my business to know these things.

"Some of my colleagues are convinced it was an outside hacker. That's bullshit. I've reviewed this Reka's emails. Gomulka was played. He was played by someone who knew him well. He had no social life outside the movement. That makes for a very small pool of suspects. The folks under him – that would be you, Amit Patel, and Madison Grant. His colleague, that Dean at Georgia Tech. His boss, Bernard. Of the five of you, only one potentially has the skill to pull off this scheme. Amit."

He paused to let that sink in and checked my reaction. I resisted the urge to babble. Finally, he continued.

"Your friend Amit has the means. Hell, he has a huge side business in selling network security software to hotels. He could easily be a secret hacker with the skill to cover his tracks from a casual check. He certainly had the opportunity. You two spent a whole year working with Gomulka and could easily have penetrated his laptop and email. This online seduction, though, took place this summer. Amit was working for the Civic Circle. Our security is airtight. No way did he perpetrate this. So, Amit had help. Who's closest to Amit?"

"You think Amit framed Professor Gomulka?" I tried my best to appear confused. Ironically, Amit had Wilson's own email thoroughly penetrated long before we hacked into Gomulka's laptop.

"You." Wilson stared at me. "You sent the emails to Gomulka, didn't you?"

"What emails?"

Wilson kept staring at me, and finally looked down at his readings. He smiled a smug smile. I was still confident I was very calm, and I hadn't given anything away.

Then Wilson looked up at me and said softly "MacGuffin."

Oh, shit. He was expanding the scope of the interrogation to include what I knew of the Civic Circle's hidden truth. Calm. Waves. Beach. Back to my happy place. I successfully remained calm.

"What?" I pretended to be confused.

"MacGuffin," Wilson said louder and more clearly. "Do you know about MacGuffin?"

I pretend to think about that. "No," I shook my head, "I don't know any MacGuffin."

"It is a term from drama," Wilson explained. "It means, 'That for which the hero seeks.' You've never heard the term?"

"I don't think so," I lied. Wilson had offered the conventional meaning of the term. Hitchcock had popularized the term in the 1930s – at a time when the Civic Circle was scouring the world for the real-life Angus MacGuffin, the missionary who uncovered the secrets of Xueshu Quan and died attempting to reveal them to the world. I still wasn't sure how Hitchcock came across the term, but he'd probably overheard it somewhere.

Wilson must have been satisfied, because he didn't press further along that dangerous line of questioning. He changed tack.

"Where were you the night before last?"

How should I play this one? Better to run with the story I knew Mr. Humphreys would tell. I decided to let him work for it, transition to short answers, to try to hide my alleged tryst with Caitlin. "I was working in the Network Operations Center with Mr. Humphreys."

"Did you leave at any time?"

He knew. Maybe he'd spoken with Humphreys already? "Yes."

"And where did you go?"

"To one of the cottages," I replied evasively, "to fix a network problem."

Wilson launched into the next question without waiting to interpret the polygraph data. "What was the problem?" He already knew the truth. He just wanted to see if I'd admit it.

"One of the access points was not responding," I continued to be evasive.

"Why was it not responding?"

"The firmware became corrupted."

"How did the firmware become corrupted?"

I paused guiltily and consciously amped up my anxiety. "Hard to say. There's lots of things that can corrupt the firmware. Cosmic rays, bad chips, software bugs..."

"Is it possible you had something to do with it? Perhaps accidentally?"

I knew that was a trap. I transitioned to shallow rapid breaths and tried my best to max out my nervous reaction. He was giving me an out to claim it was an accident instead of intentional, but since he clearly knew all about it, he'd be able to nail me for the lie. I decided I may as well 'fess up.

"I did it," I acknowledged, allowing the tension to release and starting to calm down.

"Why did you do it?"

"So I could hit on one of the women staying there."

"What happened?"

I let him pull the story out of me bit by bit – the same one I'd made up for Mr. Humphreys about seducing Caitlin, since he was probably their source. I could see he was enjoying my account, but it wasn't the sexual aspect that turned him on. It was my humiliation he relished. No time to think about that. I had to focus on my story and simulate a modest level of physical discomfort in being forced to tell these "embarrassing secrets" about myself. The experience was creepy enough that it wasn't difficult.

"It's a good thing you were so forthcoming Peter," Wilson replied. Was he being sarcastic? I couldn't tell. His partner standing behind him glaring at me was deeply unnerving. "You can't hide anything from us," Wilson continued smugly. "We captured the whole thing. Here's a little sample."

A monitor flicked on in front of me.

Caitlin, in her sexy green kimono leaned over to kiss me. "Thank you," she smiled. "I'll show you out."

The monitor flicked off.

Oh, shit.

That was the end of my meeting with the Ordo Alberti. They had a camera I hadn't spotted in the network closet. What other surveillance had I missed? Somehow their video cameras had been working, after all. They had everything. They had me. My thoughts raced. Did they have Rob too? Amit? Maybe I could convince them I was working for Uncle Larry?

"Yes, Peter," the interrogator smiled, glancing down at the furiously scribbling needles. Damn. I'd completely forgotten to even attempt to control the reactions from my stress and fear. "We have you," he answered my unasked question. "We have it all. Your pitiful attempt to defeat our surveillance failed. We have every moment of your little adventure documented." He stared at me. Reveling in my defeat. Letting the words sink in.

It was end game.

Rob was rather fond of a poem about an old Roman named Horatius who, with two comrades, held off an army to buy time for a bridge to be destroyed behind them. His favorite part went like this:

Then out spake brave Horatius,
  The Captain of the gate:
"To every man upon this earth
  Death cometh soon or late.
And how can man die better
  Than facing fearful odds
For the ashes of his fathers
  And the temples of his gods...

I may not have subscribed to his creed, but Bulldog
demonstrated for me how a man was supposed to die –
standing, alone if need be, against the overwhelming threat,
buying precious time for his friends. Deus vult, Bulldog, my
comrade. I will pick up your banner from where it fell. I will
fight my final battle under your banner, your battle cry in my
heart: "Deus vult." God's will. I accepted my fate and made
myself ready to buy as much time as possible for Amit and
Rob to get away and save as much of the Reactance as
possible.

CHAPTER 15: THE TEMPLES OF THEIR GODS

I felt the weight of my fathers behind me, as I prepared myself for my final battle. Would my enemies dispose of my remains in their 55-gallon drum of acid in the warehouse next door? It seemed a pitiful but strangely appropriate altar, though, for a temple to the false gods of the Civic Circle's new Babylon. I silently resolved to my fathers, "I will make you proud that I am your son."

"Nothing to say?" Wilson mocked me.

I accepted my fate.

I was calm.

I was ready.

Bring it on.

I would not give that bastard the satisfaction of a reaction. I met his gaze.

"We have every moment of your sad little performance captured," Wilson smirked. "Not even worth sharing the highlights around the office."

Curious... I'd have expected them to compartmentalize that information. Surely they didn't want the rank and file thugs, even at Wilson's level, to know about the Civic Circle's history or Xueshu Quan, or the secret complex under the hotel, or...

"Hard to see what that bank whore sees in that naked ass of yours," Wilson stated in a matter-of-fact manner tinged with a hint of smug satisfaction at my discomfort.

My head swirled in momentary confusion.

Then, I got it.

I was not going to die this day.

That clip of Caitlin kissing me? That was just after I reconnected the router.

Now the bastard was trying to convince me he had the full video of my "tryst" with Caitlin to extract more details and data out of me.

The weasel.

The lying little shit weasel.

He had nothing.

My fathers standing behind me? I imagined them having a good laugh at my expense. My mother, I could see standing beside Dad, wagging her finger to admonish me on my vulgar language.

"Nothing to say?" The interrogator interrupted my thoughts.

Sullen.

Trapped.

Resigned to my fate at the exposure of my "indiscretions."

I could work with this.

I put on my game face and took the field.

"Yeah? So you got me on video. So what?"

"You're some kind of hillbilly aren't you? A hick from the sticks. A backwoods redneck from Appalachia?"

"So?" His feeble insults didn't merit any more elaborate reply.

"So," Wilson continued, "they're pretty traditional back where you come from. Bet your friends and the folks back home would be mighty surprised at what you let that Holy See Bank buffoon stick up your ass."

"Yeah? Well, you do what you gotta do to get ahead, you know?"

"Exactly, Peter," Wilson said triumphantly. "Everyone's going to find out, unless you cooperate and do exactly what I say. You got that?"

I had to be careful not to get overconfident. "Ok."

"See, we know all about you," he bragged, looking through a file. "How you like to lead girls on and stand them up."

He must have been talking to Jessica.

"Your long, intimate showers with your good 'friend,' Amit Patel."

What? Oh... They were monitoring us after all. Well, embarrassing as that conclusion was, it beat them realizing Amit and I had been busy watching the video of the Inner Circle's meeting.

"Your disorderly conduct charge at that brothel in Atlanta?"

Oh, right. That little misunderstanding in my very first meeting with the Red Flower Tong where I called on the police to help rescue me. I kept an impassive face.

"And we know exactly what you did to Ashley."

Who? The only Ashley I knew... oh. One of Amit's girlfriends. After he broke up with her, she tried to get even with him by seducing me, and when I told her she was moving too quickly, she ran off in a fury and told her roommate...

"You raped her," Wilson said smugly – incongruously satisfied at his ability to pin a heinous crime on me. "We know all about it. They'll not just throw you out of school. They'll throw you in jail. Those inmates will make what that banker did to you seem like a five-star resort. Rapist and boy toy to whatever banker takes a liking to your ass. You're a real piece of work, Burdell, and now, your ass belongs to the Civic Circle. We own you. You need to appreciate that."

I hadn't realized I'd acquired such a remarkable track record for debauchery – at least in their eyes. I did my best to look way more intimidated than I actually felt. "So, what do you want?"

"What did you tell that bank whore about the Thirteen?"

"Nothing," I snorted. "I didn't have to. She knew all about my seeing them. When we were in bed together, she wanted to know about something called TARP. I kept telling her I couldn't tell her about it. That just made her more convinced that the Thirteen must have told me all about it somehow. She said what we did together was just a sample, and if I wanted more, I was going to have to find out and tell her."

We went round and round like that for a while. It was my turn to wear him down. Wilson shifted back to Amit, wanting to get me to turn on him somehow – to rat him out as a traitor to the Circle.

Then Wilson began asking me about Larry Tolliver.

"Pretty remarkable coincidence your uncle being considered for admission to Team 500," Wilson tried to lead me on. "You working for him?"

"Indirectly," I acknowledged. "I got stuck way off in Huntsville, working for TAGS this summer."

"Have you seen your uncle?"

"I see him at my Grandmother's house occasionally," I offered in a non-committal way.

"You've been working for him, though?"

"I understand Travis Tolliver, the CEO of TAGS, reports ultimately to him, somehow."

We went round and around. I finally let Wilson pull from me that I'd discussed Gomulka with Uncle Larry.

"What did you tell him?"

"I already told the Inner Circle that."

"You can tell me again," Wilson insisted.

"No, I can't," I insisted. "I was specifically instructed not to discuss it."

"As a senior member of Team 500, I am authorized to know any business brought before the Inner Circle."

"If you were really privy to that information, you'd already know what I said and you'd know I swore an oath to keep everything I said secret."

He finally gave up that line of questioning. I was confident and relaxed. I was sure his readings told him I was being truthful. The questions seemed to be winding down.

Wilson revisited his questions about Amit. Around and around we went again, with me calmly denying any knowledge of any hacking or manipulation of Gomulka. His partner continued to glower at me.

"I'm going to be late to catch the flight to Pleasure Island," I protested.

"You don't need to go to Pleasure Island," Wilson smiled. "We already have everything we need from you to ensure your loyalty." Wilson took one long last look at his notes, then he looked up at me. "We have plans for Georgia Tech this fall," he said ominously. "You're a big part of them."

He unfastened me from the polygraph and released my bonds.

"We'll be in touch," Wilson declared. "Now, get out of here."

I was genuinely relieved not to be leaving the room through the back door to the warehouse. I went up to my third floor room. Amit's stuff was gone. There wasn't enough time to get to the airport, and they probably wouldn't let me see him anyway. Maybe a text could catch him. "Not going to Pleasure Island," I sent. "Stay safe. We'll have pizza when you get back." The code word for 'you are in danger' was 'safe,' and 'pizza' meant I am fine. We'd been leaning a lot on our text codes lately, and we'd need to work out a new code set soon to avoid leaving any obvious patterns.

I wondered what kind of corruption Amit would find himself in. Then, I realized I had nowhere to go, and a week before the G-8 Summit. I packed my bag and caught a shuttle bus to the Jekyll Island Club Hotel.

Security was tight. My TAGS badge got me through the police line, but only after my bag had been thoroughly searched. They even made me turn on my laptop, and ran a check on it to confirm all the security settings were intact. "You're with the IT contractors?" the security guard stopped me in the lobby.

"Yes, sir."

"Well then, get down there," he gestured to the guards at the stairs.

The basement was a scene of orderly devastation. The ventilation had failed to clear the air of the acrid smell of gunpowder, and it was hot from more people than the designed occupancy. Forensic technicians were busy cataloging the pock marks in the walls from small arms fire. Spent brass littered the floor, each shiny cylinder surrounded by a chalk mark. Two larger chalked outlines of bodies showed obvious blood stains.

The Fidei Defensor strike team must have tried to hold off the reaction team right here, then tried to fall back and defend from behind the door. I was standing at the high-water mark of their attack. If they made it all the way here, they had to have mostly secured the Inner Sanctum, first.

The remains of an obviously blown-in door showed how their defensive position had been penetrated. I tried to look into the Inner Sanctum, but the corridor twisted just inside the blown door, blocking the view. The Fidei Defensor made it all the way here, but then lost? How?

Somehow the balance of forces suddenly changed. Somehow they got ambushed from some unexpected direction. I began to understand what happened. Backed into a corner, the Inner Sanctum overrun, the surviving members of the Thirteen unleashed their secret weapon, Spring-Heeled Jack.

Unless...

Occam's Razor.

Start with the simplest explanation that fits the facts.

Not Xueshu Quan, the rest of the Thirteen, AND Spring-Heeled Jack.

What if Xueshu Quan WAS Spring-Heeled Jack?

His minions in the Thirteen wiped out or nearly so, his own existence threatened, he launched a desperate attack on the Fidei Defensor strike team. Taken by surprise from behind, the Fidei Defensor faltered and were overcome by the Civic Circle's Response Team attacking the Inner Sanctum from the basement of the hotel. Then what?

For some reason, Xueshu Quan must have fled. Cut off from a refuge within the Inner Sanctum? Afraid his identity might be revealed? No way to tell for sure. He tried to exit down the tunnel to the Holy See Bank Cottage, and ran into the other half of the attack force blocking his exit. From what I saw of the fight with Bulldog, Xueshu Quan was virtually immune from small-arms fire. He'd have plowed right through the Fidei Defensor strike team. No way would they have any 50 cals or something heavy enough to stop him in the tunnel.

Then what? Not sure how he'd been betrayed and unwilling to take a chance with his own security teams? He'd have looked for a refuge. A place to hide out, lick his wounds, and plan his next move: the old refuge on the north end of the island under the Horton House. Xueshu Quan would have needed to reconnect and reassert power in the wake of...

"Burdell!" Mr. Humphreys interrupted my speculations, frowning. "Get your ass over here."

Humphreys and a man in an FBI jacket stood among the shattered glass and ruined IT hardware in the Network Operations Center surveying the damage. Johnny stood beside them taking notes on a clipboard.

"It's a near total loss," Humphreys was explaining. "We might be able to salvage some hardware and cables, but nothing more."

"We need you to segregate the servers," the FBI Agent explained, "particularly the hard drives, in one pile – that will go to forensics for analysis. The rest of the junk goes in another pile for disposal."

"Yes, sir," Humphreys acknowledged the order.

The FBI agent moved aside to confer with a colleague.

"Burdell!" Humphreys turned back to me. "You're just in time to help Johnny here. You heard him. Servers and drives over here, everything else over there."

I worked diligently with Johnny, yanking servers out of the pock-holed racks. Mr. Humphreys stood back and supervised.

"What's this?" Johnny pointed to an innocuous looking switch. The switch with the network tap. I wondered.

"Just a switch," I answered before Mr. Humphreys could reply. "Throw it in the junk pile."

By mid-morning, we'd made a substantial dent on the mess. A sharp-dressed caterer showed up.

"May I take your orders for lunch? Compliments of the management," he explained. It was Rob. I'd been pretty sure he and the team got away, but it was nice to have the confirmation he was OK.

"We might need take-away," I told Rob when he got to me, my hand resting on the bulky rack mounted switch that included our network tap.

"Yes, sir," he answered.

"In your dreams, Burdell," Mr. Humphreys said. "You and Johnny are staying here until the job is done. Then, you're driving the van back to Huntsville."

* * *

There was no way Rob could get his catering cart through the debris and into the ruined Network Operations Center for a pick-up. What's more, between the size of the unit and all the security, I couldn't slip the network tap into the lunch debris for Rob to cart off. That gave me an idea.

"Mr. Humphreys, can we clear out some of the clutter here?"

He looked around, conferred with one of the FBI agents, and came back. "After lunch."

Soon, Rob came with our food. When he got to us in the ruined Network Operations Center, I took the initiative. "Excuse me sir," I said, "Does the hotel have a cart we could use to clear out these ruined racks?"

"Yes, sir," Rob replied. "I'll bring one down for you."

As everyone was finishing lunch, Rob showed up with the cart. Johnny and I started grabbing the carcasses of destroyed network equipment to move them onto the cart.

"Hold on there!" The FBI agent went to confer with their superior while Johnny and I stood and waited. Rob stood by the cart. Eventually, they decided on a procedure. Johnny handed a piece of hardware to Mr. Humphreys. He handed it to the agent, the agent handed it to me, and I placed it on Rob's cart.

Mr. Humphreys and the FBI agent carefully examined each unit. I held my breath as they got to the network tap. "Another switch," Humphreys declared. The FBI guy grunted, looking it over and handing it to me.

"Dusty," I coughed to get Rob's attention. My eyes met Rob's. He got the message.

He stuck the network tap at the end of the cart where he'd be able to retrieve it easily. A few minutes later, he wheeled the cart off and was gone.

Soon, there wasn't much left for a couple of grunts like Johnny and me to do. The FBI refused to even let us near the pile of servers, for fear we might somehow compromise the data that might be on one of them.

"That's all we need from you guys," the FBI agent told us. I was a bit amused he lumped Mr. Humphreys in with the rest of us grunts.

Humphreys checked his watch. I'm going to try to catch a flight. You two," he gestured toward Johnny and me, "drive the van back to Huntsville."

* * *

I thought we'd never get through security at the hotel, but finally we were back on the road.

"I'm so glad you're going to be joining me," Johnny offered. "I'd been hoping for a chance to speak with you."

"Oh?" I had no idea what I was in for. "I thought you didn't approve of my enlightened progressivism."

"I don't approve," he confirmed boldly. "Kirin seems to like it just fine, though. She's gone off to Pleasure Island with Travis Tolliver and the rest of the Civic Youth wannabes."

Ouch! She dumped him in favor of hanging out with the Civic Circle crowd. I tried to come up with a way to console him that wouldn't tip my hand.

Johnny broke the long silence. "I'm glad we finally have this wonderful opportunity to talk about your ideology." I could see a hint of a predatory smile on his face.

"What's there to talk about?" The last thing I wanted was to spend eight hours as Johnny's punching bag. I had to shut this down, so I could brood in peace and figure out how to salvage something from the wreckage of my plans. "Surely you're not against social justice?"

"As a matter of fact, I am," Johnny spoke confidently. "Do you know what social justice is?"

"Social justice is a noble ideal," I countered, pausing to collect my thoughts. "Social justice is merely running society in a fair and just manner that ensures everyone is treated equally."

"No," Johnny disagreed. "It's a profoundly evil idea. You just have to look past the sugar coating to see the poison pill inside. Justice is treating everyone fairly, according to what is right, and doing unto them as they deserve. Now that's a good idea, a noble idea. That's all you need, really. You activists add 'social' to justice. When you add 'social' to 'justice' you negate the very concept of justice. Your concept of social justice involves treating some people unfairly, unjustly, so as to bestow benefits and favors on your friends and allies with the goal of securing political power. Social justice is a crude and barbaric form of tribalism that pits group against group with the explicit goal of tearing down the out group for the benefit of the in group."

I was impressed. That was easily one of the best definitions I'd ever heard. Of course, I couldn't tell Johnny that and maintain my cover as a leading student activist. I decided to counterattack. "Jonathan D. Rice the Third? You're merely a hopelessly retrogressive traditionalist conditioned by your privileged background to preserve and protect the very social system that created you."

Johnny snorted. "I just have to say that's mighty presumptuous of you to dismiss me as a person and disregard my positions based on your assumptions of a background that, in truth, you know nothing about. I mean, is the person who's suffered the most always the one who's right in every argument? Don't you see that's a ridiculous position to hold? Here we both are hanging out with the Civic Circle, the most elite people on the planet. If anything you're more in with them than I am. How does that make me the privileged one and you the victim of oppression whose opinions trump anything I have to say in an argument? It seems to me we're both fortunate to be where we are."

He was right, of course, but I had a front to maintain as a tireless crusader for social justice. Furthermore, I had my own anger and frustration to vent. "Every competent intellectual understands that logic and reason are merely the tools by which the reactionary white hetero-patriarchy seeks to defend its privileged position against those it oppresses," I attacked. Let him chew on that.

"My, that's a whole lot of fallacies to unpack!" he exclaimed cheerfully. "You know the 'no-true Scotsman' fallacy? That's when you dismiss evidence that would falsify your conclusion by erroneously reclassifying it. It's a form of circular reasoning in which the conclusion is assumed true, and used to refute any evidence, however relevant, to the contrary. If you claim no Scotsman likes sugar on his porridge, and I point out a counterexample of a Scotsman who does like it, you counter that he must be 'no true Scotsman.' You see, when you claim 'every competent intellectual' agrees with your position, and I point out any number of examples of respected, competent intellectuals who disagree, you're going to argue that they aren't 'competent intellectuals.' That's just circular reasoning, though. If competency is defined as agreement with your position, the fact that all competent intellectuals agree with you is a tautology, a claim that by its structure is impossible to refute. You see?"

"You're acknowledging my arguments are impossible to refute?" I countered with a smile. "We may finally be making some progress."

"The point is that an unfalsifiable argument isn't a valid argument at all," Johnny replied enthusiastically. His systematic destruction of my sophistries ended only when the security guard at the causeway checkpoint stopped us. We had to step out while they searched the TAGS van. Looking for the missing agents? I didn't know, but they were certainly thorough. My bag was rifled through yet again, and they patted down Johnny and me.

Johnny began again as soon as we started moving along the causeway once more. "You see," he confided, "I get the feeling you're really a decent sort at heart. You're not an NPC just echoing the SJW talking points. You've actually got a brain. If a couple of guys like us can just sit down and talk through our disagreements, we can reach a common ground of understanding. Maybe we won't agree, but at least we'll come away with a better appreciation for each other's positions."

The only appreciation I was getting was an appreciation for exactly how and why Johnny had gotten on the nerves of the SJWs. It was going to be a very long drive from Jekyll Island back to Huntsville.

"I don't want to understand your positions, Johnny." I had to shut him up, so I could brood in peace. "Your views have been repudiated by the vast majority of enlightened thinkers."

"Ah," he smiled, his blatant enthusiasm and joy starting to get on my nerves, "that's a combination of the Tu Quoque and Bandwagon fallacies. Tu Quoque is the fallacy that if everyone else is doing it, that makes it right, and of course the Bandwagon fallacy is the false notion that the majority is always right." He continued to explain why in annoyingly cheerful detail complete with helpful examples, so even a mind-numbed proglodyte like me could understand.

"There you go again," I replied, "attempting to use logic and reason as tools of reactionary oppression."

Johnny systematically demolished my "argument" by observing that in the very act of argument, I was conceding the point that there was a truth accessible to us both. By participation in the exchange, he claimed, I was tacitly acknowledging the validity of logic and reason to resolve disagreement.

"I'm not a willing participant in this argument, Johnny. You started it, and I'm merely defending myself. Argument is a tool of coercion by which the prevailing power structures seek to beat down any objections and silence their opposition. That's exactly what you're doing to me now."

It was obvious why Johnny had earned a reputation for mowing down the Civic Circle's NPCs. He was like a giant cuddly teddy bear, arms outstretched for a hug. With his relentless congeniality, he made you want to agree with him, want to like him, want to bask in the warm light of his comradery. If he was a teddy bear, though, he was a teddy bear with vicious fangs and razor-sharp claws who systematically shredded any bogus justifications or fallacious support for the progressive agenda. His smug superiority sugar-coated with amiability really annoyed me – all the more because I knew he was right.

You know how two bucks can fight for dominance, neither willing to back down, and they end up with their antlers locked, and they both die?

This conversation was feeling like that.

I almost wanted to let him know I was on his side. It would be easy to be friends with Johnny. My long-term program, though, required that I maintain my front as a Social Justice Warrior, and I had other things to worry about than being Johnny's rhetorical punching bag.

I threw in the towel. "Johnny, I've had enough of this conversation. I'm tired, and I'm going to take a nap now."

"Well, OK, if that's how you feel," he replied, accepting his victory over the forces of social justice with obvious satisfaction. "Always happy to expand my horizons and learn more about other people's perspectives!"

I closed my eyes, but I did not sleep. I'd escaped the wreckage of my plans, at least for now. Amit was still tangled up in the Civic Circle's web. He must have flown on the private jet to Pleasure Island this morning. He'd be there by now. I wondered if he was enjoying the Civic Circle's attempts to corrupt him. Would they be interrogating him, too? He'd probably be fine, and I'd see him at the G-8 Summit. The Albertians' failed raid on the Civic Circle? I wondered how many of the hooded figures I'd met were among the rich and prominent killed in the raid. I'd paid back a bit of the debt they owed me for my parents and the others they'd killed, but the price was more blood – Bulldog and the Fidei Defensor strike team. Would the Reactance have done any better? Or would we all have been wiped out by that remorseless thing? I'd done my best. I had blood on my hands. Could I have chosen better? Time to stop brooding, stop looking back. I had to look forward.

* * *

It was nearly midnight by the time we got back to Huntsville – and that was only with the advantage of the time zone change giving us an extra hour. Johnny dropped me off at my apartment. I set an alarm and crashed. I was up at six and began packing. By eight, I had most everything ready to go. I needed another box or two for my food – surprising just how much I'd accumulated. It made no sense to leave it sitting in my truck bed in the hot sun all day. I got the rest of my stuff loaded in the truck, and I went in to work.

TAGS was in chaos. With everything happening on Jekyll Island, I'd completely forgotten about what I'd set in motion. I got the story from Julie at the reception desk.

U.S. Robotics was not amused to discover that Glyer had helped himself to their robot designs. While I was busy on Jekyll Island, they'd filed an injunction against TAGS and Glyer personally. Then came lawsuits for theft of trade secrets, appropriation of intellectual property, patent infringement, breach of contract, violation of fair trade practices, tortious interference, the works. They had Glyer cold, including discovering he'd sent confidential software and firmware files to himself using his still-active U.S. Robotics email account the day after he'd officially resigned.

The day the lawsuits were filed, private investigators hired by U.S. Robotics photographed Glyer carrying several boxes of materials from the TAGS facility to his car. They followed him to a dumpster behind a strip mall near the Cummings Research Park, and photographed him disposing of the boxes. After he left, they examined the boxes. They were full of U.S. Robotics technical manuals, schematics, and mechanical drawings. He'd even stolen some sample components.

On the strength of that evidence, they'd secured a warrant, and the next morning U.S. Marshals had seized paper shredders and laptops from Glyer's apartment. The laptop was still running a disk wipe program when they found it. The Marshals' next stop was TAGS, where they'd seized all the company's servers.

It was a god-awful mess.

The corporate email was down and there was no telling how long it would take before service was restored – if ever. I stayed long enough to clean out my desk, handwrite my letter of resignation, and deliver it to Rachel in HR.

A quick stop back at my apartment to load up my cooler and hand in my keys, and I was on the road home to Tennessee by lunchtime. I pulled up into Robber Dell, my Uncle Rob's place, by six. A number of unfamiliar cars were parked by Rob's barn.

"Peter! My young friend! How are you?"

"Herr Doctor Krueger," I shook his extended hand, "what brings you here?"

"Hello, son."

"Mr. Burke. Sheriff Gunn. Mr. Patel." We shook hands. "What's up?"

Rob's barn looked like a computer lab. He'd set up a half dozen folding tables. Brandy looked weary.

"Barista-ing not agreeing with you?"

"No," she offered a weak smile, "well, yes. Spending all day making coffee and chatting with customers – it's hard work, but boring as hell. Living in a rented room in town with no electronics, so I'm not tempted to go online and leave a trail? Only Tigger for company? That's not what has me down, though." She didn't seem able to add more.

"I got in last night," Rob explained. "That network tap. Apparently when the Fidei Defensor compromised the Civic Circle's Inner Sanctum, it triggered some kind of fail safe. They tried to dump their files over the network. We got everything."

"Wasn't it encrypted?"

"The dummkopfs used 'encrypted' zip files," Krueger made air finger quotes around "encrypted."

"I cracked it in a couple of hours," Rob had a predatory look on his face. "Everything in their blackmail files, all neatly organized. We've been going through it all day."

"The things they done did in the dark," Sheriff Gunn shook his head ruefully, "never thinkin' someday they'd be brought to light."

"What things?" Now they had my curiosity piqued.

"All of J. Edgar Hoover's secret files for starters," Burke began.

"Ol' J. Edgar had a file on most everyone who mattered back when," Sheriff Gunn explained. "Everyone thought his files had been destroyed when he died, but the Civic Circle, they held on to them. Everything from the Lindbergh kidnapping, to FDR's suppression of internal critics, to the JFK assassination, to the real story behind Watergate."

"It doesn't stop there," Rob continued. "Remember Vince Foster, the Clinton associate and White House Lawyer? They said he killed himself with a gun shot in the mouth? Turns out he was murdered because they were afraid he'd tell what he knew. There was a second gunshot wound in the neck that was covered up, and it looks like our 'friend' Special Agent Wilson was one of the trigger men."

"Mein Gott!" Krueger exclaimed. "You must read the 9/11 files. They knew. They planned it. Only it was supposed to take out the World Trade Center towers, too. They had them pre-wired for demolition."

I was reeling from the disclosures, but that was just the beginning.

"You told us last year how they compromised the new Chief Justice on the Supreme Court," Burke explained. "Now we know why. The Chief Justice appoints the FISA judges – Foreign Intelligence Surveillance Act. They pressured him to select compromised FISA judges to approve warrants for domestic targets under weak and contrived justifications. It's usually that they have some nebulous connections to foreign espionage. They're sucking up everything from key political, business, and media figures."

Rob nodded. "Ingenious how they go about it. They pick third-tier contacts of the person they're really after, get warrants, and pick up the communications of their contacts who are in touch with the real target. It's a bait and switch."

"The worst part is all the blackmail files," Brandy was clearly disturbed. "They have videos of awful... unspeakable things."

"They're everywhere," Rob explained. "That setup at the Berkshire Inn on Jekyll Island? It's duplicated all over the place, but on an even larger scale. Hotels in Los Angeles, Chicago, New Orleans, New York, Washington. Luxury suites for the rich and powerful to go indulge themselves, complete with provisions to dispose of the evidence – and the bodies – when things go too far."

"We also have their bank records." Now Burke was the one with the predatory grin. "All the numbered accounts where the Civic Circle hides their loot."

"Ist incredible," Kreuger was shaking his head in disbelief. "Hundreds of billions of dollars in cash and investment accounts. More in less liquid assets like real estate and shares in private corporations and partnerships."

"I sent Rick and a team back to the Horton House last night," Rob had a somber look on his face, "to see what we could find out about Bulldog's fight with that... thing."

"Did you find..." I began, but Rob anticipated my question.

"No sign of Bulldog's body, or the thing that attacked us. Hell of a mess down there, but someone had already been in to clean it up. The Albertian operative at the campsite maybe? They were gone, too, along with the stash of weapons you left across the road from the Beijing Bistro. We've had no contact with the Albertians. They missed our rendezvous and just vanished, and they haven't replied to my message. We did identify that tank with fins you found, though." Rob handed me a printout with a photo.

My jaw dropped.

"Yup," he confirmed. "Missing nearly fifty years. Appears to have been thoroughly scavenged though. None of the interesting parts were still there. I figure we can pretty thoroughly disrupt the G-8 Summit whenever we want by letting the Georgia State Troopers know that baby is there."

"Oh!" Burke exclaimed. "You need to see what Mr. Patel got last night."

To: Xueshu Quan
From: Special Agent Wilson
Subject: Gomulka Investigation; Suspect Peter Burdell

Completed interrogation of Peter Burdell. No indication suspect was aware of Gomulka's activities or betrayed the Circle.

Note that Burdell was a third-tier participant in 2004 Tolliver Library incident. No indication second-tier connections, suspect's parents, were involved except by social connection to prime target, James Burleson. Suspect's parents terminated in containment operation as a precautionary matter. Both contemporaneous and *subsequent investigation shows no sign subject has pursued restricted or proscribed knowledge.*

Suspect Burdell seduced or allowed himself to be seduced by key contacts in the Holy See Bank Corporation (HSBC). Ties to the Ordo Alberti are suspected, but have not been confirmed. One HSBC delegation member remains unaccounted for. HSBC representatives approached Burdell soliciting information on TARP. No evidence Burdell disclosed confidential information to HSBC representatives. Appears to have been typical phishing effort for confidential financial data and political intelligence on behalf of HSBC.

Suspect Burdell further had lunch with a representative of the Asia Commercial Bank of Hong Kong.

Suspect Burdell is thoroughly compromised and compliant. Cleared for further access.

Wilson

Amit's father took back the intercept. Agent Wilson was the very first Civic Circle contact Amit and I had compromised, while he and his partner were staying in the hotel Amit's folks own. We'd been following all his correspondence ever since. Every once in a while we'd get an important nugget of information. Like right now.

"Thoroughly compromised? What exactly happened on Jekyll Island?" Brandy was looking at me with a suspicious look on her face.

"It's a long story," I put her off.

Everyone kept looking at me, though.

The pressure of the silence was too much.

"I had to explain why I was spending time with the Albertians. I made up a story that I'd seduced one of them."

"He managed to convince the Circle he was so corrupt, they didn't need to corrupt him further." Rob smirked. He was having way too much fun at my expense.

I changed the subject. "Interesting. Wilson's corresponding directly with Xueshu Quan. I was hoping your snipers had killed it."

"That thing that attacked us?" Rob was incredulous. "That's Xueshu Quan? That's the... the thing behind the Civic Circle?"

"The Worshipful Master of the Civic Circle, Chairman of the Thirteen, Scourge of the Ming," I confirmed. "I thought the snipers got him... it? at the Horton House."

Rob looked grim. "After Bulldog lured it down into the refuge, we took off. It popped back up a minute or two later and leapt to the dock.

We opened fire on it, but small arms fire doesn't seem to slow it down. Plus, it keeps moving – hard target to hit. It launched a few of those blue fireballs at us but we were a good distance away, and it wasn't effective. Then the damn thing took after us over open water."

"It walks on water?" Now I was incredulous.

"It was like it was hovering," Rob confirmed. "Nice straight constant velocity right towards us. Sheriff Gunn and the snipers opened up with the 50 cals."

"I heard. The Raufoss rounds."

"Yup," the sheriff grinned. "We got a piece of him. Started jinkin' around like crazy, dodging and weaving back to Jekyll Island. Last we saw of the bastard."

I explained my hypothesis that Xueshu Quan was connected to the stories from the Tolliver Library of Spring-Heeled Jack.

"Great," Rob said shaking his head. "We can add that to the list of all the other hypotheses: demon, god, alien... All we know is the damn thing has been around for centuries pulling strings behind the scenes."

"You need to see this one, too." Mr. Patel handed me another intercept.

To: Special Agent Wilson
From: Xueshu Quan
Subject: Gomulka Investigation; Jekyll Island Attack

I have reviewed the evidence and I disagree with your conclusions. The Amit Patel interrogation uncovered no sign Patel had any knowledge of an attempt to compromise Gomulka in particular or the Civic Circle in general. Patel is thoroughly under our influence, compliant, and eager to do our bidding to ensure continued access to the rewards of our patronage.

I will not have you questioning my decision to eliminate Gomulka. I will order the elimination of any initiate to the Circle who so dramatically fails in the performance of their duties. In the final analysis, it is irrelevant whether Gomulka was an active participant in the plot or was framed by others. He failed in his duties and lost my confidence. See that you avoid the same fate.

Ordo Alberti operatives were clearly involved. Among the dead we identified several former Swiss Guard suspected to be Fidei Defensor. The Holy See Bank Corporation delegation were all thoroughly vetted and have no known ties to Ordo Alberti, but it is possible some lower level members of their delegation were aligned with or influenced by the Albertians. In particular, one HSBC delegate remains missing. Our investigation continues.

It remains far more likely that Gomulka – either working alone or with more senior members of his faction within the Council of 33 – arranged the human-trafficking incident as a diversion in collusion with the Ordo Alberti in an attempt to implicate the Red Flower Tong and draw attention away from themselves.

Make no mistake, the Jekyll Island attack was a brutal attempt by Gomulka's faction within the Council of 33, colluding with the Ordo Alberti, to decapitate the Thirteen and replace the leadership with candidates of their own choosing.

Focus your investigations along more productive lines.

Quan

"There's a schism brewing," I thought out loud, "but Wilson is convinced Amit is involved.

"Amit appears to have passed this interrogation down on this Pleasure Island." The concern on Mr. Patel's face contradicted his reassuring words.

"Wilson is dangerous," I acknowledged Mr. Patel's concerns, "and he was responsible for my parents' deaths."

"If we kill him now," Rob pointed out, "it will only help validate Wilson's hypothesis to Xueshu Quan and the rest of the Civic Circle. Amit will be in more danger, not less."

"We have to stop them," Brandy spoke quietly, but with the voice of moral certainty.

I was missing something, somehow.

"What have they done?" It might take years to sift through and understand the fine details of the Civic Circle's corruption, but Brandy got me up to speed on what they'd uncovered from the Civic Circle's data breach.

One of the leading Hollywood moguls in the Civic Circle had a shell company finance the establishment of "The Church." Their "teachings" seemed to be the bastard offspring of New Age mysticism and Satanism with a pinch of Druid and Wiccan influence, but then spreading their Dark Gospel was secondary to their primary mission. As a "non-profit," they allowed the Civic Circle to launder flows of illicit cash, while keeping the finance under the radar.

The Church needed religious workers. They hired a couple dozen "pastors" from Eastern Europe under special visas. Each pastor brought in a half dozen children with a statistically improbable ratio of girls to boys and an age distribution slanted heavily toward young teenagers. Each pastor soon imported their remarkably young and attractive "wife," with a similarly statistically improbable clutch of children of her own.

They chose an area already dominated by a secretive polygamous sect that would ask no questions about the over-abundance of nubile young children in the community, particularly after suitable "donations" had been made to the appropriate local leaders.

The principal activity of The Church was a drug and addiction rehabilitation clinic. The clinic where all the politicians, movie stars, and executives go when their debaucheries become public? That's the one. Their clientele is almost exclusively male, and returns frequently for "follow-up" treatment. It was the usual Civic Circle game – the carrot of access to perversions, followed by the stick of having those perversions exposed.

Of course, The Church had to provide a cover for these activities, so they funded charitable activities in Third World countries, and set up a medical care foundation. Offering low-cost human testing of experimental medical treatments under the guise of humanitarian aid became another profit center, as unscrupulous pharmaceutical companies leapt at the opportunity to slash drug development expenses. The Church found a friendly African government willing to turn a blind eye on the foundation's human subjects testing in exchange for greasing the right palms. The Church made their human guinea pigs available to unscrupulous pharmaceutical companies for appropriately-sized "donations."

One team of The Church's doctors experimented with vaccines for tropical diseases in a remote village. One of their experiments went haywire, however. They vaccinated a few people, and within a day of the patients' first showing symptoms they were dead of a particularly virulent hemorrhagic fever – bleeding from their eyes, bloody bruises and splotches all over their bodies. It sounded ghastly.

Within a couple of days, everyone in the village was dead. Their school-age children in a boarding school some distance away were orphaned. To hide the evidence of what they'd done, they arranged for the children to be "adopted" through a "charity" in Eastern Europe. The children ended up slaves and sex workers throughout Europe and the Middle East.

In exchange, the Eastern European "charity" sent teens and tweens on "humanitarian missions" to a Caribbean country, where they got new birth certificates and passports that allow them to visit the United States.

That was just the tip of the fetid iceberg. Non-governmental organizations ostensibly set up to help vulnerable children around the world were actually fronts to exploit them – sourcing victims from all over the world.

A modern-day triangle trade in corruption.

The Church figured they had a good thing going and "vaccinated" more African villages. However, some of the villagers fled, carrying the disease to the capital, and it got out of hand. That outbreak of blood fever that killed thousands in Africa a couple of years back? The one that narrowly avoided spreading into Europe and the Americas as aid workers returned home? That was them.

The network of corruption was unbelievable, and it all tied together. Pleasure Island, the Caribbean paradise where the Civic Circle entertained favored members, rewarding them with access to these tweens and teens and documenting their perversions for blackmail had an even darker purpose.

The Church had a clinic there as well. This clinic specialized in cosmetic surgeries and rejuvenation techniques. One of their main treatments was transfusing blood from teens and tweens. They needed a constant supply of young fresh blood – literally – to keep up with the demand. Only the youngest, freshest faces were good enough for the Church and the Civic Circle. They'd use them up in a few years. Those who survived their ordeals might be promoted into staffing the operation, but they exchanged the rest through several different channels in trade for various favors.

I'd become accustomed to the Civic Circle ruthlessly murdering people who got in their way, but even I was shocked by what I was hearing – the industrial scale of their brutality and callousness defied my already low expectations of them. They managed an entire underground economy of sex and drug trafficking, illicit medical experimentation and treatment, and their clientele ran deep into the corridors of power.

The capstones of it all, though, were the rituals they performed among themselves to ensure each other's loyalty.

The ceremony to join Team 500 was appalling. The highlight was a cake that looked like an amazing facsimile of a dead body. The initiates would all chop heavy cleavers simultaneously into the cake. Red jelly filling would ooze out. They'd all get a good laugh at the ridiculousness of their simulated cannibalistic debauchery, consuming the cake before adjourning to real, if less gruesome, perversions. Every moment was documented on video.

The ritual to join the Council of 33 appeared to be almost the same. When the initiates chopped into the "cake," however, the "cake" woke up and their victim died, gasping for breath, bleeding out from the many wounds they'd inflicted. Some initiates went into hysteria at what they'd done and had to be dragged off and sedated. Others vomited. Still others stared blankly in dawning realization of the price they were paying to take their place in the circles of ultimate power. Every moment was caught on video. I was stunned at how many faces were familiar to me. The politicians, media figures, and actors who'd risen to the top in their respective fields – a disturbingly large fraction were compromised and controlled.

"There's so much here," Brandy looked overwhelmed by it all. I couldn't blame her. I felt the same. "How can we get it out?"

"We bypass the national media," Rob explained, "just like we did about Gomulka in the first place. Get the data to local media outlets highlighting the incriminating details on local figures of interest. Breitbart will be all over this. I'll get him an advance copy. He has contacts all over the place and some connection to Drudge."

"The truth will stand when the world's on fire," Sheriff Gunn noted. "Getting this out is the easy part. The hard part is when they start to trace back the source of the leak. They'll know that the Network Operations Center was compromised somehow. That'll lead straight back to TAGS and to you, Pete."

"Maybe," I acknowledged the danger. "Maybe not. Maybe this is an opportunity to kill two birds with one stone. Wilson killed my folks. Now he's chasing after Amit, too. He's dangerous, and it's high time we eliminated him. What if Wilson is more upset about his superior's decision to terminate Gomulka than he's letting on? What if Wilson realizes his superiors are about to find out he was responsible all along? That he was working with Gomulka and tipped off the Albertians. That he took out his own strike team before they could get to Breitbart?

"The man is a fanatic. He knows he's about to get caught," I considered a plausible motivation, "so he's going to take the whole Civic Circle down with him by releasing their data, pinning it on the anti-Gomulka faction, and then killing himself."

"We point all the evidence toward Wilson, and then make it look like a suicide?" I saw Rob mulling it over. "That will look awfully suspicious, even if we carry it off cleanly."

There was a solution. I knew it. I was certain. It was dancing at the edge of my conscious awareness, but I couldn't quite get it in focus. I held up a hand to silence Rob as he started to speak further. I closed my eyes and tried to understand what I was seeing. We had to make a murder look like a suicide. Of course. That was it. The pieces started falling into place.

I opened my eyes. Everyone was staring at me. I smiled back as the solution crystallized into a solid plan. "The way to make a murder look like a suicide, is to make a suicide look like a murder," I explained.

They still didn't get what was so obvious to me.

"The 'pool chemicals' in the warehouse next to the hotel — they're not specifically mentioned in the info dump, are they?"

"I haven't seen anything about pool chemicals," Burke offered, "but I can search."

Rob shook his head. "That's such a low level detail, it's unlikely to be highlighted. The info dump isn't concerned with methods so much as it is with specific dirt on specific figures."

"That's what I thought. We need a little help from Sarah." I looked at Brandy. "She rescued your cat, Tigger, for you. Think we could get her to answer a few questions for us about where she got the materials for the senior design project she completed for you and Professor Chen?"

"Sure," Brandy acknowledged, "but I still don't see what you have in mind."

"It's simple," I repeated myself. "To make a murder look like a suicide, we make a suicide look like a murder." I explained what I had in mind. "The Reactance will defile their temple and reduce their New Babylon to rubble."

My words echoed in my ears as I disclosed my idea and watched their reactions.

Rob got a huge grin on his face at the audacity of my plan. He tilted his head back, looked up at the ceiling, and mulled over the plan.

"Don't got to feather me into the fight," Sheriff Gunn declared. "I'm with you."

I saw the others looking at each other, as the obvious solution became clear to them.

"We can do this," Rob nodded his agreement. "Brandy, you need to get George P. Burdell to reach out to Sarah with our questions. Let's finish organizing this data and figure out how to make copies to distribute."

CHAPTER 16: A FATAL DISCLOSURE

The week flew by.

True, Amit and I had long since hacked Wilson's computer, but we still had to be careful he didn't get a hint of what I was about to do to him. Wilson gave me the opportunity when he left his computer on while he ran out to dinner. I used his Omnibrowser to log some suggestive searches, so they'd be waiting in his search history when someone looked. Then, I placed some online orders for delivery to an unoccupied house on Jekyll Island using one of Wilson's favorite aliases. I billed them to a prepaid credit card Rob's team had acquired in Brunswick a few weeks back.

Rick and a couple of the guys who'd stayed in Brunswick made the trip out to the island to pick up the deliveries. Now that the Civic Circle Social Justice Leadership Forum was over, security on Jekyll Island was back to normal. Securing the helium was the hardest part, but of course, it was essential to the plan. One of Rick's team went shopping in Brunswick to secure all the supplies we needed – DVDs envelopes, postage. He made the all-day road trip back to Tennessee to deliver them to us. We weren't taking any chances that a forensic investigation of our materials would lead back to us in Lee County, Tennessee.

The Civic Circle still reeled from the blow. The high profile funerals of the Jekyll Island victims became platforms for more calls for war and appeals to bring the sinister forces behind the Jekyll Island terror attack to justice. The culprit had to be Saddam Hussein and his Axis of Evil.

At the memorial service for the late Senator Paul Wellstone of Minnesota, killed along with most of his family in an "unfortunate" airplane crash, the fervor reached its peak. A crowd of 20,000 packed the basketball arena at the University of Minnesota. The nationally-televised memorial had more the flavor of a pep rally as a pantheon of Democrats came to pay homage – Bill Clinton, Tom Daschle, John Kerry, Ted Kennedy.... Even President Lieberman came to pay his respects.

The Civic Circle thought they'd silenced one of the most outspoken opponents of war, but they only emboldened Wellstone's supporters. Dueling eulogies passionately advocated war, while others counselled restraint. Some spoke out for immediate revenge. Still others called for careful consideration. Passions ran high, and the event devolved into a near riot. The Secret Service escorted the President out amid a seething hostile crowd.

It was clear that the political resolve for war was wavering, but President Lieberman still vowed to rally the G-8 nations behind his plan at the Sea Island G-8 Summit. We were too busy to do more than watch some of the highlights.

Somehow, we finished all our preparations in time.

Rob and I joined Rick's team in Brunswick for the final steps. One of Rick's team members had printed several dozen cover letters at the business center at the Jekyll Island Berkshire Inn where Wilson was still staying, working on his investigation. We carefully sealed each cover letter in an envelope with a DVD and addressed it to a media outlet.

That night Rick's team mailed the envelopes and the DVDs we'd prepared using various mailboxes around Brunswick. They'd arrive at their destinations starting Tuesday. Rob had already primed Breitbart and other friendly media contacts what to expect. They were ready to do their part.

The next step was critical.

I drafted an email message from Wilson's account and scheduled it to be sent at the time of his usual run, the following morning.

To: Xueshu Quan

From: Special Agent Wilson

Subject: Gomulka Investigation; Jekyll Island Attack

I have uncovered who was responsible for the Jekyll Island attack.

Gomulka was a loyal and trusted servant of the Circle. His enemies framed him so as to deprive us and you of his services. He should not have been so casually eliminated.

I now have conclusive evidence that a different faction within the Council of 33 allied with the Albertians. They used Amit Patel to incriminate Gomulka and by extension, the rest of Gomulka's faction within the Council of 33.

They plan to reveal the secrets they stole from the Inner Sanctum. I must act quickly to stop them.

When you have a chance to review my evidence, you will realize the hidden truth.

I will have a full report to you later today.

Wilson

"You're sure about this?" Rob asked, looking over my shoulder. "They might just eliminate Amit."

"Wilson has been pointing the finger at Amit for a couple of weeks, now," I pointed out. "We have to take the chance."

* * *

The morning of the day I had to be in Savannah for the kickoff to the G-8 Summit, I returned to Jekyll Island to complete one final task.

Rob drove a commercial van with a phony business name to the Berkshire Inn, and backed it up near the Civic Circle's warehouse of horrors. One card sweep opened the door and gave us our window of opportunity. Rob pushed in past me. By the time I got the helium cylinder unloaded and in, Rob had picked the lock to the "pool chemical" storage area. Rob took the helium cylinder from me and locked it in with the barrels of acid, while I confirmed the server room was clear and deposited one last piece of evidence.

We were in and out in under two minutes, the video surveillance of our activities automatically erased.

Using a high gain antenna from the beach parking area next door, I was able to hit the WiFi node in Room 228 and access the hotel's secret surveillance system. Wilson was still asleep. Rob and I settled in and waited for Wilson to take his final run.

"He's moving," Rob announced about thirty minutes later. "Let's go."

The dawn's early light was no match for the canopy of the Spanish-moss-cloaked trees. We traversed Wilson's usual running course backwards, guaranteeing an encounter. We timed it just right.

Wilson jogged along the path toward Rob and me.

I'd been picturing what this moment would be like for nearly two years. "My name is Peter Burdell," I'd say. "You killed my parents. Prepare to die." In my imagination, many times I'd seen the dawning realization in Wilson's eyes that the bill had finally come due for his crimes.

The reality wasn't anything like what I'd envisioned.

"Hey," Rob yelled at Wilson as he jogged past us. "You've got to see this!" Rob held up a colorful piece of beach debris.

As Wilson slowed and turned, I carefully aimed my .45 and fired. One shot. At under a dozen feet, I could hardly miss. Did he realize what was happening? I wasn't sure. It happened so fast. The back of his head exploded in a gruesome, bloody pulp, spraying red and gray goo over a small dark green palmetto just off the trail. The blood looked black in the dim light.

I felt an almost sexual euphoria at the sight of my dead enemy, and just as quickly an even more profound sense of nausea at the gory scene I'd just made.

"Look away," Rob ordered. He holstered his own pistol which he'd hidden under the weathered plastic debris and pulled out a plastic bag. "Take a deep breath. It's over."

"You're expecting me to vomit?"

"Natural reaction," he consoled me. "You doing OK?"

I took another deep breath and nodded yes.

"Then let's get the hell out of here," he commanded. "Back this way to avoid the splatter."

* * *

The G-8 Summit was on Sea Island, just north of Jekyll Island. After the attack on the Civic Circle Forum, not to mention the latest violent assault on a key Civic Circle operative, they weren't taking any chances with security. The press, and even the Civic Youth, were all sequestered in hotels in Savannah, Georgia, a good ninety minutes north of Sea Island. I figured they'd become rather tired of protesting crowds singing "Civic Circle Dandies," also.

Rob and I met up with Mr. Garraty at a restaurant just off I-95 north of Savannah. Mr. Garraty handed over our phones and the keys to Rob's truck. As far as any electronic surveillance was concerned, Rob and I had left Tennessee in the morning and headed straight for Savannah, never coming within a hundred miles of Jekyll Island. Rob tossed him the keys to our truck.

We headed back south, finishing our well-documented trip straight from Tennessee to Savannah. "Remember, they'll be on their guard," Rob cautioned me as he dropped me off at the hotel on Bay Street in old town Savannah. "No communication. Assume you're under surveillance at all times, and don't break cover."

"I know," I smiled. He was trying to reassure himself as much as me. "If the plan works, I'll have nothing to do but sit back, enjoy the show, and wait for all hell to break loose."

"Trust the plan," he returned my smile. "The storm is coming." We shook hands. Then he drove off.

Backpack slung over my shoulder, I tried to walk into the hotel where the Civic Youth contingent was supposed to stay. Security refused to let me in. I had to hike another several blocks to the Johnson Business Center on East Bryan Street to check in and get credentials. For a while, I thought they were going to send me across the river to the International Media Center, but they made a few phone calls and squared away my status.

By the time I made the trek back to the hotel to check in, I was wilting from the August heat. I dropped my bag off in my room, took a quick shower, and went down to the main lobby to hang out.

A couple hours later, the main Civic Youth contingent arrived. I looked at their sun-tanned faces back from their week on Pleasure Island. Some appeared relaxed. I saw Kirin in the crowd. I couldn't read her. I was relieved to see Amit. He glanced my way and gave a barely perceptible shake of his head – no – as he headed to the elevators and up to his room.

No. As in no contact? I decided to let him make the first move. As the group assembled for dinner an hour later, Amit stood on the far side of the lobby ignoring me. Did he know he was under suspicion? He must have some idea, given the interrogation he'd apparently passed while on Pleasure Island.

We walked as a group to dinner, as National Guard Humvees and Georgia State Patrol vehicles rumbled by on the streets.

Dinner seating was assigned, and again I had no opportunity to speak with Amit. I did find myself across the table from Jessica and Kirin. Jessica looked like she'd had a great time – much better now that she'd put the underwear and orange jumpsuit look behind her. Kirin on the other hand appeared... haunted.

"How was Pleasure Island?" I whispered to Kirin.

"The first rule of Pleasure Island," Jessica replied softly, cutting off Kirin's reply, "is one does not speak of Pleasure Island."

"Ah," I acknowledged. "I drove back to Huntsville with Johnny," I told Kirin. "I'm sure he sends his regards."

She nodded in acknowledgement, but would say no more.

* * *

We were up early Monday morning to board the bus to Sea Island. First, we met a State Department Protocol Officer for a tutorial on how to address and interact with world leaders, and we rehearsed how to stand around and form a backdrop for various photo opportunities. All day long. The organizers were taking no chances. Every last detail was planned out.

The highlight of the day was a ten-minute meeting with President Lieberman. "You young people will play a crucial role in shaping the future of our country," the President told us. A staff photographer snapped a picture of us with him.

Tuesday was more of the same. Our job was to be the background scenery as the Leaders of the World arrived in something called reverse protocol order for a Tuesday evening social gathering. It was interesting seeing such luminaries as Angela Merkel, Tony Blair, Stephen Harper, and Vladimir Putin, but we did not interact with them. We merely formed a backdrop so the photographers and reporters on the other side of the corridor would be able to show smiling young faces welcoming the Leaders of the World to the United States.

Despite being at ground zero for the biggest news events of the day, we were completely isolated from any outside news. If the plan was on track, the first disclosures would already be popping up on the media sometime that morning. Would reporters sit on the incriminating material? Surely at least some would be eager to score the scoop of being the first to disclose the secrets. Out of contact all day Tuesday, there was nothing I could do but wait and trust the plan.

The storm hit Wednesday. 'Shocking Disclosures!' read the headline. 'Senators, congressmen, judges, and high administration figures implicated in criminal human trafficking ring!' The scroll bars on the early morning news programs couldn't keep up with all the names. The media techs must have been kept busy overnight strategically blurring the most salacious portions of the blackmail pictures and videos. I grabbed a paper to read on the long early morning ride to Sea Island. The stories they reported were incredible, but I knew it was only the tip of the iceberg.

Amit looked up from his own newspaper and looked back at me, a questioning look on his face. I gave him a subtle nod – yes. I saw him nod slightly in return. He got the message – these disclosures were our handiwork.

We got to play backdrop again in the morning at the plenary session, and again in the afternoon at the Spouses' Program led by First Lady Hadassah Lieberman. By mid-afternoon, the tension was thick in the air as the revelations continued to pour forth. Angry confrontations were taking place all over. "Can't you stop these vicious people saying all these vicious things?" the First Lady was asked.

Whatever we were supposed to be doing that evening was cancelled amid the chaos and the emergency damage control sessions. We were all shuttled back to Savannah late Wednesday afternoon. We drove past bedraggled protestors who'd made the trek under the hot August sun all the way along the causeway to Sea Island. Their destination was a corral manned by National Guard soldiers, where the exhausted protestors sipped from bottles of cold water as they waited to be formally arrested and driven back in air conditioned vans for processing.

The Civic Circle's usual efficiency was breaking down. We were all on our own for dinner. I was waiting in the lobby hoping to catch Amit and go somewhere private where we might talk at long last. Out of the corner of my eye, I saw a woman sit down behind me.

"Come," a sultry voice spoke softly. "We have to talk. You must follow me."

She rose and headed slowly past the front desk.

It was Ding Li.

This was a risk. No one would know where I was. True, we were in a hotel swarming with security, but I didn't doubt that "accidents" could be arranged. Better to face the danger head-on.

I trailed her casually, a couple dozen feet behind her, as if looking for a restroom. She ducked into a door marked "Staff." I followed. She led me out of the hotel through a side exit that somehow bypassed security, and then down Bay Street. I maintained my distance, walking about thirty seconds behind her. We turned down an alley and went in the service entrance to a different hotel. She waited for me at the end of a service corridor. Two thugs moved to block my way.

"He is with me," Ding Li advised them. They stood down, but eyed me menacingly as I passed. Ding Li led me through a back door into what looked like one of the hotel meeting rooms, decorated in the same red Chinese-themed motif of the Red Flower Pavilions in Atlanta and on Jekyll Island. I recognized who was waiting for us.

"Honorable Shan Zhu," I gave a modest but respectful bow, and he nodded his head in recognition. "Mr. Hung," I acknowledged the man who was probably the regional leader of their organization. "I do not have the honor of knowing your colleagues, however."

"Mr. Burdell," Mr. Hung stood and returned my bow. "These..." I interrupted him with an outstretched hand. He shook my hand and continued. "These are my Brothers. Please be seated."

Brothers? Peers to Mr. Hung? Fellow regional leaders? "Gentlemen," I nodded in their general direction as I took my seat. Ding Li sat beside Honorable Shan Zhu.

Another stunningly beautiful waitress set four cups of tea on the table. I wondered if she harbored secret and dangerous talents, like Ding Li. Mr. Hung interrupted my train of thought, pouring tea into two of the cups, leaving two cups empty.

I took one of the cups, and poured the tea into another. I offered Mr. Hung the cup of tea and lifted the remaining cup to my mouth. We both sipped.

"What a remarkable week this has been," Mr. Hung began, "filled with revelations and exposure of corruption. It is as if someone turned on the lights and the cockroaches are too busy scurrying for shelter to remember what they had planned to accomplish."

Ding Li whispered softly into Honorable Shan Zhu's ear, translating, I presumed.

"Yes," I agreed neutrally, "Truly remarkable."

"Every action bears the chop of the actor," Mr. Hung continued, "his intent, his purpose, his means. Every action tells a story about the actor responsible."

"Chop?"

"The sign, the signature, the fingerprint," he clarified.

"Oh, I see." They were suspicious. I felt the weight of more than a dozen eyes seeking out any hint or reaction. "What does this chop tell you about the actor responsible for these disclosures?"

"There are many actors on the world stage," Mr. Hung explained. "They are cautious. They work in the shadows with modest means for modest ends. They seek incremental advantage, and improved leverage, to enhance their position and those of their patrons. They hoard their secrets greedily, using them as currency and as tools against their opponents. They have learned through hard experience that small moves are the wisest, because if they forget this lesson they are soon no more."

That sounded ominous.

Just then the waitress returned, accompanied by men carrying platters of food. The placed steaming platters of food on the rotating platform at the center of the table.

"Please, serve yourself," Mr. Hung invited me. "The duck is very good."

I helped myself to platters my hosts had already sampled and nibbled modestly at my food as he continued.

"The Ordo Alberti are as ancient as our own organization. They know these lessons as well as we do. Yet, they take a crazy chance. They move directly against Xueshu Quan, himself. True, the Albertians landed a mighty blow, even killing most of the Thirteen, but Xueshu Quan himself took the field against them, killing their elite Fidei Defensor warriors to a man. Xueshu Quan immediately moved to the north end of Jekyll Island and repelled a secondary attack."

He looked coldly at me. "Just then, you chose to impose on our hospitality and invite your friends to dinner under our roof, one of whom may have ties to the Ordo Alberti."

He paused. The silence grew longer.

This was no casual social gathering. The leadership of the Red Flower Tong had gathered to discuss last week's attack on the Civic Circle. They probably suspected my involvement what with my showing up on the doorstep of the Beijing Bistro and asking them to arrange an alibi. If they suspected I had the Civic Circle's secret blackmail files...

"My actions are my own," I explained, "but, I may not betray my own secrets or the secrets of others I have agreed to keep, just as I would not betray your secrets you have entrusted with me." Did they suspect my involvement? Or did they think I was a minor player in an Albertian plot?

"Rome itself shudders under the weight of this reckless behavior," Mr. Hung explained. "Xueshu Quan has refrained from moving directly in the past, but with John Paul II gone, his successor may be unequal to the task. It is clear this novice Pontiff endorsed the rash actions of the Ordo Alberti. Xueshu Quan will move against him. Pope Benedict will resign, or be killed."

"I thought being Pope was a lifetime position," I countered. "A Pope can't simply resign, can he?"

"That's what John Paul I thought as well," Mr. Hung answered dryly. "A remarkable amount of doctrinal flexibility is possible when the alternative is death, however. In any event, Xueshu Quan will ensure that a more compliant Pontiff will soon sit on the throne of Saint Peter. We were amazed at the uncharacteristic rashness of the Ordo Alberti. Then, some trusted agent of the Civic Circle leaked secrets that were publicized with incredible speed, defying the usual gatekeepers and controls the Civic Circle imposes on the flow of information. Now, the revelations of the past couple of days made us wonder if the prime mover behind all these events was within the Order or without.

"On Jekyll Island just three days ago, one of the most diligent and feared assassins of the Civic Circle, a man named Wilson, was found murdered just as he claimed to have uncovered those responsible for the attack. The full resources of the Civic Circle swept in to investigate who killed Wilson. Wilson's partner, a Special Agent Jack Gardner, vanished as suspicion fell upon him. They discovered Wilson had been investigating balloons. As they were investigating, local police, acting on an anonymous tip, found a half dozen partially dissolved victims and a used helium cylinder in a storage area underneath the Berkshire Inn. The Civic Circle is now convinced that Wilson shot himself, and used a balloon to carry the gun away, in a desperate attempt to incriminate your friend, Amit Patel and the faction within the Council of 33 opposed to Gomulka."

Mr. Hung took a sip from his water glass.

"Wilson is also... apparently... responsible for the shocking disclosures of the last few days. The Civic Circle's agents found the evidence in a server room near where they found the helium. As near as the agents can tell, Wilson released the entire collection of Civic Circle kompromat to the world in one reckless action. Whether his partner, Agent Gardner, was involved they do not know, for he cannot be found."

I resisted the urge to celebrate.

This was very good news.

Our plan had worked.

The Civic Circle accepted our staged suicide at face value and blamed Wilson for our disclosures. His partner – this Special Agent Jack Gardner – vanished rather than face the usual consequences of a Civic Circle investigation.

"The local police and the Georgia Bureau of Investigation are now also convinced that Wilson was part of a ring responsible for a series of disappearances of local youth over the years," Mr. Hung added. "They are resisting attempts by Federal officials to sweep it all under the carpet."

Mr. Hung waited, expecting an answer.

"Perhaps Wilson grew remorseful for the many lives he's taken over the years," I speculated. "He took his own life and released blackmail material he'd had access to over the years in an act of repentance for his crimes."

Mr. Hung didn't seem convinced.

He stared at me.

The silence grew heavier.

I resisted the temptation to jabber further.

Finally, Mr. Hung broke the silence.

"There is a new actor on the world stage, Mr. Burdell, and these actions bear his chop. This new actor is brutally direct, and ill-disciplined. He manipulates ancient powers and dangerous operatives with frightening ease, drawing them into ill-considered actions. He acts extravagantly, emotionally, expending in a moment secrets that could take many lifetimes to secure. These are not the actions of the Albertians. These are not the actions of any established power. These are the actions of someone new, an agent of chaos, someone dangerous, not only to Xueshu Quan and the Civic Circle, but to the Ordo Alberti and the Brotherhood as well. We wondered what new power was rising, moving in secret, leaving so much chaos in its wake.

"Then Ding Li told us a most improbable tale: a tale of an impetuous youxia who refused to accept the inevitable course of events and rashly vowed to bend the very powers of the Earth to his liking.

"And, of course, all that the youxia rashly vowed to do came to pass, and the murderer of the youxia's parents lies dead – blamed for the disclosures."

Mr. Hung paused, staring at me. They had me. We'd been so busy trying to hide our tracks from the Civic Circle, we hadn't thought how obvious it would appear to the Tong. Better to 'fess up than try to hide behind an evasion or an obvious lie.

"And we all lived happily ever after?" I offered a glib conclusion to his story.

No one seemed amused by my flippancy.

I continued in a more serious vein. "Ding Li told me she was authorized to speak to me with the voice of the Red Flower Tong. She told me the Brotherhood would not stand in my way. I have heard that when a Brother speaks, it is a vow. Everything a Brother says is a promise. If a Brother says he will do something, then it will be done. Have I heard falsely?"

"You heard correctly, slippery one," Mr. Hung confirmed, "but Ding Li is not truly a Brother. Moreover, she committed the Brotherhood only to stand aside and not interfere. Ding Li's words pledged us to neutrality. Some might argue that you broke that neutrality by seeking refuge under our roof. You risked dragging us into your conflict, risked bringing Xueshu Quan himself to our very doorstep. You tricked us into aiding you when our only obligation was to stand aside. We are no longer bound by a vow to you that you have broken to us. You have unbalanced the scales."

This did not sound good. People who unbalanced the Tong's scales ended up dead. I had to think fast.

"When you agreed to help me discredit our mutual enemy, Professor Gomulka, I told you I expected a shipment of illicit drugs, and I told you I expected that the outcome would be the discrediting of the Civic Circle and the disruption of their plans to trigger a Middle East war. You agreed to work with me, knowing that you would use our agreement to further your own ends by smuggling in...

workers for your organization. You further knew my expectations that war could be avoided were unrealistic. Yet, you said nothing.

"Who are the slippery ones? Who unbalanced the scales? All I asked of you was a meal and an alibi for me and my friends in a time of need, and I even paid for the privilege. I did not set out to deliberately mislead or take advantage of you. I only sought your minor assistance in an emergency. I have done much more for you and yours in your time of need, saving your nephew, Professor Chen. You, on the other hand, deliberately set out to mislead me by failing to correct my... misunderstandings regarding the nature and consequences of our collaboration.

"You would have led us into open conflict with Xueshu Quan," Mr. Hung insisted. "That is not 'minor assistance.'"

"It was minor assistance," I insisted. "You helped me establish an alibi. I paid well for the privilege. If there are unforeseen damages or consequences to the Brotherhood, I will make amends, and I will pay what I owe, but I do not see that you have suffered any harm.

"You would have seen my nation led into open conflict, my countrymen slaughtered, our strength dissipated," I pointed out. "Whose grievance is the greater?"

I turned to face Honorable Shan Zhu and waited for Ding's translation to catch up before continuing.

"The Albertians made their existence known to me. I have worked with them, as I have worked with you to harass and weaken our mutual enemy, the Civic Circle. They acted of their own free will. They acted contrary to what I advised. They won a tactical victory against our mutual enemy, but at great cost. I have no secret power to make anyone do anything except by laying out facts and opportunities and seeking mutual assistance to mutual benefit."

I waited for the translation to catch up and then addressed Mr. Hung and his Brothers.

"I value our friendship. We share a common enemy. We share a common goal – his destruction. I did not share all my plans and designs with you, as you do not share yours with me. You agreed to stand aside, and I acted alone. Now, our mutual enemy is weakened by the most direct blow he has suffered in many decades. You did not have to act openly. You did not face a significant risk in this action. You suffered no harm. Now, you stand to benefit. Perhaps I have created chaos, but chaos is inherent in the downfall of the ancient enemy. In chaos there is risk, but there is also opportunity to be seized."

I turned back to Honorable Shan Zhu and concluded.

"I have worked honorably with you to our mutual benefit. Your nephew, Professor Chen, continues to serve you because of my actions. Our mutual enemy, Professor Gomulka, is no more because we have worked together. Now the Thirteen themselves have been broken. Now Xueshu Quan knows that he is vulnerable. His control weakens. His power crumbles. All this I have accomplished at the cost of a dinner in your restaurant, for which I paid. The Brotherhood was not harmed."

I remembered something from Sun Tzu. I hoped I could paraphrase accurately. "We stand at a crossroads. Now is the time to join together with allies, secure each other's flanks and pursue the fleeing enemy, not squabble amongst ourselves."

I was out of words. I could only hope I'd made my point. I was kicking myself for coming with Ding Li with no backup and no plan. The Brotherhood of the Red Flower Tong was about to pass judgement upon me.

Honorable Shan Zhu listened to Ding's translation, and said something back to her. She stood and bowed to her master, then faced me and said. "You will come with me."

I didn't see much alternative.

My life was already in their hands.

I followed her through the door. A couple of "waiters" followed us down the service corridor and around a corner. Ding Li opened a door into a closet and stepped in. "Join me in here."

There was barely room for the two of us. I stepped in, placing a hand on her bare shoulder as the room became jet black. The waiters closed and locked the door behind us.

"My, this is cozy." I felt her moving. She turned and leaned away from me, her pert silk-shrouded rear pressing into me. "What are you...?" A crack of light appeared as the wall swung away.

"This way." She stepped into a hotel room. I followed, and she closed a mirror behind me, leaving no trace of the secret passage. "Have a seat," she gestured toward a love seat.

"I prefer to stand." I looked around the room – a large suite with a single king-sized bed visible through the door in another room. "This must come in handy," I gestured toward the mirror-covered secret door.

"You have caused me to lose face with Honorable Shan Zhu and my Brothers." She sat on the love seat, her legs crossed modestly, but her arms spread wide – one on the arm of the chair and the other on her hip. Her elbow framed a jaunty angle drawing my attention to her chest which rose and fell delightfully.

I shifted my gaze upward to meet her eyes. "Why?"

"You are dangerous. You are an enigma. We do not casually collaborate with outsiders. We use outsiders. We do not let outsiders use us. Yet somehow, it is clear that you used us. This is intolerable. The example of the Albertians shows the danger in continuing to tolerate your existence. Somehow you killed the most feared agent of the Civic Circle and twisted his death to serve your own ends. If you could do as much to the Albertians and the Civic Circle, what could you do if you raised your hand against the Brotherhood? There are many among my Brothers who would kill you out of hand and rid ourselves of the risk."

The incongruity between what she said and the way she licked her lips afterward was... disconcerting. "Their hands are stayed by my vow to you. This angers them. Because of you and what you have unleashed here, Honorable Shan Zhu has had to travel a second time this season. This angers him.

He had to summon many of my most senior uncles to advise him. This angers them."

"Are they angered by the blow suffered by the Civic Circle?"

She smiled. "There are those who would prefer to stand aside and allow Xueshu Quan to make the Celestial Kingdom the agent of his global power and only then claim what he will have won for us. There are others who recognize that Xueshu Quan in control of China and the world would be an even more formidable foe, perhaps invincible. The inevitable course of history dictates the decline of the West and the growth of Chinese power with or without Xueshu Quan. Many of my brethren are pleased at the setback our ancient enemy suffered at the hands of the Albertians. Others are fearful of the chaos that will result. Still others are both."

"The old sometimes fear change," I offered, "even when it's for the best and makes for a better world. We are all individuals. We must act as we see best."

"You are right," she replied, "and you are wrong also. We are all individuals, but we are individual links in a chain stretching from our ancestors to our descendants. We must live up to the legacy of our ancestors and build upon it so as to leave a world that will make our descendants proud of us.

"There is a village on the Yangtze River where the baiji, the river dolphins, once played," she looked into the distance as she shared her story. "For generations our ancestors lived beside them, but now we fear the baiji may be extinct. My people built a preserve and sanctuary to keep safe any baiji who might remain. They built a hospital and holding pools to treat sick or injured or newly-captured baiji. They built a fish farm across the river to ensure the baiji would have plenty to eat. All this was not only very expensive for my poor village, but also, likely to fail to save the baiji, for as best we can tell, the baiji are no more."

"Why do they sacrifice in this fashion?"

"If we fail to do so, we will shame ourselves in the eyes of our ancestors and our descendants. While there is shame in failure, the greater shame lies in failing to try. We seek to redeem ourselves in the eyes of our ancestors and our descendants alike by doing all we can to save the dolphins. We are a great people, because we have great ancestors to live up to."

"One's ancestors and their accomplishments don't make one great," I countered. "It's still an individual choice."

"Yes," Ding Li nodded, "but you miss the point. Your ancestors present you with their example. They say to you, 'look what we accomplished. We started with far less than you. We worked hard to create the legacy upon which you rest. We did all these great things. What will you do?' They ask, 'What is your excuse? What legacy will you leave to your descendants? Will you live up to our example and be good stewards of that which we leave in your care? Or will you squander the opportunity we have bought for you in sweat and blood?' Great ancestors inspire you to make the right choice and to live up to their example. If you follow their path, you earn a share of their greatness."

I could see her point.

"I have failed my ancestors," she continued, "by binding the Brotherhood's hands when they need to be free to deal with you."

"I disagree," I couldn't let that stand. "You've succeeded in making an alliance with a capable new ally in the Red Flower Tong's fight against the ancient enemy. You committed the Tong to a policy of neutrality in a battle that inflicted great harm upon the ancient enemy and your Albertian rivals alike, with no harm done to the Brotherhood. You are the Brotherhood's liaison to a powerful and promising new ally. You've advanced the Brotherhood's goals with minimal risk and cost. You should be honored among your Brothers for what you have accomplished."

"I do not know if they will see it that way," she smiled, "and in any event, surely you have noticed I am not even a 'Brother.' My power is more limited than theirs. And they may well choose to dishonor me and renounce the word I gave to you."

It was my turn to smile. "You know the power you possess, and you wield it skillfully. You have the ear of the Honorable Shan Zhu, and the wit to know what to whisper into that ear."

Just then the mirror opened and one of the thugs said something to Ding. "They have decided," she said. "Come with me."

My tactical position with only Ding Li on this side of the mirror was far better than it would be once I crawled through to where the thugs awaited me. No matter how skilled she was, and I wasn't about to underestimate her, I was much larger and stronger. I might be able take her in a fight, if I acted now, and struck with surprise. Once we were on the other side of the wall with the two thugs, I wouldn't stand much of a chance.

The room was probably locked and guarded. I kicked myself mentally for allowing Ding Li to distract me when I should have been working on an escape. I hesitated.

"I am sure it is good news. Come with me." She stepped through the aperture.

I didn't see much alternative, and somehow, I trusted her. I joined her in the closet. I hoped I wouldn't regret my decision. She slid her way past me and closed the mirror. I intercepted her hand as it moved for the closet door. "Wait," I commanded. My hand swept up her bare arm in the darkness to the back of her neck, my fingers grabbed hold of her dense hair and twisted her against me.

I heard her take a deep breath as she melted into me, her scented hair tickling my nose.

"For luck," I said, pulling her head back to kiss her.

She lingered a moment, reciprocating my kiss with her own, her hands pulling me hungrily toward her. Then, she pushed me back, took another deep breath, and released a contented moan. Then she whispered, "Save your luck." I could hear her smile in the darkness. "You will need it soon, but not today."

She flowed past me sensually to open the closet door. I followed her out, and we were escorted back to the Red Flower Pavilion.

Honorable Shan Zhu pronounced his judgement on me. Ding Li translated.

"All that Mr. Hung has said against you is true. You are dangerous, undisciplined. You leave chaos and confusion behind your passing. You put us at risk." He looked at me. Ding's head was bowed. She did not meet his eyes or mine.

"However," she continued translating as he looked at me, "you hide order beneath the chaos you create, and you mask your strength with your apparent weakness. You won a great victory against the ancient enemy. Perhaps we were exposed to some risk, but you did us no harm. And we are bound by the words..." The others shifted in their seats. I saw some eyebrows raised in surprise, and a few heads nodding in agreement. She paused a moment, the flow of words temporarily interrupted by disbelief, before continuing. "...by the words of Ding Li, our Brother."

He continued, and Ding Li paused a moment before translating. "You are dangerous, but far more to the ancient enemy than to ourselves. We do not doubt your motives, only question your wisdom. You are young. You have many lessons to learn, Mr. Burdell. I hope you will live long enough to learn them. Go in peace, Mr. Burdell."

I bowed. "Thank you, Honorable Shan Zhu. May the winds be with you in your journey home."

He barked a command, and Ding Li escorted me out of the Red Flower Pavilion.

"A token of our renewed friendship," I said to her once we'd cleared the room. "The Civic Circle noted your meeting with me. They are unaware of your connection to the Brotherhood. Also, the Civic Circle intends to deport your workers to Pleasure Island, unless you can intervene. They have something on the judge."

I didn't like being a party to the Red Flower Tong's human trafficking, but with the Albertians out of the picture, it beat the alternative of letting the Tong's "immigrants" fall into the Civic Circle's clutches.

"Oh?" Ding Li looked at me in surprise. "Thank you. I will pass that on."

By now, we were back in a public area of the hotel. I had to ask, "I thought you were convinced they would renounce your word. So, how did you know everything would be fine?"

She smiled. "Because the only reason they would have summoned you was to share good news. If the decision had gone against you, you would have remained in the room. With me."

She moved closer and whispered in my ear. "In a way, it is a pity," she offered. "I would have made it the most pleasurable death I have ever inflicted." She took a step back and smiled sweetly. "I think I like you. See you around, Peter Burdell." She turned and departed without another word. I watched her receding hips sway seductively back and forth.

I took a deep breath as I felt a load of tension lift from my shoulders. At that moment, I finally got what Amit had been saying about crazy and hot. No, "crazy" wasn't the right word. She wasn't "crazy," just extremely dangerous and unpredictable. She'd kill me in a heartbeat if she were ordered to do so, or if she thought it was required by her duties to the Tong. I had to get a good night's sleep if I was going to be effective at the G-8 Summit tomorrow.

* * *

On Thursday, it became clear that the previous day's revelations were merely a prelude. The full force of the storm hit. 'Disgraced!' read the bold headline on *USA Today* in the hotel lobby. An epidemic of suicides and disappearances had struck the corridors of power – The Chief Justice of the Supreme Court was found dead from a gunshot wound to the head in his study at home. Suicide? Murder? Who could tell? Who would you believe?

There were also several skirmishes the previous day on the streets of Savannah between protesters and the police and National Guard who were there maintaining order. We saw none of it because we had all been herded onto a shuttle bus at five in the morning for the drive to Sea Island.

The world reeled from the weight of the previous day's disclosures. More were coming out almost hourly as hundreds of reporters sifted through the source material, finding and publicizing even more guilty figures. I checked my watch early Thursday morning as we were bussed across the long causeway to Saint Simon Island and Sea Island.

Back in Sherman, Tennessee, Uncle Rob was busy orchestrating the largest theft since the creation of the Federal Reserve in 1913. Mr. Burke, Dr. Krueger, and Mr. Patel set up in a conference room at the Berkshire Inn where they'd have good connectivity. They began systematically working their way through the Civic Circle's numbered accounts at banks around the world, transferring funds to accounts we controlled, and then on to still further accounts elsewhere. They began early – tapping European accounts and moving funds to the Caribbean and Panama. As the day progressed, they would be clearing out accounts from the Caribbean and transferring funds to Asian banks.

For now, I could only trust the plan. Later, I would learn the details. They were not entirely successful. The numbered accounts had elaborate safety protocols in place. Even though we had all the access codes and passwords, some prudent and suspicious bankers made calls back to the account owners – those who were still alive – to confirm the transfers. Most of the ostensive owners were dead, killed in the raid on Jekyll Island. Others were distracted in the futile efforts at damage control.

It would be days before the final total could be known, and the complexity of it all defied an easy accounting, but the total amount was easily in the tens of billions of dollars.

Meanwhile, back on Sea Island, the final day of the Summit was yet another waste. I kept waiting for the explosion of activity – for the security teams of the most powerful leaders on Earth to execute their contingency plans, swoop in and evacuate their respective heads of state from the danger zone on Sea Island as Rob executed the final blow against their meeting.

I wondered if they'd also rescue the Civic Youth, the young men and women they kept claiming were the future of the world, or if we'd be abandoned while they saved their own skins. Nothing happened, though, except for lots of waiting around for opportunities to serve as scenery.

The Civic Youth served as a backdrop for the world's leaders to issue a joint proclamation endorsing unity, peace, and better relations amid furtive glances and quiet, but angry discussions about the continuing revelations. All talk of war was abandoned. Instead, the discussions were on how to mitigate the damage inflicted by the revelations of the previous days and whether the info dump would include... details best left unspoken around Civic Youth like me.

I wondered why Rob had failed to act. He must have realized we'd already won, and stayed his hand for some reason.

The closing ceremony made the day's ordeal well worthwhile, however. As host, the Governor of Georgia presided.

"Time capsules are a Georgia invention," the governor boasted proudly, "Why, in 1940, right here in Georgia, Thornwell Jacobs sealed the first and still most elaborate time capsule ever constructed – a 'Crypt of Civilization' to preserve a record of our people and our times into the distant future.

"We bury this here time capsule here on Sea Island in commemoration of this meeting, that it may remind our descendants, a century hence, of our times and of these historic past few days."

The crowd and assembled dignitaries applauded. The audience began to disperse around me, heading for the buses back to Savannah, or for the closing press conferences from each of the world leaders.

I stood still a moment, studying the program for the closing ceremony and the background information on the Crypt of Civilization.

Of course.

I finally had the answer I'd been seeking.

Why had it taken me so long to figure it out?

Amit and I joined a select group of Civic Youth – those who had demonstrated the right combination of talent and compliance – to join the Presidential Motorcade to Hunter Army Air Field near Savannah. I was dying to whisper my secrets into his ear, but I had to assume we were under constant surveillance by professionals. We flew from there to Andrews Air Force Base on board Air Force One. President Lieberman even autographed a box of Presidential M&M candies for me. Then, we rode into Washington in yet another van, following in the wake of one of the two official Presidential motorcades.

We attended a State Dinner at the White House where more platitudes were mouthed. The mood was somber. Conversation was hushed.

"Did you see the latest?"

""Do you think they know about...?"

"What else is coming?"

Last minute cancellations left the State Dining Room noticeably below capacity.

It was at the State Dinner that Rob played our last card.

A pair of tuxedoed men swiftly escorted President Lieberman out of the room. Several others abandoned wives and husbands to follow. The rest of us only found out hours later in the lobby of the hotel where we'd been bussed.

"Lost nuclear weapon found on Jekyll Island," scrolled below the talking heads on CNN as they breathlessly conveyed the latest updates.

The peculiar "tank" with fins we found under the Horton House? It was a Mark 15 nuclear bomb "missing" since a 1958 "accident" off Tybee Island. Stripped of its high explosives and plutonium core, it had been abandoned there for a while, but it would take hours for the investigators to discover what Rick and his team had already figured out. They'd be operating under a worst case assumption – if the bomb detonated at the rated 3.8 megaton intensity, it would leave a gaping crater in the north end of Jekyll Island, wipe out most every building on the island, and devastate not only Brunswick, Saint Simon, and Sea Island as well. They were already evacuating the entire area before sending in a Nuclear Emergency Response Team to secure the site.

The pattern was obvious once we'd looked into it.

Despite all the security, The U.S. had lost a number of nuclear weapons. In 1956, a B-47 carrying two cores for a Mark 15 thermonuclear bomb vanished on a flight from McDill Air Force Base to the Mediterranean. The flight path was just off Jekyll Island. In 1958, a complete Mark 15 bomb was lost off Tybee Island, a hundred miles north. In 1961, a B-52 carrying two 24-megaton nuclear bombs crashed near Goldsboro, North Carolina. One bomb was never found. "Buried and never recovered," the official reports said. In all, over the course of five years, The U.S. lost four nuclear bombs, and all four were lost in the southeast, not far from Jekyll Island.

Why had Xueshu Quan masterminded the thefts? What had he – or it – done with the missing nuclear material? We had no idea. Records like that were not included in the material we'd stolen from the Civic Circle.

After the dinner, a Civic Circle representative went around to book flights home for the Civic Youth. "We'll both fly into Atlanta," I pre-empted Amit. Amit knew something had to be up. Knoxville made more sense. He said nothing and went off to his own assigned room.

I spent an hour watching the news. For once, the 24-hour news channels had no trouble finding enough content. Pundits and politicians alike were busy trying to save their own skins and explain away what had been dubbed the

"Wilson Files." The revelations of the past few days had obliterated any momentum toward war. The disclosure that a missing hydrogen bomb had been found next door to the G-8 Summit was just making the rubble bounce – yet another momentous disaster as the cherry to top a heaping mound of just desserts.

I sent a text message to Rob asking him to pick us up in Atlanta. The message included a coded passphrase so he'd know where to meet us. I went to sleep under the watchful eye of a smoke detector.

"What's going on?" Amit whispered as we waited at the gate at Washington Reagan International Airport to depart.

I shook my head no. "Later," I whispered back.

Our last-minute flight did not include adjacent seating.

I caught up with Amit as he lingered, slowly moving up the jet way.

"OK," Amit whispered. "Now what's going on?"

"Leave your phone off and unplugged," I whispered back. "Follow ten seconds behind me."

We'd arrived at the C Concourse of the Hartsfield-Jackson Atlanta International Airport and caught the underground PlaneTrain toward the main terminal. I waited until the last moment and jumped out at the stop for the A Concourse. Amit narrowly missed being caught by the door. I led Amit along the underground tunnel, making sure no one was following us. When we got to the T Concourse, the terminal Gates, I hopped on the escalator. Amit followed, closing the gap.

"The main terminal is actually the next stop," Amit noted.

"I know," I explained. "The terminal gate concourse has a separate exit. If anyone is waiting for us at the main terminal exit, they'll miss us."

We caught a cab to Centennial Park, just south of the Tech campus. I paid cash. We met Rob there, and climbed in his truck.

"OK, Pete," Amit said. "'Fess up. What's the big mystery?"

"Where are we going?" Rob asked.

"I'm going to take you to where Angus MacGuffin hid the Nexus Detector and the Red Flower Tong's secret scrolls."

I pointed off to the east. "Thataway."

CHAPTER 17: EPILOGUE

The gothic gray granite towers of Phoebe Hearst Hall loomed over the meticulously landscaped grounds of Oglethorpe University. The building radiated an impression of permanence in the bright August Atlanta sun, a sense it would stand forever.

The Oglethorpe coat-of-arms perched above the door – three boars' heads on a field granite, slashed with a stone chevron. Below, the builders carved an inscription, just above the entrance, into the solid rock: "A search is the thing He hath taught you, For Height and for Depth and for Wideness."

We walked around the building. I tried the side door; it was open. I motioned to Amit and Rob to join me. We went in and down the stairs to the basement. The building was quiet, except for the hum of a vending machine's refrigerator. There was no obvious sign that this nondescript academic hallway hid a terrible secret: a secret that the Civic Circle would kill to keep. No sign, that is, until we reached a polished steel door that looked like it would be more at home in a high-security vault instead of an academic building. What we were looking at was not a vault, however. It was a crypt.

The Crypt of Civilization.

An engraved steel plaque was riveted to the door.

THIS CRYPT

CONTAINS MEMORIALS OF THE CIVILIZATION WHICH
EXISTED IN THE UNITED STATES AND THE WORLD AT
LARGE DURING THE FIRST HALF OF THE TWENTIETH
CENTURY. IN RECEPTACLES OF STAINLESS STEEL, IN
WHICH THE AIR HAS BEEN REPLACED BY INERT
GASES, ARE ENCYCLOPEDIAS, HISTORIES, SCIENTIFIC
WORKS, SPECIAL EDITIONS OF NEWSPAPERS,
TRAVELOGUES, TRAVEL TALKS, CINEMA REELS,
MODELS, PHONOGRAPH RECORDS, AND SIMILAR
MATERIALS FROM WHICH AN IDEA OF THE STATE AND
NATURE OF THE CIVILIZATION WHICH EXISTED FROM
1900 TO 1950 CAN BE ASCERTAINED. NO JEWELS OR
PRECIOUS METALS ARE INCLUDED.

WE DEPEND UPON THE LAWS OF THE COUNTY OF
DEKALB, THE STATE OF GEORGIA, AND THE
GOVERNMENT OF THE UNITED STATES AND THEIR
HEIRS, ASSIGNS, AND SUCCESSORS, AND UPON THE
SENSE OF SPORTSMANSHIP OF POSTERITY FOR THE
CONTINUED PRESERVATION OF THIS VAULT UNTIL
THE YEAR 8113, AT WHICH TIME WE DIRECT THAT IT
SHALL BE OPENED BY AUTHORITIES REPRESENTING
THE ABOVE GOVERNMENTAL AGENCIES AND THE
ADMINISTRATION OF OGLETHORPE UNIVERSITY.
UNTIL THAT TIME WE BEG OF ALL PERSONS THAT THIS
DOOR AND THE CONTENTS OF THE CRYPT WITHIN
MAY REMAIN INVIOLATE.

Franklin Delano Roosevelt, President of the United States
Eugene Talmadge, Governor of Georgia
Oglethorpe University by Thornwell Jacobs, President
Anno Domini, 1936, Ab Universitate Recondita Anno
Vicesimo Tertio

"Allow me to introduce MacGuffin's 'thorny' friend, and fellow Presbyterian, Thornwell Jacobs," I explained to Rob and Amit. I could see the realization dawning on their faces.

"But, it says 1936," Amit began. "MacGuffin was murdered..."

"In 1940," I interrupted him. "Just weeks before Thornwell Jacobs sealed the vault permanently." I pointed to another poster next to the door:

The Oglethorpe University Crypt of Civilization

From 1936 until 1940, Oglethorpe University executed detailed plans to build an extraordinary time capsule designed to store records for more than six thousand years. The result was the Crypt of Civilization, which the Guinness Book of World Records (1990) hailed as the "first successful attempt to bury a record for any future inhabitants or visitors to the planet earth." The visionary of this quest was university president Dr. Thornwell Jacobs, who has been called "the father of the modern time capsule."

While engaged in teaching and research, Jacobs was struck by the scarcity of information on ancient civilizations. In November 1936 in Scientific American Magazine, he explained an idea to store contemporary records for posterity. Jacobs wrote of a unique plan to show the manner of life in 1936, as well as the accumulated knowledge of humankind prior to that time. His plan was to preserve consciously, for the first time in history, a thorough record of civilization in what he called a "Crypt."

"One of those stainless steel cylinders," Rob said, studying the photograph of the Crypt's contents, "contains MacGuffin's scrolls and the Nexus Detector. We're standing just a few feet away from it..."

"...on the other side of a vault door," Amit studied the dome over what was probably the lock and handle. "Who has the combination?"

"I understand it's been welded shut," I offered.

"So near, and yet so far," Amit examined the polished steel door. "The walls?"

"It used to be a swimming pool," I explained. "Two-foot thick stone floor. Seven-foot thick stone roof. The whole thing is carved out of granite. The crypt is ten feet high, ten feet wide, and twenty feet deep."

"Granite," Rob was shaking his head. "Damn hard stuff. We'd have to blast. It'd be easier to get in through the door. Explosives might damage the contents in that confined space. An arc welding rig, or maybe even an oxy-fuel torch..." his comment trailed off as he analyzed how he might cut open the door.

I looked at them both. "I've been thinking about something Rick told me. Rick said, 'They won't give back our country without a fight.' He was mostly right, but not the way he, and you, Rob, have been thinking."

"What do you mean?" Rob looked puzzled as I interrupted his analysis of fuel mixes and melting points.

"It's not your kind of fight, Rob. Not a fight of weapons and violence," I caught him before he could interrupt me. "True, the Albertian attack weakened them, and I'm sure force and firepower will have a place in what's to come.

"This is what it's about." I pointed to the vault door. "It's a fight of ancient puzzles and fantastic new technologies. It's going to be a fight of ideas, of propaganda, of persuasion, and of new discoveries.

"The Civic Circle has been weakened by scandal," I pointed out. "Many of their minions in government are compromised. The Albertians even managed to kill a few of them. The organization as a whole is far from dead, however. They're going to be back, rebuilding their team, seeking out their enemies, securing their hold on power. They'll redouble their efforts to infiltrate Georgia Tech. We have to be ready for them. We have to access this vault and retrieve MacGuffin's cache. We have to design, debug, and implement a Nexus Detector of our own."

"We beat them last year when we were the rookies playing against the veterans," Amit pointed out. "We wiped out Gomulka, literally. We'll chew right through their second-string agitators and spit them out."

"Don't get cocky," I cautioned Amit. "Last year all we had to face was Gomulka, and he still came close to victory. In a sense, he won. We may have kept him from placing Cindy Ames in charge of the Engineering School, but he removed Chen and Graf. Two for one isn't a great exchange rate, not when we're so badly outnumbered. Now Ames is coming back, too, and the whole attention of the Civic Circle will be on the Georgia Tech campus trying to complete the convergence they attempted last year. They'll be trying hard. We have to shut them down, harder, so they don't try again."

"Getting into the vault, I can do." Rob examined the shiny steel door. "The challenge is doing it quickly, finding what we want among the clutter," he gestured to the photo of the crypt's contents, "and getting out without being detected."

"So," Amit summarized, "the ride never ends. We have to win another ideological battle on campus, secretly break into a vault that's supposed to be sealed for the next six thousand years, identify and retrieve MacGuffin's cache, design and build a Nexus Detector of our own, and somehow do all this without getting caught or detected by the Civic Circle."

"Who now have their guard up," Rob cautioned. "It won't take the Civic Circle long to realize some third enemy is on the rise, rallying the Albertians and the Red Flower Tong, taking the fight to a new level."

"How are we going to do all that?" Amit asked.

"I don't know, exactly," I acknowledged, "but one thing is clear."

I looked at Amit and Rob.

"It's going to take a hell of an engineer."

The End.

Look for Pete's continuing adventures in
A Hell of an Engineer, Book 4 of The Hidden Truth.

ABOUT THE BRAVE AND THE BOLD

This is the section of the book where I provide the tips, hints, and clues needed to begin sorting out where the fiction ends and the underlying facts start.

First though, I have a request of you.

Please leave a review.

I like five-star reviews that gush about how my book was perfect as much as the next author, but if you didn't like something for some reason, or if something just didn't work for you, please feel free to explain why and mark it down accordingly. I'd rather have a one-star review with some helpful feedback than no review at all. You won't hurt my feelings, let alone with a three- or four-star review that expresses some criticism.

Here's what I'll do for you in return: not only will I read every review, but also I will provide a reply to everyone who leaves a review. Leave a review, ask a question, leave a comment – I will reply, although depending on the volume of reviews, it may not be immediately.

I'm delighted you chose to honor me with your book reading time and money. However, I have many demands on my own time, and lots of projects more remunerative than fiction writing I could be spending that time on. I'm going to take a vacation from fiction writing for a while to prioritize those other projects. I cannot at present say when to expect *A Hell of an Engineer*, the next installment of *The Hidden Truth*. I'll get around to it. Eventually.

I make my readers this promise, however. If I have at least one hundred true fans who like *The Brave and the Bold* enough to leave reviews, I will begin working on *A Hell of an Engineer*. You can expect to see *A Hell of an Engineer* within a year of the hundredth review posting for *The Brave and the Bold*. You'll find updates on my blog at aetherczar.com or my Twitter and Gab feeds where I am @aetherczar.

Don't cheat, though.

It's not going to help to leave phony reviews from phony accounts. All that will accomplish is to get me in trouble with Amazon. The integrity of the review process is very important. Honest reviews from honest readers only, please.

This is a work of fiction, but *The Brave and the Bold* draws heavily on real-world history, science, philosophy, and events within our own timeline. Here are a few of the more interesting examples.

Did the NSA actually kill ultrawideband (UWB) radio technology? Technology columnist and raconteur, Robert X. Cringely, thinks so, and said as much in a column a few years back.

Kenneth A. Norton, the FCC engineer, played a critical role in justifying the FCC's suppression of Edwin Howard Armstrong's FM radio technology at the behest of industrial giants who felt threatened by it. See Ken Burns' documentary, *Empire of the Air*, or the book by Tom Lewis. Norton really did also come to an erroneous conclusion on the nonexistence of Zenneck Surface Waves (ZSW). ZSW technology does hold the promise of realizing Tesla's vision of global wireless power distribution, a technology strangled in its infancy by J.P. Morgan, who refused to finance Tesla's scheme to fruition and cut the funding. In Morgan's defense, the "free power to the world" concept is a tough business model to justify, yet there may well be a way to make it a viable business. I expect we'll all be hearing a lot more about the incredible potential of ZSW technology in the next few years. Assuming the Civic Circle doesn't successfully suppress it, of course.

Now that's two real-world strikes against Norton in my fictional universe which by my rule makes it merely coincidence. However careful readers will note there is a third subtle clue from Book 1 Pete has overlooked which elevates Norton's role to "enemy action."

Pete's adventure with the safety suggestions and the fire hoses? That comes straight from my own summer intern experience as a nineteen year old. Disappointed by the lack of real challenges, I memorized the Corporate Safety Manual and snagged a handful of $50 safety suggestion awards. A month before I had to go back to school, I hit the motherlode with the discovery that every firehose in every modular building was in violation of the guidelines, nearly thirty in all. I was looking forward to clearing enough money to actually buy a computer to use when I returned to school. Alas, although my manager was very supportive, the facilities manager stone-walled my request. He delayed acting until I was back to school and unable to effectively appeal. I would have to wait another couple of years to afford my first computer.

My former employer cheated a poor college student out of over a thousand dollars. I certainly wouldn't want to embarrass this company by disclosing their name in public, but their initials are "IBM."

Quotes attributed to Ted Turner, David Rockefeller, and Steve Jobs are verbatim or very close to it from real world sources. In particular, some of the remarks attributed to David Rockefeller are reported to have been presented at a Bilderberg Group Meeting in June 1991 and were quoted in *Programming, Pitfalls and Puppy-Dog Tales* (1993) by Gyeorgos C. Hatonn, p. 65. The individual revealing what were supposed to have been confidential remarks has never been identified, and the validity of the remarks has been disputed. Other remarks are taken from Rockefeller's 2002 *Memoirs*, and a 2007 interview with Benjamin Fulford.

The Report from Iron Mountain appeared in the late sixties. Ostensibly the findings of a secret government panel,

384 THE BRAVE AND THE BOLD

the report concluded that a perpetual state of war was essential for governments to maintain their power. Officially the whole thing was a satire. That's what they tell us, anyway.

The weird opening ceremony for the Civic Circle's Social Justice Leadership Forum? Check out the Gotthard Tunnel opening ceremony where orange-jumpsuit-clad performers ended up stripping to white underwear as they cavorted about in a neo-Babelian ritualistic ceremony for European heads of state and other dignitaries.

An intern with iRobot allegedly stole the company's intellectual property, colluding with a large defense contractor in an attempt to land a larger Army robot. Private investigators caught the principals throwing away iRobot proprietary materials in a random dumpster. Look up the fascinating story of Robotics FX versus iRobot.

In January 2018, a 71-year-old man, Alan J. Abrahamson, appeared to have been murdered in Palm Beach Garden, FL. A police investigation subsequently demonstrated that he faked his own murder using a weather balloon to carry off the murder weapon.

The 30th G-8 Summit really was held in Sea Island, Georgia, United States, on June 8–10, 2004. The hydrogen bomb lost off Tybee Island remains safely lost – so far as we know.

The many anecdotes and stories of elite corruption are adapted largely from the *Crazy Days and Nights* blog. Additional sources of inspiration came out of the interpretations of "*Q* drops" by such online luminaries and Anonymous Conservative and Neon Revolt.

The electromagnetic physics originally discovered by Heaviside and suppressed by the Civic Circle? Those are my own discoveries, and a significant part of my motivation in writing these stories was to make my scientific ideas available to a wider audience. My next project will be a non-fiction exploration of physics, tentatively titled *Fields: The Once and Future Theory of Everything*.

The Crypt of Civilization remains sealed in the basement of Phoebe Hearst Hall on the campus of Ogelthorpe University. Please see that it remains so. If you are reading this, I can assure you that on your timeline, Pete, Amit, and Rob have already removed the scrolls and the Nexus Detector. They are far too dangerous to be left unattended on any timeline.

ACKNOWLEDGEMENTS

Paul Blair pointed out the remarkable synergy between my story and the career and writings of the pioneering author of speculative fiction, Jorge Luis Borges. Borges' tales of Scotch Presbyterians bearing magical books (*The Book of Sand*), and his prescient description of the Many Worlds Interpretation of quantum mechanics (*The Garden of Forking Paths*) almost make me believe he really did socialize with Angus MacGuffin and Ettore Majorana in Buenos Aires.

Campus Reform (campusreform.org) does a brilliant job documenting the irrationalities of the contemporary college scene. I relied on the excellent reporting of Toni Airaksinen for many of the ideas and ideologies ascribed to Cindy Ames.

I am grateful to Keith Weiner of Monetary Metals for permission to use and adapt his special report on bank manipulation and ascribe it to Brother Francis and the London Office of the Holy See Bank Corporation. No relation to the real HSBC Bank is implied or intended. Keith is pioneering a revolutionary scheme to allow gold investors to earn interest in gold, on gold. Check out the details at monetary-metals.com. And keep in mind the April 1 publication date of Keith's special report on bank manipulation for a hint to his actual views on the subject of market manipulation!

Commenter "Delta" on the RooshV Forum contributed the interesting connection between monogamy and the

Prisoners' Dilemma. I adapted his analysis for the Albertians to explain to Pete the game theory of promiscuity.

I am indebted to John C. Wright for his sharing the "point-deer-say-horse" story and its relevance to progressive politics.

The insightful Vox Day shared the interesting story of the Chinese village and their efforts to save the river dolphins, the baiji.

I borrowed some epic lines from "Horatius at the Bridge" by Lord Macaulay. Read, or better yet, listen to a reading of this heroic poem in its entirety.

I'm grateful to the blurb gurus at the Conservative Libertarian Fiction Alliance who helped me update and fine tune my previous and current book blurbs. These include Adam Weissman, Dave Leigh, Scott Hoffman, and particularly Paul Allen Piatt.

I adapted the hilarious "Social justice tongue fu" from the Amazing World of Gumball for some of Johnny Rice's dialog. Check out the original – it's great.

My Alpha Readers gave generously of their time to review my early drafts and provide their suggestions and corrections. Alpha Readers included Brandy Harvey, Jack Gardner, Declan Finn, Francis Porretto, Jeff Koistra, June Coker McNew, Daniel Humphreys, Edward McLeod Jones, and Robert Tracy. Foremost among my Alpha Readers is the amazing Barbara McNew Schantz, whose talents, not only in managing our busy household, but also in editing and proofing my novels are much appreciated by her husband.

In conclusion, I am deeply grateful to all the readers of *The Hidden Truth* who took a chance on an unknown author. You joined Peter Burdell and Amit Patel on their fictional journey to discover the hidden truth and unmask the Civic Circle, followed their first steps to outwit and defeat their formidable enemies, and now you have joined my heroes in their first major victory over th sinister forces threatening to destroy Western civilization.

Your support through your reviews and word-of-mouth have been critical to the success of the *Hidden Truth* series. You are wonderfully engaged, and a remarkably high fraction of you volunteered your time to review my work and help bring it to the attention of more readers. If you enjoy my latest story, if you think it deserves a wider audience, I hope you'll let your friends know, and post reviews on Amazon and elsewhere to help spread the word.

Thank you.

ABOUT THE AUTHOR

I'm a radio frequency (RF) scientist with a Ph.D. in theoretical physics. My research aims at understanding how bound or reactive electromagnetic energy decouples from a source or an antenna and radiates away. This theory has been helpful in understanding and designing not only antennas, but also near-field wireless systems. I "wrote the book" on *The Art and Science of Ultra-wideband Antennas*. In addition, I'm an inventor with about forty patents to my credit, mostly antennas or wireless systems, but I was also a co-inventor (with my wife, Barbara) on a remarkably effective baby bowl. Barbara's Baby Dipper® bowl and feeding set (see http://babydipper.com) helps parents feed infants and helps toddlers learn to feed themselves through a clever, ergonomic design. With Bob DePierre, I co-invented Near-Field Electromagnetic Ranging. I conceived the idea and Bob reduced it to practice and made it work.

I'm an entrepreneur, as well. I co-founded The Q-Track Corporation. Our company is the pioneer in Near-Field Electromagnetic Ranging (NFER®) Real-Time Location Systems (RTLS). Q-Track released the first NFER® RTLS a few years ago. Q-Track products provide precise (40cm rms accurate) location awareness that enhances the safety of nuclear workers. In other installations, Q-Track products let robotic overhead cranes know the location of workers to avoid collisions. Q-Track's new SafeSpot™ systems help keep people safe from collisions with forklifts. NFER® RTLS provides "indoor GPS" by providing location awareness to the most difficult industrial settings. See https://q-track.com.

Furthermore, I'm an amateur radio operator (KC5VLD), and a Cubmaster in Huntsville, Alabama, where I live with my wife, Barbara, and our four children: twin boys, and twin girls.

No author can possibly write as fast as his readers can read. Fortunately, there is an amazing abundance of great fiction emerging every week – I can hardly keep up with it. Here are a few suggestions I personally recommend to my readers to tide them over until the release of *A Hell of an Engineer, Book 4 of The Hidden Truth*.

In *A Rambling Wreck*, I noted Russell Newquist was an emerging talent to watch based on his fast-paced, clever, horror short, *Who's Afraid of the Dark?* Jim Butcher's Harry Dresden collides with Larry Correia's Monster Hunter International in Russell's *War Demons*, a supernatural thriller that goes straight to Hell. A soldier must face and overcome both figurative and literal demons that followed him home from his service in Afghanistan. Allying himself with elite special forces, a Holy Knight, and determined friends, Newquist's hero tackles demons, monsters, warlocks, even a dragon. Hardcore Georgia Tech fans will appreciate Newquist's shockingly true-to-life depictions of hordes of barely sentient shambling zombies, stalking the University of Georgia campus. The tenacious courage of my hero, Bulldog, was inspired, in part, by the example of Russell Newquist bravely marketing a book with no pages to color to UGA fans.

I'm actually not a big fan of zombie stories, but Daniel Humphreys is such an excellent writer, I make an exception. His Z-Day series, *A Place Outside the Wild*, *A Place Called Hope*, and *A Place for War* examine what happens after the zombie outbreak, when the greatest enemy the survivors face is themselves as they must band together to tackle a new emerging threat and rebuild civilization.

As if that's not enough, Humphreys also has an amazing urban fantasy series. The Paxton Locke series is a bit like

Harry Dresden on a road trip, except real tech gurus named Hans don't "giggle like a schoolgirl" at their handiwork. Well, not usually.

Any resemblance between this distinguished author and Peter's fictional boss, Mr. Daniel Humphreys, is entirely coincidental. Readers in any way troubled with my fictional character's behavior may console themselves with the thought that it was better than the fate that befalls arch-villian and nano-technology guru, Dr. Schantz at the end of Humphrey's *A Place for War*.

Jon Del Arroz followed up his young adult steampunk adventure, *For Steam and Country*, with two more entries in his adventures of Baron Von Monocle series, *The Blood of Giants*, and *The Fight for Rislandia*. His fun pulp adventures are worth checking out, and his new *Flying Sparks* comic series is simply amazing.

One of my favorite Heinlein stories, *Gulf*, featured a secret society of superachievers who banded together to save humanity from itself. Heinlein's story didn't quite live up to the promise of its premise, but Neovictorian's *Sanity*, does. Recruited since high school by a similar secret society, Cal Adler has to figure out their motives and decide whether to enlist their aid to avenge his friend's death. Written in an interesting non-linear style, Sanity is part mystery, part thriller, and part anti-modernist critique. Neovictorian constructs a well-grounded and plausible secret history of the Cold War and the behind-the-scenes struggle to control the destiny of our society. I find it a bit reminiscent of my own work.

Fenton Wood's *Pirates of the Electromagnetic Waves* is an amazing young adult techno-adventure reminiscent of Bertrand R. Brinley's classic *Mad Scientists Club*. Set in an alternate universe nostalgically reminiscent of mid-century America, Wood tells the story of a boy and his young friends as they struggle to build and operate a radio station. I highly recommend this book, and I look forward to more *Yankee Republic* tales.

Loretta Malakie's *Love in the Age of Dispossession* is a quirky and nostalgic tragicomedy about an upstate 1990s New York girl who loses herself in the big city but finds redemption in returning home. I hope there will be a sequel so we can find out what happens to the heroine. Worth checking out.

Want some good old-fashioned rip-roaring pulp fiction? John Taloni offers a nostalgic homage to the vintage science fiction of H.G. Wells, Jules Verne, and Edgar Rice Burroughs in his *The Complete Martian Invasion: Earth's Defense Awakens*. C.A. Powell's *The Last Days of Thunder Child* revisits H.G. Wells *War of the Worlds* from the perspective of the brave crew of the titular ironclad that bravely defends Victorian England from the alien invaders.

Want to read an epic tale complete with rocket ships that – in the words of the legendary Arlan Andrews – take off and land as God and Robert Heinlein intended? Check out Karl K. Gallagher's Torchship trilogy, finalist for the 2018 Prometheus Award for best libertarian SF novel.

John C. Wright blurs the border between science fiction and fantasy in his amazing *Superluminary* series, and his charming young adult fantasy *Moth and Cobweb* series is worth checking out as well.

Declan Finn actually does appear to write faster than his readers can keep up with him. Not only are there now five books in his *Pius Thriller Trilogy*, he's now completed his Dragon-Nominated *Live and Let Bite* series.

Peter Grant continues to entertain with his latest military science fiction trilogy, *Cochrane's Company*. Grant spins a remarkably interesting tale of a mercenary who must assemble and finance his forces with an equal mix of tactical cunning and fiscal legerdemain. Grant also demonstrates he's a cross-genre threat with *King's Champion*, an epic tale of an aging warrior whose honor and courage remain undaunted. James Alderdice's, *Brutal*, is a similarly grim but deeply rewarding sword and sorcery adventure.

Adam Smith's, *Making Peace*, is a magnificent debut novel. Hired by an enigmatic patron, a romance novelist must unravel a mystery, and survive a bloody civil war on a brutal planet where conventional technology is forbidden and swords and sorcery reign. Starting from an ingenious premise, this first person narrative cleverly ties together science fiction, fantasy, and mystery in a novel and engaging fashion. The story is dark at times, and may be too violent for some readers' tastes, but the end result is an inspiring tale of hope, loss, redemption, and perseverance. Don't forget to read the amazing afterward, and here's to long shelves well-stocked with incredible books like this one.

Here's a forgotten gem I only recently discovered (at Daniel Humphrey's suggestion). Joseph Garber's *Vertical Run* vividly demonstrates that it's not paranoia if everyone truly is out to kill you. Designated a threat to be shot on sight, a business executive must elude a team of assassins and figure out why they're targeting him. This non-stop action thriller combines, murder, mystery, and conspiracy in a thoroughly satisfying package.

Mikhail Voloshin's *Dopamine* is the best cyber-crime thriller I read all year. His company taken away by unscrupulous investors, an entrepreneur must thwart a high-tech criminal conspiracy to prevent a novel genetic engineering technology wreaking havoc. This is an amazingly well-grounded portrayal of the sometimes cut-throat world of venture-backed entrepreneurship and includes the best and most realistic portrayal of hacking I've read. Amit and Pete could get some good lessons from this book!

In Robert Bidinotto's long awaited *Winner Takes All*, a vigilante journalist and his CIA agent fiance must defeat powerful and unscrupulous enemies in a no-holds-barred battle for the ultimate stakes: the presidency. The Vigilante Author does it again! In this third Dylan Hunter book, Bidinotto builds on the foundation from the previous two installments to deliver a masterfully crafted tale of a crusading hero's quest for justice. His characters' choices all have well-thought-out consequences, for better or worse. The multiple plot strands come together beautifully at the end, leaving the reader guessing until the very last moment. Bidinotto tied up all the loose plot strands that have been hanging around since his debut novel, *Hunter*, to create a very well-unified trilogy. I look forward to his next narrative of vigilante justice versus unscrupulous lusters after power.

E.C. Williams *Westerly Gales Saga* is a fantastic nautical adventure set in a post-apocalyptic future where the tenacious remnants of human civilization have made a home on Kerguellen Island in the south Indian Ocean. His heroes venture forth in search of trade and other survivors, and do battle with pirates.

A variety of great non-fiction works informed my writing as well. Vox Day's *SJWs Always Lie* and *SJWs Always Double Down* are modern political classics and must reading for anyone who wishes to understand SJWs and how to defeat them. Anonymous Conservative's *The Evolutionary Psychology Behind Politics* and his r/K theory present a fascinating correlation between personal psychology and political outlook. Kurt Schlichter's caustic, no-holds-barred *Militant Normals* explains the conflict between what he terms "normals" and the self-styled "elite." For a less polemical and more historical look at conspiracy theories, check out Jesse Walker's *United States of Paranoia*. Akron Daraul's *Secret Societies A History*, was my prime source for information on Tong lore. I reviewed Dave Grossman's classic *On Killing: The Psychological Cost of Learning to Kill in War and Society* for insights to the psychological impact on Pete for killing Wilson.

The writings of pickup artists and "game" theorists are readily available online and at Amazon. I'd like to particularly recommend the writing of Roosh Valizadeh. So long as Roosh wrote about his sexual exploits and offered pick-up tricks in books like *Day Bang: How to Casually Pick Up Girls During the Day*, or wrote his pick-up themed tourist guide books like *Bang Iceland*, Roosh was largely ignored. As Roosh began to tire of the pick-up artist lifestyle, his far-reaching experience gave him deep insights to contemporary sexual culture. He forayed into political activism with a lecture tour that became the center of international controversy. You'll find the details in *Free Speech Isn't Free: How 90 Men Stood Up Against The Globalist Establishment -- And Won*. He's regarded as such a threat that he's been banned from the UK. In fact the UK forced a London-bound flight to return to Iceland when they realized Roosh was a passenger. More recently, Amazon banned Roosh's best-selling new release, *Game*, and nine other titles. You can order Roosh's works directly from his store at https://www.rooshvstore.com. I recommend *Game*. As my children mature, I plan to give my boys a copy, so they can hold their own against their peers, and I'll share it with my girls, too, so they appreciate the tactics their suitors might employ against them.

Where do I find all these wonderful books? The Conservative Libertarian Fiction Alliance on MeWe is a great place for readers and authors to mingle and learn about the latest great releases. The Sunday Morning Book Thread at Ace of Spades HQ (http://ace.mu.nu/) is usually full of good reading suggestions, as is the Book Horde blog (http://www.bookhorde.org). Finally, check out the conversation at John Walker's Ratburger for reviews and reading suggestions (https://www.ratburger.org).

For more current suggests and updates on my progress, check out my blog at http://aetherczar.com, or follow me at https://twitter.com/AetherCzar on Twitter or on Gab at https://gab.ai/aetherczar.

Thanks again for your interest in *The Brave and the Bold*.